Will gibson

Because there is a tipping point.

# Paradigm Time

## Will Gibson

**One Planet Press**

Second Edition

ISBN  09830099170
ISBN-13  978-0-9830991-7-8

Library of Congress Control Number
2013914888

Printed in the United States of America

# Paradigm Time

# Two Tales of the Future

## Resource Wars                           Pages 1–136

"Three generations had passed since the beginning
of the new century and for each, the struggle for survival
had become harder."

"It is such a world in which Damian Schneider finds himself
trying to support a family, trying to make his way in a world
gone mad, in a world short on rations and reason."

## Resolution Days                        Pages 141–318

"Three generations had passed since the beginning
of the new century and for each, the struggle for survival
had become safer and saner."

"It is such a world that Annie Sullivan lives in, grows and
flourishes in, and gives back to on a daily basis."

# Resource Wars

THREE GENERATIONS had passed since the beginning of the new century and for each, the struggle for survival had become harder. At the turn, warnings and alarm bells had been sounded for years by scientists, environmentalists, thinkers, and those of conscience about our perilous position on a fragile broken planet. There were some small changes, an increased awareness perhaps, but a concerted call for deliberate action by governments and by their populations had never occurred. People had continued to concentrate on their own small sphere of family or region or culture and had failed to pull together toward any common purpose. With the urgent necessity of those in the world to view all of humankind as being in this together somehow never having come into fruition, we had continued to think only of ourselves and our immediate families and even more jealously protect what we had from those that might need it, too.

Sufficient and quality water sources and safe, adequate food production had become seriously compromised because of an accelerated environmental degradation when the wasteful world had continued to pump dry the irreplaceable ancient aquifers, had continued to poison and deplete the agricultural lands, had continued to cut forests and to pollute and overfish the oceans, had continued to gash and rip open the earth to pull out the oil and coal, and had continued to pave over and urbanize our open spaces. We had neglected our stewardship of the earth in favor of short-term materialistic benefits. Ignoring severe signals at the beginning of the century had taken us past the point of recovery and now, sixty years later, we were paying the price.

Food supplies had reached a breaking point within the first twenty years of the new century when no effort at controlling population growth throughout the world had led to an inability to feed the many mouths that now over-peopled the planet. Adding seventy million to our numbers every year was insanity and a blindness, a breakdown in intelligent thought. For religious or cultural reasons, no attention to policies or management to keep the numbers of humans at sustainable levels was ever pursued. Even though resources were becoming more scarce, very few felt the need to address this issue and the three billion people added in the first fifty years of the new century had brought unbelievable pressure on a now untenable position for civilization.

The poisoning of our atmosphere had brought devastating weather changes to every region of the world. Violent hurricanes pounded our shores, massive tornadoes tore our cities and towns apart. As no rain fell in the previously strong agricultural areas, too much rain flooded areas that had been relatively more arid in normal times. Now, extreme and severe and powerful weather events were to be expected. We were being treated as the short-sighted, self-indulgent children that we were and Mother Nature, as any mother can after so very many disappointments and bad behavior, had grown tired and impatient with us. And no longer could she take care of us or could support us or could protect us. We had been part of a throwaway society and that is exactly what had happened, we had thrown it all away.

Conservation had never been valued as a personal virtue or pursued as a national goal and we were paying dearly for this lack of altruism. As people became more affluent, the material and physical side of life became all encompassing and had become the paragon of the good life. And it was promoted, it was touted as success, it was sanctioned by society. The consumer lifestyle of the wealthier nations had finally forced its way into the rest of the world. Those that previously had exported freedom and democracy for the world's benefit now export over-consuming and materialism to the world's detriment.

For many decades, only the few developed nations had placed consumerism on such a high level. But, as several other countries and particularly the most populous ones had also achieved this economic and material success, the race for resources to retain that lifestyle became intense. With so many now wanting what only a small percentage of the world had been able to afford previously, the selfishness and the battle for possessions had become heated and had reached a kindling point.

And with those resources decreasing and with populations increasing, there was no formula and no amount of technology that could solve the problem now. An extreme and a desperate competition for life sources existed at almost every level of society and eventually had turned into armed conflict. The new wars were not fought over land or oil or ideologies, the new wars were fought over food and water. The wealthier, more powerful nations and governments had consolidated their grip on their own production and then went looking for easy takeover targets. And of course, having that overwhelming military superiority, it was no contest. But, after years of this, the spoils of war were not much more than that, spoiled, with lands that could not produce because of unpredictable drought or floods, with breakdowns in societies and infrastructure that had led to chaos and anarchy, with famine and disease and hopelessness. There wasn't much left to win as everyone became a loser.

It was a shallowness to life that had led to this disaster, a simple equating of possessions held to one's personal worth. The constant consuming and drive for material goods had everyone running a race that could never be won. Those with much had always sought to protect it and those with little had always sought to obtain it. But, the gap between these groups had now become a gulf, an abyss, and a canyon that became impossible to cross. With physical conditions deteriorating rapidly, there simply was not enough to go around anymore. Those with much had less each day and those with little now had nothing.

Throughout the years of the Resource Wars, strange alliances had been easily brokered as national boundaries were crossed and erased whenever suiting the needs of those still wielding the power. Countries that had been opposed either religiously or culturally or ideologically now readily joined forces when an advantage to each presented itself. Being African or Asian or European or Latin American or North American didn't matter anymore, what mattered was food in your stomach and a safe and secure place to exist. For most of the twenty first century, the breaking apart of culture and language and lifestyle had led to a more homogeneous but less interesting world. Gone was the diversity of the world's population, gone were the benefits of tradition and culture and heritage, gone were the different foods and arts and customs, gone was the color of life.

Economies had broken apart with the severe shortages of fuel and raw materials and markets that had simply evaporated. As prices climbed exponentially with these acute shortages, only the very wealthy were able to maintain any type of familiar lifestyle. Basic necessities had taken on the pricing of previously appointed luxuries. Massive unemployment from this reduction in overall economic activity resulted in fueling widespread international depressions, and with it, followed the collapse of the consumer economy. It had always been an economy based on the absurd anyway, where one is encouraged to consume as many resources as fast as one can.

The world had also failed to rise to the issue of eradicating poverty. Instead of addressing the root problems of crime and wasted lives, we had continued in a winner take all mentality that led to tremendous inequality. We had failed to bring even clean water or sanitation or crop production to the poorer countries of the world in order to better their lives and ours. By failing to bring dignity to all humans, we had disgraced ourselves as a species. By failing to provide education to the rest of the world, we had suffered for the ignorance.

The situation had become an extreme, sad reality of the haves versus those have nots. It had always been a world of givers and takers, and the takers had taken and taken and taken until nothing was left. And solely because we had never risen to our potential as an intelligent and thinking and understanding species, we had continued killing each other because of things, because of ideas, and because of our differences. And, of course, there still existed greed and the need for power in the world.

We were short-sighted, self-interested, and seriously stupid. Our ignorance was bliss and then devastating as we didn't care about our fellow human, didn't care about creating a climate for fairness and sharing and a working together. It had always been competition over cooperation, self-interest over selflessness, and entertainment not enlightenment we had sought in our lives.

Shallow, superficial, self-indulgence had blindly led us down a predictable path to disaster. And all the money and possessions and power in the world could not fix our air and lands and water now as the life planet of the universe was dying and departing with it was our future, and more sadly, our children's future. It is such a world in which Damian Schneider finds himself trying to support a family, trying to make his way in a world gone mad, in a world short on rations and reason.

*     *     *

Damian quickly closes the gate behind them and peers out into the approaching nightscape. He then scans the darkening hillsides one last time before turning to his men. The security group has just finished their patrols for the day. "Alright, that's it," he says. "Get some sleep and be ready for the meeting at eight in the morning. Tomorrow will be a busy one again." The men turn and one by one go in their different directions toward their housing. Damian will move on to his office to write his reports before returning home to his wife and son.

It has been an uneventful day and the kind of day for which they always hope it can be. And seldom did any problems arise anymore but, on occasion, he and his men would come across others making their way up the mountain and they would have to be chased away. The Perimeter stretches a few miles in every direction from the mountaintop compound and patrolling is a daily requirement. Most Groupings have been able to maintain and protect their immediate surroundings with adequate arms and sufficient manpower. Those who may still threaten are declining rapidly in numbers as death and despair increasingly prevail below. But one needs to stay on guard, just in case some foolhardy soul, mad from starvation and want, makes a last ditch suicidal assault on a well-protected and well-provisioned compound such as the Donnelly Grouping.

Opening the door to his office, Damian puts down his pack and sits down at the desk. Turning on a lamp, he rests in the low glow of a single bulb. He is tired, weary from his day's work. But he is one of the lucky ones, with a job, in a Grouping where food and water are still abundant. Damian and his family had moved here almost ten years ago when his son was only five years old. The offer had come from a friend of his deceased father, from a Mister Donnelly, a man of wealth and power who had gone in with three others to build this mountain fortification. The proposal was for Damian to join the security forces and work for the Grouping and with this allegiance came the safety and sustenance that would make life possible for his family and himself. It had been a difficult but simply unavoidable decision. Reality looked them in the face and it was either join or in time, they would also perish.

Life had become unbearable in the cities and the towns like the one in which Damian and his family had previously lived. Economies were wrecked and with that disappeared the benefits from having steady and regular employment. People had used up their savings and sold nearly everything they had to purchase the remaining necessities of life. And as chaos and unrest spread through the streets, safety had become a main issue. In the early years of The Decline, crime and theft had increased enormously. Those that had provisions would hide them from view, hide them from others as no one was to be trusted, not your neighbors, not your friends, and not that person beside you. It was simply everybody for themselves. Families clung ever tighter to each other, grasping at any life preserver that floated past, and then hanging on for dear life. But dear life was an image of the past, near death being the more real present.

Filing his last report, Damian quickly looks over tomorrow's work schedule. He checks the duties being required, the staff that will be working with him, and the recent reports from other companion Groupings about any warnings or areas of concern. Clearing the screen, he signs off and prepares to return to the housing unit where his family awaits him. Damian rises slowly, and looking about the room, sees his reflection in the glass of the front door. Peering back at him, he sees a man in his late forties with tousled black hair and a moustache and with a countenance of complacency and acceptance. And that bothered him, having that countenance of constant complacency.

Damian had always prided himself on his initiative, on his drive, and on his own inventiveness. They had always burned brightly within him, creating dreams and giving direction to his life. The last few years, though, has seen a flickering, a withering and dimming of those dreams and hopes. It has been replaced by that damned acceptance of things the way they are. His greatest fear now is not that he may be turned out or may succumb to the inevitable as so many others are doing. His greatest fear is that the light will go out of his life, that the fading flame will finally lose all heat. Damian worries that he may truly cease living as his life continues in front of him.

But for now, he looks forward to returning to the family's apartment where his wife, Sarah, and their fifteen year old son, Christopher, are waiting for him. Damian turns out the light, locks the door, and hurries home. Their apartment is in the lower section of housing that has been constructed for the employees and for their families. Each worker is allotted rations for three people, no matter how many are in the family. It's not that one isn't allowed a larger family or other members, it's simply that no more food is given to them beyond their rations for three people. And with such a provision, careful thought is given to family size, hard decisions in hard times.

Rounding the corner of the building, Damian walks past the first two apartments before he reaches his living unit. He enters through the front door and sees his wife sitting at the kitchen table, working on one of her projects. Sarah, looking up at him as he enters, says, "Hi, honey, I'm so glad you're finally home. I've just been waiting for you to get back to eat dinner. Christopher went ahead and ate just a little while ago."

"I'm sorry," says Damian. "We had to do some extra patrols today so something must be up and I was told to expect an even longer day tomorrow." He then walks into their bedroom and places his pack on a chair before continuing on to his son's room. Damian pokes his head in at the door. "Hey, how are things?" he asks his son, sitting at his desk. Pushing the door with his foot, Christopher just closes it without giving an answer. Turning around, Damian simply walks back to the kitchen.

"So, what's up with him?" he asks his wife. "He slammed the door right in my face."

"You know," she sighs.

"Oh, not that again," says Damian. "We've been over that a hundred times, what did he expect us to do?"

"Nothing, but you can't blame him. It's even harder on him, you know that," says Sarah.

"I know, but taking it out on us doesn't help anything," as he bemoans their disappointing circumstances.

"He's just a child, Damian, and it's not fair to him and he has to express it somehow. He doesn't mean it, leave him alone for a while. I talked to him earlier about it."

Damian then pulls out a chair and wearily sits down beside his wife. "I don't know, I just don't know. We've got it a lot better than others. What else could we have done?"

Sarah gets up from the table and begins filling a plate for herself and her husband of over twenty years. They had met at a summer picnic held by the company that Damian had worked for at the time. She had come with a friend who also worked there. Sharing in games and laughter for the afternoon had led to a romance, a marriage, and then a life together. So much promise, so much planning had given way to sorrow and simple surviving as the world had come crashing down around them. Christopher was born after five years of marriage and, although wanting another child, they like so many others had forgone the possibility. The idea of one more mouth to feed is a hurdle that not many are willing to jump over anymore.

"Maybe we could have one of Christopher's friends stay over tomorrow night," suggests Damian as a possible improvement to their situation.

"He hasn't wanted to spend time with any of them lately," says Sarah. "There's only two boys his age here and he doesn't really get along with them. Don't worry, he'll be okay."

"But he knows that if we had stayed below, there is a chance that we wouldn't have any food now. From what I hear, things are only getting worse down there. And Johnston said the other day that he heard several Sectors were expelling less desirable members to cut down on the number of people they had to feed. That could have been us," says Damian.

"I know that and you know that, but it doesn't make the day to day existence for Christopher any easier. He wants more out of life and I can't blame him. I'm getting a little tired of the whole thing myself," she says. Placing the food on the table, Sarah sits down beside her husband.

At the time of the Schneider family's move into the Grouping, the breakdown of governments and of social order had created particularly perilous scenarios for those without means or reserves. Very few could afford to pay the extremely high prices required to obtain food supplies and often, even with money, there were none available. Production had been dominated by those with wealth and influence. Large, global corporations had merged and united in attempts to control food supplies, water sources, and any other worthwhile resource.

In the many preceding decades, the extreme consolidation of money and of power had resulted in a very small percentage of the world's population owning or controlling almost all of a country's, and then the world's, wealth. Alliances between these corporations and extremely wealthy individuals had existed only for the benefit of those players. Corporate ownership had been narrowed to only the very few who could afford to buy 'shares' in what really had become personal businesses. But there was no concern for profit or return or appreciation anymore; what was wanted was just a piece of the action. And the action was now food and water and security.

What they wanted was one last chance for life. So, those with power and means had generally banded together and built protective compounds in which to live and house supplies. These compounds or 'groupings of members' were often built in mountainous regions near water sources, near areas that could be defended easily, and in areas away from the coastal regions that were now the scenes of climate catastrophes.

Damian picks up his fork and begins eating. The day has been long and the hunger and fatigue now come to the foreground. He eagerly eats, digesting the food and the just completed work day. He is concerned about subtle comments that he is hearing from superiors and wonders if there is a potential threat or problem on the horizon for him and his staff. Lost in thought for a moment, Damian looks up from the table to his wife. She is sitting idly, stirring the food on her plate. "I thought you were hungry," he says. "Aren't you hungry?"

Sarah sighs and puts down her fork. Her dark green eyes peer up at him from behind the strands of curly brunette wisps of hair that fall down her forehead. She gazes at her husband but no words come from her.

"What's wrong, Sarah, what's wrong?"

"I don't know," she says. "Everything, I guess."

"What do you mean, everything?"

"Just that, I mean, what isn't wrong today? What is left that is good or is fun or is meaningful? No wonder Christopher gets so disillusioned and disappointed all the time. If this is what living is going to be for the rest of his life, what is there to look forward to really? We're like prisoners here."

"It's not that bad, we have food and water and each other. We have much more than others and at least we have a chance to keep on going and maybe things will get better someday. Maybe things can still change and everything will just return to normal again someday," he says.

Looking deeply into the eyes of her husband, Sarah then says, "You know they're not going to change, Damian, and you know they're not going to get better, just stay the same if we're lucky or get worse probably. We've had a life but what's in it for our son, a chance to live in a Grouping for the rest of his life. What kind of future is that for a child?" she asks him.

Damian doesn't answer Sarah for a moment because he does know it, has always known it, but on the surface puts a good face on the situation for others. His job is to care for his family, to provide for and protect them, and with that task in mind, he has more or less gone through the last few years without thinking on those things. His own ennui would surface from time to time but he would fight to overcome it, not for himself but for his family, not for now but for the future. 'What future?' he thinks.

"I know what you're saying and I know we don't have a great life, but when we made the decision to come here, we all knew what it would be like. And, you know, we talked about staying behind with the others and giving it a try but it just wouldn't have worked. The situation was getting worse quickly and if we hadn't done something who knows where we'd be now," says Damian to his wife. "There was really only one choice for us to make, so we shouldn't spend too much time revisiting it," and he then reaches over to hold on to her hand.

A small, single tear appears at the corner of one of Sarah's eyes and then slowly snakes its way down her cheek. A weariness and weight pushes her down in the chair until her head reaches the table and then rests on his hand. Gently stroking her hair, Damian looks down on his mate, his companion of these many years as the love and respect he has for her swells inside him, and then the loss and regret of things that might have been deflates the moment and Damian is saddened. "I want things to be better for all of us," he whispers to her. "I do, I really do and if I could change things to make them better, I would."

Sarah, slowly raising her head, moves closer to Damian and says to him, "I know, dear, I know you would. I'm sorry and I shouldn't be so ungrateful. It's not just me, though, I feel so bad for Christopher and sometimes I don't know what to say to him. I hear myself saying things that I don't really believe just to make him feel better. And that seems wrong sometimes."

"No, that's okay. We have to stay strong for him, we have to stay happy and hopeful. We have to try," he says.

*     *     *

Clare's shift is over for the day and she prepares to return home. Gathering her things, she quietly exits her workplace and enters the darkened streets. Moving quickly along the sidewalks, she stays close to the buildings, trying to avoid being noticed. Although the area around the desalination plant is relatively safe, the bounty she carries home each night can be greatly coveted. If others knew that she was carrying pure clear drinking water, it might be a different story. Clare doesn't want to unnecessarily tempt anyone at this time of the night.

Her shift remains long, from early at eight in the morning until eight in the evening, four days a week. She is one of the lucky ones, though, with a good job and extra rations. Years ago, the desalination plant had been built by the local municipality in cooperation with state and federal agencies. With the collapse of order and government, those remaining with wealth and power had been able to commandeer it and to use it for themselves and their members. Also cordoned off by security perimeters, these last vestiges of modern cities acted as isolated islands for any remaining civilization. Unable to produce or sustain life sources for themselves, many had joined these quasi-organizational groups that fortified certain cities into protective zones. Those with money or needed talents could join a Sector, pay fees, and be granted basic protection, housing, and rations. Knowing the main manager at the plant had enabled Clare to get a job there and had allowed her to survive with her two children. And she hurries home anxiously to them now.

Crossing the last deserted intersection, she ducks into the third staircase from the corner and climbs the two flights to her apartment. It is dark, no electricity for the stairs or hallways, and she navigates by memory of repetition until reaching her door. Clare knocks once, waits, and then knocks twice. She hears the footsteps of one of her children running to open the door.

"Mommy, is that you?" asks a small voice.

"Yes, Jenny, it's me, you can go ahead and open the door," says Clare. And the door opens quickly and widely as the little girl throws her arms around her mother's waist and hugs tightly. "It's okay, dear, I'm back now," she says.

The room is mostly dark except for a single candle burning on a kitchen table. Only a flickering half light breaks the darkness and illuminates a sparsely furnished room with just the basics of furniture. Clare sees her son sitting quietly in a chair. "James, is that you, what are you doing?"

"Oh, not really anything," answers a rather indifferent James. "Jenny and I were just playing some board games but one of the candles burned out and we couldn't see anymore. We've been waiting for you to get back home."

"I'll get dinner going, you kids must be hungry," says Clare. The electricity is strictly rationed for each member household of the Sector. Those going over their allocations get a reduced amount for the following month and so on until, quite possibly, all electricity can be shut off to willful violators. Clare and her family save their electricity for the refrigerator, for operating fans for the now daily extreme temperatures, and for that one Saturday night a week. Then they will use the lights for an evening of nostalgia and normalcy, playing games or reading books or just sitting and enjoying the ability to see each other clearly, removing the dreariness of the dark. The rest of the time they will rely on candles for their light as did their ancestors almost two hundred years ago. The path of progress had gone full circle and had curved back on itself.

"I am, Mommy," chirps in Jenny about the hunger question. "Can I help?" she then offers. Everything is better now that Clare is home. On her work days, the children must spend the time on their own. She is fortunate, though, to have James to look after his younger sister. He is a caring, understanding eighteen year old who is hardened beyond his years. He misses going to school and having a normal teenage life but never complains or causes his mother any problems.

James sees his purpose in life as keeping things as regular as he can for his younger sister and in helping his mother. As with others his age, complaining and crying had exited early in his childhood. The young now learn early the lesson of age, that one needs to stand up to the trials of life, that action not complaint makes things better, lessons being learned the hard way.

Clare prepares a simple meal and sets the table. After calling Jenny and James over, they sit down together. "Can you move the candle to the center of the table?" she asks her son. Reaching behind him, James pulls it from the counter and places it near so they can see to eat.

"This is the only one left, Mom," he says.

"Okay, dear, I don't have work tomorrow so we can go over to Mr. Brannan's in the morning. I told him last week that we were going to need some more candles and he said that he had a shipment coming in."

"Could we see if he has any crayons or markers, too?" asks Jenny. "I want to do some more drawing and the others are so short and worn out, they don't work anymore."

"We can pick up a few things," their mother cautions, "but he's been charging more and I only have the two large bottles of water to trade now. If he'll take those for the candles, maybe I could spend a little bit on other things. Is there anything that you might want to get, James?"

Looking up and gazing into his mother's eyes, he only shakes his head. "No, not really, I don't need anything." A statement that wasn't true but true to his nature. James has come to not expect much from life and in that way protects himself from its simply unavoidable disappointments. It can be disappointment at not having a life that now only exists in memory and in pictures from previous generations. There are no Friday night football games, no cruising with friends, no summer weekends at the lake, no dreams of 'what do I want to be when I grow up?' There is only a day to day dreariness, a sorrowful sameness, and few opportunities in these limited lives.

"Are you sure?" his mother asks again, reaching over to rest her hand on his. "Maybe he will have something new that you would like, we can look tomorrow."

James rises from the table and carries his plate to the sink. Scraping the remaining crumbs into the trash, he reaches for a damp rag to wipe the plate and stacks it on the counter with the others. The dishes will be washed every three days, using a very small amount of water. Showers are taken every other day and can't last for more than five minutes. And toilet use is only when absolutely necessary.

The water supplied through the aging municipal system is limited and somewhat intermittent. And the quality of the water coming through the pipes is poor, very poor, unfit for drinking. That is why Clare's job and her extra rations of drinking water are so valuable. It is a difficult life but her family is surviving for now and Clare is grateful for that situation.

\*   \*   \*

The next morning comes and James is the first to awaken. Clare enters his room to see him combing his hair in the mirror, two shirts are lying on the bed. "I can't decide which one to wear. I like the blue one better but look, it's got a hole right in the front. Damn it," he lets out.

"I can mend it if you really want to wear it," offers his mother. "What's the occasion?"

"What do you mean?" retorts James.

"I just haven't seen you pay much attention to the way you look lately. It doesn't have anything to do with Mr. Brannan's daughter, Sophie, does it?" teases Clare.

"I don't care anything about her. I just want to wear my blue shirt. What's wrong with just wanting to wear a blue shirt?" he then says to her.

"Oh, nothing, nothing at all," as his mother smiles broadly. "Here, let me fix that hole." And she takes the shirt from James and carries it into the kitchen to mend it.

\*   \*   \*

The three are ready to leave the apartment and Clare pulls the door tightly closed, turning the knob again to make sure that it is locked. Descending the stairs, she instructs both her children on the route that they will take and about the need to move quickly. Clare and James each carry a large cloth bag in which a gallon container of pure drinking water is placed.

Crime is not as bad as it was years ago, those surviving don't have nearly as much to steal as was previously the case but still it is important to be vigilant. Also, in the new order of things, theft is seen as a capital offense, a social taboo, an abhorrent crime. When there was a value to consumer goods, it was not seen as life threatening to steal a car or shoplift a store or take someone else's possessions. But with the only goods with value worth stealing now being food and water, the rules had changed because the world had changed.

Exiting onto the street, Clare and her children begin the walk to Mr. Brannan's residence. He lives on the other side of town, a considerable distance away, and they make the trip only when necessary, usually about twice a month. Brannan is a trader who can often obtain goods that others cannot. Trading with another Sector or buying from smugglers coming into the area allows him to support his family through barter. And it allows Clare a place to get her candles.

"Come on now, Jenny. You must keep up with your brother and me" says Clare hurriedly. The three then move through the mostly deserted streets, only a few buildings are still occupied. With the large exodus of people from coastal cities years ago, they had become empty and hollow places. Those remaining had been allowed to live in only certain sections where water and electricity is still supplied. But within those areas, one could pick anywhere they want, squatters' rights, and one may find themselves the only residents of a three story apartment building like Clare and her family.

Storefronts lie abandoned as normal commerce had ceased. Small business had disappeared years ago with the failure of local economies. Consumerism had stopped being a life pursuit but had also ceased being the economic engine that had been the driving force behind misdirected economies in the past. The production of unnecessary and unneeded material goods had finally been stopped, out of necessity and out of reason. But it had come too late, it had come too late.

Jenny goes skipping by her mother and brother, a young girl with the immediacy of youth protecting her from a fear of the future. James is older and knows the score but both he and his mother take comfort and joy in the innocence of the other child. "Hey speedy, I'm going to have to chase you down," says James. Catching Jenny, he grabs her around the waist and spins her around several times until both are dizzy and fall to the ground, laughing. Clare smiles to herself as she enjoys the moment and now hurrying herself, she walks briskly to catch up.

"Alright, you guys, James, pick up your bag. We need to keep moving." And the family continues down the street. Turning the next corner, they see two figures coming toward them from about three blocks away. "Quick, get in here with me," says Clare, ducking into a darkened doorway. Holding still and listening intently for a minute, the family looks out as the men pass by, walking in the center of the street.

"Hey, why don't you let me carry that bag," James says to his mother when they are gone. "You can take Jenny's hand then." And the boy who was forced to quickly become a man is looking out for his women.

After twenty minutes more, they arrive on the street where the Brannans reside. They live in an older home with a large porch and a gated front yard. At one time, Mr. Brannan had owned four houses in the area and because of this was allowed to stay and live in one of them. It is the only section of the city with single family homes that is still provided water and electricity.

Pushing the gate aside, Clare, James, and Jenny make their way up the steps to the front door. Clare gently knocks and then waits, no response, so she knocks again. Not knowing if they are home, she leans to look in the window when Clare notices the curtain being pulled to the side and a face peers out.

"Hello, Mr. Brannan?" she calls out. "It's Clare Thompson." The door opens slightly and Sophie peers out at them through the crack. "Sophie, is that you?"

The door opens wider and the tear streaked face of the young girl appears before them. "Oh, no, Sophie!" cries out Clare when seeing her there. "What's wrong, what's the matter?" And the three of them quickly enter the living room and close the door behind them. "What's wrong, dear?"

"They took them. They came to the house last night and just took them away," she blurts out.

"What do you mean, girl, what did they take away?" Clare asks her. Sophie seems to be very upset and almost hysterical by this point in time.

"My parents, they took away my parents!"

"Who took them?" asks Clare.

"The security forces. They started asking my dad all sort of questions and then they just took him and my mom. I don't know what happened to them. I don't know if they're coming back," says Sophie and then she breaks down.

Clare moves closer to comfort her and Sophie wraps her arms around the older woman and continues crying. "Don't cry, dear, it's going to be okay. They're probably not going to do anything to your parents."

"But they know my dad trades things. What if they don't like that and they do something bad to them?"

"The security forces know about traders and it's mostly okay with them. They just have some rules that have to be followed," she says. Clare motions to James to take Jenny and sit down on two chairs near the couch. She moves slowly, holding onto Sophie, and then both sit down near them. Stroking Sophie's hair, Clare holds the young girl close and attempts to calm her. "Would you like for us to stay with you until your parents get back?" she then asks.

Stopping her crying for a moment, Sophie looks up and says, "Would you?" 'Of course, we will,' is everyone's answer. Sitting still for a few minutes longer, she regains her composure and soon jumps up to be the good host. "Can I get you something to eat? We have some crackers and a piece of fruit."

"Sure," answers James. "I'm a little hungry."

"Can I help?" Jenny asks and follows Sophie into the kitchen.

"What do you think they want with the Brannans?" James asks his mother after the girls have left the room. "Do you think they're in trouble?"

"I don't know if they are or not, honey. There is a chance that they could be, I guess," says Clare.

The two girls reenter the room, each carrying a plate of food. Jenny sets hers down on the table and then runs back to the kitchen to retrieve the glasses that Sophie had set out. "We have drinking water," she had told her new friend.

All of them sit quietly sampling the treats until James asks, "Has your dad been trading for a long time?"

"Yeah, for quite awhile. He used to work at a regular job but that company closed down so he started doing this. He says we have enough money to pay our fees to the Sector but not for the other things that we need. Sometimes I don't like it because we have all these people coming around, but it's always been okay before," she starts to choke up again, "before now."

Jenny moves closer to Sophie and then says in her diminutive voice, "Don't cry, Sophie, we'll help you."

A smile crosses Sophie's face and she hugs the small girl next to her. "Thank you, sweetie, you're so nice." And Jenny beams with grown-up satisfaction at having been able to help out.

"You know, I've heard of them taking in others to the security department and then they just wind up letting them go, without doing anything to them. A guy on our street has been taken in twice and nothing ever happened to him," offers James as more evidence that things will work out for her parents.

Clare slowly sips on her glass of water while pensively gazing in Sophie's direction. She is slightly worried that Mr. Brannan and his wife may very well have gotten themselves into trouble. She has traded or bought goods from him for over a year with no problems but she has the awareness to know that traders are always walking the line between a necessary reality allowed by the authorities and their need to control the distribution of goods without favoritism or unfairness. Clare hopes that they don't decide to set an example with the Brannans.

Sophie then stands to carry the plates back into the kitchen. James jumps up to clear the glasses and follows her. Shortly, they both return and James gravitates toward a bookshelf and begins looking through some of the books. Sophie turns toward Jenny and asks her a question. "Would you like to come up to my room? I have some dolls from when I was younger and I could show them to you if you want."

"Oh, yes, I'd really like to see them. I'm going to go upstairs with Sophie now," Jenny pronounces to the others. "Mommy, you and James stay down here."

"Okay, we will," answers her amused mother. "I'll make sure that we stay down here." Clare looks over at Sophie and they exchange broad smiles with each other. The enthusiasm and the excitement of younger children can ameliorate any situation and all are grateful to have Jenny around today.

*　　*　　*

Dusk is approaching and James moves closer to the window to better see what he is reading. Then hearing the sound of an approaching vehicle, he looks out it and gazes down the street. Very few vehicles move about the city anymore, fuel is solely available for patrols and a few delivery trucks. As it nears, James can distinguish that it is from the security department.

"Mom," he whispers. "It looks like a security car is coming down the street, maybe it's the Brannans." Clare gets up quickly and goes to the window to see for herself.

Peering from behind the curtains, they watch as the car slows and then parks near the front gate. A large man in uniform exits the passenger side and opens the back door for Mrs. Brannan and her husband to get out. The officer spends several minutes talking to them while gesturing and making his seemingly strong points. The older couple remain quiet and just nod their heads repeatedly as if acknowledging that they understand. Soon, the vehicle pulls away from the curb and the Brannans make their way up the sidewalk toward the house.

Clare and James move from the window to greet them at the door. Surprised by their appearance there, the couple is taken aback at first. "Mrs. Thompson, is that you? What are you doing here? Where's Sophie, is she okay?" asks the father.

"Yes, yes, everything is fine," Clare hurriedly assures him. "She is upstairs with my daughter. We came to buy some candles early this morning and found Sophie here by herself. And then she told us what had happened. Is everything okay?"

"Mostly, I guess" says Mr. Brannan. "They sure asked us a lot of questions and then they kept us overnight. They might have been trying to scare us a little bit."

"Scare us?" a fiery Mrs. Brannan jumps in. "They were trying to bully us. That one big guy kept saying that they could kick us out if they found out that Bob is trading with people that aren't allowed. I felt like kicking him."

"Now, now, Marion," interjects her husband. "Take it easy, they were just doing their job. It's over."

The weary parents enter the house. Mr. Brannan sits down on the couch as Mrs. Brannan quickly rushes upstairs to find her daughter. He looks exhausted and beaten down. Clare and James join him in the living room and sit quietly until he speaks. "I want to thank you for staying with Sophie, we were worried sick about her. I didn't think they would keep us overnight."

"That's fine. I'm glad that we came by," says Clare.

"What did they say you were doing wrong?" asks James.

"Oh, they had been told that I was trading with other Sectors. There's kind of an unwritten rule that it's okay to trade with the East Fork Sector but not any others. They have an agreement with ours to look the other way if it is coming from one or the other. They just don't want any of our goods that the authorities don't know about benefiting any other Sector. I told them that I wasn't doing that, told them that over and over again. I know they believed me but they had to put up a tough appearance for a while," says Mr. Brannan.

The girls and Mrs. Brannan then come down the staircase with Jenny leading the way. She excitedly runs over to where her mother is sitting. "Mommy, Sophie let me draw with her. She's really, really good at it and she showed me how to draw a horse. Look...look!" And Jenny eagerly shoves the piece of paper in front of her mother.

"Oh, Jenny, that's really good. I like your picture," says Clare as she passes it over to James to add his approval.

"And look, she gave me these to take home." Jenny opens her hand to reveal the two felt tip markers and three new crayons. "Can I keep them?" she pleads politely while asking permission for such valuable gifts.

"If it's okay with Sophie and her parents," says Clare as she looks over at the Brannans.

"Of course, it's okay," says Mrs. Brannan. "We so appreciate that you stayed with Sophie while we were gone."

With things settling down, Clare and Mr. Brannan make their trade of water for a few candles. She also buys some items that she knows they will need soon. Turning to James, she asks him if there is anything that he might want. He says no that he doesn't need anything. "Are you sure, honey, a book or something?" says Clare, knowing of his love for reading.

"No, Mom, I don't need anything. I can always go back to the school if I want to get another book."

"You go to a school to get books?" Sophie quickly jumps in. "Which school do you get them from?"

"The old high school over by our place. The library is full of them and nobody goes there anymore. A lot of classrooms still have science and history books in them, too."

Clare mentions that it is getting late and if they want to get home before dark, they had better start now. Both of Sophie's parents thank them again as they all walk to the door. The day has been filled with much more than any of them had expected. But the Brannans have returned safely and that is the most important thing. Saying good bye on the front porch, Clare and her two children turn to leave.

But then a request comes from Sophie that is addressed to James. "If you ever go back to the school, I would like to do that. I would like to go with you."

"Sure," he says, feigning no interest in the matter.

And then the three of them make their way back through the darkening streets to their building. Climbing the stairs to their apartment, all are glad to be home again.

\*     \*     \*

Michael has been traveling with the same group of Outsiders for the past two weeks. As they enter the city, he knows that he has had enough of the current situation. The benefit of numbers for protection and companionship is outweighed by the lack of resources that they have come across recently. Not finding much in the way of food for the past few days has created tensions among the men. Moving into a new area now, Michael feels it is time to strike out on his own again.

This ragtag band of men has walked for the past five days to get here. Rumors had spread that this town had escaped much of the ransacking and might still have some goods worth pillaging. As they enter the edge of the city, Michael decides that it is time to make his move. And almost simultaneously with the others, he suddenly begins running toward the buildings that now appear in front of them.

Sprinting in a pack, each now breaks off in his own direction, following his own instincts. Michael turns a corner and begins down a side street. He passes several vacant storefronts with broken glass and debris spilling onto the sidewalk. Slowing down, he stops at an intersection to plan his next move when he hears footsteps coming toward him. Quickly glancing around, Michael sees a single tall building with its windows intact and a large majestic doorway rising above the street. He makes his way to the front door as the other person also crosses the street and comes toward where he is standing.

Backing into the doorway, Michael retreats like a cornered animal. Tripping over some boards that are lying on the ground, he picks one up and shouts at the person now in front of him. "Get away, get out of here! This is my building!" With Michael raising the board above his head, the other person takes the threat seriously and decides it is not worth a fight. He turns and then runs down the street to find his own.

Lowering the board and breathing heavily, Michael wearily collapses against the side of the building. 'Oh, my god,' he thinks to himself. 'What is happening to me?' Having always abhorred violence, he is now disgusted with himself for resorting to it. But in a crazy mixed-up world, things tend to become crazy and mixed-up, nothing makes sense anymore. There is no purpose or direction to his life now, only the need to move on, to find something to eat and to find clean water to drink.

Michael is one of the Outsiders, one of those who hasn't the connections to be in a Grouping or who doesn't have the means or skills to pay and work in a Sector. They are simply 'outside' any of these still sustainable living situations. Forced to scavenge off the land and forage in the deserted towns and cities, they struggle to survive. The resourceful ones keep moving, looking for new opportunities. The lesser ones grow tired of the fight and give up and die. Michael isn't giving up, not yet.

He pushes hard against the heavy door and slips through an opening into the entry. As with most deserted buildings, dusty debris litters the interior. The items previously used in running a business lie uselessly, without purpose, on the floor. With the decline in regular commerce, these buildings and businesses have simply become superfluous. There was no need any longer for retail stores offering endless aisles of consumer goods that had driven a world into waste and now want. This building, as with many others, represents a shell of that former world, of a previous life that no longer exists. But for Michael, it may offer shelter for a few days as he explores the surrounding area for anything that may be useful to him.

He makes his way across the dusty, dirty lobby and through a door leading to the staircase. It is one of the taller buildings in the city, of probably six or seven stories in height. Climbing the first set of stairs, he exits onto the second floor. Walking the hallway, Michael looks into each room but only broken furniture with more debris littered about is the scene that greets him time and time again. But he searches each floor while working his way toward the top of the building.

When reaching the last level, Michael opens the door into the hallway and is met by more desks and chairs and bookcases piled in front of him. Each room has been emptied of its contents and they now reside recklessly in the hallway. Climbing over the pile, he makes his way halfway down the hall before deciding that it is useless and turns around to return to the staircase.

But just at that moment a sound is heard, a faint sound, not clear or understood but a sound in this now usually still world.

Stopping his retreat, Michael listens closely to see if he can hear it again. Yes, there it is, a whimper, a crying out, soft but distinct, unearthly but human. It is coming from the end of the hallway where he notices the door to the last room is closed.

Beginning again, he climbs his way over the obstacles and makes his way down the hallway. Michael now stands in front of that closed door and with some trepidation, he slowly opens it. Then seeing furniture neatly arranged and bookcases filled with household goods, he looks about the room. Sunlight streams from open windows and artwork adorns the walls. It is obvious that someone has been living here for quite some time.

Michael takes a few more slow, cautious steps into the room. The cry, the whimper, can be heard again and is coming from a corner behind some furniture. Moving carefully, he then peers around a large bookcase and sees a woman lying on the floor. She is on her back with her head fallen to the side and with her eyes closed. She doesn't move.

Standing still for a minute, Michael hears again the now clear and very distinct crying. He sees the figure of a small boy, about eight to ten years old, sitting on the floor with his back against the wall. The young child sits with his head between his legs, his hands covering his face, and his body convulsing rhythmically. Lost in his anguish, the boy is unaware of his surroundings and he doesn't notice Michael near him.

Approaching him slowly, the older man calls out to the boy, "Hello, are you all right?"

The boy jumps and a look of terror is on his face as he sees Michael near him. He reacts by arching his back and pressing harder against the wall.

"No, no don't worry, it's okay," says Michael. "I'm not going to hurt you." And he then stays where he is so as not to physically scare the young boy. Michael crouches lower to the ground and allows him to calm down for a moment before speaking again. "I'm here to help, I'm here as a friend."

The boy then looks up at him and breaks into sad tears again. Moving closer to him, Michael sits down and reaches out a hand to soothe him when the boy suddenly grabs wildly onto it and holds on tightly. Surprised by this reaction, the older man just sits quietly beside him on the floor as the many tears and the apparent travails then necessarily pour out of him.

The body of the woman, obviously deceased, sits across the room from them. A red-haired, fair-skinned woman, somewhere in her mid-forties, lies among the furnishings in the room. There is no visible evidence of an injury or of any blood from a wound. Sitting there on the ground so near to a dead body is unnerving and uncomfortable for Michael and he wonders how the boy can cope with it and Michael wonders who she is.

The boy is quieting now. His crying has become intermittent and his grip has loosened on Michael's hand. But he continues to hang his head and to hide his face.

Michael asks, "Are you okay? Is there something that I can do for you, anything at all?"

The boy slowly raises his head and his pale blue eyes look up at him. The redness and weariness in them startle Michael, so much sadness and sorrow on such a young face is hard to witness. Michael forgets about his situation, his hunger and his problems retreat to the background as the older man concentrates his energy and attention on the boy. Concern and care for another is a soothing balm for an already aching individual.

Simply shaking his head 'no' to Michael's question, the boy continues to vacantly gaze at him and then moves his eyes to the spot on the floor where the woman lies. His languid and listless stare at the body is without emotion.

"Who is she?" asks Michael.

"She's my mom."

"What happened to her?"

"She fell a while ago and cut the back of her leg really bad," says the boy. "I thought she was getting better but it got infected. My mom said that we didn't have anything to treat it and then she started to get really sick. I tried to help her but I didn't know what to do. I tried to help her."

"I'm sure you did," says Michael. "And you did all you could for her, it wasn't your fault." The two of them continue sitting on the floor as the conversation lapses for a minute. "So, have you and your mother been living here?"

"Yeah, for a long time. And for a few months by ourselves since my Dad's been gone."

"What happened to him?"

"I don't know. He went out on one of his trips one time and never came back home to us."

"One of his trips? What did he do?"

"I don't really know what he did. He just used to say that he was helping people move things from place to place. He would leave and be gone for a couple of weeks. My dad always brought back things that we needed, like food and stuff. But after one trip, he just never came back. My mom said that something bad must have happened to him because if he could, he would have come back to us," says the boy.

"I'm sure he would have," says Michael. 'And now his mother is gone, too,' he also thinks to himself. Looking about the room, he sees the corpse lying near them. "Do you want to get out of here for a while?"

"Okay," says the young boy and the two of them stand to leave. Walking past his mother, the boy looks down and then turns his face toward Michael's body and puts his arms around the man's waist. Holding him, Michael ushers him to the door. The hallway full of furniture greets them and Michael begins to again climb over the pile.

"No, this way," the boy quickly says to him. At this end of the hallway is a large steel door that opens into a second staircase. "We can go down this way." And both begin their descent from the seventh floor of the building.

"So, you use this staircase instead of the other one? Why is everything emptied out of those rooms?" asks Michael.

"My dad did that, he put all that stuff there to stop people from coming on to this floor. He said that everybody would just think somebody had already gone through the rooms and there probably wasn't anything left worth looking for."

They continue making their way down to the ground floor. When Michael begins to open the door leading to the outside, the boy stops him. "Wait, I want to show you something first," he says and then goes down the final flight into the basement. The dark and dampness greet them as the boy reaches to retrieve a candle and a book of matches from a shelf. Lighting it, he directs Michael to a room at the back. It is a storehouse with shelving against the walls but nothing on them.

"What's this for?" asks Michael.

"I'll show you, will you help me move this," and the boy points to a table resting on a large steel plate. Moving it to the side, both reach down and push the heavy cover from its resting place. The candle illuminates a set of stairs leading down into the darkness. They both walk down and when reaching the bottom, the boy lifts the light over his head to reveal shelves filled with row after row of canned goods and foodstuffs. Lined against one wall are several plastic bottles for carrying water. It is an amazing scene, a pharaoh's tomb of riches to a hungry person, and much more valuable than any gold or jewelry or treasure.

"Unbelievable! How did you ever get this much food? Where did it all come from?" says a surprised Michael.

"From my dad," answers the boy. "He would bring back cans of food for us from his trips. He always said, 'At least, I'm going to make sure that my family has enough to eat.' Sometimes, my mom and I would ask him to stay longer before making another trip, that we had enough for a while. But he would say, 'No, we are going to need more and I have to find it while it's still out there,' and he would leave again."

"And is there water in these?" asks Michael about the large storage bottles.

"Not right now. Before my dad went on a trip, he would fill all of them and then store them down here for us. We carried them one at a time up the stairs to the room. We just ran out and my mom was too sick to go fill them up again."

"Where do you fill them?"

"A place up in the hills a few miles from here where there's a spring. That's where we go to get water."

The sheer magnitude of food that is stored in the room is impressive and overwhelming. Michael admires the drive of a father who was doing as much as humanly possible to secure the existence of his family and to provide them with the necessities for survival. Whatever his job, he must have taken risks for their benefit. He must have lived his life for them.

"Will you show me the spring?" Michael asks the boy.

"Yeah!" is his first lively response. "My dad took me with him there a couple of times. I know exactly where it is." And the boy seems revived and refreshed and glad to have something to do. Grabbing two containers for water, both begin climbing the steps when the boy stops for a few cans of food. Reaching behind a post, he retrieves a can opener hanging there. "Would you like something to eat first?" he offers.

"Let's take them upstairs with us and when we get back, we'll have some," says Michael. And the two make their way out of the building, into the sunlight, onto the street.

Leaving the city, they follow a dusty side road and then a trail into the hills. The walk proves to be long and very hot as the heat of the day builds to an almost unbearable level, necessitating several stops along the way to seek shade. For years, the daily temperatures have risen to unheard of highs, commonly reaching over a hundred and fifteen degrees in previously more reasonable and temperate areas. Many now simply avoid the middle of the day, seeking relief and refuge from the penetrating and devastating rays of an oppressive sun.

Once again, humankind and its quibbling governments had been short-sighted and without any common cause or purpose. The destruction of rainforests for cattle production and one time resource extraction contributed to unhealthy accumulations of carbon dioxide in our atmosphere. Continued use of petroleum based fuels has accelerated the problem of climate change that had finally gone too far, so far that it could not now be reversed. The few degrees of increase that had been predicted for the first fifty years of the twenty first century is double that now, triple in some locations. Ice caps which act as our global cooling systems have now almost disappeared. The natural regulating systems on Earth that had evolved over eons had sadly crashed in just a microscopic period of geological time.

And what had taken a divine creation hundreds of millions of years to develop was dismantled by ignorant self-serving human stewards in a matter of a few hundred years. Corresponding sea level rises from previous predictions were also underestimated with several island nations and the world's great cities simply disappearing under the tides and becoming uninhabitable. The forward thinkers of the race, those that advocated for the communal good and for considering the social benefit of our actions, had continued to remain in the minority.

Michael and the boy begin climbing a ravine that sits between two hillsides. The trail is now indistinct and rocky. Wondering if they have lost their way, Michael asks, "Are we getting any closer, how much farther is it?"

"See that big tree up there," answers the boy, pointing to a large willow near the top of the ravine. "It's right at the bottom of that tree."

"Do others know about this?"

"I think they do. My dad said he saw a couple of guys on the trail one time and had to hide from them. But my mom and I haven't seen anyone in the city for a long time. That's why my dad brought us here, he thought it would be safer for us when he was out of town."

The two soon reach the tree and a small gurgling spring that surfaces and then quickly disappears into the ground again after only flowing a few yards. The dry, dusty terrain around them belies the possibility of finding water in such an arid spot. Filling the two containers, each shoulder the heavy load and begin the descent down the hillside, occasionally losing their footing under the weight of the water. They begin the long trek back into town with Michael occasionally carrying both bottles as it is truly a heavy load for such a small boy. But as soon as he is rested, Michael hears the words again. "No, give it to me. I can carry it," Sean says with an earnest determination. They would proceed in this manner all the way down the trail.

Coming back into the city after nightfall, the streets are dark and silent. An ominous and eerie feeling pervades the many now deserted towns and cities. Places of previous activity and life have now become tombs of stillness and death, an apocalyptic arena in which the last scenes and chapters of civilization are being played out. The curtain has come down on many of them. Only places like Sectors and Groupings have enough left to keep the play running. But all know that they are nearing the last act and that a revival is unlikely.

Eventually, they make their way back to the building. The stars still shine brightly in the sky, the planet continues its rotation, the moon still rises in the east. On such a night, one might wonder if not the nightmare that is upon them will just disappear in the morning light. And it is a feeling worth pursuing and worth enjoying, if only for a moment.

"Okay," says Michael setting down the two containers. "Want to get the cans of food?" and the young boy disappears into the staircase. Reemerging quickly, Sean joins Michael and they walk to the other side of the building and sit down, leaning their backs against the wall. The boy reaches for the opener and expertly opens the two cans. They take turns gulping down the kernels of corn inside. For dessert, they will pull out slices of syrupy peaches with their hands and dine delightfully into the evening. When finishing, both become silent and stare into the night sky. Several minutes pass before Michael speaks again.

"You know what? I don't even know what your name is," he says to the young boy.

"Sean Andrew Walker," comes back the formal reply.

"Well, Mr. Sean Andrew Walker, my name is Michael, and it is a real pleasure to meet you."

Shaking hands, the boy says, "Nice to meet you, too," as he offers back the small, soft grip of a child.

Michael's thoughts then return to the room upstairs and to the woman lying dead on the floor there. "Why don't we just sit out here for a while longer. It's cooled down quite a bit and I think that the moon will be coming up over that hill pretty soon. Is that okay with you?" he asks.

"Sure," says Sean, "that sounds good to me."

The two sit leaning against the wall, side by side. Sean will eventually fall asleep and slump heavily against Michael's body. The man will put his arm around the boy's shoulder to keep him warm and to keep him safe. Michael will stay awake for over an hour, lost in his own thoughts, thinking of a life passed with little purpose and with little achievement. Had it all been wasted and why is he still living when so many others have passed?

Sean will stir and then fall across Michael's lap as the older man changes position, gaining some relief from the hard ground.

Gazing down at Sean, he sees a young boy like himself so many years ago, a young person with his life ahead of him. He knows the future is uncertain, unsettled, he knows the boy will face difficult times but for now Michael vows to do everything that he can to help the child make his way in the world.

The next morning they return to the room where Sean's mother lies dead. They will bury her with tears and kind words coming from the small boy. "She always said it was her fault," Sean will say as they put her body in the ground. "It wasn't your fault, Mom, not your fault I was born into this world."

And then Michael and Sean will move on with their lives and will begin the new day upon them, together.

\*      \*      \*

Damian has worked overtime hours for the last two weeks. A raid on a nearby Grouping placed the security department on high alert and he has worked almost every day since that time. It had been an attempt by a desperate group of seven men to climb a fence and break into a warehouse. They weren't successful, they never were. Without many resources or firepower, the pack of Outsiders was quickly routed. The word had gone out, though, and the Donnelly Grouping deemed it important enough to be vigilant. But the next day is a day off and Damian looks forward to time again with his family.

"So, what do you want to do tomorrow?" he asks his wife, Sarah, as they both lie quietly beside each other in bed that night before falling asleep.

"What do you mean?" she says.

"I don't have to work tomorrow."

"I'll make us a nice breakfast and you can sleep in if you like. You've been working so much lately."

"But what should we do with the day?"

"Watch a movie or go to the rec center, I guess. What else is there to do?" answers Sarah.

"Well, I thought about taking a hike. We haven't done that for a long time," Damian reminds her.

The Grouping is bordered by a large mountain and although fenced, it is possible to exit a gate and reach a trail that takes one higher into a tree shaded and cooler canyon. There is only one trail but members are allowed to use it if security conditions are good and they sign out. And over the years, especially when Christopher was younger, they would hike it often, to escape the enclosure that they have voluntarily put around themselves. And he had loved it, as any child would, scampering ahead, picking up rocks and hurling them back down the mountainside, grabbing a stick to draw in the dirt or to use as a walking cane.

"Is it okay to take a hike? asks Sarah. "I thought the threat level was too high for that right now."

"No, it's been brought back down. I could go and sign us out in the morning," volunteers Damian.

"Well, if you want to, it's fine with me. We would have to ask Christopher, though, he doesn't care much about that anymore. He didn't go the last time that we went, don't you remember?" Sarah cautions her husband.

"I'll talk to him about it in the morning," Damian confidently ends the conversation. The light goes out and husband and wife say good night with a kiss.

'Tomorrow will be a good day,' Damian thinks to himself as he lies in bed that night. For some reason, Damian looks forward to tomorrow morning coming and looks forward to a new day, a feeling that rarely overtakes him anymore.

\*     \*     \*

Changing positions, Damian rolls onto his other side. One of his sleepy eyes opens slowly, seeking the clock. It is almost eight in the morning. Turning back, he sees the empty spot on Sarah's side of the bed and then notices the sounds and smells coming from the kitchen. Rising quickly, he slips on a pair of pants and a shirt and makes his way into the other room.

"Good morning," he says to his wife who is standing by the stove watching over the breakfast potatoes.

"Hi, dear, I'm so glad that you were able to sleep in today," answers back Sarah.

"Where's Christopher?" asks Damian.

"In his room. He ate something earlier this morning and then just went back to his room," she says.

Damian makes his way down the hallway. Gently knocking on his son's door, he asks if he can come in when Christopher answers, "Sure, come on in, Dad."

"What's up? It seems like we haven't seen much of each other over the past couple of weeks. I'm sorry that I've been working so much lately," says Damian.

"Oh, that's okay. It's not such a big deal, don't worry about it," says Christopher.

"What are you going to do today? Do you have any plans with the other kids to do something?"

"No, I haven't talked to anybody since last week. So, I don't know what they're doing today," he says with, unfortunately, his all too common indifference.

"Well, your Mother and I talked about hiking up the canyon this afternoon and we would like you to come with us. How about doing that? We could take a lunch and maybe hike to the Point," as Damian lays out his plan.

"It's just the same trail, just the same things to look at," says Christopher as a reason not to participate.

"I know, but we haven't done it for a long time and it would be good for us to get outside. And we could spend some time together. Mom and I would really like you to come with us," says Damian again.

"I don't know, maybe. Yeah, I might go."

And taking that as good enough for now, Damian leaves the room and returns to the kitchen where Sarah is just putting his breakfast on the table.

"What did he say?" she asks her husband.

"I think he'll probably come with us," is the father's guardedly optimistic reply as he sits down to eat.

\*      \*      \*

Christopher is leading the way with the energy and drive that comes easily to a fifteen year old boy. He is setting a blistering pace and fairly soon, Damian and Sarah let him go ahead as they are unable to keep up.

"Well, he seems to be doing okay. At least, we were able to get him to come with us," says Damian.

"But I don't know if he is doing it out of spite or enjoying it. I haven't heard him say two words since we left the compound," answers Sarah.

Directly ahead of them, the trail soon enters a grove of trees and Christopher disappears into it. "I don't want him to get too far ahead of us," worries the concerned mother. "You go ahead, Damian, and catch up to him."

"But I don't want to leave you," he protests.

"I'm fine and I'll be right behind you. Why don't you just go ahead and make sure that he's doing okay."

Damian is a large man, physically fit for his age, and he forges on ahead. Soon entering the same grove of trees, he continues on the trail now winding around fallen boulders. The trail is less distinct here and much rockier and one needs to keep their head down to watch their footing. Rounding the next bend in the trail, Damian almost trips over Christopher who is sitting on a fallen tree and hurling stones at a distant target.

"Hey, Mom wanted me to catch up to you, everything okay?" asks a cautious Damian as he sits down nearby.

"Sure," answers Christopher right away. "I had forgotten how good it felt to be outside and I just took off."

"So, you're glad that you came?"

The young boy smiles back sheepishly at his father. "Sorry, Dad, that I've been kind of grumpy lately."

"You've been fine. It's been hard on all of us cooped up here, but it's probably the hardest on you," Damian confesses.

"Well, you have to work and Mom is always busy doing things for us. I don't have it very hard," says Christopher.

The father appreciates his son's unselfish comment and his mature outlook. And indeed, the day is proving to be a good one, validating Damian's initial optimism from last night. Sarah has arrived at the place where they are sitting. She is also enjoying today's diversion and some time off from her duties. Ever since moving to the compound, the mother has acted like a mother, taking care of others, doing what is required of her, and making the best of the situation. She generally tries to hide her personal feelings, subjugating them to what is best for her son. Sarah isn't generally a complainer and both of the men in her family love and respect her for that attribute.

"Phew, I'm sure glad that you two are finally taking a break," says Sarah breathlessly when reaching them. "I need to sit down. The trail just seems to keep going up and up."

"It isn't great to be outside, Mom!" says Christopher.

"Yes, dear, it really is. And it hasn't gotten that hot yet. We're pretty lucky. We got a good day for it."

"Remember when we used to walk up that little hill behind our house," he says. "I always called it 'the mountain' and you guys would go along with it and call it the mountain, too."

"Well, you were only three or four at the time, and to you, it was quite a mountain," says Damian.

"But didn't you guys buy me a backpack or something that I would always take along on those hikes?" asks Christopher of days long lost from his childhood.

"Yes," laughs Sarah, remembering now. "And we also got you a walking stick, one of those telescoping ones that are made for hiking. You would use it in the back yard and march around with your backpack on. You were always climbing up and down anything that you could find."

"And all your favorite books were always about adventurers. People who were either climbing mountains or crossing deserts or running rivers. You would tell people that when you grew up you were going to climb every mountain in the world," Damian adds with a smile at the remembrance.

"And when people would say to you 'Every mountain, that's going to take a long time, there are a lot of mountains' you would answer firmly, 'Yes, every mountain, I've got time,'" says Sarah as all laugh at the retelling of the story.

The camaraderie is good, the break is needed, and all three sit quietly for a moment, removed from the realities of their current situation. Up here, things seem more normal, more real. The sky is still blue, the trees that are standing are still green, and the blackness from the hole humanity has dug itself into is absent. For this brief interlude, a peacefulness and calm envelop them. It is Christopher who speaks next.

"What do you think it's like down there?"

"What do you mean, son?" asks Damian.

"I mean, what it's like for the people still living down there. Do you think it's like it used to be, with towns and neighborhoods and people moving around or is it all just weird with guards and criminals and empty buildings?"

"I've heard that certain Sectors are often better than others. In some of them, things are more normal if they have access to the resources that they need and they manage it well. In others, the people who run it are in it for themselves and the members get only small rations and the protection. The Outsiders are fewer in number every year. Some of them find food and a place to live but most are always moving around trying to scavenge whatever they can."

"Didn't your sister join a Sector, Mom?" asks Christopher.

"Yes, the last thing I knew she had joined one somewhere down south but that was years ago. I don't know where she is or what she is doing or if..." and then Sarah's voice just trails off as she considers the possibilities.

"What happened to the Richardsons and the Millers, Dad?" asks Christopher of the neighbors that had lived near them. "Do you know if they stayed or what they are doing?"

"No, I don't know. A lot of them didn't have many choices. Some were moving to different parts of the country where things might be better and others just stayed and tried to make it work. That's why we decided to join the Donnelly Grouping. It seemed like the best chance to keep going," says his father.

"Yeah, I know we had to do it. But do you think in some areas things are normal where kids go to school or businesses are open or where people can just walk around the neighborhoods?" asks the teenage boy, somewhat hopefully.

"Probably not, son, probably not," says Damian.

They will continue their hike up the hillside until reaching a lookout point from where you can see for miles over the dry and mostly barren landscape. You can look east toward a rising sun that sends its unwelcome heat into the day or to the west where a sunset occurs that no longer offers solace at a day's end. It represents only the unending cycle of life that is now to be endured and accepted with resignation and complacency, that damn complacency that so bothers Damian.

As Sarah and Damian lie quietly beside each other in their bed that night, they exchange few words. It had been a good idea, the hike. Christopher had enjoyed it and had gone to another boy's house when they returned home to see if he would go hiking the next afternoon. But Sarah is unusually quiet, more quiet than is healthy, and Damian knows that something is bothering her. "Are you okay, honey? You're a little distant."

She moves closer to her husband and then rests her head on his shoulder. Damian puts his arm around her. "We left all our friends behind," says Sarah. "We left everything that we knew, everything that we thought was important to us." She pauses and attempts to control her quivering voice. The tears well in her eyes and begin cascading down her cheeks. "I don't even know if my sister is alive or dead. I don't even know that," says Sarah with abhorrence and despair.

*　　*　　*

Two days have passed and Damian is now back at work. He and three other security officers are making the rounds on the access roads near the compound. Their mission is to patrol the boundaries within two miles of the fencing. Also on delivery days, vehicles are sent down to the main road to escort the trucks carrying supplies up the mountain and into the Grouping. Security officers are part of that contingent.

Commodities are now obtained through an elaborate system of production and delivery developed by alliances involving up to ten different Groupings. The owners and benefactors of these Groupings all have connections to either vast stores of goods or have appropriated land and production facilities. Through an exchange system of currency and barter, these organizations are able to provide for the survival needs of their members and their employees and their families.

Today is such a delivery day. Damian and other guards are to meet the truck at two o'clock at the main intersection below the compound. They make their way toward the meeting spot as the time nears. The heat is extreme today and very uncomfortable, soaring near one hundred degrees. Mountains that offered relief and coolness from the dry, hot valleys in times previously have become extreme themselves. As Damian and the others hug the side of a rock outcropping, they seek the shade and a respite from the piercing rays of the afternoon sun.

"Where's this shipment coming from?" asks one man.

"I think it's from the Platt Grouping. They're the ones down south that still have grain fields out in the middle of the country somewhere," answers a security officer.

"It seems like they're about the only place to get that stuff anymore," says another.

Damian sits quietly, only partially hearing the conversation. His thoughts have been solely about his wife for the last two days. Sarah had expressed her sorrow at leaving their friends and about the worry for her sister's safety the other night. And since that time, he has only been able to think on that one thing. Damian also misses their friends but his parents are dead and he has no brothers or sisters. This is his only family and they had come with him. He understands the closeness that had existed between the sisters before everything disintegrated. They had seen Sarah's sister just before leaving for the Donnelly Grouping and the two had talked of trying to stay in touch and of hopefully reuniting at a later time. But Shannon had not been heard from after the first year, only rumors that she had moved south to join the Marshfield Sector.

"Did you say the Platt Grouping is down south?" Damian asks, coming back into the moment.

"It is," says one of the men. "I made a trip down there about a year ago with a couple of the bosses. They went down to make arrangements for increased shipments and I went along as one of the security, don't you remember?"

"I remember your leaving last year, I didn't remember where. Is that anywhere near the Sector known as Marshfield?" Damian asks the man.

"Never heard of any Marshfield when I was there."

About that time, the guard on the rock above shouts down to them. "I can see some dust on the road. It looks like two trucks are heading this way." The men ready themselves and wait for the approaching vehicles. When they arrive at the intersection, one security guard joins each truck. Damian climbs into the cab of the first truck and shuts the door behind him. The others place their vehicle at the front of the procession as they make their way back up the hill.

"Has it been a long drive?" asks Damian of the driver as they start the climb toward the compound.

"Yeah, but we left early this morning, so it wasn't too bad. Though it's getting hotter than hell now. We had to stop about an hour ago to let the engines cool off. I was afraid we wouldn't be able to climb this hill if we didn't."

"So, how long have you been working for the Platt Grouping. Have you been there very long?"

"About seven years now. I tried making it on my own for a while but you know how that goes."

"I sure do, I don't know if we'd still be around if my family and I hadn't moved here. I wonder how those people down there make it these days," says Damian.

"I don't think most do anymore. Just driving between there and here today, we hardly saw anyone. We used to see at least a few people moving around. It sure has changed from just a few years ago. It's safer for us but kind of weird, you know, there's no sign of life out there, nothing."

The truck continues its bumpy climb up the roadway. Dust plumes rise high and obliterate the view of the truck in front of them. The sun beats down hard and the rays burn through the fabric of Damian's shirt. He removes his arm from resting on the window and shifts his position as he angles his body away from the bothersome sun.

"Can I ask you a question?" says Damian.

"Sure, fire away."

"Ever hear of the Marshfield Sector?"

"Yes I have but that place hasn't been in existence for years," answers the driver.

"Oh, but was it near where you're from?"

"Not very far away. It was out on the coast, in one of the old cities. We're back up in the mountains, kind of like you guys are. It was probably about four hours away if you drove it."

"What happened to it?" asks Damian.

"Well, it wasn't managed very well and most people in it really couldn't contribute much either. It was a second rate Sector at best and eventually it just fell apart. We picked up a couple of guys from there when it closed down."

The caravan approaches the Perimeter fencing and the trucks come to a halt. Damian then jumps down from the vehicle and assists in opening the gates. The trucks enter and are ushered to the other end of the compound to the storage warehouses. Employees come from the buildings to aid in unloading and the trucks are emptied in less than an hour. Damian approaches the driver with whom he had ridden when they finish.

"So, you said that some of the people in your Grouping had come from the Marshfield Sector?"

"Yeah, one of the guys had been their logistics manager and had worked for them for a long time."

"Could I maybe get ahold of him? Do you think there is some way that I could talk to him or get a message to him?" Damian asks the driver.

"Probably, why?" the man asks.

"Well, I think my wife's sister used to live in that Sector and we haven't heard from her in years. I'd like to try to find out something about her and try to find out where she might be now," explains Damian about his emerging plan.

"What do you want me to do?" he readily offers.

They then make arrangements to contact each other over the security communication system when the driver talks with the other man. Damian thanks him and tells him that he will wait for word from him. He leads the trucks back to the gates and opens them. Waving to the man as they depart, Damian follows the truck down the hill with his eyes. He watches for a long time, looking out to the vastness and emptiness that lie below. Gazing upon the disappearing figures in the distance, his spirit rises and a mild excitement comes over him.

*   *   *

Two nights later, Damian is about to leave the office when he is informed that he has a call on the communication system. Turning around and sitting back down at his desk, he picks up the receiver and the driver's voice comes over the line. "I had a chance to talk with Tom Foster today. That's the guy I told you about that used to work for Marshfield. He said he'd be happy to talk with you," is the good news over the radio.

"That's great!" exclaims Damian. "Thanks so much for doing that for me."

"No problem," the man answers. "Well, how do you want to go about it?"

"Would he be able to use this same system tomorrow night to call me?" asks Damian.

"I could ask him. What time do you want to shoot for?"

"Let's say, seven o'clock."

"Alright, I'll let him know," confirms the man and the call is ended with Damian, once again, thanking him.

Leaving the office and walking to his apartment, Damian is flooded with thoughts. Among them, a perilous plan to go below and search for Shannon continues to ferment and strengthen in his mind. Realizing that it would relieve Sarah to know more about her sister would be a main reason for his taking the risk of such a trip. It would bring some comfort to his wife, especially if everything is fine with Shannon. But what if it isn't, what if something bad has happened to her, what kind of news would that be to bring back?

And Damian thinks of the planning required for what he is now proposing. It has been years since he was out in the world, away from the compound. Things must certainly have changed and probably have deteriorated. Damian has never asked for time off, there simply isn't any reason anymore. But there are provisions in his employment contract for it, usually used to care for someone sick or simply for rest. With Damian's work record and friendly association with his immediate supervisor, there shouldn't be any problem taking off for two weeks. After speaking with the man from Marshfield tomorrow, he will talk to his boss about maybe getting a leave of absence.

Damian has been extensively trained as a security guard and is used to taking care of himself. He would have no fear of the trip, for his personal safety, but he is unsure about what he may encounter. Reports are always filtering back about the situation in the various Sectors and about the general state of those on the Outside. He knows that with each day, reserves and resources are becoming scarce in several areas. He knows that with each day, more and more must be succumbing to the inevitable death of those without means. Damian wonders if things have turned violent or if there simply isn't any fight left in anyone anymore, with there being nothing really left to fight over. One part of him would look forward to the adventure and the chance to know more about Shannon, but the other would fear what he may see happening to his fellow human left at the mercy of an unloving and now unforgiving world.

Coming through the front door of his apartment, Damian is greeted by his wife with a kiss on the cheek. He looks lovingly into her eyes and sees the strength of her character and a resolve to her spirit but he also sees the sadness to Sarah's soul that bothers him. Damian wants things to be better and he is more determined than ever to do what he can to make that happen.

\*     \*     \*

The next day Damian is sleep walking through his duties. His thoughts are on the phone call that night. Having said nothing to his family about the idea of finding Shannon, he feels it is best to get more information before telling them. The day passes and Damian returns to his office to file the daily reports. Finishing his tasks quickly, he sits at his desk and watches the clock. It is almost seven when the loudspeaker announces an incoming call for Damian. Reaching hurriedly for the receiver, his heart races slightly as he says, "Hello, this is Damian Schneider."

"Mr. Schneider, this is Thomas Foster. I was asked by one of the delivery drivers from our Grouping to give you a call," says the voice on the other end.

"Thank you, Mr. Foster, thank you very much for taking the time," responds Damian quickly.

"I understand you are trying to find out about a relative or someone that used to live in the Marshfield Sector. Is that right?" says Mr. Foster.

"Yes, it's my wife's sister. Her name is Shannon Dempsey. The last time we heard from her she was living in Marshfield. My family and I moved here to the Donnelly Grouping about ten years ago and we haven't known anything about her since that time," explains Damian.

"We never were a large Sector, only about two thousand at the most. Can you tell me a little about her?"

"Well, she would have been in her early thirties at the time. Very tall for a woman, thin, with red hair. I'm sorry, I can't offer much more than that."

"I do remember a Shannon in the first few years that I was at Marshfield. She was an attractive woman, very quiet and soft spoken. Does that sound like your wife's sister?"

"Oh, yes," comes an excited, quick response from Damian. "We used to joke that it was a good thing Shannon was pretty or nobody would ever notice her. She was always really quiet and stayed in the background. So you knew her?"

"I knew of her through her husband and I did meet her a few times. I had business dealings with her husband for a while, everybody did business with him."

"Her husband? So, she was married?"

"Yes, her husband introduced me to her as his wife and made a point of mentioning his son, too."

"Oh, my gosh," says Damian. "A son?"

"A very young infant, she was carrying the child in her arms the first time that I met her. I also saw her and the child on one other occasion, she sometimes traveled with her husband."

"And who was her husband?"

"I forget his name, everyone just called him Runner. He was originally employed by our Sector but after some questionable dealings, he was let go. I believe they stayed in Marshfield for only a short time after that. I heard about him a few times over the next couple of years, though."

"Questionable dealings, what did he do?"

"He was a smuggler and that became bigger business to him than his job. He violated the trading rules of Marshfield and basically was kicked out. He stayed close, though, as I know he was running goods between other Sectors for quite a while after that," explains the man.

Exchanging a few more words, the call is ended and Damian finds himself still sitting at his desk, somewhat numb and dazed. 'That had to be the right Shannon and with a husband and child,' are his thoughts. Thinking of the right way to tell his wife and of his next step, a half hour passes with Damian's mind spinning. Slowly and still deep in thought, he finally rises and reaches for his pack. Turning off the lights, Damian leaves the office and heads home to his family.

\*       \*       \*

The front room of the apartment is empty upon his return. Sarah and Christopher are in his son's room, playing a game on the computer. Laughter rolls from the room as the novice Sarah tries her hand at the new game.

"Look out, don't go that way and watch out for the guy on the right," are Christopher's directions to his mother. "Oh, Mom, that's it. You're done, give it to me," he demands with a smile. Damian waits quietly while standing in the doorway.

"Hi," he then says.

"Hi, honey," and "Hi, Dad," are returned by the two of them. Damian will just enjoyably watch as his wife and son are still very engrossed in the playing of their game.

"You're home a little late tonight, aren't you?" says Sarah when they finally finish playing their game and she gets up from her chair. "Christopher and I went ahead and ate dinner. Let me go make you a plate."

"Yeah, yeah, that would be fine," says Damian. "But I've got something that I want to tell you about first."

"What, is something wrong?" worries his wife.

"No, it's not anything like that. I might have some news about Shannon," says Damian.

"About my sister, Shannon?" says a surprised Sarah with her mouth dropping open as Christopher also quickly turns his attention from the monitor to listen to their conversation.

"Yes, I was in contact with a man who used to live in the same Sector as she did. He described someone that he knew there with the name Shannon and it sounded like your sister."

"I don't understand," says Sarah. "He knew about Shannon, how did you know about him?"

"I met one of the delivery drivers the other day from down south and asked him about Marshfield. He knew this guy who used to work there and I asked him to call me. I just had a chance to talk with him tonight."

"Dad!" says an excited Christopher. "You were able to find out something about Aunt Shannon? That's great!"

Sarah looks into Damian's soft, calm eyes. But she is almost afraid to ask the next question. "What did he say about her?" she asks with slight trepidation.

"I told him we were looking for information about your sister and that her name was Shannon. He said that he had known a Shannon in Marshfield and his description of her sounded like your sister," and then Damian doesn't go any further.

"And..." says Sarah.

"And he said that he knew her husband, had dealings with her husband, and on a few occasions had also met her."

"Her husband?" interrupts Sarah.

"Yes, her husband and her child."

"Are you sure, a husband and a child?"

"That's what he said," says Damian.

"Oh my, Shannon got married and had a baby! She always wanted that, she always wanted to have a child."

"Then I have a cousin," reasons Christopher. "Is it a boy or a girl?" A boy is the answer. "Cool! I've got a boy cousin."

The questions then come fast and furious as Damian replays the conversation for both of them. Christopher is particularly interested. Sarah is guarded but listening keenly to what Damian has to say. The enthusiasm from Christopher is contagious and soon all are active in the conversation. The son remembered some about his aunt but now wants to hear everything about her. Damian and Sarah take turns telling funny to heartwarming stories about Shannon. The stories go on for an hour.

That night, Damian and Sarah are both getting ready for bed when Sarah walks from the bathroom with toothbrush in hand and questions her husband. "So, just what are you planning to do with this information?"

"You mean with the information about Shannon?" answers Damian. "Don't know yet, I'll tell you when I do."

And he reaches over to turn out the light.

*　　*　　*

The following morning Damian goes into work earlier than required, intending to see his supervisor before having to start his own duties. Reaching the door to his office, he quietly knocks and then identifies himself when asked to come in by his boss. "Good morning, Damian," he says. "What can I do for you so early today?" The man, a Mr. Weatherly, is about sixty with that rather weathered face but a comforting countenance. He also had become associated with the Donnelly Grouping because of a personal contact, having previously been a firefighter in the times before change. Being a kind man, he is liked by all of his subordinates and by all of his fellow workers.

"Jack," says Damian, "I need to ask you a favor. I would like to put in for a two week leave. There are a few things that I want to deal with and I need some time off to do them."

"Well, that can probably be arranged. As you know, we do have provisions for that kind of thing and you're one of my best," he offers positively. "What is it that do you need to do?"

Damian then tells the story of his contact with the man from Shannon's Sector and of his desire to find out more about her. He explains that he wants to do it for his wife and in some ways, for Christopher and the family. With that amount of time away, he would be able to go to her last known location and then spend more time searching other leads. Damian states that it is a long shot, but he feels that he needs to try.

"You know things have changed down there," Mr. Weatherly then cautions. "The conditions in some of the Sectors are quite dire now. Violence may be minimal but there are still dangers, still unknowns. Are you sure you want to attempt something like this, have you given it enough thought?"

"Yes, I know it may sound a little crazy and I might come up empty handed but I want to do it. So, if it's okay with you, can you put in for a leave for me?" asks Damian.

Jack Weatherly agrees and offers his assistance in any way that he can help. Thanking him, Damian then leaves the room. He walks to his office on automatic, thoughts and plans flood his busy mind. He will wait until hearing back about his leave before discussing it with his family but his being is already in motion. In his soul, he has already begun the trip.

\*     \*     \*

Three days pass before Damian is given the good news that his leave has been approved. During that time, he has kept quiet about his decision and the home routine stayed the same. His demeanor has changed, though, a slight bit of excitement has surfaced in him and his companion of so many years has noticed but respected his privacy. Damian said that he will let her know when the time is right. And Sarah knows that he will.

Requiring secrecy from his staff until notifying his family, Damian has informed them of his plans and of the departure dates for the two week period that he has requested. He begins by asking each to carry an extra three to four shifts while he is gone. As a good man and a likeable leader, all easily agree to help during Damian's absence. There are even a few who express envy at this adventure and the change of scenery that will come with the search for Shannon. Others share the boredom and lack of control that exists in all of their lives. Men that were doers and thinkers have been reduced to simply doing as they are told, with their destiny and fate now in the hands of others.

The day is spent making preparations to be absent from his post. There is much to do and the day passes quickly. Soon, work for the day is over. Reaching for his pack and taking home a few extra papers to work on tonight, Damian leaves the office and makes the short walk back to the apartment.

"Hey, everybody, I'm home," he shouts upon entering. Then Sarah walks in from the back bedroom. "Hi, I'm home," he says again when seeing her.

"I can see that," she says with a laugh. The usual routine for Damian is to walk in quietly and give her a light kiss on the cheek. "What's gotten into you?"

"What do you mean?"

"Well, you're a little revved up, that's what. Did something happen at work today?"

"Yes, it did as a matter of fact, something did happen at work today. They gave me the two weeks off that I had requested," answers her husband.

"You're going to take two weeks off, for what? I didn't know you were taking two weeks off."

"I didn't know if I could get it but they gave it to me."

"Yeah, well, what are you going to do with two weeks off? Just get in my way probably," teases Sarah.

Damian then reaches for his wife's hand and has her sit down beside him. "I've been wanting to talk to you about it but I had to wait to see if it would work out. Sarah, I want to see if I can find out anything about Shannon. I want to go below and see if I can track her down, find out what she is doing, how she is doing."

Sarah is taken aback and words don't come quickly to her. Then slowly, she says, "Oh, Damian, that would be wonderful. I do think about her often now and admit that I am concerned but you can't do that. It's just too dangerous and I would be worried about you the whole time you were gone. You're sweet," she continues and caresses his chin with her hand. "But it's okay, I don't want you to do that."

"No, just listen a minute," says Damian. "We know where she was and I talked with the guy from her Sector again and got more information about her husband. That's where I could start. There must be someone out there who knows where I can find Shannon. I just need to find them."

"But, honey," Sarah protests, "we don't know what it's like down there now. Things are bound to be worse."

"Sarah, you know that I can take care of myself. I will give myself two weeks to find out something and if I don't come across anything, I'll just come back. I really want to do this," he ends firmly and with conviction.

Christopher opens the door from his room and walks into the kitchen where his parents are sitting. "What are you guys talking about?" he asks, noticing the serious expressions on their faces. "Is there something wrong, Mom? Is there a problem or something, Dad?" he says, turning toward his father.

"No, Christopher, it's nothing like that. I've been given two weeks off from work and I want to see if I can go back down and find out anything about Aunt Shannon," he says.

"You're kidding me," says Christopher. "Are you really going to go back down there and try and look for her?"

"I think so," answers a cautious Damian.

"Wow, that's great!" says Christopher. "Isn't that great news, Mom! That's really cool, Dad," and Christopher gives his father an unanticipated hug. He reaches for his mother and wraps his arms tightly around her. Sarah smiles back weakly as she looks over her son's shoulder toward her husband sitting across the table from them. Damian flashes back a big grin.

"Isn't that great?" says Christopher to her again.

"Yes," answers Sarah, nodding her head, realizing that at two to one she has already been outvoted. "Yes, it is, dear," and she hugs back with the strong bond of familial love that can hold us together in lonely and desperate times.

That evening, Sarah and Damian have more of a chance to talk about his going. She expresses her concerns and her fears for his safety and he returns assurances to each protest. Many things need to be done in the next few days to be ready for the trip. There will be much planning and preparation if everything is to turn out okay. Damian stays awake that night thinking as Sarah finally falls off to sleep beside him.

*　　*　　*

Clare has been working extra shifts for the past two weeks but today is a day off for her. She is in the kitchen washing dishes when James walks in from the bedroom, yawning and stretching while still in his pajamas. "Good morning," is the greeting from his mother. "Is Jenny still sleeping?"

"Yeah, she's still out like a light," James answers as he sits down at the table.

Rising early, Clare has prepared a special breakfast and now offers it to her son. She presents him with an extra large portion, having eaten less herself that morning than usual. "What's all this food for?" James asks as the full plate is set in front of him. "I'll save some for Jenny."

"No, that's all for you," says his mother. "I just thought that you could use the extra calories, you're getting bigger everyday," she says lovingly as she runs her hand through her son's hair. Clare doesn't know what she would do without James. He has been her rock, her savior. His unselfishness and positive attitude has helped her tremendously over the past few years. Without the young man to lean on occasionally, Clare is not really sure that she could have made it.

"Are you sure we have enough?" he asks again.

"Yes, go ahead, honey. Rations are issued again the day after tomorrow, so we'll be just fine."

James is, indeed, quite hungry and dives into the plate of food. At eighteen now, he is beginning to add weight and fill out his teenage frame. With each passing day, Clare feels as though she can witness the changes in him. Forced to grow up quickly, James has become the man of the house.

He has accepted the position without hesitation and Clare is extremely proud of his character and his goodness of heart. She considers James and her daughter, Jenny, as the blessings in her life as have connected parents throughout the years. But in this period of desperation and decline, it has taken on even more meaning. Without much good left in the world, Clare looks to them to give her the strength to carry on.

Finishing the last bit of food on his plate, James puts down his fork and continues to sit at the table, watching his mother cleaning the dishes. "I finished reading the book on geology," he then says to her. "It was really, really interesting. The earth is so old and so ancient. I can't even imagine millions of years. First, the planet was really hot and barren, then it was a tropical rain forest, and then it was covered in ice. It's unbelievable the changes it has gone through." James has always been an avid reader. A book accompanied him wherever he went, sometimes reading an entire book in one or two days if it really interested him. Without schools functioning now, Clare encourages James' love of reading as a way of educating himself.

"I think I'd like to go back to the school today and get some more books. Is that okay with you if I do that this afternoon?"

"Yes, sweetie, I just want you to be careful walking on the way there," says his mother.

"Sophie's going with me. We're supposed to meet each other at two, near the old theater. We thought that was probably about halfway between our houses."

"Oh, that's good. I'm glad that you have someone to go with, how did you arrange that?"

"Jenny and I were out front the other day and Mr. Brannan walked past. I asked him to see if she might want to go with me this week and he said he would ask her. Yesterday, he stopped by again and we set it up."

Clare continues working at the sink. Her back is turned to her son as James stays seated at the table. A few minutes will pass before he says starts talking again. "Mom?" the teenage boy quietly says his mother.

"Yes, dear," answers Clare.

"Do you think that it's going to get worse here on Earth? You know, like get hotter or have even weirder weather? I mean, do you think that it's going to happen really quickly or something?" says a disheartened James.

Clare immediately stops what she is doing and turns toward her son. It is a concern for her as it is for all families now. And it is a subject not often discussed by anyone anymore because things seem so out of control and so utterly hopeless. But now, the question is being directly presented to her by her son and James deserves a straightforward and honest answer.

She begins by speaking slowly and thoughtfully to her son. "I don't know, James, no one does for sure. It has happened faster than people used to think it would. But maybe the worst is over for now, maybe things will kind of level out for a while," Clare says, offering hope but staying realistic.

"But what's going to happen when I'm forty or fifty years old and when Jenny is older? Is there still going to be enough food and water for everybody?" asks James.

Clare moves from the sink and sits down with her son at the table. She looks deeply into his eyes and can sense his fear, his worry of what life may hold in store for him. She knows that the future isn't bright, that the plans and dreams for today's youth lie wasting away and buried under the debris and destruction of poor choices by adults over the past fifty years. Clare wants to break down, bury her head in her hands, and just cry but she won't, she can't. Her job as a parent is to stay strong.

"We'll be together for a long time, you and me and Jenny," says Clare. "Things will work out, I think things will work out." But the anger then rises in her again as it does in others about the stupidity, the short-sightedness, and the selfishness of the human race. And now her children and all other children are simply on the last lap of that race, running toward a certain end that will declare no winners.

\*　　\*　　\*

The afternoon arrives and James goes to meet Sophie. They soon rendezvous and start off for the high school. Situated near the edge of town, this large building had operated as the last functioning school for a number of years, combining all grades into one location as the population had dwindled. With the collapse of communities and cities, volunteers had kept the traditional institutions functioning for as long as possible. An attempt at normalcy was preserved for a short period of time with students attending classes three days a week. The practice was finally abandoned after so many had fled the cities and when the other basic demands of life took precedence. People had simply walked away from them one day leaving everything behind: desks, tables, hangings on the wall, and books.

"Thanks for taking me along," Sophie says to James as they walk the mostly deserted blocks toward the school.

"Oh, thanks for coming. It's great to have someone to go with, I usually make this trip alone."

"How often do you go there?"

"Sometimes I go every couple of weeks and sometimes not for a month or two. It kind of depends on how much reading I've been doing," answers James.

The two turn the last corner and can now see the school in front of them. He and Sophie climb the steps to the front entry. The heavy front doors are partially open and James pushes hard on one to allow them into the building. The halls are dusty with pictures and posters hanging at odd angles on the walls.

Occasionally, a chair or table rests on its side blocking their path and they step around it. James knows his way around, though, and they walk first to the science rooms.

"What are you looking for?" asks Sophie.

"I want to try and find some more books about geology and then maybe get another one on astronomy. I thought we could start there. I might want to pick up another history book, too. What are you interested in?" says James.

"I don't know. I'll just look around," she answers.

They enter the classroom and James heads to a bookcase on the far side of the room. Sophie surveys the scene with its rows of empty desks and dusty chairs. Walking the perimeter of the room, she stops to read old posters and look at scientific charts still hanging there. Sophie makes her way to the front of the room where the teacher's desk is placed. Pulling out the chair and wiping off its seat, she sits down.

The top of the desk still has pens, papers, and notebooks that are lying there. Sophie looks through the assorted material and stops when she comes across a particularly dusty sheet of paper entitled 'Morning Announcement' with the caption 'Please read to first period class.' Sophie begins reading aloud.

"All students please note that the pep rally this afternoon will be held at two p.m., one hour earlier than scheduled," she says in a louder, deeper, and more authoritative voice than her own and James turns around to look in her direction. "Sixth and seventh periods are cancelled so we may all take part in a special treat. Playing at the rally this afternoon will be The Firebirds, our favorite rock and roll band, from two thirty until three thirty. Come one, come all, as The Firebirds take off and rocket us into a win against the Cougars tonight. Go Cardinals!" Sophie ends with a cheerleader's exuberance.

"Go Cardinals!" shouts James from the back of the room and both break into laughter. James makes his way to the front of the room and sits down in a first row desk opposite Sophie.

"That must have been fun," she says to him.

"Yeah, I asked my mom one time about her high school. She said it was one of the best times in her life." And then both sit quietly and pensively for a few moments, never having known such things. They will never know what they have missed.

After James selects two of the books, the pair move on to the history and the social studies classrooms. James now becomes immersed in looking through all the different selections and begins making piles on the floor of books to take with him now and of others to come back for later. Sophie drifts off and begins wandering the halls. Soon, she enters a separate room in the back of the building with a large bank of high windows lining one side of the room. It is not a traditional classroom as large flat top tables and easels fill the space.

Dried paint brushes and markers rest silently on the tables with large sheets of paper and posters also piled there. Sophie slowly circulates the room, looking at the paintings and sketches still posted on the walls. She makes her way toward one easel near the window with a heavy posterboard clipped onto it. Standing in front of it, Sophie looks around to find a large pencil nearby that she can use. She begins to draw and then time slowly slips into the background.

James takes three more books and gets up from the floor. He pushes the stack of the others for which he will return later against the wall. Having been engrossed in what he was doing, he realizes that Sophie has been gone for quite a while. James goes off in search of her and soon finds her in the art room. Entering, he sees her standing in front of an easel.

"Hi, I didn't know where you had gone. What are you doing?" he asks her.

Sophie doesn't look up at him while continuing to work and answers, "Oh, nothing, just drawing."

"Can I see?" asks James as he steps around the easel.

In the center of the picture, a building is drawn, institutional in design. On the left side of the paper, there are several flowers of different heights blooming in the foreground, progressively getting larger until reaching a group of flowing trees with their limbs cascading to the ground. The sun and the birds are in the sky behind them. Looking to the right, he sees a few withered stems listing bleakly to one side in the foreground. In the back of the picture, the sky is darkened with heavy bold strokes. There are no trees between the sky and the ground, only large rocks, cold and hard and barren rocks.

It's a simple and quick rendering but it is spatial and artistic. James is impressed that Sophie is able to draw so quickly and accurately. The flowers look real and expressive, the trees bold and majestic, and the building clear and in proportion. Sophie finishes with a few more strokes and lays down her pencil.

"I didn't know that you could draw so well!" exclaims James. "You're really good at it."

Sophie smiles back at him. "Thanks."

"What's the building in the center?"

"The school," she says.

"And what about the flowers and the trees? Do you mean anything by them, do they represent something to you or are they just flowers and trees? I really like them, I mean, they don't have to represent anything," as James ends awkwardly.

"I don't know. I just started thinking about all the kids that have gone to school here, how they got bigger each year, like the way flowers grow. The trees are the teachers."

"And the difference between the two sides?"

"Before and now," says Sophie simply.

"Oh," says James with a full understanding.

He and Sophie leave the high school with books in hand and make their way back across town. James walks her all the way home this time. Exchanging conversation on the way there, they learn more about each other. Finding out that they think alike, they make plans to soon get together again. James then walks home quickly and quietly, carrying the now heavy books. And he forgets for the moment how pretty Sophie is, only thinking about how good a friend that she might become.

*   *   *

Michael and Sean work together to move the heavy desk to the other side of the room. By rearranging the furniture, they have made two separate areas in the large room that the boy and his mother had shared. Sean's mattress is moved beside the window and Michael has set up near the door. With boxes and furniture in between, the dormitory room setup is complete.

For the past few days since burying Sean's mother, Michael has made a point of taking Sean with him whenever venturing outside. They have become inseparable, with Sean showing him the lay of the land and with Michael offering him the needed companionship. It has also been good for the boy to be outside and to become active again. When his father became missing, Sean and his mother had mostly stayed inside the building and had remained hidden from sight.

Sean has kept a few things of his mother and he now places them safely away in a box. The rest of her things have been taken to another room by Michael, to get them out of sight of the young boy. Sean now works to create a space of his own, to create his own place in the world. The boy is getting a taste of independence from the hunger of separation.

Michael, too, is arranging his area and goes to another room to obtain a straight back chair to place beside his mattress on the floor. He returns and says, "Alright, that's it. My decorating is done, how is yours coming along?"

"Really good," says Sean. "But you gave me the side with the view. I can trade with you later if you want."

"No, I like my side just fine. Plus, I don't want to have to pay extra just for the view. People like you must have all the money," jokes Michael.

"Yeah, I got a lot of money," answers the boy playing along. "I just wish I had someplace to spend it."

Michael likes Sean and greatly enjoys having the young boy's company. While traveling with the other Outsiders, connections of friendship and mutual support did not exist. One could not let his guard down, even for a moment, and this lack of relationship would become a large hole in most lives.

"Hey, how about a game of basketball?" Michael asks of his young roommate.

"A game of basketball, what do you mean?"

"I think that I'm probably a better shot than you, want to take me on?" he says. Sean just looks at him and laughs, not knowing what he has in mind. "No seriously, I'll play you in a game of Horse and if you lose, then you cook dinner tonight."

"You mean, I open the cans tonight."

"Right, you open the cans."

Smiling broadly now, Sean nods his head agreeably. "Okay, tell me how you play," he says.

"Got a pair of socks?" asks Michael and Sean pulls a pair from a box near his bed. Rolling each into a ball, he hands one to the boy and keeps one for himself. Grabbing a nearby wastebasket, he places it in the middle of the room. Five books are placed on the floor at different spots and at different distances from the basket. "Alright," Michael begins, "the first one to make it from all five spots wins. You have to make the basket to continue and when you miss it's the other person's turn. You can challenge for a second try but if you miss, then you have to start over. Got it?" he asks his young challenger.

"Yeah, I think so," says Sean.

"Okay, you first," offers Michael.

Sean steps to the spot on the floor and pausing momentarily to steady himself, takes aim and lets the sock fly. Moving toward the basket in a perfect arc, it drops directly into the middle for a score. "Yes!" comes the loud exclamation from Sean.

"Lucky, that's all, it was just a lucky shot," says Michael with his good-natured and intended ribbing.

Sean then sets himself at the second book, a bit farther away. Also a good looking throw, this one hits hard at the back of the wastebasket but drops in. Another whoop exits Sean's mouth as he goes to the can to retrieve his sock.

"So, you're a ringer, acting like you didn't know how to play to set me up. I guess I know when I'm being taken," says Michael, adding more fuel to the fire.

Sean goes on to the win the first game and, of course, Michael will challenge him to a second. And then it moves on to the best two out of three as the afternoon wears on lazily. Laughter and banter continue as the two of them play in a room high above the deserted streets of the lifeless city below. They wage the battle against themselves, against their still innate competitive nature, and against the unseen forces that are trying to take that very life away from them on a daily basis.

"Okay, I give up," says Michael. "You win."

And they sit down on nearby chairs, resting and recalling the game just finished. It has been a good break, a good reprieve, and has continued to build a connection between the two. Sean is particularly excited to have a guy around again, someone to act as a buddy, someone with whom to have fun. Having his father go out of his life so early, and often absent even when he was with them, Sean has missed the companionship that a male friend so easily and naturally offers a young boy.

"Well, what do you want to do next?" Michael asks his cohort. "We've got some daylight left."

"I know," quickly jumps in Sean, in a flash of thought. "Let's go somewhere and look for a ball."

"A ball?" says Michael, not really understanding his point. "Go somewhere and look for a ball?"

"Yeah, a ball, any kind of ball. If we could just find one, then maybe we could have a real game. Maybe we could play outside or do something like that."

Michael looks over at his young partner and just smiles. "Capital idea, my dear boy, capital," is his goofy response.

They make their way down the back staircase and out the heavy fire door leading to the street. Taking the time to close it securely, they pile some debris in front to make it look unused, uninviting. The area that surrounds them is mostly businesses and commercial interests, the old downtown section of the city that now sits as an eerie empty shell of that previous commerce. Storefronts have been looted and anything worthwhile, anything small enough to be carried away, is gone.

Large items such as furniture or appliances sit in the same place in which they were left when the owners had simply walked away from their stores. On occasion, an entire display area has been left untouched with a dining room still staged, an inch deep in dust, waiting for those absent dinner guests that will never arrive. At other locations, there are entire buildings filled with products standing in an unreal and unearthly monument to stuff and to the once earnest striving for things.

Michael and Sean then enter several buildings on their search but in the many offices and businesses, the search for a ball is proving elusive. "I don't know, Sean, it doesn't seem like we're going to have much luck around here. Let's check out a few more, though," Michael says as they emerge back on the street.

"Alright," says the youngster. "But if we don't find any here, we should go out to where the houses are. Somebody's got to have a ball in one of those places."

"I think you might be right," agrees Michael. "Where do you think we ought to start?"

"Well, my dad and I went that way one time," says Sean, pointing in a northerly direction. "We found a place that looked like it used to be a nice neighborhood with really big houses in it. We saw a few people still living in them and still using them. But that was a long time ago."

After looking in a few more buildings, the pair decide to take their search to the suburbs, what was left of them. Walking the deserted, abandoned streets is always disconcerting. No matter how many times you may see the wasteland of rotting cities and decaying towns, it strikes at the human soul. It resonates with the hopelessness and despair and disgust at a world driven into want by those that had tread too heavily upon it. It represents the death and destruction of lives. And you must remain vigilant if desirous of avoiding a similar fate.

Sean is falling behind as he stops to check out the contents of a car resting on the sidewalk with its doors open. He is inside the vehicle now. From a distance, Sean then hears Michael calling to him and he quickly gives up the search to hurry back to where the older man waits for him.

"You better stay up with me," says Michael. "We should stick together in case we come across somebody. I don't really know what to expect out here."

"Okay," is Sean's dutiful reply.

They now enter that area of larger homes with their expensive automobiles rusting in the streets. When food supplies became extremely scarce and the production was taken over by large corporate or wealthy concerns, anyone outside of a Sector or Grouping simply had no way to obtain food on a regular basis.

People gave up their residences and personal property to move to places where food could still be purchased. Consequently, neighborhoods such as these were simply abandoned.

Moving from one house to another, Michael and Sean begin their search for a ball. Each residence is quite different, some have been stripped of all belongings or have been taken away by the former tenants. In others, except for the dust, it looks as though the owners had left earlier this morning, with closets full of clothes and dishes left on the table. The problem for ball searching, however, is that very few people in the last generation were having children. So, the lack of toys and games is apparent in each house that they search, until they get to the last house on this one particularly long block.

They walk through a back door into the garage. They notice several bicycles hanging from the ceiling. Michael and Sean then make their way into the kitchen. Surveying the scene, Sean is the first to spot a smaller table with two chairs near the window. "Look at that, these people must have had some kids. And look over here," he says as he rushes toward a baseball bat in the corner of the room.

"Yeah, we might get lucky," says Michael.

The home is completely furnished but they find nothing in the rooms or closets downstairs. They remain optimistic as they make their way to the second floor bedrooms. At one end of the upper hallway is the large master bedroom with its own bath. But at the other end are two smaller bedrooms that must have been used by the children and this is where they concentrate their search.

"I'll check this one out and you look in the other," Michael says to Sean.

Each starts the process of searching a room, looking under the bed, inside the cabinets and dressers, and in the closets. It is Sean who makes the discovery. In the back of what must have been the boy's closet, under a pile of dirty clothes, is a partially deflated volleyball. "I got it!" yells Sean. "I found a ball."

And Michael comes running from the other room to join him. "Good work," he says to the boy.

"But it's flat," says Sean disappointedly.

"That's okay. There's probably a pump here somewhere," says Michael and they go downstairs to head to the garage. With bicycles hanging there, the two stand a good chance.

They both look through the debris and clutter until Michael comes up with an old but functioning pump that they will be able to make work. Feeling good with themselves for successfully completing their mission, they fail to hear the voices in the street coming toward them until it is almost too late.

"Wait, be quiet," says Michael in a hushed and serious voice. "I thought I just heard something." The two stand quietly in the garage, listening, until the voices are heard again. "Hurry, back in the house," Michael says with a sense of urgency. Both rush in and quickly close and lock the door behind them. Telling Sean to stay where he is, Michael moves to the front window and peers out to the street from behind the curtain.

"What do you see, who is it?" asks Sean.

"It's three guys. They're in front of the house now, be quiet," he says. "Oh, shit," are the next words out of his mouth.

"What?" says Sean. "What!"

Michael moves from the window and checks the lock on the front door. He then motions to Sean to follow him and the two run up the stairs to the second level. "They started walking up the front sidewalk toward the house. We locked the door into the kitchen, didn't we?" he asks hurriedly.

"Yeah, we locked it," says Sean.

"Alright, just stay here. Let's see what they do."

Michael's concern is starting to scare Sean. He can sense the worry in his voice. "What do they want?" he asks Michael with a slight quiver in his voice.

"Probably just looking for food." Both are listening intently when they hear someone trying the doorknob on the front door. "Ssshh, quiet," comes Michael's warning again. The next sound is frightening as they hear the banging and pounding on the door getting louder. They are trying to break it down.

"Hurry, get in here," Michael says to Sean and leads him into the master bedroom. Looking about quickly, Michael opens the door to the large closet and they both disappear inside. It is filled with many clothes, long women's dresses and long men's pants.

Michael instructs Sean to stand behind them so his feet can't be seen and then he does the same on the other side. At that time, they hear the front door come crashing in.

"Oh, no," says the terrified boy. "I think they're inside the house now!"

"I know. Just be quiet and try not to move and make sure that you stay behind the clothes," says Michael as he tries to comfort and reassure Sean.

Voices rise from downstairs as the men ransack the house, concentrating on the kitchen. 'Get a chair and look above the refrigerator' and 'Nothing's here, just like all the other houses' and 'Shut up and keep looking.' Cabinet doors are opened and slammed shut as drawers are emptied onto the floor and their contents crash to the ground.

They then hear the sound of footsteps on the staircase. "They're coming up the stairs," whispers Sean to Michael.

"Sssshhhh, let's just try to be quiet and see what they do," he says. The men are searching the other bedrooms for something of value or something for which to trade. They even search the bathroom for any medicines or bandages that might be of use. One of the men enters the master bedroom.

"Damn it, let's get the hell out of here, there's nothing here," comes the loudest voice, the one who has been doing most of the talking. Michael thinks to himself this must be the leader.

"But I haven't checked the closet yet," complains the man that is in their bedroom.

"What are you looking for anyway, a cashmere sweater or a fancy suit or something?" says the other one.

"That's it, Maury's looking for a suit," taunts the leader. "I know, Maury's going to the ballet tonight. He's going to get all dressed up 'cause he's got a hot date," and both men break into peals of laughter as they descend the stairs.

"Aw, screw you guys," says the man in their bedroom as he then follows the others down and out the front door. In a few minutes, quiet once again falls over the house.

"Are they gone?" asks Sean.

"Yeah, I think they're gone," says Michael coming out from behind the clothes. Sean rushes over to him and throws his arms around the bigger man's waist. Michael puts one arm around the boy's shoulders and the other cradles the back of his head. They stand in the darkness of the closet, huddled together. Michael realizes that Sean was scared, very scared, and that he needs to make him feel safe again. Michael knows that he has a new purpose with his life. He must offer the boy comfort and hope in a world now very empty of either one.

The two will stay in the house until dusk has fallen. Taking a different route back to their building, they move hurriedly through the streets. Fortunately, the three men are nowhere to be seen and Michael and Sean soon reach their building. They will dine on a simple meal, exchange light conversation, and retire early for the night. Sean falls asleep quickly while Michael lies awake for an hour. Many thoughts visit his mind, mainly about his boyhood and his now lost family. Looking out the window, the still ever present stars twinkle back at him.

\*      \*      \*

The preparations for the trip are progressing well. Damian has everything at the security department finalized and all the shifts are covered. He needs to finish some reports this evening and then his work requirements will be met. He leaves in just two days and now the tasks are focused on packing and preparing for his absence from home. Over the past few days, Damian has spoken often with Christopher about watching over his mother. The husband knows that Sarah is worried for him and hopes that Christopher can support her while he is gone.

Christopher assures him that things will be fine. A change has come over his son recently that Damian has noticed. Instead of his normal teenage sullen self, Christopher has been more animated, more positive, and has volunteered his help whenever the opportunity has presented itself. It is a welcome change and convinces Damian that he is doing the right thing, if for no other reason than elevating Christopher's mood and optimism about life. Luckily, Damian is already reaping some rewards from his decision and this drives him on.

Deciding to only carry but one smaller backpack, he now has the challenge of packing it lightly but with all the essential equipment. Most of the weight inside the pack will come from two fairly large water bottles and enough food to offer a scant but sustainable daily diet for the two weeks. Items such as a compass, maps, flashlight, and a folding multi-tool will be packed into the side pouches. Damian will take a jacket, another t-shirt, and a few pairs of socks. Other than that, he will wear what he has on his back for the two weeks as it is not a vacation, it is a mission.

Sarah easily lends her help whenever asked but there is a reluctance, a hesitation to her actions. While wanting to know more about Shannon's situation and having accepted Damian's decision, she can't help but be nervous and worry about his leaving. Sarah feels guilt and responsibility for having had this come to pass. If she hadn't complained, if she had remained strong about their situation, then her husband might not be taking this risk now. It is something that Damian has told Sarah over and over again that he is doing for all of them, not just for her, but she still feels those pangs of guilt.

And Sarah worries that she may be trading the surety of a husband for the unknown of a sister, already gone for these many years. If anything were to happen to her husband, to her son's father, Sarah feels as though she would never forgive herself. This thinking has cast a long shadow over her rays of hope about Shannon. But the anticipation and excitement shown by her husband and her son pull her along with them.

Damian has made an arrangement with the same driver that had previously helped him. When their regular delivery occurs this week, Damian has been granted permission by both Groupings to receive a ride back down the mountain. He will then continue with them to the south before reaching his road west toward the coast. It will enable Damian to travel the greater portion of the distance by truck before he must find a way on his own for the rest of the journey.

Damian first plans to visit the site of the Marshfield Sector and to see if anyone still lives there and then if that proves futile with no leads, he will travel to other Sectors. There are at least three others that are still functioning within a reasonably close distance from Marshfield. It is possible that Shannon's family had found work or protection in one of these nearby organizations and are living there now.

"So, do you have maps, Dad?" asks Christopher. He and his father have Damian's pack laying on the floor, with all necessary items arranged nearby. They are in the middle of a practice run to see how everything is going to fit.

"Yes I do. Look in the small pocket on the front of the pack, Chris. I think I put them in there," says Damian as he continues working on his checklist.

Christopher pulls out the map and begins looking it over. Continuing a trend, most Groupings have retreated to higher elevations for better security protection, for the availability of water sources, and for the cooler daytime temperatures that they offer. But often Sectors are still located in the previously large coastal cities, making use of their infrastructure.

"Where is the place Aunt Shannon was living?" Christopher asks his father while perusing the map.

Damian looks up from what he is doing and slides over beside his son to show him. "Down in this area," he says, pointing to a spot on the map. He and Christopher then continue surveying the lay of the land, discussing his plans, and exchanging ideas about the trip. It is an older map with state parks, attractions, and points of interest still clearly marked on it.

"What are all these?" asks Christopher.

"See this place here," says Damian. "It's a deep canyon that cuts through a ridge of low hills. There is a river there, or was, that had a series of waterfalls on it. When you were just a little boy, your mother and I took you there and we have a picture of you standing near one reaching your hand into it."

Christopher is silent for a moment. Pensively gazing at the map, he then looks over at Damian. "Do you think I'll ever get to see some of these places?" he asks.

Damian doesn't know how to respond to his son. It is the same old dilemma, to tell the disheartening truth or to offer some fabricated hope so as to not crush any of the remaining optimism of youth. Damian is unable to do either and simply answers by saying, "I don't know, Christopher. I don't know."

The subject is changed quickly. "How about some lunch?" offers the father.

"Sure, that sounds pretty good to me," says Christopher, coming back into the moment. And they walk into the kitchen together to make something to eat.

*　　*　　*

Two days have now passed and the morning that Damian is to leave arrives. Sarah is up early, preparing a special breakfast for her husband while he finishes the packing. Coming out of the bedroom now, he sits down at the table and watches his wife working at the kitchen counter. The admiration and love that he has for her swells within him as he thinks back on the years that they have spent together. Theirs has truly been a partnership with a sharing and a mutual respect that strengthens marriages and enables them to last. Damian knows that he was lucky to find a mate such as Sarah.

"Are you hungry?" his wife asks, putting down a full plate of food in front of him.

"I'd better be," answers Damian. "I won't have to eat again until the second week with all this food. What are you trying to do, make me fat?"

"I'm just trying to make you miss me, so you'll hurry back," says Sarah.

"Come here," he says to her and she comes to sit on his lap. "You don't have to do anything to make me want to hurry back to you." And they embrace and exchange a short kiss before Sarah moves to the other chair to sit down with him.

"Damian, I want you to take something with you, something to give to Shannon if you do find her," Sarah asks of her husband.

Reaching into her front pocket, she pulls out a plastic ring, a toy ring, the type that were popular in bubble gum machines and candy boxes in the old days.

"What is it?" he asks.

"When we were young, I was about nine or ten and Shannon was seven or eight, we would play that it was a wedding ring. Both of us would talk about who we were going to marry, where we were going to live, and how many children we would have. For some reason, both of us really got into the marriage thing for a while and we would take turns wearing the ring, pretending that one of us was already married.

"Not long before we moved away, Shannon gave me the ring. She had kept it through all those years. When she gave it to me, she said, 'Here, you might as well keep it. I don't think marriage or children are going to happen for me.' It was one of the last times that I saw her. And that was when I realized how important it was to her and how disappointing it was to still be alone. But now she has a husband and a son, just like I do. When you see her, tell her it's her turn again," ends Sarah as she hands him the ring for safekeeping.

"I will," says Damian. And he places it carefully into a small pocket in his pack, precious cargo to be protected.

"I think I'll go wake Christopher. I told him last night that I'd get him up early enough to spend time with you before you leave," says Sarah as she gets up from the table.

\*     \*     \*

The early morning hours then drift slowly away. Damian has packed and repacked a few times until all is ready. Everything is in its place and he now shoulders the pack to adjust the straps. With Christopher helping from behind, they work on it until the fit is comfortable and the weight is distributed.

"What do you think? I kind of look like you, although I'm not going to climb any mountains," says Damian in reference to their earlier recollection of Christopher as a small boy.

"Oh, I wouldn't say that. I think you're climbing a pretty big mountain if you ask me," returns his son with a rather grown-up and mature analysis of what may lie ahead for his father.

"Well, I'll try to do you proud," says Damian.

"You already have," answers Christopher and the two of them exchange a firm, meaningful handshake, looking long into one another's eyes. A pride is felt on Damian's side, for a son growing into a man, for a son now also becoming a friend.

Sarah has baked a special treat for Damian to take with him. Usually all that is provided to the members are the staples, foodstuffs that offer calories and protein to keep a body going. But occasionally, the Grouping will have the opportunity to purchase some sugar or other sweet item and then it is doled out in small portions to each family. Sarah usually saves such treats for a birthday or a special event, usually only two or three times a year. She has decided that now is one of those times.

"Here, these are for you," she says to Damian, handing him a small bag of cookies.

"You shouldn't have done that. You guys keep them, I won't need them," he protests.

"I saved some for us, these are for you. I figure you can live it up some night," and then Sarah falls silent. She moves toward her husband and puts her arms around his neck. "You be careful, you hear? Don't do anything stupid and don't take any risks that you don't have to." They embrace and hold each other tightly, hold each other close as neither one wants to let go.

"Alright, are you guys going to walk down with me?" Damian then asks, trying to lift the mood.

"Sure, we will," answers Christopher, reaching for his pack. "I'll carry it for you, Dad."

"Thanks, Chris," says the appreciative father. And the three of them leave the apartment with Damian winding up in the middle, his arms around both Christopher and Sarah. They follow the road leading to the warehouse, making their way toward his departure, together as a family.

The walk is spent in easy, casual conversation about only simple things. There will be no big good-byes spoken and no big concerns discussed, they are past that now. And they all notice the sense of adventure and change that is in the air. Each knows that today is at least different from all the others that have come before and from all those that will surely follow again.

The delivery truck is parked at the dock with the unloading nearly complete as they approach the building. Damian sees the driver inside the front entrance and hurries off to meet with him. Christopher stands with his mother and the pack.

"Do you think everything is going to be okay for Dad?" he asks with a bit of trepidation in his voice.

"You know what, sweetie," answers Sarah in a matter of fact manner. "I'm starting to think that everything will probably turn out just fine," she says, putting her arm around Christopher and giving him a slight squeeze.

Damian comes from the warehouse and walks back to where his family is standing. "The driver says that they're almost ready to leave." Damian then takes the pack from Christopher and straps it on his back. He shakes his son's hand and pats him on the shoulder at the same time. Sarah and Damian embrace and exchange a few private words.

"So, I'll see you both in two weeks," says the soon to be absent father and husband.

"Promise?" says Sarah.

"Yes, I promise," and Damian turns to join the other two men heading for the truck. There is room in the cab for four and as he climbs into the backseat, he turns to look to where his wife and son are standing. Smiles cross their faces as they wave good-bye. Damian smiles back at them.

\*     \*     \*

Their truck has now been traveling for almost five hours. They are down and out of the mountains and onto the flatter, straighter sections of highway. The hot dry air of late afternoon blows through the inside of the truck as they bump along the deteriorating roadways. Nearing the junction where Damian is to be dropped off, the truck slows to the side of the road. Exiting the cab, he thanks the driver for the lift.

"Sure, see you in two weeks. Is that right, pick you up two weeks from today, right here?" shouts back the driver above the engine noise of the vehicle.

"Yes, so don't forget to stop when you see me by the road. I'll probably be anxious to get home by then," quips Damian.

"Yeah, if we're not running behind schedule, we might be able to stop for you," jokes the driver in return. Pulling away with a roar of the engine and in a plume of rising dust, the truck quickly disappears into the distance.

The intersection is an odd collection of dilapidated buildings in various stages of disintegration. On three of the corners sit the hulking shells of gas stations that pumped their last drop of fuel years ago. The remaining corner has an L-shaped building that declares 'Restaurant' on one side and 'Nan's Nook' on the other. Damian makes his way toward the restaurant.

Pushing open a broken door, he enters into an eerie scene, one covered in thick dust. A menu still stands posted high on a wall, broken appliances and dishes are strewn across the room, and utensils with napkins underneath still sit on some tables. Damian surveys the scene around him with a feeling of despair and disappointment, with a sense of loss and regret. Life has left this landscape long ago and in its place one can sense the desolation and loneliness that has replaced it.

Now placing his pack on a table, Damian sits down in one of the booths to rest and reconnoiter. He is still a fair distance from the coast but his connecting road heads west from here. Knowing that early morning is the best time for traveling, he decides to rest for the night and then start his trek a few hours before daybreak. Gazing out the large windows of the restaurant, musing for a moment, Damian observes the dead and deserted surroundings in front of him.

Obviously in the previous years, this must have been a busy intersection, the convergence of a major north-south corridor with an important one leading to the west. Commerce would have flowed through here with trucks stopping to refuel, with travelers taking a well-earned break, and with locals moving from home to work to friends. Now all that exists is a void and an emptiness of humanity. And wherever life may still flicker, the cold hard winds of despair blow harder each year and make those still lucky enough to hold a candle wonder how much longer even they can protect the flame.

Damian continues sitting at the table while eating something and washing it down with a few large gulps of water. The sun lowers in the sky and will soon disappear below the horizon. Knowing the need for rest if he is to start early the next morning, Damian searches for a place to lie down. The heat of the day still oppressively permeates the building. Finding the cooler tiles of the bathroom floor to offer some relief, he places his pack on the floor and using it as a rest for his head, lies down. It will take some time but eventually he falls to sleep. The stars climb in the sky as restless dreams dance in and out of Damian's mind throughout the night.

*　　*　　*

Four a.m. and the noise of doors slamming on a vehicle jars Damian from his slumber. Sitting up abruptly, he is disoriented, not understanding where he is for a minute. Then the reality settles in quickly. He hears voices and rising from his place on the floor, peers out the bathroom window. Directly across the highway at one of the deserted gas stations, a large delivery truck has pulled to the side of the road with its engine running and lights on. Damian sees two men standing in front of the truck engaged in conversation. He strains to listen.

"We have to be there by daylight and if we keep stopping for Jenkins, we'll never make it," says one.

"I know, I know, but what are we supposed to do? Have him do it in the truck?" says the other.

Damian looks at his watch and sees that it is time for him to be getting up anyway. Putting on his pack, he moves from the bathroom and out the front door of the restaurant. Taking a circuitous route, hiding behind abandoned cars and the various buildings, he eventually makes his way to a row of gas pumps that are directly behind the truck. Having noticed that the vehicle is headed west, down the road that he needs to travel, Damian has quickly formed a plan in his mind.

Crouching low behind the pumps, he is waiting quietly when Damian sees a third man come walking back from the other side of the building. "Finally," says one of the men to him. "Why don't you just put a cork in it, you're going to make us late."

"Yeah, well, it ain't no fun for me. Why don't you just put a cork in your mouth?" he counters.

"Shut up, you two," says the man climbing in on the driver's side. "Let's get this thing moving again." And the other two quickly scramble back into the cab. A slight grinding of the gears takes place as the driver revs the engine.

Without hesitation, Damian springs from behind the pumps and begins running toward the back of the truck as it pulls back onto the roadway. Luckily, it is a large truck and takes some time to gain speed. Damian is close now and reaches for a handhold on the side of the rear cargo door. Firmly grabbing it, he jumps from the pavement onto the rear bumper of the truck.

Safely on, Damian fumbles at the door latch with one hand while holding on tightly with the other. He is able to release it, can open the door slightly, and crawls underneath into the back of the truck. The fumes of the exhaust rush in at him so he closes the door again, being careful not to lock it. Sitting down, Damian looks around the dark interior of the truck while bouncing down the hard road. But for him, it is a soft landing, realizing that he will now be traversing miles in minutes, miles that would have taken hours by foot.

The monotony of the highway noise soon lulls Damian back into a light sleep until a bump in the road brings him back into consciousness. 'Oh, no, better not do that,' he thinks to himself and straightens his back while repositioning his seating arrangement. Pulling a map from his pocket, he uses a flashlight and is able to see the route toward the old Marshfield Sector. He notices that the present road will turn north before reaching the coast. If he is to make his way on west to Marshfield, he will have to watch for this intersection. Damian figures it is about two hours away so he must stay awake and alert.

In the darkness, his thoughts turn inward to his previous life on the 'outside.' The past ten years have slipped by quietly and quickly, with very few frames of reference and without any significant changes or events. Damian now feels like someone who can't afford vacations, who can't afford to leave town or to take time off and simply exists within their own small sphere, day after day and year after year. Like a pauper who doesn't have the ability to enjoy life's sweetness, one's existence today is a bitter substitute for real living.

Time passes until Damian then hears the downshifting of the truck's engine as it slows down. Moving toward the rear door, he opens it quickly. Early morning light is filling the sky as he looks out on the landscape moving past. The truck continues to reduce speed and Damian grabs his pack and moves to the edge of the truck bed. Looking around the side of the truck shows him that his intersection is just ahead.

When the vehicle slows to make the turn, Damian leaps from the bumper onto the roadway. Then running to keep up with his feet, he stumbles but doesn't fall as he makes his way to the side of the road and ducks behind some rocks. Peering over the top, Damian sees the truck disappear down the highway with its occupants never knowing about their hitchhiking guest.

Standing up again, he looks out upon a dry and desolate scene with no signs of life. The road leading toward the Marshfield Sector stretches out in front of him. Damian is close now and with an energetic determination, he begins walking toward the coast and walking toward his goal.

*　　*　　*

The second afternoon is the hardest. Damian had walked for almost eighteen hours the day before, only stopping to escape the heat of the midday and its dangers. Having slept only a few hours, he arose early that morning and began walking again, before daylight. It is now past noon and the heat and the fatigue bear down on him. Damian stops and seeks shelter in a small grove of spindly trees. Placing his pack on the ground, he leans against it and removes his shoes and socks, letting his feet cool. Damian nibbles a small amount of food and drinks more water than usual, trying to replenish his body. Resting, he closes his eyes while sitting on the ground. Drifting away in thoughts, he comes back into focus with the sound of wind in the trees above him. A slight, cool breeze from the west then brushes his face and offers some relief. The silence of a lifeless world is lessened by the noise of the wind and of something else, a new noise that now becomes louder as he strains to listen. It has a rhythmic cadence to it, a very familiar rhythmic cadence to it.

'Oh, my god,' Damian suddenly realizes. 'Those are waves! That's the sound of waves!' He reaches for his shoes and socks and hurriedly putting them on, scrambles to his feet. Wasting no time, he moves toward the rise in the road, almost running now. Cresting the hill, he is witness to an exciting but bewildering scene spread out in front of him. The ocean lies before him with its blue horizon and its rolling waves. Damian has made it. He has reached the coast but it is a very different coast from the one that he remembers from earlier times.

Jagged, eroding cliffs line a now radically altered coastline that reaches much deeper into the interior. Small bays appear everywhere as previously dry land is now under the spoilage of salt water. Several buildings can be seen on the hills, still above the water line, but many are at the water's edge, half submerged, half alive. Debris litters the coastline, moving in and out with the waves. Peering out to sea, he sees remnants of larger buildings barely rising above the water as they are continually being pounded into submission and obscurity.

Damian makes his way down the road. Reaching the city's edge, he is greeted by fencing and a guard station on the road, long since abandoned. The fencing is mostly down but the gate is still intact. A sign dangles from it and flaps in the wind, banging against the metal. Turning it over, Damian reads the faint and faded lettering, 'Marshfield Sector...Present Papers.'

Not having to present anything, Damian then walks around the gate. Entering the outskirts of the city, he walks slowly and deliberately, unsure of what lies ahead for him. Is anyone still living here? Are there any clues or records that he might find that would tell him something? And where should he start looking? The dreary facades of the deserted buildings look down on him as he passes beneath them.

The next few hours are spent searching the city, looking for a headquarters or an abandoned security station or an official building that might give him some leads. It is proving fruitless, though, as it seems several years have passed since anyone has lived here. Weary of the walking and of the growing futility of his search, he sits down on the steps of a building that stands away from the water and remains intact.

Damian needs to formulate a plan now, to move ahead and to keep progressing. It is much too early in the search for despair or disappointment to surface in his thinking and he fights it. The solitary man and the dark hollow streets rest silently in the late afternoon sun when a curious high-pitched single note reaches his ears as he sits there.

It is coming from the direction of the water and is increasing in its volume as Damian rises to his feet and retreats into the doorway. Soon, he sees a long shadow against the sunlit side of a large building opposite him, growing in size as it nears. Both an excitement and a concern rise in him as he entertains the idea of how to approach what is obviously another person moving towards him.

Damian silently continues peering out from his hiding place and the staccato, single notes continue drifting through the air. Suddenly, the figure turns the corner and is visible to Damian. Long, flowing white hair hangs below the shoulders of an older, slightly built man who carries a bucket with one hand and holds onto a flute-like object with the other. The man nears and is soon passing directly in front of him.

Damian has to act. "Hello, hello," he calls out first quietly and then louder. The man stops blowing on his instrument and looks around him. Damian comes out from the shadows and motions to him. "Excuse me," he says. "I need to talk with you. Can I talk with you for a minute?"

After the old man stares back at him with wild eyes, he starts walking away. Damian follows and quickly overtakes him. "No, wait, I won't hurt you. I just want to talk."

"You want my food!" the man yells in a frenzied voice. "This is my town and my food. I own everything here. So, get out, get out!" he says in an angry tirade.

"No, I don't want your food," says Damian quickly to allay his fears. "I just want to ask you a few questions."

"Oh, questions are free, I can always answer questions," the old man says, calming down immediately. 'Toot, toot, toot' goes his instrument. "I'm ready for the first one, what's the first one? If I get it right, what do I win?"

Damian is taken aback slightly. He recognizes that the man must have misplaced part of the deck and that a few screws probably need a little tightening. "Well," he begins by speaking slowly. "How many people live here?"

"That's easy, that's really easy, one. This is my land. I own everything, everything. Yes, own everything."

Damian turns to survey the devastated dead city and believes that he is probably right. One could easily own everything when there is nothing anyone else would want. And this old guy might as well be the one to make the claim on it. "When did the last people leave?" is his next attempt at information.

"They left yesterday, left last week, last year. They left, all of them," says the old man. 'Toot, toot, toot...toot, toot.'

'It's just my luck,' thinks Damian to himself. 'I finally come across someone and he's obviously crazy.' He knows that to continue the conversation is pointless but Damian asks one last question of the sad looking but apparently happy old man. "Which way did they go when they all left?"

The man lifts a very thin arm and with a now quiet solemnity, just points a finger toward the hills to the north. "They went that direction?" Damian asks again of the old man. He continues pointing north without saying a word, his eyes now glazed over and all the animation gone from his body.

"Well, thank you. Is there anything that I can do for you?" Damian then asks him.

The old man stands silent and motionless, with his arm still raised and his finger pointing. Damian takes his cue and turns to walk away. Two blocks away, he stops to look back and sees the now frozen figure still dislodged from the moment, drifted away from reality, and transfixed in his personal thoughts. He is, indeed, one of the fatal figures in this now futile world.

But Damian realizes that most probably did head in that direction. In his discussions with others, he knows that two of the three still functioning Sectors in this area lie north of here. And he knows that he needs to get started, now. Damian cinches the straps on his pack a little tighter and with his head down, begins the journey again with a very determined first step.

\*     \*     \*

Over the next two days, the terrain steadily becomes more difficult to traverse. Having followed a series of roads and then trails, Damian continues crossing from one canyon to the next. The dry, dusty conditions are demanding and he has been careful to conserve his energy and to conserve his water. Resting in the middle of the day has proven to be the best plan and, although difficult walking at night, a waning quarter moon has provided him the needed light.

Morning arrives as Damian makes his way down the side of a large hill on a narrow trail. He sees the sun rising over the eastern horizon, spilling its rays into the far end of the valley, then climbing toward him. Several trees still dot the landscape and the hills, although dry and brown, remain beautiful in their graceful undulation and in their shadows and their layers. It is a changed nature but it is still nature, and the power that it invokes to the human spirit is still strong in Damian. Pausing to gaze at the scene, remembrances and memories come back to him. He is reminded of similar hills that had surrounded the family's home. He feels as though that was a different lifetime from now.

Reaching the bottom of the canyon, Damian removes his pack and sets it on a flat rock. A rest is needed as the walking is taking its toll on his feet. As he sits, the exhaustion and weariness move over him in waves. He has been pushing himself hard for the past few days. The amount of time allocated for the trip is limited and he knows that reaching the other Sectors as soon as possible is paramount if he is to succeed in finding Shannon.

Damian pulls the map from a small pocket of his backpack. Looking over his route options, he also notices that he may be approaching the first inhabited Sector, possibly only another half day's walk. This encourages him along with the rediscovery of the cookies that Sarah had given him on the morning of his leaving. Breaking one in half and returning the other half to the pack, he slowly munches on the sweet treat.

The sun now reaches the rock against which Damian rests. The early morning rays already burn into the exposed skin on his arms and neck. Today will be hotter, Damian knows that. The trail that he has been following since yesterday is getting less distinct as he becomes faced with making a decision as to which direction to proceed. A mistake now would have serious consequences as his water supply is getting dangerously low. If it is a half day's walk, he will make it. And if it is farther, he then doesn't allow his thoughts to go there.

Damian has lost sight of the ocean since yesterday as the route has taken him a few miles inland. The cooler coastal winds from the west are beginning to be replaced by the hotter furnace blasts coming off the inland wastelands. This lone traveler knows that his will be a solitary fate, a singular destiny, in a world empty of aid or assistance. Damian has himself, and only himself, to rely upon this time.

With extreme environmental degradation, humans are not the only form of life to be affected by this new norm. Vegetation is limited in previously lush locations and wildlife has retreated to only a handful of areas that still offer habitat. Rarely does one see or come across any animals anymore. They had been pushed to the edges for decades and then driven off the cliff as we now followed closely behind in the bus, headed for the same fall.

It is because of this sad reality that the shadow moving on the ground near Damian startles him slightly. Glancing up, he searches for the source. The white bright light of day bears down and blinds him momentarily as he stares skyward. But now he sees it, a large black bird circles directly overhead. It is the first living thing that Damian has seen since leaving Marshfield and he relishes the presence of another soul.

He continues watching as the bird then soars high above, surveying the ground below and perhaps himself. For several minutes, Damian watches as it hunts and then is surprised when the immense bird circles and lands on a larger dead branch of a tree quite near him. The two figures stare at one another with curiosity and interest, asking the same question of each, 'What are you doing way out here all by yourself?'

Damian remains sitting when the bird suddenly spreads its wings to take flight. He watches as it first glides down the valley, then floats back on the thermals toward the upper end. The bird rides the crest of the hills opposite Damian and then with one long low turn heads directly back in his direction. With the bird coming down fast, Damian scurries to the side as it dives toward him, turning away at only the very last moment. Emitting one long loud scream and then climbing again, the bird disappears over one particularly rocky gray and brown hill that lies directly across the valley from him.

A thrill and excitement come over Damian's spirit. For that one moment, he was not alone. And for that one moment, there was a connection and a relationship with another living being. Quickly getting to his feet, he is revitalized and ready to move again. Damian doesn't know where things will lead but for now, at least, he has someone to follow.

Damian crosses the valley floor and climbs to the same ridge over which the bird has just flown. He will continue walking for three more hours before stopping to rest and to stay out of the heat until nightfall. He will continue walking and continue his quest while hoping for the best.

\*      \*      \*

With Damian's head drooping and rolling to the side, he jerks back into consciousness. Around him, the blackness of evening has settled in deeply. He has slept longer than he had wanted and the hour is late. Fatigue won the battle for hours between himself and sleep this time. But Damian is upset with himself for not having awakened earlier.

The trail that he was following before stopping for the day had mostly disappeared. Damian was then faced with bushwhacking his way through the hills, down the steep canyon walls, and across the narrow valley floors. The loose rocks under his feet had proved to be slippery footing. As he nears his goal, the drive to continue is intense within him. And without much hesitation or thought, he strikes out again through the darkness.

Damian works through the stiffness of his first few steps but the going is increasingly difficult so he takes his time. Slow progress is still better than no progress and Damian is grateful for the coolness that the cover of night provides. With several hours before daylight, he is hopeful that he can still travel a fair distance yet this evening.

As Damian walks alone in the darkness, the faces of Sarah and Christopher float in and out of his mind. His thoughts of them are selfless, the only concern being their worry about his safety. He wishes that there was a way to let them know that he is fine, that things are okay. But there isn't and Damian knows that the best way to care for them is to take good care of himself. The father and husband needs to safely return home to them. He needs to return because they need him.

The last section of the hill is particularly steep and Damian drops to all fours to carefully feel for handholds. His feet slip a foot backward for every two feet gained but he is near the top. Damian can discern the faint ridgeline in front of him, the border between the absolute blackness of the land and the star-filled blackness of the sky. Reaching the crest, he looks over the other side to a surprising and welcome sight. Lights from an obvious city shine back at him in the distance and the outline of buildings can be clearly seen. Below him lays a continuum of life, an outpost of living, that may provide some answers and may give some direction to his search.

Damian walks the ridge looking for a good way down. In the darkness, only the silhouettes of the larger trees and the rock outcroppings are visible. The route down is not apparent but being in a hurry, he makes his decision. Following a rocky spine of vertical stone, Damian inches his way down with hands dragging along their rough surface. Not known to him, the quarter moon of the last few nights is silently rising behind the hills to the east. In a matter of minutes, it would grant the much needed light but in his impatience lies the problem.

The next step becomes a tragic misstep. Tripping over a large rock, Damian's feet go out from under him and he begins to tumble down the steep terrain. Gaining speed rapidly with each rotation, he is unable to stop himself. The slide continues for fifty feet, a hundred feet, then his body slams into the base of a large tree directly in his path.

The moon now rises and spills its light onto the disheartening scene. Damian's cut and bruised body lies limp and motionless. His head has struck the tree hard, very hard, and it has knocked him unconscious. The stars will rotate in the sky and the moon will traverse its nightly route as the quiet, still body remains sprawled on the hillside.

At home, Sarah awakes with a start from a deep slumber. An unsettling and uncertain feeling haunts her as she is unable to fall back to sleep.

\* \* \*

Sophie and James walk side by side toward the school. They have become good friends and James often finds himself at her house. Sometimes, he will sit and read while Sophie draws at her easel. They share a love of thoughts, of ideas, of concepts larger than just the day to day existence of living. And to have one another to share in these is important to both of them.

In previous times, these older teenagers might have been making plans for their next step, the next stage of their lives, whether it was college or vocation or adventure. They might have been dreaming their dreams, weighing their possibilities, and welcoming their opportunities. But not James and Sophie, not these soon-to-be young adults, it's not what lies in store for them. They will possibly live the rest of their lives in this or a similar Sector, if they're lucky, if they're allowed to stay. Otherwise, they face the same fate as all, a limited life in a deadening world.

And as a species, we had fallen embarrassingly short of our own potential and of our own possibilities. Continuing to kill each other in the pursuit of possessions or to defend ideology, humankind had sunk to its basest instincts as circumstances worsened and as shortages increased. Empathy, selflessness, and a mutual respect among peoples never materialized in our increasingly competitive world. These and other attributes that could have uplifted us and nurtured us and aided us in bringing dignity and basic life necessities to all never received attention. And now it was too late as the fight for dwindling resources has guided us down a path of only narrowing choices. We had failed as intelligent, enlightened thinkers to see that the way forward should include all, that what was good for those at the bottom was in the end, good for those at the top. By not addressing the problems of social inequality, ecological destruction, and massive over-consumption, humans had turned their backs on the real issues, preferring to wrap themselves in self-serving blankets against the coldness of an approaching hard reality.

But for now, Sophie and James at least have each other. Their trips to the school continue as they find solace and comfort in this place for youth, in this place that previously offered unfolding opportunity and new direction. And just being within that environment somehow nurtures them. It is their own space, their own world in which to create and dream of a life that might have been. For that short period each time they visit, the real world and those very real problems dissolve away.

Perusing the available books to make more selections, James is content pausing to look through another section on one of his many interests. Sophie has adopted the art room as her own and it has become her gallery. She hangs finished compositions on the walls, next to those left behind by others that she enjoys. The large windowed wall with light streaming in opens herself to better thoughts. Occasionally, she has witnessed a solitary bird passing that lifts her spirits as she shares in the freedom of this still living symbol of farther horizons.

*     *     *

The increasing temperatures of midday bear down hard on Damian's body and with a slight jerk, he begins coming back into consciousness. Now waking in a state of confusion, his sore body allows him to only crawl into the shade at the base of the tree. Slowly, achingly, he pulls himself up and rests his back against the trunk. Clearing the dust and dirt from his face, Damian's hand passes over the gash in his forehead now pasted shut with dried blood. The brightness of day blinds him and he shields his eyes with one hand while surveying the scene. He remains near the top of the ridge with the rest of the hillside falling away below him. In the distance, he sees the buildings and city that he now remembers seeing the night before. Many minutes will pass as Damian struggles to regain his thoughts, as he struggles to reframe his references.

Then he stands on wobbly legs with a now throbbing head. Looking up the hill, he sees his backpack about thirty feet above him and climbs to retrieve it. Retreating again to the shade, Damian searches for his bottle of water. The liquid washes the dirt and dryness from his mouth and helps him come back into the moment. Soon, he begins cautiously and carefully making his way down the hillside.

The terrain remains steep and loose with rocks. Damian is careful and takes his time as he threads his way around the obstacles, moving towards the edge of the city. The portion of the urban area that is coming into view lies on a slightly higher plateau than the land near the ocean. Unable to view the water, he estimates that he is possibly two to three miles inland. Although mostly deserted with no visible signs of life, Damian notices that the buildings remain intact and still standing. Reaching the bottom of the hill, the terrain is much more level and provides easier walking. He comes ever closer to the fencing that surrounds this Sector.

The cut on his forehead begins to bleed again. Reaching to wipe away what he thinks is sweat, Damian is startled when looking at his now bloodied hand. His shirt is used to clean his hand and he now appears as a walking wounded. The fatigue and soreness reemerge with this vivid reminder of his fall. Damian's steps slow as the walking of the past three days is taking its toll on his body. Then finding a hole in the fence, he begins crossing a large open area toward some buildings.

*　　*　　*

Sophie is finished with her drawing for the day. She carefully hides her precious pencils and her paints in a deep desk drawer. Gathering the paper and stock from the table, they are also put away for safekeeping. It is now late afternoon and both children have promised to return home at an appointed time. That hour nears and Sophie prepares to leave. Walking from the room, she glances back one more time at her 'studio' when she notices a figure outside the room's large windows. A man is crossing the abandoned athletic field towards the school with an uneven and stumbling gait. He appears to be injured.

"James, James!" yells Sophie as she runs out of the room and down the hallway to find him. "James!" she calls out again as the worried boy then comes running out of a classroom.

"What!" he says when catching up to her. "What's the matter, what's wrong, Sophie?"

"There's someone out in the school yard and they look like they're hurt," she says quickly as they both run out the side door. Moving past the broken down play structures, they race toward the dazed and stumbling figure of Damian as his feet continue their now unstoppable motion. But Damian doesn't look like he is doing very well and both children rush to his aid.

"Are you okay, mister?" asks James as they approach.

With his head down and feeling very weak and disoriented, Damian doesn't notice them coming toward him. To hear voices is slightly unearthly to him and he takes some time to focus and to respond to them. "Yes, I think so," he says.

"You need to come inside and sit down," says Sophie and they lead him into the school building. Clearing an area, they pull up a chair and encourage Damian to sit down. The two teenagers stand back a distance and look at him. Dusty, dirty, with blood splattered on his shirt and face, he is a disturbing sight.

"What happened to you?" asks James.

"I fell and hit a tree," says Damian.

"Where were you when you fell?"

Damian turns and points back up toward the hill. "Up there, I was trying to make my way down last night when my feet went out from under me. I fell and hit the tree and it knocked me out. I just came to a little while ago."

"What were you doing up there?" asks Sophie.

"I was coming from the south. I've been walking this way for the past three days. What's the name of this place?"

"It's called the Alta Sector. We live here with our parents," says James.

Damian is relieved to know that he has reached an inhabited Sector. And he is appreciative of Sophie's and James' assistance. "Thanks for your help. I'm feeling better. I should be going."

"But you're hurt," says Sophie.

"I'm okay," says Damian as he attempts to stand. Swooning momentarily, he grabs onto the back of the chair. He is unsteady and unstable on his feet.

"No, you're not," says James.

"No, you're not." echoes Sophie right away. "Let's take him to my house," she then says to James.

After some protestation, Damian gives in and follows the two through the streets back toward her house. Nearing the Brannan residence, Sophie runs ahead to tell her parents. Her mother and father exit the front door as James and Damian are coming up the walk to the house.

"Oh, my goodness, what happened to you? Now, you come right inside with me," says Mrs. Brannan with a firm authority when seeing the battered man. As she reaches for Damian's arm, all walk back inside the home.

She leads Damian to the dining room table and has him sit down. Mrs. Brannan then rushes upstairs to the bathroom and the medicine chest. Returning with wash cloths and bandages, she begins working on the gash on his forehead. Soon, she has the patient bandaged cleanly and offers him something to drink. Mr. Brannan sits across the table from Damian.

"So, you sure look like you've been on quite an adventure. Where are you coming from? I don't think I've ever seen you around here before." asks Sophie's father.

"No, I'm not from here. I live with my family in the Donnelly Grouping," says Damian.

"Yes, I've heard of that place. It's up in the mountains to the north of here, isn't it?" says Mr. Brannan.

"That's right."

"What are you doing way down here? Most people don't leave a Grouping once they get in."

"I'm looking for someone," starts Damian as he then explains the reason for his trip. All around the table listen intently to his story with his finishing, "And now, I'm trying each Sector to see if anyone knows anything about Shannon or her husband."

James jumps in quickly when Damian stops talking. "What's it like living in a Grouping? Everyone says that it's pretty easy, with food and supplies and stuff."

"Well, that's true," says Damian, feeling better and a bit more talkative now. "We are fortunate to have enough to eat and are given a place to live. But it's not all that great, we are kind of stuck there. It can be a little confining."

A pensive Mr. Brannan has remained relatively quiet during the discussion. But now, he slides forward in his chair, resting his hands on the table. "So, you said that this guy, your sister-in-law's husband, was a smuggler?"

"Yes, that's what I was told. Supposedly, he got kicked out of Marshfield and then maybe worked in some of the other nearby Sectors. That's why I'm here, I thought I would just check in each Sector to see if someone knew him."

"And what was his name?"

"The person I spoke with only knew him by his nickname. He said people called him Runner."

Pausing for a moment before he speaks again, Mr. Brannan then says in a straightforward manner, "I know him."

Everyone at the table begins talking at once. "Dad, you know him? That's amazing, that's really great!" says Sophie.

"Mr. Brannan, that's unbelievable!" adds James.

"Well, maybe not quite so unbelievable," he returns.

"But how do you know him?" asks Damian.

"Well, let's just say that I've been known to do a little trading myself," answers Mr. Brannan. Laughter then arises from those sitting around the table, from those in the know.

"When did you last see him?"

Pursing his lip and knitting his brow, Mr. Brannan pauses to remember. "Oh, I would say it was about eight or nine months ago. I know it's not been more than a year."

"Do you know what his real name is? Do you know anything about his family?" asks Damian, keen with interest now.

"His name is Frank Walker and, yes, he works as a smuggler. A smuggler is often called a runner. So, Walker, Runner, get it?" says Sophie's father. "He didn't have a very good reputation but I liked him. I always got along with him and actually did business with him quite a few times."

"Do you have any idea where he was living?"

"No, I don't know. He usually kept things to himself. I know a few people I can ask, though."

"Can you tell me anything about him?"

"He was smart and shrewd but he had double-crossed people a few times. When I confronted him about it, he had just said, 'I got a family to take care of and they come first.' But like I said, he always did okay by me. Strange thing, though, as tough as he was, he would trade almost anything for just a few cans of food," says Mr. Brannan.

Damian accepts their offer to stay the night and Mr. Brannan will then contact a few people first thing in the morning to see if he can find out anything more about Walker. Damian will fall asleep that night with a roof over his head instead of the stars and with the help of others instead of only relying on himself.

He will consider himself fortunate. The pain from the cut on his forehead is already going away.

*　　*　　*

The next morning Damian is awakened by the sound of the back door slamming shut. As he quickly rises from the couch, Mr. Brannan and another man emerge from the kitchen.

"No, sit down, sit down. I have someone I want to introduce you to," says Mr. Brannan. "Damian, this here is George Davis. George, this is the guy I told you about." The two men shake hands and George takes a seat opposite Damian.

"So, you're looking for Frank Walker?" begins George.

"Yes, that's right." says Damian.

"Well, you ain't gonna find him," he states flatly.

"Why not?" asks a puzzled Damian.

"Because the guy's dead. That dirty double-crosser wound up crossing one too many people and the last guy didn't take very kindly to it and he killed him."

"Are you sure?"

"I'm sure, 'cuz I was there."

"When?"

"I'd say it was only about two or three months ago. I never did trust the guy and can't say that I'm sorry he's gone. Bob here says he was married to your wife's sister."

"Well, I think so, but I don't know that for sure. So, did you ever happen to meet his wife?"

"No, but I saw a picture of her, plenty of times. He was always dragging it out to show everybody. She was right pretty, too, with all that red hair and everything."

"Oh, that's just got to be Shannon," says an excited Damian. "Do you know where she is?"

"I know where she was because me and Runner had done a deal together and on our way back up, he wanted to stop by and see them," says the man.

"Them?" interrupts Damian.

"You know, his wife and kid. Anyways, we had stopped at the edge of this deserted city down south and he made me wait there while he went ahead to visit them. He was always a secretive son of a bitch. Well, that's about all I know about him."

"And this city?" asks Damian.

"Yeah, I can tell you how to get there."

Damian thanks the man as he stands to leave. Mr. Brannan exchanges some words with George outside before returning to the table. "So, does that help any?" he asks Damian.

"I can't thank you and your family enough. You have all been so nice to me. I didn't expect I would receive help from anyone on this trip," says Damian.

"It's been my pleasure. We don't get many chances to help each other anymore and it feels kind of good."

Damian then reaches for his pack and brings out the map. The city that George is talking about lies farther south than the Marshfield Sector and more inland. The route is less challenging than coming over the coastal hills but it is quite a distance away. Damian plans to start today, this morning. He is already nearing the end of the first week and he needs to move quickly if he is going to meet his ride back to the Grouping. Damian exchanges his torn, bloodied shirt for a new one and stuffs it along with the map back into his pack. Putting on his shoes, he is readying himself to leave and start off again on his journey.

"So, where are you off to so quickly?" asks Mr. Brannan who wonders what's the hurry with Damian.

"I need to get going. I appreciate your help but I'm going to run out of time unless I go now," says Damian with an urgency to his voice. He is truly concerned about missing his ride, and besides having to wait for another delivery day and risk running out of food and water, he doesn't want the truck to return to the compound without him on it. Damian doesn't want to put Sarah through something like that.

"But Mrs. Brannan is planning a dinner tonight for you. It's kind of a treat for her. She's been saving some special food items for just such an occasion. I have been ordered to go to James' house this morning and invite his family."

"You'll have to accept my apologies. I can't afford to waste any more days. I don't have that many left," says Damian.

"Oh, I wouldn't be so sure about that," is the curious response from a smiling Mr. Brannan.

"What do you mean?"

"Well, let's say that I know a few people and a few of them owe me favors. I'm just going to collect on one of them. George is working on it already," says the man who has stepped into Damian's life at the right time. He goes on to explain that he knows someone with access to a vehicle and that he is arranging a ride for Damian to the city down south.

Even in these crazy and mixed-up times, a guiding hand can appear to point one in the right direction and down the right path. And even now, things can still happen by serendipity and fateful chance. Even now, one can get lucky.

\*     \*     \*

That evening then becomes a celebration of sorts, of people coming together and of those people caring about one another. The times are few these days when anyone feels like celebrating, when there is really anything worth truly celebrating. But the Brannans with Clare's family have found an excuse to seek that escape now and they make the most of it.

Damian has a chance to meet James' mother and to express his gratitude to her for the help that her son had provided him. He talks about Christopher with Clare and about their shared challenges as parents. Although existing in different settings, their concerns are the same, a better life for their children.

He sits next to Sophie at the dinner table and learns more about her. She discusses her enjoyment of drawing and art but worries about a shallowness and pointlessness to it. "Don't know why I waste my time with it," she says to Damian.

"Because it's important to you," he tells her. "Keep it up, keep that passion inside you, Sophie. We all still need that."

And the crowning highlight of the evening is a pie delivered to the table as dessert. Mrs. Brannan has kept two cans of pumpkin set aside for quite a while and has spent the day innovating a crust to receive the rare sweet treat. Conversation and a now too often absent lightheartedness continue around the table when there is a quiet knock at the back door. Mr. Brannan rises from his chair to see who it is and then quickly returns. "It's all set," he says simply, turning toward Damian.

*     *     *

Clare and her family have gone home. Sophie and her mother have retired for the evening. But Mr. Brannan stays awake with Damian downstairs as they pour over maps. They discuss the route to be traveled tonight by the vehicle that Mr. Brannan has arranged and about a possible route for Damian to reach the meeting spot for his return ride to the Grouping. Sophie's father's knowledge of the local area is extremely helpful and the two of them are able to estimate the walking time from the desert city to the south to his connection on the highway leading north. It will take four days of walking, leaving Damian just three days for searching the city before the necessity of giving up that search comes before him. He knows of his good fortune so far, he earnestly appeals to the still omnipresent feeling of a greater power to allow it to continue for just a little longer.

A horn can then be heard honking outside. Damian gets up from his chair and picks up his pack. The time has come to leave, his ride is here. "Whoa, I guess I haven't lifted this for a while," he says to his host about the weight of the pack. "Maybe, it's just that I'm getting old."

"Oh, there are a few extras in there. Marion took the liberty of packing some things for you. Hope that's okay."

"You didn't have to do that. I don't want to take anything, your family needs it, too" says Damian.

"Nonsense," says Mr. Brannan. "It would have been tough going with only that much food. And we put in an extra bottle of water for you, too."

The darkness then greets them at the back door. In the street waits a vehicle with its engine running but lights off. The driver motions for Damian to hurry. Taking his leave quickly from Mr. Brannan, he stumbles for words to express his gratitude. "I don't know how to thank you. I never expected that—"

"It's fine," Mr. Brannan quickly cuts him short. "Like I said, it's a good feeling just being able to help someone. Now go, see what you can find, and someday maybe our paths will cross again, in a better time and on a better day for all of us."

After peering in the window first like a hitchhiker seeking approval, Damian is quickly motioned in. "Let's go, let's go," are the rushed words out of the man's mouth. "This ain't no taxi." Sitting in the front seat, Damian turns to look back as the vehicle speeds away from the curb. Mr. Brannan stands in the doorway with his hand raised in farewell and as a sign of good wishes.

The vehicle moves through the city with its lights off. The driver is concentrating on the road in front of him and Damian's knows to avoid conversation for now. This man must be taking a substantial risk for him and he will just allow him to do his job. Soon, though, the buildings and city fall away behind them and the driver reaches down to turn on the lights. Relaxing back into his seat, he turns toward Damian. "Rogers, Buck Rogers," he says, extending his hand to his passenger.

Damian offers his hand and his own name back to the man. He then says, "Buck Rogers, huh? So, is that your real—"

"Yeah, yeah, I know," answers Buck. "It is actually Quentin Rogers, but it's always been Buck for as long as I can remember. Don't blame me, do you?"

"No," says Damian with a laugh. "I want to thank you for your help in giving me this ride."

"Ah, it's no big deal," says the driver. "I owed Bob a favor and I got something out of it. Plus, I don't mind getting out of town for a while if you know what I mean."

"Yes, I do, indeed," is Damian's response as the man reflects momentarily on his trip and on the adventure that it has become. There is something liberating, something exhilarating in having a daily change of landscape and routine. It is something that is innate in us, something that has driven humankind for years, wondering what lies over the next horizon or around that next bend and it is something that has now dried up in the human condition from a lack of nourishment, from a lack of opportunity. The 'juices' were flowing again through Damian's body and it did feel good. And it did feel right.

The two men continue traveling the open road, occasionally passing what was a small town or a refueling center similar to the one that Damian first encountered. Besides these deserted outposts, there is nothing. Dryness and heat have shrunk the vegetation to the occasional bushes or weeds under the shade of a tree. As the sun rises over the hills to the east, the deadness stretches on and on into the distance.

"So, does anyone ever travel out here very often? Do these roads ever get used very much?" asks Damian.

"No, sometimes a convoy will move between the Sectors. We deal with East Fork occasionally and goods are shipped back and forth between the two of us. But no, most everybody stays put. Fuel is precious, you know," explains Buck.

"How do you get to use this then?"

"I'm a driver for the security forces so I have authorization. Bob Brannan went ahead and took care of my boss. So, as long as no one else finds out about it, we're cool."

"What do you mean Mr. Brannan took care of your boss?" asks Damian.

"You know, money and bribes. The world's not that different, those things still work." And Damian realizes that he now owes an even greater debt to his benefactor. "Bob's a good guy and he's a one of a kind," says Buck.

"Yes, he is," Damian quickly agrees with him. "Yes, he is," he says again as he suddenly realizes his good fortune.

\*     \*     \*

After a few more hours of traveling, Buck tells Damian that they are approaching the city. Opening his pack to retrieve the map, Damian smiles as he sees a piece of pumpkin pie resting on top. Mrs. Brannan, like every good mother, couldn't help packing something extra for 'her boy.' Soon, buildings and the cityscape come into view. Stopping on the outskirts, Damian is let out to walk the rest of the way. Before taking his leave from Buck, he takes the piece of pie from his pack and gives it to the appreciative driver.

"Wow, think I'll stop and have a little picnic on the way back. All in all, not too bad of a day," says Buck.

"Well, nice talking with you," says Damian.

"Yeah, you too." And then pausing for a minute, this Buck Rogers adds, "We didn't really think it was going to be like this, did we? We didn't think it would turn out this way."

"What didn't we think was going to turn out this way?" asks Damian, not understanding the comment.

"You know, the future, the future," he ends solemnly.

"No, we didn't Buck," says Damian with equal gravity.

The vehicle turns around in the road and heads back on its return trip. Damian stands still in the rising dust, staring down the road and thinking about Buck's words. He watches it move away for a long time until finally disappearing over the last hill, carrying away another kindred spirit that misses the old days, carrying away someone who also weeps over the new reality.

The walk begins into town with a long, low hill descending from where he stands down into the city center. Damian can see large buildings there still reaching into the sky, still standing as sentinels over the surrounding suburbs. It is a desert town with no limiting boundaries, with the endless sprawl of a human footprint stretching for three or four miles in all directions from its center. It is a big city and searching through it all will be an even bigger job. The searcher needs to get started.

*     *     *

Damian will spend the rest of the day walking up and down the deserted streets of the neighborhoods on one side of the city. If only he can ask questions of someone, if only he can see some signs of life, he will feel encouraged and remain hopeful. But initially, it is discouraging as the city seems truly empty of anyone. Abandoned cars, abandoned homes, with only debris from abandoned lives, greet him at every turn.

A dismal dusk is rapidly approaching as he now makes his way toward the downtown section. Entering into the darkened concrete canyons, the only sound is the wailing and woeful wind that eerily sweeps around the corners of the buildings. This ominous, heavy tone that fills one with dread and despair is overpowering in its sadness, in its disappointment at life bled away by humankind's self-inflicted wounds. Damian needs to find shelter and eat and rest so that tomorrow he can start the process all over again.

Entering a building, he finds a place to lie down for the night. He is once again alone and his thoughts drift back to last night, to the festive dinner table with the Brannans and Clare's family. We are all ultimately alone, in our own essence and in our own being. Damian knows that and over the years, he has welcomed the solitary times for the challenges offered and the insights gained. But not tonight, tonight, Damian only feels the loneliness.

\*    \*    \*

It is now early morning and the sky has already lightened with the coming day as Damian peers through the dirty glass of the storefront into the empty streets. Opening his pack, he pulls out something to eat while sitting on the floor, planning his day. The downtown area is several blocks wide and about a mile long. Most of the buildings are two to three stories tall with about a half dozen of them reaching six or seven stories. He will simply began at this end and go street by street, block by block, looking for...'looking for what?' he asks himself.

The day is long and exhausting and the routine is the same in each building visited, walking through broken glass and littered rooms, around dusty corners and into only lifeless scenes. 'Why would anyone come here? Is this really where Shannon and her husband were living? Why here?' thinks Damian as the heat of late afternoon wears his body and his spirit down.

Seeking the sheltered shade of one of the buildings, Damian will end his search for the day and spend the night. Tomorrow and the next day, he then explores the other residential areas that surround the downtown area. The man will travel through the deserted neighborhoods like a wayward traveler, not really knowing his direction or his destination. Damian isn't giving up but a part of him is beginning to give in.

\*　　\*　　\*

It is the end of the third day, Damian finds himself back in the downtown section. He is out of time and tomorrow, Damian must begin the trek to his meeting point with the delivery truck. Why did he undertake this? How did he hope to pull off such an impossible task? Who was he kidding and who was he going to let down? He thinks of Sarah and Christopher waiting for him at home. He thinks of the excitement on his son's face when telling him about the search for Shannon. He has offered false hopes and now feels the heavy weight of guilt from it.

Walking in the center of the forsaken street, a weary and worn out Damian breaks down and with a primal scream yells at the heavens. "Where in the hell is everybody! Why in the hell did this have to happen!" Falling to his knees, his head lowers and in only whispers between soft sobs, the weakened man repeats over and over, "We screwed it up, we screwed it up."

\*　　\*　　\*

Michael and Sean are up rather early this morning. They had stayed inside the last few days, simply passing the time and enjoying each other's company. Having found a deck of cards, Michael has taught many different games to his eager student.

The hours fall away as they sit in their high hideout, staying above the problems down below.

Both gain from their developing relationship. For Michael, the benefit is the connection to a family situation that he thought he would never get a chance to have and for Sean, Michael can now become the replacement father and protector. Fate or necessity has brought them together to face the challenges of this new order so neither will have to do it alone.

But cabin fever has set in and they make plans to spend the day outside. The late morning is reserved for a trip to the spring. They haven't gone since last week and although still well stocked, they make the trip regularly to even out the back breaking work of hauling water. Two large bottles filled per week keeps them ahead of the game. And it provides them a change of scenery, if only into the hills, if only for a few hours.

Before hiking to the spring, the boys plan a rematch of last night's basketball game. In searching the city, Michael had found a suitable 'basket' and has constructed a 'goal' on the paved area behind their building. They play often for exercise and release and friendly competition. They play for the fun of it.

\*　　\*　　\*

Damian wakes slowly. A melancholy had crept over him last evening and he had simply crawled off to the nearest doorway, curling up and seeking the escape of sleep. But the night had been unkind to him as he restlessly moved about, trying to reach a physical comfort and a mental solace. He found neither and the disappointment weighs heavily on him and drags him down. The expectation of success is being rapidly replaced with an acknowledgement of failure.

Lying in the doorway, Damian feels like a bum, alone with those failures. He now greatly misses his family and the return to them hangs in the air as consolation. There is nothing left to do but head back, but it is hard to be in a hurry. Damian's body is sore from all the walking and blisters have appeared on both heels. The prospect of four more days of walking is also painful to his spirit and to his resolve. But he needs to begin if he is to succeed in meeting the delivery truck on time.

The rays of early morning light rise above the building across the street and shine down on him. Damian knows that the heat will have to be dealt with today, the dry dead heat of the sunlight hours. It can be an oppressive feeling that can easily blacken the day and can remove the optimism from your thinking. These overpowering emotions of despair, futility, and hopelessness are not just reserved for clinical depressives anymore. All now have these symptoms daily, if not hourly. Gone is the zest for life and the dream of a better tomorrow as dealing with today is all that one can manage now.

When getting up, Damian searches his pack for breakfast and some water. If he must leave immediately, then he had better replenish his body if he is going to ask so much of it. Inside the pack, he finds another of Mrs. Brannan's treats that had been sneaked in. A cathartic, appreciative smile crosses Damian's face as he thinks back on the friends that he has made. It has been an adventure of sorts, a chance to see life outside of the Grouping, and at least, he had tried. Yes, maybe it hadn't worked out but, at least, he had tried.

Moving past that negativity now, Damian stands and reaches for his pack to begin the trek east, toward a rising sun and toward a reunion with his family. He should be able to reach the meeting place on time, even taking breaks during the day if his plan is right. It is time to go and Damian begins his walk out with a first step into an empty street but then the sound is heard that abruptly stops his departure.

Shbong...shbong...shbong goes an intermittent but rhythmic beat. It is the first noticeable sound besides the occasional call of a bird or the howling of the wind that he has heard since arriving in the deserted city. 'Possibly a door or window just banging in the wind,' thinks Damian to himself, but it wasn't really windy. Shbong...shbong...shbong goes the sound again. It seems to be coming from across the street, not far away, from behind some buildings. Damian moves in that direction as curiosity and interest overtake his immediate plans.

Shbong...shbong...bang. "Alright, a really nice shot," rises a voice above the silence. Damian is taken aback and presses his body tightly to the building. 'People,' he thinks to himself. 'There are people here.' For a minute or two, Damian remains standing like a statue, frozen from action as thoughts race through his mind. But then, he begins cautiously and slowly moving in the direction from which the sounds are coming.

Damian is now only a few feet from the edge of the building. Getting down low on all fours, he crawls the rest of the way and with a pounding heart, takes a one-eyed peek around the corner. A man and a young boy appear before him and in amazement, he sees that they are playing a game of basketball. 'Basketball, way out here in all this nothingness?'

"Okay," yells out Michael. "Fourteen to fourteen, the first one to twenty is the winner and then we'll play Horse, okay? This old guy needs to take a break from your overpowering court play," he jokes to his youthful companion.

Damian continues watching surreptitiously from his hiding spot. The game is soon over and the two idly bounce the ball and exchange conversation before beginning again. Rising to his feet, Damian takes a deep breath and then walks around the corner of the building into view. "Hello," he calls to them.

Both of the surprised players then immediately turn toward Damian as he approaches them. "Stay where you are!" shouts Michael as Sean hides behind him. "Don't come any closer. Who are you, what do you want?"

"I'm from the Donnelly Grouping, I'm looking for someone. I just want to ask you some questions. I mean no harm, really, I don't mean any harm," quickly says a respectful Damian who now keeps his distance from them.

"Looking for someone, there's nobody here. I don't believe you," says Michael as he tries to comfort a scared Sean. "Just get out of here, we don't need anybody bothering us."

"If I can just have five minutes of your time, then I'll go. I was told that a person I knew was living here at one time. I just want to ask you some questions. I've traveled a long way to get here and you're the only people that I've seen."

"That's because we're the only ones here so whoever you're looking for isn't here anyway," says Michael. "There's no reason to waste our time with it."

"No, wait, please. I'm looking for the wife of a man named Walker. They also called him Runner?"

"Did you say Walker?" interjects Michael.

"Yes, that's right. His name was Walker."

"Stay there!" warns Michael as he turns toward Sean who is still hanging on to his back side. "That's your last name," he says in a hushed voice. "Do you know this guy?" Sean just shakes his head that he doesn't.

"I don't think we can help you stranger," Michael then calls out to Damian.

"But I was told that he had just lived here recently. He was married to my wife's sister and we haven't seen her for years. I'm trying to find her. Her name is Shannon and she has red hair," offers Damian with more information about her.

Michael flashes back to the scene on the first day that he met Sean, with his dead mother lying on the floor beside him, lying still and cold in a bright green dress with her bright red hair. He turns his back to Damian and leaning over to gently grasp Sean by his shoulders, quietly asks the question, "Sean, what was your mother's name, son? What was her first name?"

"Shannon," answers Sean.

Michael stands and turns toward Damian. "We don't want any trouble. Do you have any weapons?"

Damian drops his pack to the ground and opening his shirt while turning around says, "No, nothing, nothing at all."

"Okay then, we can talk."

Quickly relieved, Damian approaches the man and the young boy. Reaching out, he shakes hands with Michael. "I'm Damian. Thank you, thank you very much."

"My name is Michael and this is my son, Sean," explains the 'father.' Damian extends his hand to the boy but Sean turns away and hides farther behind Michael. "So, you said that it's your wife's sister that you're looking for?"

"That's right. We moved to a Grouping about ten years ago and haven't seen her since then. I want to find out more about her so my wife will know that she is okay. At the Sector north of here, someone I met knew her husband and said that this was the city that they were last living in. I've been walking the streets for three days but haven't found anything or anybody until seeing you today," explains Damian.

"No, there's nobody else here. Occasionally, some Outsiders will come through but by now most everything is stripped away. We don't see them much anymore."

"Why are you here then? I mean, what do you do for food and water?" asks Damian.

"Oh, we get by," says Michael.

The three of them move out of the sun and into the shade of the building. Sitting down, they engage in conversation for the next half hour, talking about their respective experiences over the past few years in the struggle for survival. Michael asks about life in a Grouping and Damian explains the situation there. Michael says that he and Sean had lived various places but when they found the spring here, they had decided to stay. The discussion is welcome but Damian feels that he has come up against another dead end. Having mentioned his impending walk to meet the delivery truck, he now says that he needs to get going. Thanking them, Damian stands to leave.

"Wait a minute," says Michael quickly. "We have water and some food to share. Don't you need some water before you go? It sounds like a long walk."

"Well, now that you mention it, one of my bottles is almost empty. Yes, that would be great, I would really appreciate that," answers Damian.

"I'll fill it," says Sean as he jumps up to get the bottle from the older man. Running into the building, he will go to the cellar to eagerly replenish Damian's provisions.

While the young boy is gone, Michael turns to Damian and addresses him in a more serious tone. "So, what did you hope to accomplish if you ever did find this woman Shannon that you are looking for?"

"Just what happened to her. I thought if I could find out that she's okay, then my wife would feel better about things. We have access to food and water and shelter, but honestly, life is not much different probably for us than for you ."

"Yeah, we're all in this together now. It's just a damn shame it took us so long to come to the same conclusion."

"Yes, it is," is Damian's sad agreement.

The conversation lapses for a moment before Michael asks another question. "And did this guy Walker and your wife's sister have any children?"

"I was told that they had a son. My own son was especially interested in that and my wife said Shannon had always wanted a family. So we were excited for her."

Sean comes running from the building carrying the freshly filled bottle of water and then proudly hands it to Damian. "Thank you, that's really nice of you. Well, I'd better get going. These old bones and sore feet aren't really looking forward to the next part of this trip."

"Hold on, I want to discuss something with Sean. Could you wait here for just a minute?" With a questioning look, Damian nods okay and the two disappear into the building.

Sitting on the steps of the stairwell together, Michael says, "You know, Sean, we have to tell him. Damian's come a long way looking for your family. We're going to have to tell him about your mom, too."

"But I don't even know the guy," Sean protests. "How do we know he's telling the truth?"

"I asked him some questions while you were gone getting water. And I think he's a good man and an honest man and I believe him," says Michael.

Soon, the two reappear and walk with arms wrapped around each other to where Damian sits on the pavement. As they approach, he stands to greet them. "There's something we need to tell you," says Michael. "Sean isn't my son, he's Shannon's son," comes the bombshell. And that is how it strikes Damian.

"What!" he exclaims in disbelief. "You are Shannon's son?" he says, addressing the boy. Sean slowly nods back at him. "This is great, this is amazing," he says and then pauses. "But where is your mother, where is she?"

Sean stands silently with no response. Michael steps in. "I'm sorry," he begins. "His mother is dead. That's when I found him, she had just passed away."

Damian is thunderstruck, overwhelmed first by joy and then by sorrow. With his mind racing wildly, he doesn't know what to say next. He has found Shannon, or more correctly, a part of Shannon. After all but giving up hope, Damian has arrived at his destination. His search is over.

Michael suggests that they go back to the room and the three walk the several flights of stairs to the top floor of the building. Following Sean, Damian stares at the back of the young boy and only now focuses on the fact that he is his uncle. Of course, he knew of the possibility of Sean's existence but in the flesh and blood, he has an overpowering feeling of connection and of responsibility. Strong emotions and even tears well inside him as Damian continues the climb.

"So, this is home," says Michael as they enter the room.

Damian surveys the comfortable scene and moves toward a window to gaze down on the streets below. "Not bad," he says, "not bad at all. I see you guys got the penthouse floor."

Michael smiles appreciatively and Sean lets out a small laugh. "Yeah, it's great," says the young boy. "My dad picked it out. He said that not many people would bother searching such a large building because there probably wasn't any food here. And he didn't think anyone would see that staircase."

"I agree," say Damian with a nod of the head. "I think your dad picked a really good place."

"Please have a seat," offers Michael. The visitor reaches for a chair as Michael sits nearby and Sean sits on his mattress on the floor. Looking about the room, Damian comments on the artwork on the walls and the general pleasantness of the surroundings. Michael agrees and Sean says that his mother was always cleaning and rearranging the room.

"She always tried to make things nice for me. I really miss..." he just ends with his voice trailing off.

Damian changes the subject and inquires about Michael who spends several minutes giving a quick summary of the past few years for him. He explains the constant moving that had been necessary to eke out an existence and how he had traveled with various individuals at times but had decided to strike out on his own again when reaching this city. And, of course, Michael tells the story of finding Sean.

For his part, Damian is asked many questions about life in a Grouping, even Sean has one or two for him. The next two hours are filled with conversation. At one point, Michael comments that breakfast had been skipped in favor of the basketball game and that he is now hungry. Jumping up, Sean volunteers to run down to the cellar to retrieve something to eat. 'Something special if he can find it,' the excited young boy thinks to himself. And soon, the three of them are sharing a meal and a moment in time, high above the desolate streets below.

Michael has been quiet since lunch, thinking on one subject. "I want to talk to Damian for a minute," he then says to Sean. "Want to grab a book or just rest up here for a while?"

"Where are the cards?" asks Sean. "And what is that game you taught me called? Sola, sola something."

"Solitaire," answers an amused Michael. "I put them back in the desk drawer." And the two men stand to leave the room and go outside. Descending the stairs, Damian mentions that the father had indeed picked a good spot to hide his family. Michael tells him about the cellar full of food and about the quality of the spring. Both agree that he must have been a good father, that he must have tried hard to protect and provide for them.

Pushing open the heavy door, they enter into the daylight. Walking the deserted streets as if on a Sunday stroll, the two talk of many things, learning about each other and getting to know the character of each. Michael is impressed with this man and Damian expresses his gratitude for all that he has done for Sean. "Oh," Michael had responded, "he's done much more for me than I've ever done for him."

When passing a dusty bench in the shade, Michael suggests that they sit for a moment. In the gray grim deadness of the city, the men talk of the prospect for life. They, like everyone still alive, are bitter and angry over the failure of the human race, over the self-interest and greed that has now made everyone poor.

And then Michael, in a more serious and earnest voice says, "You know that he must go back with you."

"With me?" answers Damian. "I had thought about that but I didn't know what to say about it."

"There isn't anything to say. There's no life here for him, no life with me. I can barely take care of myself and I don't know for how much longer I can even do that. You are his only chance."

"But what will Sean think about it? He doesn't really know me. I worry what he will think about it."

"Well, let's just spend the day together and give him a little time. We can talk about it tonight."

The two return to the room where they find Sean engrossed in his card game. The young boy then jumps up to give Michael a high five when seeing him. "I won once, got rid of all the cards. Honest, I didn't even cheat."

"I believe you," says Michael laughing. "That's great."

The afternoon is slowly spent looking over some personal possessions of Sean's family, things that had belonged to his mother and his father. Sean speaks of them lovingly and without despair. The cellar is shown to Damian and they make use of the extra muscle to carry water from the spring. Sean runs ahead on the path, leading the way. Damian even joins in an early evening basketball game before they all return to the room.

Lingering over their 'dinner,' the three of them are tired. It has been an active day, an interesting day for all. Not often does anyone get to make new friends or interact with new people. For Michael, it has been good to have an adult to talk with again. Damian has spent the day with his new nephew and Sean has probably benefited the most, having enjoyed the games and the hike to the spring—normal activities taking place in abnormal times. All are appreciative for the break they have provided.

But now, before going to bed, it is time to discuss things with Sean and Michael knows that it is up to him to initiate the conversation. "Sean, there's something that I want to talk about with you, something important," he begins, looking over at Damian. Damian silently acknowledges the moment. "Damian and I have talked things over and we both feel it would be best if you return to the Grouping with him. He has told me that they are allowed to have family members join them and he wants to provide for you from now on." Both men are then quiet as they wait for Sean's reaction.

"But I already have a place to live. I live with you," says the young boy looking over at Michael. "You and I are a team, right? You always said that we made a good team, didn't you?"

"Yes, and we do, but I can't take care of you like Damian can. Things are okay for now but we don't know how long that is going to last. In the Grouping, you will be provided with food and water and you will be safe. There will come a time when the cellar runs out and we have to move from here and then what would we do? If I have to go out searching for food, I can't leave you here, and traveling around scavenging isn't easy work for a small boy," says a realistic Michael.

"No!" shouts Sean. "I can do all that stuff. I'm big enough to carry the water, aren't I? And I wouldn't be any trouble for you. I wouldn't bother you or anything. I want to stay with you," cries out the boy and he rushes to Michael's side.

Michael puts his arms around Sean and allows him to cling tightly for a moment before gently pushing back to look into his eyes. "Oh, Sean, if I could have anybody in the world to be my son, I would choose you. You're the best thing to come into my life for a long time, but it doesn't make any sense now. Damian took a lot of risks looking for you and your mom and we need to take advantage of the opportunity now that he has found you. It's the best thing, it really is," says the strong but disheartened friend of the boy. Michael knows that his life will return to the solitary loneliness of a life without close personal connections. He's not looking forward to that again. But it is not about him, it is about the boy.

"No...no, no, no!" wails the young child and Michael makes a head motion for Damian to leave the room for a moment. These two souls who were thrown together are being ripped apart and it is not easy for either one of them.

"Listen, Sean," says Michael in a soothing, comfortable voice. "Damian is your uncle, he's part of your family. Don't you think your mom and dad would be happy knowing that your uncle has found you and can take care of you now?"

"I don't know. I just don't, I just don't want to leave you," says the tearful child.

"I know where you'll be and maybe someday, I'll be able to come visit you. Someday, we can see each other again," offers Michael as solace to the situation.

"Promise?" says a more composed Sean.

"Promise," he says with a smile on his face.

Michael then calls out to Damian and he returns to the room. Looking at Michael, Damian is given a nod of the head and a calmness comes over everyone. Joining them on the floor, the three sit quietly as night settles in around them.

So, it is decided. Damian will return to his family with news, sad news about Shannon, but he hopes the arrival of Sean will provide the lift that all will need. The father and now uncle is energized by the prospect of having an addition to his family. Rations will have to be split but that will be okay, that will work out. And he's bringing home a cousin to his son and a connection to Shannon for his wife.

There is only one problem and Damian has thought about it all day. He has used up one of the days for the return trip and it will now be almost impossible to meet the truck on time. They can wait for another but there are usually several days between deliveries. With no way to inform Sarah, he worries about her concern if the truck returns and he is not on it.

"I think most of us are probably pretty tired," says Michael. "If you guys are heading out early tomorrow, we probably better get some sleep." Damian is quiet with no response to Michael's statement. "Oh," continues Michael, thinking about the sleeping arrangements. "I know where a couch is on the next floor down. You can sleep here with Sean."

"No, that's okay, anywhere is just fine with me," says a rather distracted Damian.

"Is something wrong?" asks Michael.

"Oh, just that I estimated from here it would take four days of walking to reach the highway where I am to meet the truck. Today was one of the four. I don't know if we can make it on time now. I'm not sure what to do," he says.

"How many hours of walking each day is that?" asks Michael. "Maybe you guys could walk a little more each day."

"I only figured on stopping for four to five hours during the middle of the day to get out of the worst heat. We won't be able to walk anymore than that," says Damian. And a heaviness falls over the room, a deflation.

"Bicycles!" Sean suddenly shouts out.

"What?" says Michael, turning toward him.

"Bicycles, Damian and I can use bicycles!" offers the excited boy as a solution to their problem. "Remember that house where we found the ball, there were bicycles hanging in the garage. We can go faster if we use them, can't we?"

"You know what, I think you may have something there, my dear boy. That's a great idea, that might just work. You simply continue to amaze me," he says to him. With their spirits lifted, lots of celebratory back slapping of Sean takes place by both men. They even pick him up and carry him about the room on their shoulders for a few minutes. Damian will fall asleep that night feeling better about their chances.

\*　　\*　　\*

The next morning finds the three of them walking in the empty suburbs north of the city. Without much trouble, they locate the house with the bicycles hanging from the rafters of the garage. The family that lived here apparently had no use for them in the next stage of their lives. The tires are low but in good condition. They hope that the pump back at the room will get them on the road. Sean runs upstairs to find it when they finally get back to their building.

"Can you believe he thought of these?" says Michael as they stand beside the bicycles. "Do you think that you guys will be able to make it on time now?"

"I think we can. A person walks about three miles an hour, we should be able to do two or three times that."

"I hope Sean can keep up. He's going to be on a smaller bike which makes it harder for him."

"Yeah, I know but I'll pace us. We'll still have to take breaks during the middle of the day. If we can just see the road well enough to travel at night, it should work out."

"Well, he's a go-getter and a hard worker. I know Sean will give it his best," says the other man. And then he falls silent as he is lost in thought for a minute.

Michael is reflective and Damian knows what he is thinking. After a few moments, he says, "This must be hard for you."

Michael purses his lips and then just nods his head. Sean had come into his life at a good time. With only real despair and futility nipping at Michael's heels, the young boy had given him a purpose and that connection to another that he so desired. And admitting the truth to himself, Michael had wanted that role of a replacement father for Sean. With the boy out of his life now, he worries that the senselessness of it all will return.

Sean comes running out with the pump in hand. Michael then takes over and says, "I can do this, you guys go upstairs and pack your things. And Sean, I put a few things under your pillow. Don't forget to pack them, too."

Earlier in the morning, Michael had written a letter for Sean with 'do not open until you reach your new home' scribbled on the envelope. In it, he says everything he had never taken the time to say, thinking that he had time. But now, he writes about the love and respect that he has for Sean. Michael also places his lucky coin there, an old worn out silver dollar he has carried with him for years. Sean would repeatedly ask to see it, enjoying its look and feel. And he includes the deck of cards, hoping Sean thinks of him each time he plays or teaches somebody one of their games. It is bittersweet, a sorrow from separation mixed with true best wishes for the boy.

Soon, the two return to Michael standing outside. "So, you got everything?" he asks as they approach him.

"Yeah, I think so. I guess we're set to go," says Damian.

"The tires seem to be holding but here, take this along with you," and Michael hands him the pump. "Strap it to the bike, you might need to add some air."

"But you need it for the ball," says Sean.

"Oh, I don't think I'll be playing much ball."

And that is when the reality of the good bye strikes Sean and he rushes over to give Michael a hug. "Are you going to be okay?" asks the empathetic young man.

"Are you kidding me? answers Michael, now knowing to put a good face on the situation. "I've got a whole cellar full of food, a spring basically all to myself, and don't forget the penthouse. You might say that I'm living the high life. And I would say that I owe it all to you," he says to Sean, lifting the boy off the ground and planting a kiss on his forehead.

Damian walks over and reaches out his hand. "Thank you, thank you for everything," he says.

Michael shakes his hand and returns, "It's been my pleasure. Say hi to your family for me when you see them again."

Damian and Sean get on their bicycles. The sun has climbed higher in the sky and the day is quickly progressing. Three days and miles of traveling are in front of them, one man and lives soon far apart are behind them as they pedal off down the street. Before making the last turn, Michael sees the two of them wave to him as they disappear around the corner. He waves back before making a slow and now solitary climb to the room.

*   *   *

The heat has become overly oppressive and Damian motions to Sean following behind that they are going to take a break. They have been riding for a few hours and both are hot and tired. Two withered but large eucalyptus trees offer some protection from the sun with their massive trunks. It will be their main stop of the day. Eating, drinking, and resting are needed now.

"You doing okay?" asks Damian as he gets off his bike.

"Yeah, fine," the young boy answers. And he has done fine, keeping up with Damian the entire way. Sean has even passed him on the downhills, letting out a whoop as he goes flying past. Damian has maintained a steady but not unreasonable tempo.

He knows that if they are going to make it, pacing themselves will be very important.

Sitting in the shade, they exchange food and conversation. "So, you said that your kid is a boy?" asks Sean. This is the first time that he has talked directly about Damian's family and the opportunity to discuss them is welcoming to him.

"That's right. His name is Christopher and he is fifteen years old. He likes hiking and there's an area behind where we live that is great for it. You guys will have to take some hikes there. I'm sure he's going to be really glad to have someone to go with," says the father.

"And your wife is my Mom's sister?"

"Yes, your mother and Sarah, that's my wife's name, were very close until we moved away. We used to spend a lot of time together. She lived in a town that was very near where we lived. I really liked your mom, she became a good friend of mine, too." Damian looks over at the boy and flashes a big smile.

"Oh," says Sean, smiling back, "that's cool."

They will take a three hour rest before climbing again onto their bikes. It is now late afternoon and the sun is to their backs, providing some relief. They will benefit from the cooling and from a slight west wind that is blowing them gently down the roadway. The pavement stretches out in front, leading them on, providing a path to reunion.

\*       \*       \*

The darkness has closed in all around them. Stars have come out but no moon appears to grant them any light. Luckily, the white center stripe on the road can still be seen and they use it as their guide. The terrain has been rolling with very few large hills for which Damian is grateful, for both himself and Sean.

It is past midnight and Damian feels that it is a good time for a break. Sean rides in front and coming alongside of him now, Damian says, "We got a good stretch in that time. I think we're doing pretty well, let's stop for a while."

Sean just nods his head and quickly pulls his bike to the side of the road. Finding a bank to lean against, the two sit down for a rest. "I think you're doing great. I'm not pushing you too hard, am I?" asks Damian. The young boy just mumbles something like a no and then leans a little more heavily against Damian's body and in a few minutes, Sean is fast asleep. Damian realizes that the day has already been long for the young child and that the best course for now is to stop for the night.

Damian knows that tomorrow will be the push if they are to meet the delivery truck on time as they only have a day and a half left to cross this desert stretch before reaching the north-south highway. And maybe only a day and a half until Damian is reunited with his family. 'If everything goes according to plan,' he thinks as sleep also finally overtakes him.

*     *     *

"Sean," whispers Damian to the boy as daybreak begins filling the sky. He doesn't move. "Sean, I'm sorry, but you need to wake up now," and Damian gently shakes him.

"What?" he answers sleepily.

"It's morning and we need to get going."

"Okay," says the boy and he immediately stands up and walks over to his bicycle, resting against the bank. Still not completely awake, Sean puts one leg over the bike and sits down on the seat. His head droops down, his eyes still half-closed.

Damian quickly runs over to him, quietly laughing to himself. "Wait a minute, wait a minute. We'll eat something first and give ourselves a little time to wake up," he says while smiling broadly. 'Michael was sure right about that,' thinks Damian to himself. 'This kid is no slacker.'

And he isn't. Like all young people now, there is no ability to avoid dealing with the harshness of life until the later years, until given that chance to 'grow up.' The realities of life have simply become too real to avoid. And like others, Sean simply digs in and doesn't complain. Gone is childhood, gone is the innocence, gone is the grace period.

The sun begins to clear the hills to the east of them. Early morning rays shine down on where they sit by the side of the road, eating breakfast. The rest was long enough and each begins to feel the surge of energy again from having taken the break and from having gotten some sleep.

"So, how much farther is it?" asks Sean.

"I don't know for sure. I think it's probably about eighty or ninety more miles maybe," says Damian.

"Is that a very long way? I mean, on bicycles, for us to travel that far on bicycles?"

"You know, we should be able to cover that much distance in time. We do start hitting some more hills when we climb the other side of the valley up to the highway to meet the truck but we should be okay."

"Well, let's go then," says Sean.

"Alright," answers an again amused Damian. He is enjoying this time spent with his new nephew. And he realizes that he will, indeed, treasure being an uncle and a provider to the boy. The young child will come into his family's life and Damian feels all will benefit because of it.

*    *    *

The highways have deteriorated greatly over the last several years as no repairs to infrastructure or roads occur anymore. There are no resources to repair them, no entity to take charge of them, and really, no need anyway. The very few vehicles that travel them are basically just delivery trucks shuttling between Groupings and Sectors. Drivers have the roads to themselves and they simply use the entire road to steer around the damaged sections of pavement.

Damian and Sean need to navigate the same potholes and are on the constant lookout for them. They use a system of bicycle etiquette in which the front rider tells and signals the rider behind him about any obstacles in the roadway. After hitting one particularly bad section, Damian had thought of the idea and with Sean usually riding in front, had given him the job. And he hopes that the task will take the boy's mind off the more laborious job of pedaling.

Sean relishes the responsibility and has taken on the job with a passion. "On the right," he yells as he moves over to the left side of the road.

"Okay, thanks," shouts back Damian. Riding a little faster so that he can come beside Sean, he says, "It looks like we have a long downhill coming up. Do you see it?"

"Yeah," answers Sean. "It looks really long."

"Do you want to take advantage of this section to go a little faster? Maybe we could have a little bit of a race," says Damian. "The road seems to be in pretty good shape but we still have to watch out. Is that okay with you?"

"A race, sure," accepts the boy immediately and then adds, "I'll be careful."

The bikes are now parallel to each other on the road.

"On your marks, get set...go!" shout out the two racers loudly and in unison.

Both riders then take off with a flurry of legs pumping hard on the pedals, especially Sean with his little legs and his little bike. They both gain speed quickly and are soon hurtling down the highway, two solitary figures in a lonely landscape, driving forward and leaving that other world behind.

Damian plays it up. He will let Sean get ahead and then catch up and pass him slightly. With Damian then pretending to have to brake to get around a rough section of road, Sean will take the lead again. The race goes back and forth as they bottom out and begin to climb again.

"See that big rock on the right up there," Damian yells over the noise of the wind rushing past them. "First one there, wins." With his head down and every ounce of concentration on the goal, Sean reaches it first and lets out a howl of victory and one of accomplishment. Going uphill now, they gradually come to a stop, get off their bikes, and begin pushing them.

"Ohhh," exhales Damian. "I guess you're just too fast for me. You about wore me out."

Sean beams back at him and flashes a big smile. "I was going fast, really fast, wasn't I!"

"Yes, you were," says Damian.

The two walk side by side exchanging light conversation and a little good-natured ribbing. They decide to continue to the top of the next hill before riding again. The sun is higher in the sky and the rays are intense. With the daytime temperatures climbing, Damian worries about their exposure. He has forced water on Sean at every break. He knows that they will have to be careful, have to take precautions if they are going to make it.

"Okay," says Damian when they reach the top of the hill. "Are you ready, Sean? Here, take another drink of water." And they begin pedaling down the road again.

The terrain is dry and desolate. They are crossing the worst part of the desert in the middle of the day. Damian had hoped that by riding through the night, they might be past this section by now, but they're not. His concern remains masked and hidden inside as he follows Sean down the road.

The long stretches of lifeless, barren landscapes offer little contrast and small measures of progress as each section takes what seems hours to cross. With one hill conquered, another only rises in front of them. The riding is becoming more difficult and the riders are already running on empty. The shimmering of heat on the asphalt in front of them offers just false horizons of cooler and watery goals.

Damian says to take a break and both of them pull over to the side of the road. Sean gets off and simply drops his bike on the ground as he walks quickly toward the shade of a scrub brush. Collapsing on the ground underneath it, he lies outstretched and lifeless. Damian, with great concern, rushes to him.

"Sean, Sean!" he says. "What's wrong!"

The boy doesn't answer. He is sweating profusely and his face is very red and flushed. Damian's worst nightmare is coming to pass, the heat and exertion may have been too great for the boy's small body. Damian lifts him gently and pours water over the top of his head, allowing it to run down his back while hurriedly fanning his face. He is urgently trying to bring down Sean's body temperature. Damian holds him carefully, lovingly, as his worry mounts about the boy's possible condition.

They lie underneath the bush for several minutes as Damian blows gently over his forehead while continually pouring the water over the top of his head. He then lifts Sean beside him and encourages him to drink. To Damian, it seems like an eternity passing but soon the boy begins to sip gingerly.

Within a short time, Sean begins to look better. The redness is diminishing from his face and he moves to sit up. Damian looks into the boy's eyes that only minutes before had been rolled back into his head, blank and distant. Damian continues holding him as Sean turns toward him to speak.

"Okay, I'm ready, is our break over?" he says bravely.

"Not for you, son, not for you," answers Damian. They will stop for their midday break, seek the shade, and rest their bodies before beginning again later in the day. They will stop with their goal in sight but still so very far away. Damian sits quietly watching the two large birds circling overhead as he caresses Sean's head that now rests comfortably in his lap.

\*     \*     \*

Three hours have slowly passed and the extreme heat of the day is diminishing. Sean had fallen asleep and Damian had then decided to let him get in a few hours of rest. The temperatures are brutal today and any energy expended now would only deplete them unnecessarily for later in the day and Damian knows that tonight they will have to keep moving if they are to meet the truck tomorrow morning. The young boy will need every ounce of reserve that he can gather to accomplish that task.

Sean stirs and begins waking. Sitting up, he looks about him as if trying to remember where he is and it takes a moment for the fog of sleep to dissipate before the boy can regain his references. "Did I fall asleep?" he asks.

"Yes, you slept for a few hours," says Damian.

"I'm sorry," says Sean.

"No, it was the best thing, it was good that you got some rest. Are you feeling any better?"

"Yeah, yeah I am," answers the young boy.

The two share a bite to eat and Damian makes sure that Sean drinks enough and stays hydrated. Reaching into his pack, he pulls out the bloodied tee shirt from his fall and rips the clean part from it. He then takes the water bottle and carefully, without wasting any, soaks the cloth. Although cooling some, it remains quite hot and Damian feels that Sean is still susceptible.

"Here, turn around," says Damian. He places the wet rag over his head and ties it securely in the back. For the next few hours of riding, Damian will continually wet the cloth to insure that Sean stays cool. They are down to one bottle of water and Damian has begun skipping his portion to conserve what is left for them.

As the hills become steeper, Damian resorts to riding beside Sean on the climbs so that he can use one hand to push him up those harder sections. It is working and with the young boy still aggressively pedaling away, they are making fairly good time. Night is approaching, though, and the darkness will make it more difficult to move quickly on the downhill sections because of the poor road conditions.

"So, everything going okay?" Damian yells ahead to Sean.

"I'm doing just fine," answers back the young boy. "For some reason, I don't even feel that tired."

Damian moves closer so that they can hear each other better. "People used to race bicycles in the old days," he begins. "Back then, they would have races that would take over three weeks and the riders would ride over two thousand miles during the race, which means they rode about a hundred miles every day."

"Wow, that's amazing!" says Sean.

"They were professional bicycle racers. They used to have professional football players and professional baseball players and professional tennis players, all sorts of sports."

"What does professional mean?"

"That means they did it for a living, that's how they made their money," explains Damian.

"People used to be able to play sports as a job? How about basketball?" asks Sean.

"Yeah, they had professional basketball players, too."

"That's cool, I bet I could have been a professional basketball player. Michael said I was really good at it, but you know what?" Sean then says to his uncle.

"What?" is Damian's response.

"I'd rather have been a professional bicycle racer. I'm a really, really fast bike rider, aren't I?"

"Yes," answers Damian with a smile and laugh. "Yes, you are. I bet you're one of the fastest there is."

"If I had lived back then, that's what I would have done for a job. I could have been a bicycle racer," says Sean.

Damian looks over at the boy but no words come to him as the emotion overcomes the man for the moment. Opportunity or vocation or life direction is simply not within young people's possibilities anymore. And that realization is demoralizing to think about, it is what bothers him so much with his own son. What can Damian offer Christopher for his future and for his life? What he can offer to him is nothing, flat out nothing, and that is hard medicine for a parent to swallow.

*　　*　　*

It is well into the night. Damian has resorted to pushing Sean for certain sections as he sits on his bike while walking his own. It is becoming increasingly hard to follow the faded center stripe as the darkness is now complete and overpowering. But they must keep moving, they are down to hours before meeting the truck. They have no choice but to continue.

"Okay, it feels like we've leveled out. I'm going to get back on my bike. Can you ride on your own for a while?" asks Damian.

"Yeah, I can pedal by myself," says Sean.

"We'll have to be careful, the road's in pretty bad shape here. You go first and I'll follow you. Ready?"

"Ready," says the boy. And they start riding again.

\*    \*    \*

The two are moving slower than at any other time of the trip but they haven't stopped for food or rest since late afternoon. Damian is beginning to feel the effects of not having enough water as he continues to skip his ration to save it for Sean. The big man is running dry, but still running. Damian knows this is one challenge that will have to be met head on and faced down. And that this is one race that cannot be lost.

The terrain continues undulating with only slight downhill sections but no really steep hills either. Earlier in the day, they had climbed through most of the elevation gain and now sit on a higher but more level plateau. Damian feels that at least they are over the worst part. The road begins to descend slightly and the pair pick up speed. Sean is ahead and Damian calls out to him, "Not too fast now." But Sean is gone and Damian strains to see through the overpowering darkness in front of them.

Trying to catch up, Damian begins pedaling faster but soon hits a piece of broken pavement and almost has the handlebars ripped out of his hands. "Sean!" he yells out loudly but with the wind in his ears, the boy hears nothing. The rush of the moment and the coolness of the night drive him on, recklessly, but with determination. Sean wants to take advantage of the descent to make good time. He wants his uncle to be proud of him.

The crash occurs with the sickening thud of a body being slammed onto the pavement. It is accompanied by the sound of the bicycle careening down the highway and by the appearance of a few sparks as the steel grinds into the pavement. Sean has hit a very bad and a very deep pothole in the road. Unable to see where he was going, the poor boy had simply pushed too hard and had taken too many risks. His scraped and bleeding body lies on the ground a short distance from his bicycle.

Damian is worried about Sean's taking off and continues to try and catch up to him when he runs over something on the road. He stops and gets off his bike to investigate when he sees that he has run over Sean's bicycle. Panicked now, he calls out loudly, "Sean, where are you? Sean...Sean!" A moan then comes from the side of the road and out of the darkness in front of him. Damian rushes toward the sound.

Reaching Sean's side, Damian hurriedly says, "Are you okay? Sean, can you say something? Oh, my god," he continues with an agonizing worry.

The young boy is dazed but conscious. Damian has him sit up and feels the dampness of blood on one arm as he holds him. Reaching to brush back the hair on his forehead, he feels more blood there. The boy is hurt and maybe very badly. 'I'm pushing him too hard. I should have seen this coming,' thinks Damian to himself about the accident.

"Sean, can you say something?" he says.

"I guess, I'm too fast," he finally whispers.

Relieved that he is talking, Damian replies, "Yes, a little too fast maybe." Damian will remove the t-shirt from his head and use it to wipe Sean's wounds. He encourages the boy to eat and drink something. Sean is scraped and battered but seems okay otherwise. Damian knows it could have been much worse.

\*　　\*　　\*

A few hours have passed and early morning light is filling the first half of the sky. Unable to continue because of the dark and Sean's injuries, they simply sit by the side of the road waiting for daybreak. As it approaches, Damian is able to see Sean's bicycle for the first time, resting about fifteen yards away from them. It doesn't look promising with the front wheel badly damaged. 'Now what are we going to do?' thinks Damian.

With only one functioning bicycle, Damian has gone over the options in his mind continually while allowing Sean to sleep next to him. They can both ride on his or he can put Sean on the seat and walk the bike, both slow and awkward methods for making any decent time. Looking down at the boy, he sees both of Sean's knees are badly scraped and have been bleeding. The boy is simply in no shape to travel anywhere, by any method.

They are to meet the truck in four hours, in only four hours. It is decision time and Damian knows it. There is only one option. He will have to leave Sean and go ahead to meet the truck. If he misses it, he will turn around and come back to Sean. Damian doesn't know how much farther it is but he knows that he needs to get going and now.

Damian gently nudges Sean to awaken. The boy begins to stir and come around. "Hi," he says, looking up at him.

"Good morning," replies Damian as the two sit quietly for a moment. Although just surface scrapes, Sean looks rather beat up and it is slightly unsettling for Damian to see. His road rash is worthy of any professional bicycle racer and it now forces him to withdraw from his first race, short of the finish line.

"Do you see your bike over there?" asks Damian.

"Oh, no, I really bent up the wheel, didn't I?" says the boy. "What are we going to do now, don't we have to meet the truck this morning? I really messed things up," says Sean with obvious regret about having the accident.

"I tell you what, this is what we are going to do." And Damian fills in the boy on his plan to ride ahead, meet the truck, and come back for him. He says that he is not sure how much farther the north-south highway is but he thinks that they must be fairly close. With any luck, maybe he can still reach the meeting place and the delivery truck in time.

Damian then spends a few minutes cleaning Sean's wounds. He will move him to another place that can offer more shade and leaves his backpack with him with plenty of food inside. Damian passes the last water bottle over to him. With kind, soft instructions to eat something and to stay hydrated and out of the sun, he goes to retrieve his bike. Damian unleashes the pump and fills his tires with more air as he prepares to leave.

Walking the bike back over to where Sean sits, he begins to say good bye, promising to return quickly. "Here, you take the water bottle. You're the one who's going to need it," says Sean, holding it out to him. Politely refusing, Damian assures him that he will be fine. "At least, take a drink before you leave," the young boy insists. The same refusal comes from Damian.

Sean unscrews the cap on the bottle and prepares to turn it upside down. "Either take a drink or I'm going to pour the whole thing out, right now. You hear me? I'll do it, really, I'll do it." And realizing that he does mean it, Damian gives in. The coolness of the liquid sliding down his parched throat is blessed and Damian quickly gains new energy and a new determination to strike out, to strike out to save himself and this incredible boy that has now come into his life.

Facing directly into the morning sun, Damian squints and keeps his head down. He is watching the road to avoid any bad sections of pavement but he is also trying to avoid the searing rays that have baked into him over the last few days. With or without humankind in it, this desert world has always been inhospitable. With the increased daily temperatures and almost non-existent rainfall and nearby mountain snowmelt of the past few decades, it is about as barren and bleak as anywhere on earth. And Damian is riding a bicycle through it, only a crazy person or a father would attempt such a feat.

\*     \*     \*

"Everything is loaded. You guys better take off, that middle stretch is going to be hotter than hell today," says the warehouse man. "I'll radio ahead and let them know that you are leaving. Should I tell them that you'll be there around three?"

"Yeah," answers the driver. "Tell them we are on the way." He and the other worker climb into the cab and start the engine. Pulling out of the gates, they wave to the security personnel while passing. They begin the long, hot drive to the Donnelly Grouping that lies about three hundred miles north of them.

Soon, the truck pulls onto the main road that will lead them there. And the road toward which Damian is furiously pedaling at the very same moment. "Aren't we supposed to meet up with that guy we gave a ride to a couple of weeks ago?" says the worker to the driver.

"Yep, today is the day."

"Do you think he's going to be there?"

"I don't know. I hope he makes it, he sure seemed like a nice enough guy."

"Well, I know I wouldn't want to be trying to cross that desert on my own in this heat."

"No, driving through it is bad enough, huh?" says the driver as he looks over at his fellow worker.

"Yeah, you sure got that right," the other man returns as the first furnace blasts of the morning rush in the windows at them as the truck speeds down the black, hot highway.

\*     \*     \*

Damian's initial burst has dwindled to a slow, steady grind. His body is simply running down and the toil of the last few days is becoming all too obvious as his legs are heavy and his back is aching. The cramping of his thigh muscles is proving especially uncomfortable and more than once Damian has simply had to jump off the bike, let it fall to the ground, and agonizingly try to walk out the cramps.

But then Damian immediately gets back on and painfully and awkwardly continues riding. He is trying to fight through that pain and discomfort and trying to keep making progress as one more mile conquered is one less mile to travel. It has come down to mind games to keep himself going and Damian is inventing a new one every few minutes now.

\*     \*     \*

Within a few hours, the truck approaches the intersection where they are to meet Damian. Slowing down, the driver pulls to the shoulder directly opposite the road from which the traveler is to return. Shutting down the engine, both men disembark from the cab to survey the scene.

"He's not here," says the one.

"No, he isn't," replies the driver.

"So, what are we going to do?"

"Wait," is the one word answer.

"What do you mean we're going to wait? For how long?" asks the other man.

"Don't know, we said that we would meet him at ten o'clock. It isn't ten yet."

The other man returns to the cab to pull his cap over his eyes and rest. The driver remains outside and paces back and forth down the side of the truck. He anxiously glances every few minutes in the direction from which Damian should be coming as the heat shimmers off the empty barren stretch of road in front of him. He stands with his hand raised to cover the eyes as he peers into the distance, hoping to see something moving toward him, hoping to get some good news.

The man in the truck awakes from his nap. He is sweating heavily as the heat in the cab has risen substantially. Getting out, he comes around to the other side of the truck. "Phew it's hot, do you see anything?" he asks of the driver who is still gazing down the merciless road.

"No, nothing."

"What time is it?"

"Eleven fifteen," answers the driver.

"Eleven fifteen! We've got to get going," says the other man. "We're going to be late with the delivery. They're going to have our butts if we don't get there soon. Let's go, the guy's not going to show up anyway."

"No, we'll give it a little more time."

"Give it a little more time? You're going to get us in trouble, you know that we have to make these deliveries on time. We could lose our jobs and I'm not going back to scavenging again just because of this guy. Come on, let's go," he says somewhat more aggressively.

The driver spins around and faces him. "I said that we are waiting. We can't help it if the truck overheated and we had to stop to let it cool off."

"What?" comes the bewildered response.

"I said, the truck overheated, got it," the driver states firmly and with authority.

"Oh, shit," says the other man. He then retreats to the shade underneath the truck and sits down while grumbling to himself, "The son of a bitch is going to cost us our jobs."

\*　　\*　　\*

Besides severe cramping, Damian is approaching the serious need for water. By skipping his ration over the past two days, he now risks dehydration and his clarity of thinking is fading. 'I must be close, it can't be that much farther,' he thinks to himself. 'Just a little more, just a little more,' becomes the mantra.

The pain of pedaling is intense. Using one hand to physically push down at the knee, he continues moving, continues turning the cranks but barely, only just barely. Each hill crested offers the same vista, just more of the same seemingly endless road. But Damian has now noticed the mountains in the distance are getting closer, the mountains that have the highway at their feet. It gives him hope, it is enough to keep him going.

The driver continues his vigilance near the truck. For some reason, his eyes remain fixed on the road to the west. He can't turn away, something tells him to keep watching, to not remove his optimism from the moment. But he begins to doubt his judgment about waiting for Damian and now seriously considers that he may, indeed, be jeopardizing their employment and their means of survival.

Pacing back and forth, he checks his watch and decides that they must be going. The driver stops to look one more time down that long stretch of straight highway when he sees something moving, something cresting the top of a distant hill. "Charlie, Charlie!" he yells out to his companion. "Come here, come here quick!" And the other man jumps up and runs to where Tom, the driver, is standing.

"There, on the top of the hill, do you see that thing? That's somebody coming down the hill, isn't it? Isn't that thing moving toward us?" he says.

"Damn, I think it is. But what is it?"

"I don't know but it's headed this way."

Damian is nearing exhaustion. The last stretch of road before rising to the old battered stop sign at the intersection is slightly downhill. The bicycle weaves a crazy path as Damian is simply hanging on, barely able to recognize what he is doing anymore. The two men run toward him and meet him as the road starts going uphill again. As the bike rolls to a stop, they reach it in time to catch Damian as he nearly falls to the ground.

"Are you okay, mister?" says a concerned Charlie. "You don't look so good." His forehead is blistered from the sun and his eyes are shallow and vacant. Damian is cramping so badly that he is unable to walk under his own power.

"Come on, Charlie, hurry!" Tom says with an urgency to his voice. "Put his arm around your shoulder, we've got to support the guy. We got to get him out of the sun."

For the next few minutes, Damian is basically unaware what is happening as the two men carry him to the shade of the truck and have him sit down. While the other man goes for water from the cab, the driver stays with him. "I started to think you weren't going to show up," he says. Charlie comes back with the water. Damian grabs at the bottle and begins drinking compulsively, choking on a mouthful.

"Whoa, slow down. You're going to be okay, you made it," says Tom. And the two men wait until Damian becomes more lucid, until he is able to speak.

"The boy, we have to go back to get the boy!" Damian finally blurts outs.

"What?" asks Tom. "What boy?" And Damian points back in the direction from which he has come and tells them about Sean. "Quick, let's get him in the truck," he says to Charlie.

The vehicle pulls away from the side of the road and with a roar begins heading back to get Sean. Within the hour, they have reached him and found him to be safe, in the same spot where Damian had left him. Soon, the two of them are sitting in the back of the cab, resting comfortably and relieved to be reunited again. It is now the middle of the afternoon as the truck speeds toward the mountains and a return to the Grouping.

\*     \*     \*

"What time is Dad supposed to get back?" Christopher asks his mother as they sit at the kitchen table eating lunch.

"The deliveries are usually around three in the afternoon. I'm going down to the office in a minute and see if they have heard anything. Do you want anything else to eat? You didn't eat very much this morning," says Sarah.

"No, I'm fine. Can I go with you?"

"Sure, let me just clean up the dishes and we'll go."

Sarah and her son walk to the security department and ask the person on duty if they know anything more about the delivery truck. They are just informed that a call was made earlier this morning that estimated their arrival between three and four in the afternoon. The two exit the building.

"That's good, that's only going to be a couple of hours from now," says Christopher. "It sure seems like he's been gone for a lot longer than just two weeks, doesn't it?"

"Yes, dear, it does," answers Sarah as two weeks is a longer period than the husband and wife have been separated in the last ten years. Without vacations or trips for business or visits to relatives anymore, the couple has consistently been together each and every day. And Sarah likes it that way. She has missed her husband more than she could have imagined and is anxious for his return, anxious in more ways than one.

"It's going to be great to see him again. I can't wait to hear what he found out about Shannon," says Christopher.

Sarah smiles back at him but doesn't say anything. She is slightly sullen and somewhat distant and her son picks up on it. "What's wrong, Mom?" he asks.

"Nothing. Why?"

"It seems like something is bothering you."

"Oh, I just want to see him back here again. I guess that I'm just a little nervous until I see him get out of the truck," she says. And Christopher remembers the risk that his father has taken. The reality of something possibly going wrong looms larger for him now and his joviality is less.

"Dad knows how to take care of himself. Don't worry, Mom," says Christopher, trying to comfort and reassure her.

"Yes, I'm sure you are right. Why don't we just go home and wait until three, then we can come back down to meet the truck," says Sarah, and they return to the apartment.

\*     \*     \*

"So, you look like you been in a fight," says Charlie, turning around to address the young boy in the back seat.

"You should have seen the other guy," ribs Tom.

Sean laughs at this new joke for him. He is feeling fine but is quite a sight to see. Besides two skinned knees, he has a bloodied right arm and a serious scrape on his forehead and one cheek. His shirt is torn and dirty. And Damian, for his part, doesn't look much better. Unbathed, sunburned, with a two week growth of beard, he is one grisly looking guy.

It is now getting later in the afternoon with nightfall being only a few hours away. They still have a fair amount of distance to cover before reaching the Grouping. The conversation has been minimal as the two men have allowed Sean and Damian to rest and regain their strength. With plenty of water now and something to eat, both are feeling better although Damian continues to cramp rather badly.

"How long have you guys been riding those bikes?" asks Charlie of the two travelers.

"Three days," says Damian.

"Oh, my butt can't take one of those things for an hour, never could. I don't know how you guys did it. And in that heat, too," he says.

"Well, we always stopped in the late afternoon and we tried to pace ourselves. Sean was the one leading the way. I just followed him," offers the proud uncle.

"Have to hand it to you, kid," says Tom. "You did what most grown men wouldn't have been able to do." Sean smiles broadly, from ear to ear. The grin will stay permanently pasted on his face for the next thirty miles.

In a few minutes, Damian says, "Let me ask you a question," directing the comment to the driver. "I was supposed to meet you at ten o'clock in the morning. It must have been almost two when I made it. Why did you wait for me?"

"Oh, Charlie and me here just kind of had a feeling that you'd show up eventually, didn't we, Charlie?"

"That we did, Tom," he says with an appreciative wink.

The truck with all of its supplies and human cargo continues the trek toward the mountains. Just before nightfall, they reach the last windy stretch of road that will transport them the final forty miles to the compound. Damian and Sean are nearing the end of their journey but are also approaching a new beginning at the very same time.

With silence in the truck, the father's thoughts for the first time drift to his own family and to the surprise that he has brought back with him. Damian knows that Sarah will embrace Sean completely and will become a surrogate mother to him. He remembers Christopher's excitement at finding out about his boy cousin. The risk has provided ample reward.

Remembering something, Damian asks Sean to pass his pack to him that is resting under the boy's feet. Digging through one of the front pockets, he feels for the ring that Sarah had asked him to give Shannon, the plastic ring from their childhood. Damian tells the story to Sean and says that he should have it now, that he has earned it. With pride and a slight sadness of remembrance for his mother, Sean slides it over his finger. The young boy will feel the ring often as they continue into the night.

\*　　\*　　\*

Christopher has gone back down first and is waiting by the front gate when Sarah arrives. "Nothing yet?" she asks her son. Christopher just shakes his head from side to side and continues looking out through the chain link fence that surrounds the compound. He asks his mother for the time. "It's only about three thirty," she answers.

Sarah and Christopher will wait as the next two hours slowly pass. At one point, Sarah returns to the apartment to get water for them. The two will share the bottle while both continue their unending gaze down the hillside to the road below, the road that leads to the Grouping. A security guard passes and Sarah asks if they have heard anything more about the delivery truck.

"No, there's nothing new. We radioed to their Grouping and they just confirmed that the truck had left early this morning," the guard informs them.

"Are they usually late?" asks Christopher.

"No, not usually. They could have had mechanical problems. It's really hot down there this time of year," says the guard as he then continues making his rounds.

"I don't like this," says Christopher to his mother.

"I know," answers Sarah as her concern is rising, too, but she needs to mask it for her son. "We shouldn't worry, everything's probably okay. They're just running late."

"But what if Dad didn't make it on time? What if he didn't meet the truck?" he asks.

Sarah is frozen for a moment by fear and by similar thoughts. She has been fighting the very same idea ever since Damian left. 'What if he doesn't make it back in time to meet the truck, then what?' She pushes it still farther into the back of her mind. "He made it," she says half-heartedly, half-believing her own words. "We just have to think that he made it."

Sarah then says to Christopher that maybe they should just go back to the apartment for dinner and then come down later. "The security department will notify us just as soon as the truck gets to the warehouse."

"You can go," he says. "I'm going to stay here." The dedicated son worries for his absent father and worries for the man who is more important to him than he had previously understood. Damian's absence is becoming a large hole inside him, one that he feels would never fill if his father failed to return. Christopher now realizes what he has always possessed as the threat of its loss rises precariously in front of him.

"I'm going to go back home and make us something to eat. And then I'll bring it right back. I'll go quickly," says Sarah as she lightly touches her son on the shoulder. Without turning around, Christopher simply answers 'okay' and continues staring out into the blackness of the night.

\*     \*     \*

Sean has fallen asleep and Damian is forced to constantly shift positions as both his legs continue their painful cramping. "Okay back there?" asks the driver. Damian answers, 'Yes,' just a little out of shape he guesses. "Well, its not much farther, we'll be there in about twenty minutes."

After a few miles more, Damian asks the two men, "Do you guys have any family?"

"Charlie does," volunteers Tom. "Me? I don't think anybody would put up with me. I can be an ornery cuss at times."

"Any children?" Damian says to the other man.

Charlie is slow to respond to the question and Tom jumps back in. "Charlie had some bad luck recently. It's kind of hard for him to talk about sometimes."

"Oh, I'm sorry," says a sincere Damian. "I probably shouldn't have asked."

"No, no, that's okay," as Charlie begins. "We had decided not to have any children, you know, with trying to feed them and everything. But Sherry got pregnant and I had gotten this job so we were excited. It looked like we could pull it off." Charlie pauses for a minute, pensive and reflective. "When it came time to have the baby, we couldn't find anybody to help us, anybody who knew about that sort of thing. We tried to do it on our own and Sherry was wonderful, she was great. But the cord got wrapped around its neck and when the baby came out it wasn't breathing and it wasn't moving," and the emotion momentarily chokes off any further words.

When he can regain his composure, Charlie continues talking about it. "Can you believe it? A person can't even find a doctor anymore. What kind of crazy, mixed-up world is this? You can't even find a god damn doctor anymore," the man repeats as his voice then just trails away sadly at the thought.

From then on, silence remains in the cab as the truck begins climbing the final hill to the compound.

\*     \*     \*

Sarah returns from the apartment and has brought dinner for Christopher. But he refuses it, even with her encouraging him to eat something. She lays down the food and stands beside her son at the gate. Sarah reaches for his hand and grasps it gently, lovingly. Having past her in height a few years ago, Christopher drapes his arm around her shoulder in return.

"There!" he suddenly yells out. "Look, those are headlights!" and then they disappear. Sarah peers into the darkness until the truck comes out from behind another curve in the road. "See, see!" Christopher says again to his mother.

"Yes, honey, I see them. I can see the headlights now," says Sarah with a great feeling of relief as Christopher then runs to inform security that the truck is coming up the road. Two guards come from the office and make their way toward the front gate. One man begins opening it.

Downshifting of the gears can be heard as the truck prepares for the last steeper section into the compound. Soon, it is passing and Christopher sees his father in the back of the cab waving to his son. "There he is! It's Dad," and Christopher goes running after the truck as it heads toward the warehouse.

Coming to a stop, the back door opens quickly and Damian gingerly gets down from the truck. Christopher comes running up to him as the father stands still and waits for him. "You made it! You made it back, Dad!" says Christopher as he then throws his arms around his father.

Sarah soon joins them and Damian reaches out to her but she is taken aback at the appearance of her husband. "Oh, Damian, you look awful. Are you okay, dear, are you okay?"

"Yes, everything is just fine," he says. And it is, now that he has seen his family again.

Charlie and Tom exit the truck and then come over to where Damian is standing with them. "Is this your crew?" asks Tom of his former passenger.

"Yes, this is my son, Christopher, and this is Sarah."

"Nice to meet you, ma'am. I'm Tom and this here is Charlie." Both of the men will shake hands with everyone and then excuse themselves as they need to get that truck unloaded.

Sarah goes up to each of them before their leaving. "Thank you," she says to them. "Thank you very much."

"Our pleasure," replies Tom. "You've got quite a guy there. Take care of him, take good care of him." And the two men turn to walk back toward the truck.

"Come on," Sarah says to her husband. "Let's get you home. I think you might need a shower." And she reaches for his hand to start leading him away.

"Wait a minute," says Damian. "I have a surprise for you, for both of you." And he climbs back into the truck to wake Sean. "Time to wake up, son. We're here, we're back at the compound." A groggy and sleepy Sean slides across the seat and climbs down from the truck.

The mother and the son are beyond words and just wait for Damian to continue. "Sean, I want you to meet Sarah." And the young boy extends his hand as Sarah does to him. "And this is Christopher." 'Hi,' say the two boys to each other. Sarah glances over at Damian with a puzzled look on her face.

"Show her the ring," he says to Sean. The young boy puts his hand out in front of him and Sarah looks down to see the ring that she had given to Damian. A wave of recognition sweeps over her and she rushes to him, puts her arms around Sean tightly, honestly, and holds on for a few moments. Pushing back slightly, she gazes into his soft eyes. "Are you Shannon's son?" asks Sarah. The battered boy looks back at her and nods his head.

"Hey, we're cousins," quickly jumps in Christopher excitedly. "That's cool, really cool!"

"Christopher, why don't you and Sean go grab our packs out of the truck," Damian then asks of the two boys. They complete the task and begin walking back together toward their housing. Sarah helps Damian as he is having trouble with the discomfort from the cramping. They follow behind more slowly.

"I've never had a cousin," says Christopher to his new friend. Sean says that he doesn't think that he has either. "Come on, let me show you where we live. You can share my room, there's plenty of space for two of us."

And the boys begin walking more briskly.

"Ever play hearts?" asks Sean.

"What's that?" says Christopher.

"It's a card game, it's one of my favorites. I really like playing it, I'll teach you," offers the young protégé.

"Cool," says Christopher again. And the two boys are the first to return to the apartment.

Damian is walking carefully and painfully and Sarah is a bit concerned about him. "Are you sure that you're okay, honey? You look a little worse for the wear. And Sean, what happened to him? He has scrapes all over his body."

"Oh, he wrecked his bike," says Damian.

"His bicycle?" asks Sarah, not understanding.

Damian laughs, laughs very loud. Pulling his wife closer and holding her tighter, he says, "I'll tell you everything when we get home. We have time, we have time."

And they do.

# Resolution Days

THREE GENERATIONS had passed since the beginning of the new century and for each, the struggle for survival had become safer and saner. But disappointingly, it had not come without a high cost and, of course, it had not come without first a crisis. Twenty years into the new century, critical food shortages had placed unbelievable pressure on several governments to support and feed their people. Food rioting had started in areas where the shortages were causing pain and suffering. As the wealthier world watched, mass hunger and starvation had occurred in many areas and to many peoples throughout the world. It was severe, it was intense, it was devastating. And to some, it was something that they could no longer endure or tolerate.

While several of the more developed nations were still able to keep the life-sustaining levels of foodstuffs on hand for their populations, this bred an even stronger contempt from the have nots toward the haves, from the poor toward the rich. And in that one corner of the world, in that one desperate moment, a core of individuals planned the unthinkable and dedicated themselves to carry it out. With their backs against the wall, with nothing left to lose, they wanted revenge and they wanted to even the score. A nuclear weapon in the hands of such a group could only have negative and very serious consequences.

These perpetuators would become the source of the world's first 'loose nuke' but they were determined to give it someone else's ownership. This highly technical, highly political faction had succeeded in creating the appearance of a nuclear attack on another country by one of its enemies. And before the deception was uncovered, the two countries retaliated with nuclear strikes of their own, coming down on a major city in each nation.

Three atomic weapons had been unleashed upon the planet. And the accompanying devastation and the horror and the pain had been felt the world over whether one was an actual victim or had only been a witness. Besides the many deaths, radiation sickness affected hundreds of thousands more and rendered large areas of land uninhabitable for hundreds of years.

But because of the Great Mistake, changes had finally come to all governments and all nations. With the complete abhorrence by the world of this event, conferences had then been urgently arranged and agreements quickly reached to prevent any such occurrence from ever happening again. Also, in addition to the destruction of all remaining nuclear weapons, formal treaties were signed by every sovereign nation in the world promising never again to wage war or to resort to violence or military intervention to settle disputes. The world had almost killed itself and all knew the Mistake must never be repeated.

This real peace dividend would reap real rewards as no longer would nations spend great percentages of their wealth on defense or on military buildups or on the bullying of weaker counterparts. Because war is never waged only on countries or governments, war is waged on people, that is why it has always been wrong and even immoral. And now governments did not have to waste their money on these destructive and unproductive areas within our society and we could finally turn our attention to solving the more basic problems of the human condition. Food production, health systems, education, and infrastructure could finally take their rightful place at the top of the spending list. Money is now directed toward people's lives, not toward their deaths.

And with just this one basic change, a truly new world of possibilities had broadly opened before us as it was no longer country against country, culture against culture, or class against class. The world had finally embraced its diversity, appreciated its differences, and celebrated its various viewpoints. We had looked into each others' eyes, into the depth of each others' souls, and found similarities not differences, love not hate, and respect not disdain for one another.

The first step was to provide efficient sustainable agriculture to the entire world. Because of the disasters of the early part of the century, few areas of concern received as much attention as the pure and simple feeding of our populations. In the developing nations, many successes of subsistence farming and husbandry had been achieved. In the developed nations, the failure of large scale and corporate agriculture to provide a safe and quality food supply had finally brought about change. We had realized that these overly processed and easily contaminated and nutritionally deficient products had been the wrong recipe for a healthy human diet. With a return to family farming, better stewards of the land than any corporate board, came an awareness of the benefits and the cost savings of a more localized production and distribution of the food supply. And we had finally stopped pouring poisons on the lands and had protected the waters and oceans to allow us, once again, to utilize the vast resources of our seas.

After several decades of empty rhetoric and false promises on education, the world had finally recognized that in this one vital area may lie the answers to many of our social problems. Ensuring that our young people were able to freely and easily obtain early quality education became a main purpose of every government in every country. And with this accomplishment, we could finally move forward from a position of understanding and intelligence, not from one of only false beliefs or defended ideologies or perpetual ignorance. By producing fully informed individuals, more progressive and far-sighted public policy had followed and, indeed, had been demanded by its enlightened citizens. Better educated people make better lifestyle choices, make better contributions to society, and create better solutions to the problems that exist in the world.

Energy and environment had linked together into a coherent and sane plan for supply and survival. A successful transition from industrial age fuels to new age renewables had occurred rapidly with the realization that any other path forward would be a journey into decline. With the degradation of the environment occurring at a much more rapid rate than previously predicted, countries and governments finally realized the urgency for action that was needed in this arena. If we were to maintain a healthy home planet for future generations, sincere and earnest action by the citizens and the leaders of the day was required. Conservation in all areas of commerce and lifestyle became the new paragon. By reducing usage, we had been able to make the transition to renewables easier. And with this conversion, innumerable jobs had been created in the research and development of alternative energies and in the caring for and the renewing of the lands and the rivers and the lakes and the oceans.

Another major area that had finally received attention was controlling the numbers of humans that lived upon the planet. Also because of our experiences with the food riots of the early century, all finally knew that something had to be done about the out of control, burgeoning human populations. Programs were developed throughout the world to educate people on the benefits of having a reasonable family size and on the responsibilities of that parenthood. Adding two billion to our numbers in the first seventy years and then again in the next thirty years during the previous century had been a foolish formula for disaster and with the weight of that human activity treading heavily upon the earth, the number of footsteps had to be reduced.

Additionally, a new economic system had evolved in this new world. The constant growth that was rapaciously required by so-called modern economies had been replaced by the reason and predictability of a sustainable and more socially valuable system. The New Economy has become a needs based economy and not a wants based economy. The production of necessary goods and services on a global level provides sufficient economic activity for all without the requirement of that 'growth industry' or that next hot thing or another sanctioned scam. The boom, bust, and bubbles of market economies had blown up in our faces, time and time again. An economy based on growth is an economy digging its own demise in a world of finite resources. And we no longer look favorably upon using those resources to produce goods for only conspicuous consumption as we are no longer judged by the things we own but by the way we lead our lives.

The Old Economy had simply been a numbers game where the numbers just didn't add up anymore. The 'bigger is better' group had finally been pushed from the top and had been replaced by the more reasonable and rational thinking on smaller and more local levels. And with the inability of big business to solve our big problems, individuals had regained the reins of commerce to make it work for everyone. It was time for the bigger part to end and for the better part to begin. It was time for a new paradigm. Although larger operations such as those necessary to produce economies of scale still continued in many areas of production, those now leading these companies could no longer inordinately enrich and empower themselves at the expense of others.

Valid social and environmental costs had finally been added into the formulas of the free market and with these adjustments, the true cost for all goods and services could now be determined. Unnecessary, frivolous, and harmful material goods had finally stopped being produced; essential, socially beneficial, and safer goods and services now prevailed. Because of an improvement in basic living conditions, that excess consumption was no longer needed to fill those empty holes in people's lives.

With population problems coming under control, with the end to war making, and with all countries and peoples of the world working together, we were able to better our lives and those of others. By addressing the urgent issues of ecological destruction, of societal inequality, and of intensely needed economic reform, the world had finally grown up and had taken responsibility for its actions. We started thinking long-term not just short-term, we became concerned with the social value of our actions not only with the personal benefits, and we had acted out of conscience instead of conceit. Success had come to all by making sure that none were touched by failure.

And we all had no greater a responsibility than to protect the planet for the children, that was our job and that was our reward.

Fortunately, we had finally started working on the real problems facing humankind, together and in time. It is such a world that Annie Sullivan lives in, grows and flourishes in, and gives back to on a daily basis.

*　　*　　*

Annie's plane lands on the runway and slowly makes its way toward the terminal. Having only been assigned an eight day trip this time, Annie, for some reason, feels as though she has been gone from home for much longer. She had enjoyed the trip, traveling to a part of the world that she had always wanted to visit. The tour had been successful and the group of people traveling with them this time had been exceptionally interesting and very appreciative of all that the touring company had provided for them. But always at the back of her mind, in the more responsible recesses, Annie has regretted being absent from her grandmother for so long at this particular time. She is her caregiver and her provider. And although the grandmother does fine by herself and always tells Annie not to worry, she does. And now, walking toward the baggage claim, her granddaughter gives her a call on the phone.

"Grandmother, this is Annie. My plane just landed and I'll be home within the hour," she says.

"Oh, hello, dear," comes back the sweet and sincere response from a gracious Martha Goodman. "I'm so glad that you're back. Did everything go well this time?"

"Everything went fine, the trip was a lot of fun and we had a completely booked group this time. All of the guides received small bonuses and East Africa was really beautiful, just beautiful. But what about you, how are you feeling, are you doing okay?" asks Annie, with a worried tinge to her voice.

"Why, sure, I feel okay," answers a not quite honest Martha. "Julia has come by almost everyday to check on me and she brought me dinner last night and even stayed to watch a movie. She's so nice, you have really nice friends, dear."

"Yes, Julia is a sweetheart. I'll have to thank her for helping out so much," Annie reminds herself about her closest friend. "And you're sure that you're doing okay?" she asks again before hanging up. The assurances come back and until getting home to see for herself, Annie accepts the situation for now. Hurrying to the waiting transport, she is anxious to get back into town and to the house where her grandmother waits for her.

Annie is a tour guide and works for a travel company. Guides must be trained in basic medical procedures, be knowledgeable about local history and customs, and be able to speak at least two other languages. Whenever a particular language or regional expertise is required, those who were qualified are offered the tour. Trips vary in length but generally run from a minimum of eight days to as long as five weeks. It is a good job, an interesting job, but Annie is on record for a maximum length trip of only two weeks. Her other job is much more important to her.

Martha Goodman was a vivacious twenty four year old at the time of the nuclear disasters. Living near one of the epicenters, she had been exposed very directly to the blast but, because of her location within a strong concrete structure, had avoided being killed. Several days had passed, though, before she eventually had been pulled from the rubble. Having suffered severe thermal burns to one side of her body, Martha was also exposed to the radiation that had remained over the area. And now, after forty more years of life, she was in the final stages of bone cancer, leukemia, and her health was failing very rapidly. Annie worries constantly about her while being gone from home and that is where the friends come in.

Endearing herself to many with her positive attitude and her good nature, Marty, as Annie likes to call her, has always been everyone's favorite. The people who cross her path greatly enjoy her company and come to visit often. Some of the luscious limes and lemons that she grows so well in their backyard and showers upon visitors probably also has something to do with it. But those who had survived the Great Mistake and continued living held a special place in the entire world's heart. Many offered their help to these last symbols of one of humankind's greatest inhumanities. Martha was one of the more fortunate survivors, in a way that is, as her life continues to be a daily painful struggle for that very survival.

Tragedy had struck this family more than once. Although war and famine and disease had been conquered, accidents were, of course, still part of life. Annie's parents lost their lives in a house fire almost fifteen years earlier. Marty had lived near them at the time and with their loss, Annie moved back to the area to help take care of her mother's mother.

The taxi pulls to the front of the small house located at the end of the tree lined cul de sac. After handing the money over the seat, Annie exits the vehicle and makes her way up the sidewalk. Opening the front door, she calls out to Marty.

"I'm back here, Annie" answers the grandmother from her bedroom at the rear of the house.

Relieved to be home, Annie places the suitcase in her room as she moves on to Marty's. Entering, she sees her grandmother sitting quietly in a chair near the window with a few letters and pieces of paper on a table near her. Annie goes over to give her a hug and a kiss on the forehead. "Everything okay?" she wants to know as she looks down on the disfigured and slight woman of over sixty years of age.

"Sure, you're home again, right?" says Marty and then smiles impishly. Annie pulls another chair near her so that she can sit down with her grandmother.

"So, what have you been doing to keep yourself busy?" asks Annie, looking about the room.

Marty says that she has been talking with one of her best friends almost daily. "Jessica may come to visit next month." Jessica is also a survivor of the Great Mistake and had turned activist soon after the catastrophe. She lost her husband and two children in the disaster. Her organization and many similar ones had been instrumental in increasing the outcry against military solutions to world problems and conflicts, against forcing one's beliefs or values or interests on another, against creating evil in the name of good.

"That's sounds great, when will you know if she can come?" asks Annie.

"Within the week, probably," says Marty.

Annie stands to attend to unpacking when she glances down at her grandmother's leg. The entire side of one calf is black and blue and very severely bruised. "Marty, what happened to your leg? It looks awful!" she moans in true concern for what appears to be a very bad injury.

"Oh, it's all right. I was out back repotting some of the flowers and one of those big pots fell against it. It didn't hit very hard, it's okay, it's just a little bruise."

'It's just a little bruise,' Annie thinks to herself. This happens way too often now to her grandmother and each time, it troubles her greatly. Only a small bump, a slight scratch, and the result is large amounts of bleeding with dark, purple, sickly bruising. Annie scolds her each time and tells her not to lift things, not to do heavy work, but she is determined to stay busy, to stay active. After what she has been through, shutting down life is not an option. Marty will continue her gardening, her sweeping of the walks and patio, and the attempting of any repair that comes her way. Martha Goodman is a fighter, a survivor, and that fight is what keeps her going, bruises and all.

Annie will then empty her suitcase yet again but leave it close so that it will be ready for that next time, for that next call which will surely come soon. But, for now, she will make herself and her precious grandmother a light dinner and spend the evening telling of her most recent travels. She will speak of the places that she visited, of the people that she met, and of the adventures that it brought. And Annie will relax, now that she is home and now that she is near again.

\*     \*     \*

Watching his efficient team move the last section into place, Alex Galway checks the time. Seeing that it is already past three o'clock and being a Friday afternoon, he announces the end to the work day. "Alright," says Alex. "Bolt it down and we'll wrap it up, maybe get out of here early today. Ryan and Alison, start putting the tools away, will you?"

"Sure, boss," the two workers reply quickly. They are anxious to end the day as both are meeting their sweethearts at the Friday Dances. With enough time to return home and shower, they may well be the first to arrive and claim a spot up front, near the band, and they hurry to finish the task.

Alex rolls the plans back into the tube and stores them away in the desk inside the construction shed. The week has proven productive with no major obstacles to overcome and they have been able to underground nearly three miles of utilities in just this week alone. And with public money funding infrastructure projects, the workers are also the owners so what is good for the project is good for the people. And, of course, there is always the possibility that the tax rebate next fall will be larger if they and others stay under budget and stay productive.

The tax system had gone through a major restructuring and simplification as a much needed and necessary part of the New Economy. Three basic taxes now fund the spending on both the federal and the local levels. An income flat tax of seventeen percent, or an optional eighteen percent rate that offers a savings plan with matching contribution, has been implemented for federal expenditures. Property taxes support state outlays and sales taxes with rates determined by the individual city and county jurisdictions fund local needs. With the end of corporate and business loopholes and to any minimum income level, all citizens now gladly pay their share because the benefits of government spending are now both real and fair.

With the first two percent of the federal tax rate supporting health maintenance costs, the remaining fifteen percent funds general expenditures. Because of easily accessible preventive care and a newfound peer pressure to lead healthier lives, a 'good health rebate' is very possible if costs are controlled. With instantaneous accounting procedures in place, this is issued in March of each year. In a similar manner, if a country lives within its means and meets its budgets, a tax rebate can be issued in October. Money is returned to the citizens, to be spent again, to drive the economy even further down the road.

Alex's public works team is one of the best. Being comprised of Conversion Core employees with several private contractors and small businesses participating, his group produces well, year after year. Several awards have been issued to them and Alex is one of the most knowledgeable, respected managers at the Core. Looking out for the best interests of the projects, the employees, and the citizens is a win-win situation that is reflected throughout the New Economy. Doing what is right, doing what is best for all, and performing honestly and diligently is, once again, revered and rewarded. And success is no longer simply measured by the making of large amounts of money for a few, it is measured by the making of a better life for the many.

With the workers gone, Alex checks next week's production schedule before exiting the trailer and locking it on the way out. Making his way to the parking area, he gets in his peetee and begins the short trip back to his home. Descending the hill, he enters the flow of other peetees moving along the cruiseway.

Because of population decreases and the promotion of urban revitalization programs, many previously busy and congested highways have been retrofitted for thoroughfares to be used solely by the peetees, by only 'personal transports.' These are extremely simple and efficient and small profile vehicles that run on short distance power supplies. The devices offer economical and clean transportation to the majority of workers who now commute an average of less than ten miles to work. With a steady speed of forty five miles per hour, these narrow and lightweight transports move safely and quietly through a network of peetee exclusive pathways throughout all metropolitan areas. There are even designated bad weather routes that offer retractable enclosures that can provide safer routes during inclement times. Combined with the bicycle and walking paths, these new roads carry the bulk of commuters on their daily trips to work and for its citizens moving about town shopping or running errands. With the improvements to inner city environs, those who work there now also choose to live there. The insanity of hours' long commuting with all its personal and social costs has disappeared as cities have become truly livable again.

Alex arrives back home and parks his peetee in the garage. Plugging into the charger, he then enters through the side door. "Hey, anybody here?" Alex shouts out to a quiet house.

"Upstairs, Dad," his son, Aaron, calls back.

Climbing the steps, the father reaches Aaron's bedroom and sees him sitting on the edge of the bed, fingering a guitar. "Hey there, what's new? Have you been home very long?"

"Not long, I didn't have a seventh period. So, yeah, I've been home for about half an hour," he says.

"Where's Katie?" Alex asks about his daughter and Aaron's much younger sibling.

"Oh, she's next door at Emily's. One of their friends is having a birthday party tomorrow and they're making decorations or something. I don't know much about it, she's been over there a while," as the seventeen year old boy continues looking down and finding chords on the guitar.

With his son back in his own world, Alex turns to leave but asks one more question. "And Mom?"

"She said something about having to go to her exercise class. She was on her way out when I came home," ends the exchange of information between the two of them.

Alex makes his way downstairs and moves on to the kitchen. Sitting down to a light snack at the kitchen table, he hears Katie coming through the back door. "Daddy!" she yells out excitedly when seeing her father already home and rushes over to where he is sitting. "Look, Emily and I made all these decorations for the birthday party tomorrow. Every balloon cutout is a different color and each one has somebody's name on it that's going to be there. And then Emmy and I drew these butterflies and colored them in, her mom helped us cut them out. Here, I did this one," she says as she shows her father.

"Katie, that's a good job," says Alex and he gives his daughter a hug. Katie beams back at him with a satisfied smile. "Hey, are you hungry?" he then asks his seven year old.

"No, thank you. Emily's mom made us some cinnamon toast and it was really, really good," says the young child. "Why don't we ever have cinnamon toast?" she asks with true concern about this serious omission in their lives.

"I don't know, there's no reason that we can't," says Alex. "Would you like to have cinnamon toast sometime?"

"Oh, yes, but ask Mrs. Martin how to make it first. I think she probably makes the best cinnamon toast there is," says Katie about their next door neighbor.

"Okay, I'll ask her first," says Alex and Katie hurries upstairs to show her brother her creations.

\*     \*     \*

Another hour slowly passes before Alex's wife, Laura, returns home. Alex had noticed the absence of one of their peetees when parking but at the time, he had thought that Aaron was still at school. Laura makes her way back into the house now, coming in through the garage.

"Hi," Alex says as she passes the doorway into the living room where the husband sits watching television.

"Oh, hi," Laura answers, slightly surprised to see him there. "You're home already. When did you get back?"

"A while ago, what have you been doing?" he asks. "I thought classes were on Wednesday."

Coming into the room, she says, "I caught an extra one today. Fridays are for a more advanced group and Phillip felt that I was ready for it. And it is harder, a lot harder."

"Well, I like the results," the husband teases and reaches out to have his wife come sit with him.

"No, no time for that," says Laura, moving away quickly and hurrying into the kitchen. "I have to get started on dinner." Alex follows her into the room.

"So, Katie has a birthday party tomorrow. If you want, I'll take her. What time does she have to be there?" asks the often busy father.

"Eleven thirty, but that's okay. I already planned on taking her. I have some errands to run, so I'll just drop her off and then come back later to pick her up."

"But I would like to take her. And then I could stay and help out with it. They always need more parents at those things and I missed out on the school program last week, remember? I kind of want to make it up to her and spend some time with her," he offers as more reasoning for him to get the job.

"No, I'm going to take her," Laura states flatly.

"Okay," says a disappointed and curious Alex.

\*     \*     \*

Jeremy Lucas sits quietly at his desk on the fifth floor of the Simmons Insurance and Investment Company building. He is a paper pusher, an order taker, who is responsible for answering questions on policy provisions, for providing claim forms and service, and for processing payments. It is a simple job, a dull job, absent of any real need for intelligence or creativity, but Jeremy is a rather dull mundane individual and it suits him fine. His only real passion in life is fishing and with the work week completed, almost every weekend is spent at a lake or a river or that special stream angling against his watery adversaries. Only keeping an occasional fish for a fresh dinner, he releases all back into the wild, to continue their lives, to perhaps provide action for himself or for others again.

But it's not about the fishing. It's about being outdoors and communing with nature, as the saying goes, because communing with people has always been more difficult for him. While in the outdoors, there are no judgments from others, no awkwardness from within, and no expectations not to reach. With the blue sky as his canopy and the green earth as his foundation, Jeremy is content and does not miss human companionship. But on the long work week nights, he struggles with the emptiness and loneliness that is constantly pushed to the back of his mind. He has come to expect less, to accept what life offers, and to make no plans for improvements. Jeremy is forty one years old, single and solitary and lonely.

Now looking at the clock, he notices that in only ten minutes the weekend will arrive. His mood lifts as he clears his desk before departing. On his way home, he will stop at the beverage store to pick up a quart of beer, a ritual and tradition, done more out of habit than desire. Jeremy doesn't really like the taste of beer but coupled with his takeout dinner of fish and chips, it seems to complement his Friday nights. On most evenings, he makes a simple meal and retires early. But on Fridays, Jeremy feels the need to reward the week's work. The little buzz that he gets from the beer increases his excitement for his weekend excursion as he sits watching, what else, fishing shows.

Turning the lock on the front door, Jeremy enters his small but adequate first floor apartment. It is located on the end of the building and allows him private access to a pleasant side yard that doubles as a casting area where he can practice for hours. The yard would also be perfect for a dog, a companion, and Jeremy has thought about getting one for years now. But he won't, he can't. Being gone during the day and most weekends, he feels as though he simply couldn't offer the poor animal a very good life. And coming with him on his fishing trips is an impossibility. One doesn't spend that much time and money on a hobby to have a well-intentioned dog running up and down the banks scaring away the fish.

It is a two bedroom apartment, sparsely furnished with idyllic posters of far off rivers and lakes adorning almost every wall. In his bedroom is only a single bed and a chair and a nightstand and not much more. With an efficiency kitchen, an adequately sized front room, and a second bedroom turned into a fly tying studio, all his needs are met.

As he pulls a side table nearer to his easy chair, Jeremy sits down to his bagged dinner and carefully pours a tall, cool glass of beer. He watches the bubbles moving upward and shimmering from the light coming through them. The television comes on and switching quickly to his show that will be starting in ten minutes, Jeremy begins eating his dinner. The fishing show is directly followed by a travel show that garners his attention and causes him to remain seated for nearly two hours more before rising to carry the dirty dishes to the kitchen.

Travel, now that's something he would like to do, if it wasn't so daunting, so intimidating. Jeremy often looks at the posters on his wall with all those perfect, peaceful streams and rivers and lakes from around the world. He envisions himself casting into this still corner of a stream or from a simple boat sitting comfortably in the middle of some picturesque lake. And Jeremy can afford to do it, gets his five weeks off, but can't commit to something so out of character, something so demanding of social interaction and personal involvement. At the core of his being, he wishes that he could but Jeremy just lets go of the thought while reaching for a map. It is time to plan tomorrow's fishing, nearby and close to home.

*     *     *

Annie rises early the first morning after her return. Leaving her room, she peeks in at Marty still sleeping comfortably and quietly makes her way to the kitchen. First starting the water for tea, she then searches the refrigerator for breakfast. Reaching for the milk, she closes the door and takes a box of cereal from the cabinet's top shelf and a banana from the fruit bowl on the counter. Annie goes to the back yard to retrieve a lemon for use in her tea along with the orange blossom honey that is always kept in stock. It is a clear and peaceful and beautiful morning and Annie is, indeed, glad to be home again.

The required traveling that is necessary has been both an upside and a downside to her employment. Annie has had the chance to explore much of the world and to witness its rebirth. In the last decade especially, traveling to see nature's splendors and to take part in flourishing cultures different from one's own is an opportunity that many take advantage of now. Learning of others, respecting and exploring their unique perspectives and traditions, has increased the desire of people to travel outside their own safe sphere of experience. And having been with the travel company for almost twenty years gives Annie the seniority that allows her to choose only the shorter tours, to minimize that downside of being away from home

But sitting at the kitchen table now, she mulls over the same nagging worry that follows her on those long journeys from home. For years, her grandmother has lived with the discomfort and the scars from her exposure to the nuclear blast. She has adjusted and it is simply part of her life. But in the last few months particularly, Annie has noticed a fatigue and weakness coming over her beloved Marty. Accustomed to having her more active, seeing friends or going out for a special event, Annie worries when Marty now passes on these activities.

And she sees the weariness on her grandmother's face, in her sighs and in her movements. Annie's greatest fear now is that she will be on one of her trips when something goes wrong at home. That is the reason Julia and others make a point of stopping by or calling each day while she is gone.

Absentmindedly stirring her tea while just staring out the window, Annie seriously considers the possibility of taking a one year leave of absence from her touring job. She is truly afraid of receiving that late night phone call while in some far corner of the world that prevents her from rushing to her grandmother's side. The income would be missed, her flexibility in employment might be jeopardized some, but Annie feels that she would never be able to forgive herself if something went wrong and she was not at home when needed. And that is a cost she is unwilling to bear, a cost that would be too high. Lost in these thoughts for a moment, Annie then hears Marty stirring in her room and goes in to check on her precious grandmother.

Struggling to sit up, Marty is slowly and painfully rising from the bed when Annie goes to her aid. "Oh, thank you, dear," the soft spoken women says. "Have you been up long? I think I slept a little longer than usual."

"Not very long, I just finished eating my breakfast. Can I get something for you?" asks Annie.

"Did you happen to see those tangerines in the refrigerator?" Annie answers that she did. "Could you maybe peel a couple of those for me? I've almost gone through the whole bag already, they're really delicious."

"I'd be happy to, let me just help you up first." And then Annie takes her arm to support an unsteady Marty. "Are you okay? You seem to be moving a little slower."

"In the morning, honey, I'm just a little stiffer in the morning now." And the two of them make their way to the kitchen where

Annie pulls out a chair for Marty to sit down at the table. And then she turns to attend to the tangerines and to make another cup of tea for her grandmother.

"It's so nice to have you home again, dear. Are you seeing some of your friends today?" asks Marty.

"No, I'm going to give it a few days. I called Julia from the airport yesterday to tell her that I was back and that she didn't need to come over today. I'm going to spend time with you," she says and comes over to kiss Marty on the cheek.

"Oh, that's not what young people are supposed to be doing, hanging out with us old relics. Now, you call somebody today and go out, have some fun. I'll be just fine, just fine," she says, somewhat more adamantly.

"I will Marty, in time, but I have a few things around here that need attention first. And I'm kind of looking forward to having nothing to do for a while." Except for sleeping, the tour guides are basically on call around the clock while on the trips. They see to the tourists needs, dine with them, run errands for them, and are available for private tours or side trips when arranged. Only having to look after one person is like being on vacation anyway and she is home, finally home.

A single woman, Annie is now in her late thirties. Having attended college with an emphasis on foreign languages opened many doors for her and eventually led to a job with her first position as a tour guide. With a career in teaching as an early direction, for purpose and giving back, Annie had decided after just two trips with the touring company what she wanted to do with the next phase of her life. A romance with a fellow guide fueled her personal life for a few years, with both often staying in their locales at trip's end to simply enjoy the area and each other. Marriage was spoken of and even planned for but with the death of her parents and her need to become the main caregiver for her grandmother, Annie was forced to make one of those difficult life choices. She had to let go of her lover, of her future, to have to deal with a demanding present. And although disappointed, her boyfriend had respected her decision. To others, Annie had made a sacrifice but because of Marty's unique situation, she felt it had been small in comparison.

And even now with her many friends and many adventures and a good life, Annie can still feel that empty hole inside her but she always quickly fills it with yet another responsibility. Although staying in contact for a few years, her lover had moved on to his own marriage and to his own family. Thinking that she had let the best one already get away, the young woman had simply quit looking. With Annie unconsciously walling herself off from any other romantic connection, she makes her way in the world by herself except, of course, for Marty.

*　*　*

The weekend continues for Alex. Aaron is spending Saturday night at a friend's house and, of course, Katie is attending the birthday party. Laura has taken her and Alex does chores around the house waiting for them to come home later in the day. When they return, Katie brings home balloons from the party and she and Alex spend quite some time trying to set new records on the number of times they can hit it before touching the ground. As they laugh and fall over the furniture in their attempts, the remaining afternoon passes quickly. With the day coming to a close, they talk about dinner.

"So, honey, what do you want to do for food tonight?" asks Alex. "How about going out to get something, we haven't done that for quite a while. You might need something good to eat. What did you eat at the party?"

"Oh, Daddy, we didn't eat a lot of junk food. We just had the cake at the end of the party and Sally's mom made it herself. It was so good, it was choc...o...late."

"Oooo, where's my piece?" he asks.

"It was just for the kids," says Katie.

"I see," says her father playing along. About that time, Laura comes in from the laundry room with an armful of dry clothes as she heads upstairs to put them away. Catching her on the steps, Alex tells of their plans to go out to eat tonight.

"You guys go ahead. I'm just going to make something here for myself tonight," says Laura.

"No, we want you to come. Aaron's going to be spending the night at Jason's and it'll just be the three of us, it'll be fun. Your pick, maybe we could head over to Charlene's. I know you like her food," says Alex.

"I don't want to go out to eat. Just go ahead and take Katie," and Laura turns to continue climbing the stairs.

Reaching out to touch her arm and try to talk her into it, Laura spins around and in a firm tone says to her husband, "Alex, I told you that I don't want to go. You and Katie can go, just leave me alone," she ends abruptly.

"Okay," he says. "I'll leave you alone."

\*       \*       \*

Katie and Alex are at her favorite restaurant, by default the choice of dining had become hers. It is a small cozy place tucked into a tree shaded hollow near a main road and not far from their house. The owners are of French ancestry and have named their eatery The Crepe Place. Katie enjoys going there because the owner, a friendly woman with a sweet countenance, always rushes over to greet the blond-haired, blue-eyed seven year old with a kiss and a 'look how you have grown' comment. Gushing over the small girl makes her feel special, an honored guest, but Alex thinks it is probably also the sweet berry crepes served as dessert that make her want to return. But first, they will share buckwheat dinner crepes of fish and chicken and a salad.

This restaurant is similar to many that now populate our bustling cities and small towns everywhere. Simple and healthy and affordable dining has been a welcome result of the Food Revolution that had evolved after the food riots and the collapse of corporate agribusiness in the first part of the century. With agriculture returning to a local level, freshly prepared and nutritionally valuable meals in a variety of ethnic and regional cuisines are readily available. And many people, like the owners of The Crepe Place, can be successful and can easily supplement their income by not having to rely on ambiance or presentation or exclusiveness in their restaurants but by providing fresh food at reasonable prices with neighborly service.

As Mrs. Verlaine exits the busy kitchen to make the rounds of her diners' tables, she sees that Katie and her dad are just finishing their meal. Coming over to them, she addresses the small girl. "Well, look at that, a clean plate. I guess I know what that means," she says with a wink toward Alex.

"You know, she did mention something about a berry crepe. I told her that I didn't know if you had anything like that," says Alex, continuing the good-natured teasing.

"Well, she might be in luck. Mr. Johannson stopped by this morning and said something about having just picked his first crop of olallieberries for the season and he mentioned something about having a few blueberries, too. I guess I'll have to look in the back," says Mrs. Verlaine.

"Oh, would you?" asks an excited Katie, with her eyes opening wide at the thought.

"Sure, I'll see what I can come up with," the robust, energetic woman says as she turns to return to the kitchen. Katie flashes back a big smile in her direction and an excited 'oh boy' exits her mouth as she looks over at her father.

"Why didn't Mommy come?" Katie asks when Mrs. Verlaine is gone and the two are sitting quietly at the table.

"I don't know," Alex begins slowly. "I guess she just felt like staying home tonight."

"Let's take some of the dessert home for her, she'll like that," says the little girl.

"That's a good idea, we'll save some for her."

*     *     *

The father wakes early, it is Monday morning. The weekend has come and gone, always a little too quickly, but the break has been good. Besides spending time with Katie at dinner, he and

Aaron had attended a tennis tournament in a different city on Sunday afternoon. Having played competitively when younger, Aaron still greatly enjoys watching the sport and knew one of the local players who competed over the weekend.

The event was held in one of the larger cities on the coast. With the ability to take the Express Rail from Travers, the two hundred mile trip is now a relaxing one hour train ride that allows for easy conversation and uninterrupted viewing of the landscape rushing past. After arriving in the city, Alex and Aaron had time before the matches started to take local transit out to the beach and have lunch at one of their favorite restaurants. The food was good, the tennis was exciting, and the time spent between father and son had been appreciated by both.

Alex's job requires his leaving the house by six thirty, before the other family members are awake. This morning, the quiet gives him time to reflect. The shortness of his wife's comment on the steps the other day coupled with her lack of interest in going to dinner with them has bothered him. Approaching the subject last evening before retiring, Alex was shut out again.

"I'm just going to bed," Laura had said.

Their marriage had been rough at times and before Katie was born, Laura had mentioned separation on several occasions, complaining that she just didn't think that things would work out between them. Alex, for his part, had also come to the same conclusion that their lack of sharing and having true concern for one another probably weren't going to improve. And what was important to one in life and love was not at the top of the other's list. Laura and Alex had both been preparing for the next stage in their lives, without the other being in it.

But then Katie had come along and with the excitement and the joy of another child, the real problems between them were pushed into the background. They continued taking care of their responsibilities and continued making the best of the situation. But there were no real solutions sought, no frank discussions pursued, and each knew that a time would come when they must once again face the unpleasant challenge. Alex realizes that time is now quickly approaching.

Packing his lunch slowly and thoughtfully, he has a sinking feeling in the pit of his stomach. Laura is unhappy with him and unhappy in their marriage. And to Alex, the lack of contact and distance between them is also troubling. All these thoughts flood his mind as he makes his way through the garage to unhook one of the peetees for his commute to work. The drive this morning is not spent viewing the lovely, low green hills surrounding this valley or the clear bright sun that's rising above them, spilling its morning welcome into the day. His mind is elsewhere because his attention is on other matters.

Pulling alongside the trailer, he parks his vehicle and reaches down to retrieve his pack. There on the floor is a scrap of paper that he dutifully picks up to deposit in the nearest trash can. Turning it over as he walks toward the trailer, he sees the name 'Arrowhead Cinemas' across the top and realizes that it is a movie receipt. Looking at the information on it, he also sees that it was for a movie this past Saturday at twelve twenty in the afternoon. 'Curious,' he thinks to himself. 'Where did this come from?' is the obvious thought.

Now hurrying up the front steps of the trailer, Alex quickly unlocks it and reaches for this week's production schedules and begins planning the day's job assignments. His work crew will arrive very soon and all needs to be ready when they do. For now, staying busy with the tasks at hand will take care of the worrying that has been plaguing him ever since leaving home but Alex knows that it will not stay away for long.

The Conversion Core was established early into the second decade of the new century for mainly the urban recycling land programs that had greatly enlarged green spaces within cities in attempts to reestablish natural environments. Because of the urgent need to address infrastructure and because of funds now made available for road and utility projects instead of weapons and bombers, a rapid deployment of workers and not of warriors, both private and governmental, had set about fixing the roads, repairing the lands, and improving the urban landscape. With population pressures greatly reduced, growth for growth's sake was no longer needed or even desired. What was taking its place was a refinement and a restoration of lands and lives.

And Alex's crew is an integral part of the biggest and most important undertaking of all, the permanent undergrounding of all utilities. With major advancements technologically and with the invention of a simple and efficient underground drilling machine, safe and easily accessible utility pathways are being installed all over the country. The biggest benefactors have been the cities and metropolitan areas that have become livable again, without the blight of our energy hunger constantly rearing its ugly head. And not only are storm interruptions of service a thing of the past, the visual improvement, the return of the clear horizon, is hugely popular and is supported by the people and by their taxes and by their money.

Soon, Alex is joined in the yard office by another of the Core's managers for this utilities project. "Well, good morning," is the greeting from Scott Bettencourt who is also Alex's closest friend. "It looks like you have things well in hand. Want me to do the postings or is there something else that needs attention?"

"No, go ahead and do the postings. They're over there in a pile by the door," answers Alex. Pausing for a moment, he then asks Scott another question before his exiting the door. "So, what are you doing after work tonight? Do you have time to maybe stop at Kerry's before heading home?"

"I could arrange that," answers Scott, seeing the seriousness on his friend's face. "What's up?"

"Nothing much. I want to talk to you for a minute about some things, you know, just personal stuff."

"Sure, I'll just let Jennifer know I'll be a little late coming home. But don't think that you're finally going to be able to beat me on the dart board. Let's see, I think I've lost count," Scott ribs his good friend. "Is it the last seven or eight games in a row that I've beaten you?"

"It's eight," says Alex.

\*     \*     \*

The end to the work day nears and the tools are being picked up as the driller and a few trucks are parked within the fencing.

Fellow employees take leave of one another as they peel off in their own direction home. Alex is locking the door on the trailer as Scott waits near the vehicles.

"Ready?" asks Scott as he gets into his ride.

"Yeah," says Alex, "just go ahead and I'll follow you." And both leave the yard with Alex making quick work of closing and locking the gate behind them.

They soon arrive at Kerry's, a popular watering hole. Being a pub in the truest sense of the word, the main draw is three competition style dart boards set in different sections of the bar. Local tournaments are held frequently and one time every year, usually in the early spring, Kerry's is the honored sight of a large regional tournament. It spills over to the neighboring art gallery that is reconfigured to handle as many as ten more competition boards. With people coming from miles around and with a little bit of beer drinking, both businesses usually do very well on that weekend and all have a great time.

"Do you want anything?" Scott shouts over the din.

"Sparkling water with some lemon."

Scott adds a dark draft to the order and then goes to join Alex at a table. "Want some munchies?" he asks.

"No, I'm good," says Alex.

The drinks are brought to the table. Scott will sip his beer as he quietly watches Alex squeezing some lemon into his glass and then stirring the mixture slowly. A few moments will pass before either one begins speaking again.

"So, thanks a lot for taking the time," Alex starts while looking over at his friend. With a slight nod of the head and a pleasant smile, Scott makes it known that he is glad to be there. "I wanted to talk to you about Laura. A couple of things have happened between us recently and I'm trying to get my head around them. I thought maybe if I said things out loud and talked them over with someone, it might make more sense to me."

"Yeah, it probably would," says Scott. "Are you guys having some problems between the two of you again?"

"I don't know for sure. I didn't think so but she's really pulled away from me lately. And she never really wants to talk about it," Alex begins the telling of the situation.

"I remember when you guys had some problems before, is it kind of like that time?" asks his close friend. "Wasn't that just before Katie was born?"

"Yeah, she's acting the same way but at that time, at least she would talk about things. Now she just turns and walks away and tells me not to bother her."

"How long has this been going on?"

"Not long, but it seems like the same old thing again."

"What was the deal last time, what did she say was wrong?" as Scott presses his friend a bit.

"She said that she just really wasn't happy in our relationship and that she really didn't enjoy our life together and wanted to do other things," says a dejected Alex.

"But you must have worked things out, you guys have stayed together a long time since then."

"We were in the process of making some decisions but then when Laura got pregnant with Katie, I think we just basically put everything on hold. Our life has been okay, not great or anything, but I thought it was okay."

"Well, maybe Laura wants more than okay," is the honest comment coming from Scott.

"I know, I know, but look at this," and Alex reaches into his pocket to retrieve the movie stub found earlier that morning. Passing it over to Scott, he tells the story of Laura's rather terse demand to drive Katie to the birthday party because of the need to run errands on Saturday. And he relates about finding the receipt in the peetee that she had used that day. "She didn't run errands, she went to a movie."

"And lied to you."

"Yes, and she lied to me," answers Alex as clearly upset and disappointed at that behavior as much as its ramifications.

"Well, you have to talk to her about it," says Scott, giving his frank appraisal of the needed next step.

"Yeah, I know I do," answers Alex as he stares into his glass. Without raising his eyes, he adds, "I guess that I'm just a little afraid about the answers I might get back."

Scott sits looking at his disheartened buddy and attempts to lighten the mood. A challenge is issued on the dartboard and accepted by Alex. The banter will come more easily now as the comfort of a solid friendship dispels the immediate problems of the moment. But the ride home that evening will end as it had begun that morning with concern and trepidation firmly lodged in the forefront of Alex's thinking. The heavy fog hanging around his spirit shrouds the clarity of the late afternoon sun that now comfortably streams around him.

\*     \*     \*

"You know what, Grandmother," Annie says to Marty sitting near her on their back patio. "I've been to a lot of beautiful places, but out here in the backyard, with the fruit trees and the green hills over there, I must admit that this ranks up there pretty high, too," she says, gazing out at the landscape.

"Yes, dear, it is very pretty here. And these fruit trees have really matured over the past few years."

"That's because of you and your green thumbs," adds Annie as a compliment to her gardening grandmother.

"Well, I've got one green thumb at least," says Marty, holding up her good hand as the other one is badly misshaped and fused together from the heat of the blast. "In fact, some days all these fingers seem to be quite green," she says laughing and wiggling her good hand in front of Annie's face.

"Marty," Annie then says thoughtfully after a few moments, "I've realized lately that I'm getting a little tired of traveling. When I come home, it's always great to see you and my friends. But then I turn around and I'm gone again."

"I know, dear, I know it's hard to be gone from a home. But you love your job and think of the opportunities that it has presented. You've been all over the world. And the people you've met and the places you've seen and you like the other guides, too, don't you?" asks Marty.

"Yes, both Sonia and Laurel have become very good friends," answers Annie about the two other guides who speak the same languages and who are often on trips together. "But I have been thinking about looking at job opportunities around here. That way I could be here, with you, and I wouldn't have to always ask other friends to do favors for me."

Marty is quiet and reflective. What started as a conversation about Annie's situation has come back around to being about her situation. Although failing in health quite dramatically now, the grandmother doesn't want to be a drag on her granddaughter's life. That is the last thing she wants and she fights it.

"Annie, now you listen to me," the feisty grandmother begins. "I am fine and do fine when you are away so you just stop this talk about quitting your job," and she gives Annie a stern finger wagging as she stares down her granddaughter.

"We'll see, we'll see," says Annie, not wanting to delve any deeper at this point. "It's just an idea for now."

*   *   *

In the late afternoon, Annie is running errands at a nearby shopping area. She has been home for several days and has settled in comfortably. She enjoys the time spent catching up on friends, events, and restocking the home place. With only one item left on the list of chores, Annie now drives to a fruit market that is outside of town. It is a fair distance away but knowing of her grandmother's love for a certain sweet tangerine that they produce is her impetus for making the drive.

Entering the parking area, Annie finds several others also picking from the bounty of this local orchard. She knows the owners well, having purchased from them for years, and having sought their advice for her and Marty's home edition of fruit trees. She then heads to one of the tables where she sees Mrs. Donovan weighing apples for a customer. Standing on the sidelines until she finishes, Annie approaches her.

"Oh my gosh, look! It's Annie! Come here, my dear, come here," says an excited Marianne Donovan as she throws her arms around the younger woman. "It's so good to see you, you're back in town. Have you been here long?"

"It's been a few days now," says Annie. "But I'm just getting a chance to come out and get some of the best fruit in town. What's peaking, are there any tangerines?"

"Oh, I'm so sorry, honey. I'm out of those," apologizes Mrs. Donovan, knowing of Marty's love of them. "We have two apples that are just coming in, and here, taste this," she says as she hands over a slice of a new pear variety.

"Marianne, this is really delicious! I don't think that I've ever tasted one like this before, I can't even describe it," gushes Annie, finishing the last bite.

"We're thinking about getting some trees started down by the pond. It is quite different."

Annie then continues her shopping and accumulates three bags of different fruit. Taking them to the scales, she reaches into her purse to pay Mrs. Donovan. "That will be nine dollars and fifty cents," says Marianne.

Picking up her purchases, Annie comments there are four bags and that she only had three. "This must be someone else's," she says, handing it back.

"No, that one goes with you, too," assures Mrs. Donovan. Looking into the bag, Annie sees a half dozen delightfully looking tangerines. Protesting over the extra ration, Annie is told that the Donovans had saved some out for themselves and that they are meant for Marty anyway. "We need to take care of our Marty, don't we?" says a warmly smiling Marianne.

"Yes, we do. She'll be delighted, thank you very much," says Annie and she gives Mrs. Donovan a parting hug.

On the way home, many thoughts and ideas flood Annie's mind. Ever since talking with Marty the other day about quitting her job, the concept has strengthened in her mind. She has put almost twenty years into her job, into her career as a tour guide and now, besides the traveling, other aspects of the job also bother her. Relationships, even just for friendship, are difficult to maintain as Annie rarely is in one place long enough to become a daily part of others' lives. Annie is tired of leading a half life and she is especially tired of the hotel rooms and the airports.

Coming through their front door, Annie now calls out for her grandmother. An answer comes from the back patio which is surrounded by flowers and plants and fruit trees. Marty will spend her afternoons here, puttering with the potting, doing some pruning, and watching the birds and bees. It is soothing and comforting to her to be in nature's embrace. The glory of the green world has rebounded and has replaced the rape of so many years ago. The wounds to the planet are mostly healed although Marty still sees hers in the mirror every morning.

"I thought I might find you out here," says Annie as she comes out onto the patio. "You're not doing too much, Marty, are you? Now don't go tiring yourself out."

"Oh, don't worry, I am fine. When I'm out here, I'm just fine," says Marty as she gazes about their landscaped backyard. Annie comes over to where her grandmother is sitting. She notices that Marty has a blanket over her lap.

"Are you cold? It's quite warm today," she says.

"No, not really," answers Marty. Her two legs, one still badly bruised, extend below the blanket. Annie notices that she isn't wearing pants or wearing a dress.

"Is something wrong?" Annie then asks her with a sense of seriousness. She lifts the blanket from Marty's lap to witness her large and extended belly. "Marty," cries out Annie in concern. "Your stomach, it's huge! What's wrong with it?"

"It just comes and goes some. It's always a little bigger, but sometimes the swelling is too much for me to fit into clothes," explains Marty of her recent health problem over the last month. Not known to Annie, she had decided to wait to tell her and had hidden the problem from her on purpose.

"We're taking you to the doctor right now," says Annie in a rather stern and authoritative voice.

"We don't have to do that," answers Marty.

"Oh, yes, we do and I'm going to call Dr. Granger right now." And Annie turns to go back in the house to phone.

"Annie, Annie dear. Come here for a minute, just come here," Marty pleads softly to her. Marty has Annie sit beside her again. "We don't have to do that," the grandmother repeats. As Annie's protestations arise again, she continues, "I've already talked to Dr. Granger about it, just two weeks ago."

"You did, why didn't you tell me?" asks Annie.

"There's nothing much to tell. I started getting some swelling and Julia took me to see him. It's just part of the disease. It's just something to do with the kidneys or the liver."

"Oh, Marty," says her granddaughter with a tinge of sorrow in her voice. "I'm so sorry and I feel so bad for you. Does it hurt, are you in any pain?"

"No, I'm just uncomfortable at times. I might have to pick up some of those old lady sack dresses, though. I would look quite stylish in them, don't you think?" says the grandmother with that still ever present sparkle in her eyes.

*    *    *

Night is now almost upon them as Annie stands in the kitchen preparing a light dinner for Marty. She had called Julia earlier in the day and the two of them plan to meet this evening at a nearby neighborhood restaurant. Having been back for about a week, Annie had not yet made the time to see her good friend. But now, she needs someone to talk to, Annie needs someone with whom to share her thoughts.

Walking out the front door, she tells Marty one more time to call her if she needs anything. Stepping into her peetee, Annie descends the small hill before entering the cruiseway that will take her to the restaurant. Julia is quietly sitting on a bench in front waiting for her when Annie arrives and the two friends greet each other with a warm embrace.

"I was just about to give you a call. It's been a few days since you returned and I hadn't heard anything. It's really good to see you again," says Julia.

"Oh, I know, I'm sorry. It's good to see you, too," says Annie. "I've just been working around the house and been running a few errands and it's kind of taken me a little time to get back into the swing of things."

The two women then enter the restaurant and are seated near a window. They are given a sheet of paper that lists the four specials being served that evening. This restaurant is run as a second business by the Jensen family. There are only a few tables and the family members are the wait staff, the cooks, and the dishwashers. Their specialty is fish with Mr. Jensen being a fisherman by trade. With the return of localized food production, many bakeries and cafes and take out eateries exist in every neighborhood. The Satisfied Salmon is open four days a week and fills each table every night and sells out of their catch every week. With quality high and prices reasonable, all now enjoyably and easily partake in this part of the good life.

Because of the severe problems with large scale agriculture at the beginning of the century, smaller local production has been a success all over the world. Of course, large wheat fields and corn fields and soy fields still exist but they have gone back into the hands of local farmers, people who know the earth and respect it. And no longer are chemicals being dumped on our lands to raise production while lowering our chances for survival. No longer are huge amounts of quality grains being diverted to destructive and wasteful cattle production. Also no longer do we produce nutritionally deficient processed foods that can become easily tainted and deadly. We had now come full circle from our humble agrarian beginnings and we were all better for it.

"This looks so good," says Annie as she scans down the menu. "I really miss this place."

"I don't think that you and I have been here for quite a while. Mark and I were here two weeks ago and had this great halibut. What are you thinking about getting?" asks Julia.

"The salmon. Everything sounds really good but I can't pass up teriyaki salmon." Both women will order and then relax into each other's company.

"And how is Mark?" asks Annie about Julia's husband.

"He's fine, busy. The Parks and the Youth Programs just keep expanding. They're planning some extra courses for the summer now, wilderness camps and things like that. He loves what he's doing and the city and schools have been very supportive."

"You've got a good one there," says Annie. "You guys sure are great together."

"Well, Mark has a good job, I have my three days a week at the optometrist, and we take care of each other. And we get to live in a place like this," says Julia with a broad sweep of her hand out the window toward the hills.

"Yes, a beautiful place like this," Annie easily agrees with her. "That's what I want to talk to you about, Julia. I'm thinking of making some changes with my job. And Marty said that you took her to the doctor two weeks ago?"

"I did. She didn't want me to call you about it and she asked me to not say anything about it and that she would tell you. Of course, I was going to tell you when I saw you again anyway," says the good friend.

"What did Dr. Granger say, what is the problem? I saw her stomach this morning and it's huge."

"It's the leukemia, Annie. The spleen and liver can swell and it affects their function. He said that the kidneys can be affected, too. She's also starting to have more joint and bone pain. Have you noticed it's difficult for her to get up and down now?" Julia asks her disheartened friend sitting across from her.

"Yes, I have had to help her out of bed a couple of mornings. What does she do when I'm not here?" Annie asks mournfully and with true regret.

"She's fine, she just told me that she takes her time getting up and moving about the house."

"Oh, Julia, I don't know how I can thank you for all you've done for Marty. If I didn't have you, I don't know what I would have done. And I'm always gone. What kind of granddaughter would leave her to fend for herself?" says Annie with sincere remorse at the thought.

"A wonderful granddaughter who has dedicated her personal life to the taking care of her grandmother, that's what kind of granddaughter you are. Now let's eat and I want to hear all about East Africa and maybe about any interesting talent that was in your group this time, if you know what I mean," says Julia with a wink and a broad smile.

"Same old you, always pushing me to hook up with some guy," laughs Annie as she, too, digs into her plate of food.

\*     \*     \*

The dinner then winds down and with thanks and well wishes from the Jensen family, they leave the restaurant. The cooler breezes of evening greet the two women on the steps and the last low rays of sunlight are filtering over the hills that stretch out in front of them. Annie asks Julia if she needs to get home right away. Answering that Mark is at a meeting until nine thirty, Julia says no, that she is in no hurry.

"Can we sit on the bench for a minute then? I want to ask your opinion on something," Annie asks of her friend. They both sit down out front of the restaurant.

"I'm thinking about quitting my job with the tour company," Annie begins. "I've been giving it some thought lately and I really think that I need to be here now, with Marty. She seems to be failing more rapidly and I need to be closer to take care of her. The poor thing, I feel so sorry for her, and after all she's been through. It just doesn't seem fair."

"I can understand that, I know it weighs heavily on you while you're away. But I still have lots of free time to continue helping out. I don't mind, you know that. I've come to love Marty, too," says Julia, reaching her hand over to her friend. "And you know how strong-willed Marty is, I don't know what she would think about it. She always worries about you giving up things because you're taking care of her."

"Well, it would also be for me. I'm starting to get a little tired of all the traveling. It's been almost twenty years now, Julia. And how often do I get to see you, a couple of times a month if we're lucky? If I were here all the time, besides taking care of Marty, I could settle into a life a little less transient. I don't know if it's the getting older or what but mainly I want to be with Marty in what may be..." and Annie chokes with emotion at the unpleasant thought, "the last part of her life."

Julia puts her arm around her friend and they comfort each other while watching the last vestiges of daylight in the western sky. Neither one speaks for several minutes as they each remain in their own reflective thoughts. Julia knows of the very real possibility that Marty is, indeed, failing fast and her death may be near. That is a reality that will have to be faced. Annie's mind races as she thinks of the major changes that may lie ahead for her if that were to occur.

"Did you say Mark is working on adding summer camps for the kids to the city's Parks Program?" Annie suddenly thinks to ask her friend.

"Yes, that's why he is so busy these days. School is out in just seven weeks and the funding is already in place. They just have to come up with the ideas and then present a program to them. That's where he is tonight."

"They're going to need group leaders. They're going to have to hire more people for that, right?" says Annie.

"I'll ask Mark," says Julia. "I'll ask him tonight."

\*      \*      \*

Jeremy quickly loads the last items into the trunk of his car. Pine Lake is three hours away and, of course, fishing requires that early start to the day. In the still morning darkness, Jeremy makes his way through the streets to the highway that will take him to his destination. But first he stops at Maria's, a favorite of his and one of the few places in the area that is open this early. Ordering a strong special blend of black tea that she stocks in her bakery and one of her delicious apricot scones, he happily returns to his vehicle and heads down the road.

The terrain begins to change as he leaves the open spaces of the valleys and travels deeper into the forests. Having been to the lake only once previously and that was years ago, Jeremy is careful to pay attention to his route, to not miss his turn. Glancing at the map, he feels that turn should be coming soon.

The last stretch of highway will continue for another twenty miles to the lake. Located at the end of the road, Pine Lake sits completely surrounded by dense forest. Fallen trees reach into the water at many points and have been left there as habitat for the fish, for the bass and crappie that Jeremy fondly remembers pulling from its depths. He wonders if that big one that actually did get away last time is still out there hanging around, maybe just waiting for his return. Jeremy is getting closer and getting that itch to put the line in the water again.

Pulling into a parking area a short distance from the lake, his is the only car there and Jeremy likes it that way. Not only does he get first crack at the fish, he won't have to go through all the pleasantries and the fishing talk with others. It is not that he doesn't enjoy the discussions on occasion but Jeremy definitely prefers fishing to talking about fishing. Anxious now to get going, he pulls his gear from the back of the car and begins to make his selections of flies to take with him. Soon, Jeremy is heading toward the water.

The cool and crisp morning greets him as he comes out of the trees and onto the lake's edge. This area, like many others, is in a reclamation zone. With the severe damage that had been done to the environment, great effort has come from governmental, societal, and personal commitments to bring back a balance to the planet. After the Great Mistake, the world still looked down the gun barrel of extinction in the guise of environmental catastrophes. With the time and money now available for action, countries around the world began projects of reforestation to protect the air and lands, stopped rampant pollution to protect the rivers and oceans, and rescaled the urban areas to protect our sanity and safety.

Through systems of credits and other incentives, land trades from individual citizens to social institutions have allowed for a major realignment of our lands with green belts and parkways now occupying a much greater portion of the land within our towns and our cities. Also large areas throughout the country have returned to their more natural states of prairie and forest and marshland. And the urbanization trend that had threatened to produce megacities of immense populations and immense problems had not materialized. Smaller, more sustainable, and stronger local economies have become more desirable and have become the new and more promising reality.

Jeremy sends out the first cast of the morning and watches the widening circles radiate from the spot where his fly has landed. Slowly inhaling the pure clean air of the forest, he lets out a long and low sigh that finally relaxes him into his weekend.

The morning will pass lazily as the fishing proves productive with Jeremy catching three good size fish before lunchtime. He now returns to his vehicle to take that break.

Sitting on a large rock near the water's edge, Jeremy snacks on the food that he had prepared earlier that morning. The sun streams down on the spot where he sits, offering warmth and comfort. He watches the ducks landing and taking off on the far side of the lake, watches the minnows and small creatures scurrying at the shore's edge, and watches life go on around him. For Jeremy, nature is life.

Growing up in a rural section of the country, he was always wandering the fields and spending his time outdoors. Without siblings and being very shy as a young child, Jeremy had learned to entertain himself with exploration and discovery and wonderment of the natural world. School had never been social for him, with no close friends and no real relationships. Without encouragement from others, Jeremy simply accepted whatever life handed him. Graduating in an accounting program, he had gone on to work in the financial services field that holds little stimulation for him but provides a paycheck, a paycheck to fund that enjoyable passion for fishing

The luster had left the financial services industry many years earlier and no longer did it offer the layering of money that had benefited so few and had contributed to the detriment of so many others. No longer was it accepted that capital would be the main beneficiary of increased economic activity while those that labored and created that productivity did not benefit proportionally. And no longer was the wealth of a nation held in the hands of a few as it is now shared by all its citizens. Greed, self-interest, and disregard for social responsibilities are no longer attributes that are rewarded financially.

Finished with his lunch, Jeremy walks to the other side of the lake and will fish there for the rest of the day. As the afternoon sun moves through the sky and the shadows lengthen across the lake, he hooks one particularly strong fish late in the day. Having thrown all back during the day, he decides this one will be his dinner tonight if he can land it. Jeremy plays out the line and maneuvers the fish down the bank. The battle continues for several minutes until the fish finally tires and comes into the net. It is a beauty, almost a two pounder. The sun glistens and reflects rainbow colors off the fish's shiny surface.

Jeremy carefully removes the hook from its mouth and then watches it opening and closing, gulping air. He watches the fish squirming from side to side and he watches it watching him. 'Aw, what the hell, I feel like having pizza tonight anyway,' is his reasoning as Jeremy releases the fish and watches the beautiful free creature swim away from the bank.

\*     \*     \*

Alex has avoided confronting Laura for the past two days after talking with Scott. But with the constant dread hanging over his head, he can't let it go any longer. He needs to ask what has been bothering her, what changes can happen to make things better, and why did she go to a movie when saying that she was running errands. The communication between them has been difficult for the last several years. Having not really resolved the problems, they have continued to grow apart.

Laura has her class again tonight. When she gets home, Katie is usually in bed and Alex thinks that this is when he should approach her on the matter. With the dishes cleaned and put away, he sits nervously in the living room watching the clock. Laura will be home soon.

Alex hates confrontation and the apprehension over it can be worse than the actual discussion. As in many relationships, the 'discussion' usually turns to blame and accusation rather than to one of shared responsibility for an unpleasant situation. Alex has felt that working things out is now almost an impossibility between the two of them. And deep inside he knows that Laura is unhappy and restless and knows that he is also lonely in the relationship. But they had made a life together and, of course, there were the children to consider. Alex now hears Laura as she comes through the side door from the garage.

Walking into the living room, she sees Alex sitting there quietly with only a few lights on. "Where is everybody, what are you doing?" she asks her husband.

"Nothing, just waiting for you to get home. Katie is in bed already. She went a little early tonight, she said she was tired. Aaron is over at Jason's, he is supposed to be home by eleven," Alex answers back.

"I'm going upstairs to shower," Laura then says as she quickly turns to leave.

"Can you wait a minute? I thought maybe we could talk first," offers a wary Alex.

"Talk, talk about what?"

"Well, things aren't going very well between us and I just thought that we ought to talk about it."

"Alex, we've said about everything there is to say over the past few years. Don't you remember, before Katie was born, how we had tried to 'talk' to each other. It seems to me that we didn't get very far on that subject. I don't know why you think it's going to be any different this time."

"There is something different this time," says Alex and he reaches into his pocket for the movie stub. "I found this in the peetee you used to take Katie to the birthday party on Saturday. I thought you needed to run errands that day and that is why you wanted to take her."

"I went to a movie instead."

"By yourself?"

"No, with Philip. Philip wanted to see it and he asked me to go, so I went."

"You went with Philip, why did you say that you were running errands then?" asks Alex.

"If I said that I was meeting another man at the movies, what would you have thought?" says Laura.

"I would have thought that you were having an affair unless it was for a different reason."

"It was for a different reason, Alex. It's because I enjoy his conversation and his company and he has an interest in my life, too. He is someone I can talk to, relate to, and I need something, someone like that in my life. Obviously, we don't have it," says his wife about their relationship.

"What do you talk about that's so much better with him?" he asks half-heartedly.

"Oh, Alex, I connect with Philip on so many levels and we don't. He knows that I've been unhappy for years, he knows the situation. He's just someone I can release with and relax with, it's nothing more than that. I should have told you, I'm sorry," Laura says and comes over to place her hand on his resting on the arm of the chair.

Alex is crestfallen and beaten down by Laura's sad but honest appraisal of their marriage. He is disappointed and discouraged as he looks up into her eyes. "What are we going to do, Laura, what are we going to do?" asks her husband, rather pathetically and somewhat lost.

"Just go on for now," she says and then, "I need a shower." And Laura leaves the room to go upstairs.

Alex will continue sitting in the half dark, in the quiet, as the loud echoes of his wife's words bounce around inside his head. He will contemplate the beginning of their life together, all that has transpired over these many years, and the end which now looms on a closer horizon.

*       *       *

The next morning Alex is back at his job. Nearing the end of the week, he checks the production reports. His crew continues the steady progress and is completing work ahead of schedule. Everything is going well, he feels, when finished scanning the paperwork, almost everything. But his personal problems need to be pushed to the background, he knows that. He needs to concentrate on the things at hand, he needs to get lost in his work. Alex needs action to replace that melancholy of worry.

"Scott," he calls across the room to his assistant manager. "These look great. I think we can get a start on the new section tomorrow. We might as well go for it, what do you think?"

"Let me check with the repaving crew first to make sure we can get everything covered up before moving on, but yeah, I think we could start the B-Three Section tomorrow."

"Are you headed over there soon? I need to see Jensen about some of the tubing orders."

"In about five minutes."

"Mind if I catch a ride?" asks Scott's boss but also one of his closest personal friends.

"Maybe, but only if you have the right clearance to ride in one of the project's vehicles," says Scott.

"Ha, ha, I'll meet you outside," Alex answers, taking his hard hat from the shelf and exiting the trailer.

The construction site is a busy one. For the past twenty years, the undergrounding of utilities and services has continued across the country and with population decreases and transportation improvements, many previously used roads and highways are simply no longer needed. Besides the removal of concrete from many urban areas allowing greenbelt areas and reducing runoff problems, the project has provided great pathways for energy and communication infrastructure.

Because of the many vast technological gains in developing deep and very effective horizontal drilling devices, energy and communication hubs are now buried and then connect easily and efficiently underground to individual homes and businesses within the area. In each trench is also placed two large diameter tubes that enable more or different type of services to be added later. Alex needs to make sure that enough of the extra tubing is on hand so that the landscape and repaving crew can complete their work this week. He climbs in the vehicle with Scott to check with his supply manager.

"I finally talked with Laura last night," are the first words out of Alex's mouth as they drive toward the site.

"How did that go?"

"Okay, better than I thought it would."

"Did you ask her about the going to the movie thing?" as Scott gets right to the point.

"Yeah, she told me about it. Laura said that she went to it because Philip wanted to see it."

"Her exercise guy? What is that all about?"

"It's not a physical thing. Laura just says that she enjoys his company and can relate to him. You know, better than she does to me," explains a sullen Alex.

"So, do you feel better about it? I mean, at least about the sexual part?" asks Scott.

"Not really, I almost wish she had been having an affair. At least, that would have been a little more concrete. I feel like I'm in purgatory now. I don't know what's going to happen next," says Alex about his personal state of mind.

"No, you don't mean that, buddy. If she's not having an affair, it's not such a big deal. Maybe it's something that you guys can work on again."

A strained smile crosses Alex's face and his head just moves slowly from side to side in a sad wag. "No, it's all over but the shouting. And I hope we don't have to go there," is the husband's melancholy assessment of the situation.

"I'm sorry, Alex," says Scott, placing an understanding hand on his friend's shoulder. "I'm sorry."

"Yeah," answers Alex, turning to stare out the window for the rest of the drive to the job site.

*       *       *

A few weeks have passed and Annie has turned down the two tour opportunities that had come her way. She just can't imagine leaving home at this particular time. Being able to observe her grandmother over this longer period of time has raised warning signs for her. Marty has much less energy than she did even a month or two ago.

Marty, for her part, always acts as though everything is fine. "Oh, maybe a little sore," or "Just a little tired, I guess," are the continued comments when Annie inquires on how she is feeling. Marty had seen the hell of a nuclear disaster from inside the inferno. Marty had seen the world at its worst so every day since has been a better day. And even with the constant reminder of her injuries, she looks beyond herself. Yes, she had been a victim, but thankfully, no one will ever have to live that horror again. And with this knowledge, this solace, Marty moves through the world without complaint.

"Well, Ms. Greenfingers," says Annie over their breakfast. "I think you and I need to get out of the house today. I like your company but you're probably getting a little tired of just looking at me," she teases.

"I've seen a lot worse things to look at, don't know if I've ever seen such a pretty thing, though. I'd rank you right up there with my daffodils in the spring," says Marty.

"That's me, the daffodil darling," muses Annie.

The two women are more than only just a grandmother and her granddaughter, they are also friends. Relying on each other for support and relationship, they have forged a strong bond over these many years, with a sincere concern for each other's welfare. And the mature wisdom and endless positive spirit that Marty displays is a constant source of inspiration for Annie. To give so that one may receive and to enjoy so that one may persevere in life is Marty's example to her.

"So, what should we do with such a beautiful day? Your pick," Annie says to Marty.

"Well, I do have one thing in mind. I was looking over the Art Schedule for town last week and I think, if I'm not mistaken, that today and tomorrow there's a painting exhibit at the high school. Remember Mary Watkins, that very nice woman I took watercolor classes from five or six years ago?"

"Yes, I remember her. And you said that you really liked her, didn't you?"

"She is an exceptional teacher. I was talking with Vivian the other day and she told me that for the past few years, Mary has been working with the students at the high school and doing wonderful work and that two of her students have gone on to very prestigious art schools. I'd like to go by there and look at some of the children's work."

"Done," Annie then answers quickly. "And I would like to stop by Marianne's on the way home and see what they have, maybe some of the tangerines are back in."

*     *     *

Annie pulls to a stop in front of Travers High School. Helping Marty from the vehicle, she has her sit down on a nearby bench while parking. Soon Annie returns and both enter the multi-purpose room where the art show is being staged. Lovely, lilting guitar music drifts toward them as they make their way toward the information table.

"Hello, ladies, thank you so much for coming. Let me just explain a few things to you and then, please, feel free to walk around and take your time looking at the paintings," comes the warm greeting from one of the parent volunteers. "On the walls to your right is the 'Shape Group' where each student was asked to create a picture based on using three similarly shaped objects. To the left here," she continues, pointing to the another side of the room, "is the first year students' work and on the back wall are examples of our students who have been in the program for three years. Please enjoy yourselves."

"Thank you," says Annie. "And that music is really beautiful, what a nice addition to the show."

"Yes, he is one of our students. Four young people from our music programs will be providing sounds to add to your visual feast over the next two days of the showing. The 'visual feast' part is in our promo for the exhibit," the parent explains and all three women share a laugh.

Although still moving slowly, Marty is enjoying one of her better days, physically. The swelling of her abdominal area has decreased significantly, at least for now, and she has started some new medications to reduce the discomfort and swelling in her joints. All in all, she feels more like that spring chicken today than an older hen. And it is good to get out and be around others again. Marty is very glad that Annie had proposed the change of scenery for them.

Enjoyably, they make their way around the room. Some paintings are simply incredible, marvelous, and the viewpoints expressed by the young people are intriguing and interesting. The arts have come back strongly into the schools after nearly being abandoned in the early part of the new century. The idle talk of so many years about the importance of education has finally received the attention that it deserves. And knowing that a healthy body and a critical mind are only strengthened by the self-expression and creativity of music programs and art classes and writing projects, all students now enjoy these pursuits and can make that discovery. We were finally producing well-rounded and thinking and caring people to send out into the world, to help create that better world for all of us.

Time passes quickly and after fifty minutes, they prepare to leave. "I'll go get the car and bring it to the front," says Annie as she retrieves a chair for her grandmother to use while waiting. "I'll be right back," and Annie makes her way toward the door.

Passing the teenage boy playing guitar, she stops to speak with him. "Thank you so much for playing, it's beautiful. What is it?" she asks of the music that she has been hearing.

"We have a songwriting workshop every summer and all the music over the next two days was written by students, and in some cases instructors, from those workshops. Here is a list of the songs and songwriters," and he hands over a printed sheet containing the information.

"Oh, how nice. Are any of your songs on the list?"

"Yeah, I've got two of them on there," answers the student, appreciative of Annie's interest.

"What's your name?" she asks, looking down the sheet.

"Aaron Galway," he says.

"Well, thanks Aaron, it's really pretty music," and she flashes a big smile his way. "My name is Annie," she then offers. Aaron nods his head and then an equally large grin is returned from the polite and talented boy.

\*　　\*　　\*

Now driving toward the Donovan's orchard, Annie and Marty eagerly anticipate their arrival there. "The last time I was here, Marianne had me taste a new variety of pear that they're thinking about planting. It was delicious," says Annie as they drive into the countryside. "And some of the early citrus might be starting to come in. I'm so glad you're with me, she was asking about you the last time. She'll be thrilled to see you."

"You think so? Why would anyone be excited just to see an old woman?" answers the always teasing Marty.

"Because that old woman is one of her prize pupils. Marianne has always said that you missed your calling, that you should have been a farmer," says Annie.

"She was awfully sweet helping us out when we were trying to get the trees started in the backyard. Remember that time the oranges had the lichen problem and we tried everything with no luck until she took one look and told us what to do?" reminisces the gardening grandmother.

Marty and Annie are not that unusual in today's world. Many residents have planted vegetable gardens and fruit trees on their properties. Neighbors often now trade oranges for tomatoes and walnuts for squash and sweet ripe corn for bursting berries. And in the green belt sections of municipalities, local clubs and schools and organizations grow crops and tend the public land. All share in the proceeds from the sale of these products. Fifty percent of the proceeds go to the organizations and fifty percent returns to the cities and towns for maintenance and for funding of new greenspace acquisition.

A wave of the hand greets them as they pull into the driveway. Marianne has already spotted them as she rushes over to meet the car. "Well, sakes alive, look who you brought with you this time. Marty, how wonderful to see you," says Mrs. Donovan as she opens the door for the sweet older woman. "And how are the trees doing?" she asks.

"They're doing just great and how are you doing?" comes the sincere and warm response from Marty who is of a similar age and generation as Mrs. Donovan.

"Well, I'm pretty good. The whole thing is starting to feel a little too much like work, though. It couldn't have anything to do with getting older, do you think?"

"No, I doubt it. We don't get older, we just get better, right?" answers a smiling Marty.

Annie and her grandmother will take their time making the selections and visiting with Marianne before preparing to return home. And Marty was in luck. A grower from down south had some extra tangerines for sale and has consigned them to the Donovans. She slowly picks over them feeling for that just right softness on the outside that promises that just right sweetness on the inside. Placing all carefully into their bags, Annie shoulders the load and begins leading Marty back to the car.

Mrs. Donovan is waiting on another customer at the other end of the stand. With a wave, they express their intent to leave and then Annie calls out, "Thanks, Marianne. Nice seeing you, we'll see you soon."

The older woman waves and then answers back, "Well, you know where to find me, most people think I live here," she quips as they drive away and back down the hill.

\*     \*     \*

Jeremy is rising slowly today. Looking at the clock, he notices that it is almost thirty minutes later than usual for him to get out of bed. Bothered and upset that he has overslept has put him in a foul mood to start the day. Jeremy is definitely a creature of habit, one of those who is comforted by the sameness and the routine chores of everyday living. He will awake and start the water boiling for tea, then into the bathroom after laying out his clothes on an already perfectly made bed. Then his lunch is prepared carefully with each item placed in its respective compartment. This all needs to be completed by seven fifteen in the morning if the day is going to go well, according to plan. The numerals on the clock scream five minutes after seven at him as he rushes about the apartment, in that bad mood.

Leaving his residence by seven thirty allows him the twenty minutes needed to walk to work. His office is much closer than that but his preferred route is along the river as it winds through the town. This longer and prettier path gets him near the water. It gives him that peaceful and connected feeling before entering his eight hours of confinement in his bland office. But now the choice has to be made, to skip breakfast or to simply take the shorter route. He is unhappy with either scenario. It is just not right he feels. Jeremy likes routine and that routine has been interrupted and it's just not right.

Not wanting to pay for any food near his work, he opts for breakfast at home and the shorter route. But Jeremy is off to a bad start to the day and when that happens, usually nothing can change his frame of mind. He clings to that bad attitude as the recipient of the blame for his unhappiness, his excuse for the day. Jeremy never lets it flow over to others, though, to his co-workers or to the people that he might meet on the street. He internalizes the feeling as he does with everything in his life, not by choice, not by design, but by simply having lived so many years without any close personal connections or beneficial friendships.

The elevator doors open and Jeremy is deposited on the fifth floor where Tina, the receptionist, greets him. 'Good mornings' are exchanged with maybe a 'nice day out there' or 'it's really coming down.' But that is it, that is all ever said between them. Someone whom he has seen every morning for the last nine years is actually a stranger to him. Jeremy is not good at conversation. Jeremy is not social.

His lunch is placed in the break room with the cold items on the same shelf of the refrigerator each day and his pack in an exact spot on the counter. Then all the pencils must be checked for sharpness, the thermostat in the room confirmed for the correct setting, and any paper that may still reside in the trash can must be put into the recycling bin. Jeremy likes a clean slate to start the day with everything being in its proper place. He is a bit obsessive and a little uptight.

Checking his appointment calendar, Jeremy sees the day is not busy. He meets with three clients this morning and has two scheduled for the afternoon. Usually these are new customers to the company that require assistance in determining what type and how much insurance they will need. They also receive an explanation about the various investment programs offered that allow for payment of those premiums.

With the National Banking and Savings Plan in existence for years now, individuals receive competent banking services from publicly owned institutions. And with easy and secure electronic accounting, the depositing of money and the paying of bills is a simple and cheap process that is easily accomplished without the layers of middle money men and private profit taking that had previously existed in the banking world. The simple skimming off the top that performs no beneficial function or contributes to any true increase in economic productivity is no longer deemed acceptable. Several options are also provided for the installment payment of yearly income taxes and for the contributions to the nominal but required savings plans.

The previous commissions and fees and expenses that had enabled vast numbers of people in banking and financial services to make their livings and their killings off of others are no longer tolerated. No, Jeremy is not in it for the money. Jeremy is in it because it is straightforward, easy, and yes, routine.

Sitting at his desk, he begins the day returning phone calls and checking his messages. A few people will be contacted about future appointments and he will need to solve some problems that have arisen for his clients. Besides that, the day will drag until lunch time when Jeremy can once again go outside, sit by the river, and have his lunch. And of course, the pigeons always get that last scrap of bread from his sandwich.

It is late in the afternoon now and Jeremy has just finished his last appointment for the day. Stopping by the break room after escorting his client to the door, he enters to retrieve the iced tea that he has brought for that afternoon lift. Two others are in the room engaged in conversation around a table.

"Hey, Jeremy," says Paul Douglas. "I haven't seen you all day. Have you been hiding in that office again?"

"Just doing my work, Paul, just doing my work," comes back the weary response from Jeremy. 'Why doesn't this guy just leave me alone,' is his thought as he opens the refrigerator door.

"Who are you going to bring to the party on Friday?" asks Paul as he continues with his questioning.

"What?" says an already exasperated Jeremy.

"You know, Cinco de Mayo is Friday and the whole office is going to the banquet room at Hildalgo's. It's in the newsletter and posted everywhere. Haven't you seen it?" asks the badgering and bothersome co-worker.

"Yeah, I saw it."

"So, who are you bringing?" says Paul, not letting it go.

"I probably won't make it. I have to get up real early Saturday morning," explains Jeremy.

"Oh, come on now, those fish won't miss you for just one weekend. Come to the party, live it up a little."

"That's fine, Paul, you can live it up for me," says Jeremy as he turns to leave.

"I was just trying to set you up. I had the perfect date in mind for you for a Cinco de Mayo party, too," Paul goes on slyly. "Don't know how I'm going to tell that donkey you're not available," and the bullying stupid man breaks into self-congratulatory laughter that is joined by the other person sitting at the table.

"Funny, Paul, just hilarious," counters Jeremy. He hears the laughs follow him down the hallway as he returns to his office. "Asshole," he mumbles under his breath as he begins clearing his desk and prepares to go home. Jeremy is more than ready for this day to end. Taking his time and the River Walk back to his apartment, the warm spring day removes the negative thoughts from his mind. The day is over, the night belongs to him.

Arriving at his apartment, Jeremy puts the key in the lock and opens the door. Calling out in jest, he says, "Hey everybody, I'm home." Living alone can be just that, lonely, can be deflating when returning to an empty house at the end of a tiring day, one void of conversation and connection. But, of course, no one ever returns his greeting and some days, he feels that he would just settle for a wag of that tail.

Jeremy will prepare an evening meal, sit quietly for a few minutes while eating it, and then spend considerably more time afterwards cleaning the dishes. With the kitchen chores out of the way, he will watch some entertainment for an hour or so before preparing to retire early, into the comfort and release of sleep. Of course, the bedtime ritual takes some time with the laying out of fresh pajamas on the bed, flossing first before brushing, and searching the refrigerator for ideas for the making of tomorrow's lunch.

On most nights, sleep will come quickly and his mind is not allowed to think on those things that may keep him awake. Then Jeremy doesn't have to concern himself about a lack of friends or a lack of purpose or a lack of love in his life. If sleep comes easily, he will simply be allowed to slip into slumber and awake the next morning to start the routine over again. But tonight is not such a night.

Jeremy is unable to fall asleep. Although telling himself not to look, he watches the hands of the clock move past eleven and then twelve. Staring at the ceiling, his mind is busy, noisy, keeping him from rest. 'That Paul is a real jerk, why doesn't the guy just leave me alone,' is a constant thought. But that is not what bothers him. It is the feeling that maybe Paul is right, maybe he is a loser, a failure. 'What if the guy is right and this is all it's ever going to be,' is the doubt that can creep into one's thinking and not let go, especially in the quiet of the night.

Restless and uncomfortable, Jeremy rolls to his other side. His eyes fall on the poster of one of his favorite lake settings, high in the Andes of Argentina. He has pictured himself several times at this location, standing at the water's edge in waders, and casting for those beautifully large brown trout that he is just sure live there. So, with the calming blue of the waters and the comforting beauty of the mountains looking back at him, Jeremy's eyes slowly close and he finally drifts away.

\*　　\*　　\*

Her phone is ringing and Annie reaches over to pick it up. "Annie, this is Julia," comes the voice from the other end.

"Hi, I was just thinking about you and thinking that we have to get together real soon. You must have been reading my mind," says her good friend to her.

"Yes, we'll have to for sure, but I have something else I want to tell you. Remember when you asked me about the summer camp programs for the children?" Annie answers that she does. "Well, this morning Mark said everything was approved last night and now they're in this mad dash to hire counselors and teachers. Applications are being accepted starting today and I thought you might want to know about it."

"Julia, that's great, that's great news! What type of people are they looking for, do you know anything about the jobs?" asks a truly excited Annie.

"No, I don't, but you can talk to Mark about it if you want. With your background and experience, I'm sure they're looking for someone like you. And I couldn't think of a more caring person to help out with the kids. You'd be perfect," as Julia adds her appraisal of Annie's chances of being hired.

"You're sweet, Julia. Thanks for letting me know about it," says Annie. "Hey, what are you doing Friday night, want to catch one of The Dances with me? I haven't been for a long time and it would be a chance to see some friends."

Dances are now a popular activity in municipalities all across the country. They serve as showcases for local musical talent as well as providing social networks for friends and neighbors at the end of the work week. And, of course, dancing always provides that great exercise and that great release.

Several venues are established around town at various public buildings and all ages and all types of people participate on the weekends. Rock, country, and blues bands perform on Friday nights at three locations. And on Sunday afternoons, ballroom dancing with accompanying instruction are provided in larger settings with ensembles and orchestras performing. It is not uncommon to see a young high school student shaking it up with one of her parents' friends at a Friday Dance or to see an eighty year old graceful matron teaching the basics of the waltz to a twenty year old burly carpenter on a Sunday. Dance can be a celebration of life, a celebration of movement and body and of our connection to others. Dance is a shared exuberance that can bring people and generations closer together.

The conversation soon ends with promises from each to get together on Friday. Annie makes her way to the back patio where Marty is warming in the morning sun. "Who was that, dear, one of your friends?" asks a truly interested Marty who wants Annie to get out more, to be around others more her age and situation. The weight and guilt that Marty feels occasionally is not severe, not overpowering, but she knows someday her time will come and Annie will have to face life alone. And that aloneness, that singular path, can be harder than one may expect. Marty only wishes the best for her granddaughter when she is gone. Marty knows that she will need more relationships and more friends around for support when that day comes.

"Julia," she answers. "We're going to go to one of the Friday Dances together this weekend. I'm kind of excited about seeing a band and hearing some good music."

"Good dear, I think that's wonderful."

"And she also told me about some job openings at the Parks Department. Mark is in charge of the new summer programs and they began accepting applications today," is Annie's opening line in explaining her new plan to her grandmother.

"Job openings? But you have a job, Annie, what do you need another one for?"

Annie moves closer to where Marty is sitting, to be closer for what she is going to say next. "Because I want to find a job here, in Travers, where I live."

"Annie," then comes a stern warning from her grandmother. "What are you thinking? Come on, out with it."

"I've put in for a leave of absence from the tour company, Marty, and I'm going to find a job here and stay at home for a change. I want to put that suitcase in the closet for a while and concentrate on some other things in my life."

"Like me, I suppose," as Marty then responds with obvious dissatisfaction at a possible ulterior motive for Annie.

"Like you and a bunch of other things. I'm not doing it just for you so don't go there. I miss Julia and all my other friends. I come back from my trips and it seems like I'm always starting over again. I've been thinking about it for quite a while. I just think that now might be the right time."

"But aren't you risking your career? You have always said how satisfying it is and how fun and rewarding it can be. I don't want you to risk losing or missing out on that."

"I'm not risking anything. I spoke directly to Thomas about it and he said no problem. They have plenty of guides to take my place. I can always go back and start again, it's in my contract. I'm just going to take a year off and see what happens," says Annie about her decision.

Marty is still not sure and cocking her head to the side, gives Annie a hard look. "Don't worry," Annie laughs. "I know what I'm doing." And she leans over to give her darling grandmother a kiss on the cheek, on her good side, of course.

*　　*　　*

Friday comes and Annie is at home changing clothes and preparing to have Julia pick her up for one of the Dances. Having gone to the Parks Department earlier in the week to submit her application, she had come away feeling very good about her chances. By luck, the hiring manager was the one staffing the front office when she went in to apply. After finding out about Annie's qualifications, about her having been a tour guide with medical certification, he had made it very clear that she stood a good chance of getting one of the openings. It had brightened her day, and for that matter, her whole week and has put her in a very good mood as she finishes getting ready.

"Marty, I'm going to be heading out soon. Is there anything you need before I leave?" she calls out to her grandmother.

"Yes, dear, just one thing," Marty answers from her room.

"Okay, just a minute, I'll be right in. What is it?" Annie asks, showing up in the doorway.

"Promise me that you'll have a good time tonight and that you won't worry about me while you're at the Dance."

"Oh, you old fooler, yes I promise. For some silly reason, I am really excited about going out tonight and I don't know why," answers Annie. She doesn't quite understand the anticipation and excitement that she feels tonight. "I'll be back by ten," she then says as a courtesy to her grandmother.

"You better be or you're grounded," says Marty.

\*　　\*　　\*

Alex and Scott are sitting in the office, wrapping up the week's business. Most of the other employees are gone, except for one or two who are helping to secure the job site for the weekend. "Do you and Laura have any plans for the evening?" Scott asks as he sits across the room from Alex.

"No, she and Katie have an event to go to tonight," answers Alex about the girls' activities.

"Are you and Aaron doing anything?"

"Are you kidding me, a seventeen year boy spending a Friday night with his dad. You don't know anything about teenagers, do you?" jokes Alex to his yet childless friend. "He and his buddies are practicing tonight at Jason's or something."

"So, you're free then."

"Yeah, I guess so."

"Alright then, you're coming with us," Scott pronounces, not leaving a lot of room for a refusal from his friend.

"Going with who, where?"

"With Jennifer and me, to a Friday Dance. There's a blues band playing at Harvest Hall who are really, really good. They're from Atwood and we heard them a few years ago. This is their first time playing in the area for quite a while and Jennifer's actually the one dragging me to it, she loves them. I said I'd go if I could take you, so you're coming."

"That's a nice offer, buddy, I appreciate it. Don't know if I feel like dancing, though, I think I'll pass."

"You will when you get there. So be ready at six and Jennifer and I will come by and pick you up," and Scott stares down his friend from across the room.

Alex knows that he has lost the argument and simply laughs while smiling at Scott and shaking his head from side to side. "Okay, I'll make sure I'm ready."

\*　　\*　　\*

Pulling the curtains to the side, Alex sees Scott and Jennifer arriving in front. Waving to them, he checks the house quickly and locks the door behind him as he walks toward the waiting vehicle. "Hi guys," he says, getting into the back seat. Scott's wife turns and flashes a big smile in Alex's direction.

"Hi there, Alex," says Jennifer. "I'm really glad that you're going to come with us. You won't regret it, this band is great. Do you have your dancing shoes on?" she asks, looking down at the floor in the back seat.

"Yeah," says Alex, while laughing.

"Make sure that you save a dance for me, will you?"

"After everybody sees my moves, you might have to wait your turn but I can probably squeeze you in," he jokes. Looking out the window as they drive to the dance, Alex's mood is elevated. His scenery has already changed and the night offers relief and escape from those everyday worries. He is glad that his friend had talked him into coming.

Scott drops Jennifer and Alex at the front of the building and then leaves to park their vehicle. Both wait on the steps of the hall for his return.

"Things been good with you?" Alex asks Jennifer.

"Yes, really good, busy. But we have part of our fiver coming up pretty soon, as you probably know. So, we're kind of looking forward to that."

"That's right, Scott has his next month. Are you guys taking the two weeks now or the three?" he asks about their plans for vacation time from work requirements.

"This year we decided to do the two weeks in summer, things are so nice around here at that time anyway. We'll take our three weeks in winter. We're thinking about Australia this time. I've always wanted to go there," says Jennifer.

"Oh, me, too," sighs Alex in agreement.

No longer is society hell bent on running as fast as they can to their collective grave. After years of diminishing returns from such activity, a balance between work and rest has also come back into people's lives. And with basic human needs like health care and affordable housing now provided to all, the treadmill doesn't need to be constantly moving anymore to just keep one's place in line. The treadmill can remain idle for periods of time to allow for needed maintenance and necessary retooling.

Five weeks of vacation is the new norm for all, a fiver. Most people have opted to take two separate periods during the year with roughly six months in between, split into two and three week periods. A full five week hiatus is also common in certain industries or areas of employment where the businesses can function normally in this manner. Besides cost savings to the businesses by reduced wages in slower times, it has promoted a new area of employment for temporary positions in almost every segment of the economy. This has created internships, summer employment for students and young people, and easily attainable part-time employment for older citizens wanting something to fill their days or to make a little extra money.

And with that free time, tourism has filled the void left by the decline of the consumer economy in the early part of the century. It has become the new economic engine that replaces the previous inefficient and inferior model. In every corner of the world, restaurants and lodging establishments and small businesses have benefited immensely by this new spirit of world harmony that has stimulated so many to travel. Tourist dollars have filled people's pocketbooks and have made local economies strong. And this exchange of cultures has filled people's hearts with an understanding and an appreciation of others.

Scott now joins them where they wait on the steps for him. "You guys ready?" he asks and all enter the building. The band is just finishing a song as they join the other locals streaming into the hall. Alex sees an old friend and excuses himself to Scott and Jennifer. He says that he will catch up to them.

"Eric Oldenmeyer!" shouts out Alex as he approaches his old acquaintance. "What's it been, three or four years since I've seen you?" The other man answers that it's been too long and gives his friend a hug along with a handshake. "You'd think we would have run into each other by now, Travers isn't that big of a city. So, you're still around, huh?"

"Yeah, most of us are. Tim's gone off to do a two year stint in Nicaragua but Molly's here. She's busy working at the Sheffield Bakery and learning the trade. She loves it," as Eric offers the updates on his family. "And you guys are doing good? Aaron must be in high school by now."

"He'll be a senior next year."

"Oh my gosh, Aaron is a senior already? I remember that he was really into the guitar, wasn't he?"

"Still is, it's a big part of his life."

"And how old is your daughter?"

"Katie is seven now."

"And Laura, everything's good with her?" Eric asks about the last member of the family.

Alex pauses for a minute and then answers, "Fine, she's doing just fine. Well, I better go catch up with my friends. It was really good seeing you, Eric, really good and say hi to that sweet wife of yours for me, will you?" And Alex says good-bye to him to go off in search of Scott and Jennifer.

*    *    *

"Did you make it into the office to apply this week?" Julia asks her passenger on the way to the Dance.

"I did, about a half hour after I talked with you," says Annie with a laugh. "I talked with a guy named Colin."

"Oh, good, Colin is one of Mark's bosses. And I think he's the one in charge of personnel for the Parks Department. How were you able to pull that off?"

"He was standing at the front desk when I walked in. I guess, I just got lucky."

"It's just meant to be if you ask me," offers Julia, looking in Annie's direction and giving a couple of nods of the head.

"I hope so," says Annie.

Soon, they arrive at the Friday Dance. "Here, let me get it for you. I've got a ten anyway," and Annie drops her contribution into the lock box at the entrance to the Hall.

The venues are provided by the city and budgeted under the Arts Division of the Parks Department. The bands will play for the exposure and the experience with volunteers performing the set up, the tear down, and the clean up. All dances start at six and end by nine in the evening. The contribution boxes had begun out of a need for a place to put the tips given to the musicians. The unwritten rule now is that everyone contributes five dollars at the door and at the end of the evening, the money is divided by one of the volunteers.

Fifty percent of the donations is given to the musicians and fifty percent is returned to the Arts Fund. A really good band providing a fun time can do fairly well when those leaving after having thoroughly enjoyed themselves and off to a great start to the weekend, feel only too happy to contribute another five or ten dollars to the musicians on their way out the door. A friendly competition has arisen between the local bands in the area to see who can raise the most money each week, for themselves and for the Parks Department.

"Thanks," says Julia and they enter the activities with the dance and its patrons already in full swing. The two women make their way to the side of the room where they are able to stand and see the band. Two guitar players, a very animated drummer, and a cool looking saxophone player with his dark shades and stylish hat are on the stage performing. They are producing a strong and powerful sound and many are already on the dance floor, moving and shaking things up.

"These guys are great!" Annie shouts to her friend over the noise of the hall. Julia nods agreement and with a wave of the hand toward the floor, asks if she wants to dance.

"Sure," comes back the answer. And the two women join the jostling, bouncing crowd on their edge of the room. Spotting other friends around her, Annie is already easily enjoying the evening's escape.

"Phew, I'm thirsty," says Julia after she dances through the next couple of songs with Annie. "I need something to drink." Annie agrees, but before getting the chance to leave the dance floor, she is whisked away by a Mister Bennett, one of Marty's friends who has just spotted her and whom she has not seen for quite a long time.

"I'll meet you over there," Annie yells above the din of the crowd as she is pulled back onto the dance floor.

\*     \*     \*


Alex catches up with Jennifer and Scott. "What a turnout! And you're right, these guys are really good," he acknowledges. "I'm going to have to tell Aaron about them."

"Is he still into music?" asks Jennifer.

"Oh yeah, he really likes it. Mainly the guitar but he's been tinkering with the keyboard lately, too. He and a couple of his buddies are in a group that does a lot of practicing, I know that," says the father about his often absent son.

"They should play one of these things," offers Scott.

"They want to, when they're ready they say. It's probably a bit intimidating for them right now," says Alex, raising his voice to an understandable level. Conversation is difficult above the music and after standing for a few minutes more, Scott and Jennifer hit the dance floor again. Alex makes his way about the room with an occasional handshake or a wave to friends and acquaintances. These events are well-attended by locals as they all now share in this weekly celebration of a better life.

Continuing to make his way toward the front, Alex is closer to the band and has a good view of all in the room. It is a joy to watch people having a good time, the smiles on their faces, the camaraderie with the other participants, and the complete abandon that one can experience while dancing. It is hard not to have a good time and a broad smile also sits on Alex's face as he watches the proceedings.

Scott and his wife come back to where Alex is standing. "Okay, you're next," says Jennifer when they reach his spot. A slight hesitation from Alex then gives rise to her second proposal. "Alright, Scott and I will get something to drink, but don't think you're going to get out of dancing with me. You better be ready when I get back," she warns.

"I will, I will," answers Alex.


\*     \*     \*

Alex will dance with Jennifer for two songs and then stay out on the floor for another couple of turns. One comes from a young girl from his part of town who had come over to ask her neighbor for a dance after having her own father tire out. Having fun now and moving with the music, Alex takes the initiative to ask Mrs. Webster for the next dance. A woman about ten years his senior, she had been a favorite teacher of Aaron's in sixth grade. All in all, Alex is having a great time and not once has he thought on the problems that he and Laura are having, not once has a shadow come over the bright light of fun and friends.

And now his thirst will take him off the dance floor and to the snack bar. With juices, water, and a wide variety of healthy treats, it serves to refresh the dancers and also that Arts Fund. Alex waits his turn along with several others as he nears the counter. Looking at the list of available drinks, he then selects a limeade when reaching the front of his line.

Annie leaves the dance floor and makes her way toward the refreshment stand. At the other end of the counter from Alex and also at the front of her line, Julia calls out to Annie, hanging at the back. "What do you want, I'll get it for you."

"Limeade," she shouts back.

Julia, who has already paid for her drink, orders another so her friend won't have to wait. The two volunteers manning the stand approach the cooler at the same time. Alex's helper wraps his hand around the last bottle of the requested beverage just as the other worker reaches for it. "Oh, I'm sorry," calls out the person helping Julia. "That was the last one."

Overhearing the comment and realizing the situation, Alex offers it to Julia, standing in the other line. "No, you go ahead. I'll have a tangerine juice instead," says Alex as he then orders another one of his favorite drinks.

The two clerks enjoy the easy solution and the last limeade is presented to Julia for her second payment. "Thank you," she mouths in Alex's direction. A smile and a slight nod of the head are returned from him.

It is nearing eight thirty now and the night is winding down. An appreciable part of the crowd has melted away with evening and family duties calling them home. The band is taking their last break when Alex walks past the spot where Julia and Annie are sitting. Recognizing him as the person at the counter, Julia thanks him again for his polite gesture with the drink.

"You're welcome. I think I came out ahead, though, that was about the sweetest tangerine juice I've had in years."

"I've got a grandmother you ought to meet," interjects Annie and then she explains Marty's love affair with the fruit. The three of them will engage in idle talk for the next few minutes before Alex spots Scott and Jennifer across the room. Excusing himself to go meet them, Alex starts to leave. Julia then extends a hand and says, "My name is Julia, thanks again."

"Sure, I'm Alex," he says as he shakes her hand.

Glancing over at her friend, Alex and Annie's eyes meet again and she joins in the introductions. "Hi," then comes the soft and sweet greeting from this equally gracious person. "I'm Annie." And she, too, extends her hand for shaking.

"Hi, Annie," says Alex. He reaches for her hand, grasps it, and slowly and deliberately moves it up and down a few times. Momentarily, the man is charmed by the brightness of her face, the clarity of her eyes, and the trueness of her smile. Losing track of time, he shakes Annie's hand a few times more before letting go. Awkward and thrown off guard for a minute, he strains to regain his composure. "Well, nice meeting the both of you," Alex quickly recovers and then walks away. Annie's eyes follow him across the room.

"Well, that was electric," says Julia when Alex is gone.

"What?" answers Annie innocently.

"Don't what me, you know what I'm talking about. I thought the sparks were going to catch somebody's hair on fire," says Julia about the obvious connection between the two of them.

"It wasn't like that," she protests.

"Oh, it wasn't?" her good friend teases.

Then pausing to review the episode honestly with herself for a moment, Annie says, "Well, maybe a little."

\* \* \*

Three months have now passed and these three lives have continued down their respective paths, with small changes, big changes, and no change. Annie had gotten one of the openings for summer counselors, helping with day camps and the trips to surrounding historical sites and wilderness areas. She has settled into her new job and is enjoying the work immensely. All at the Parks Department have welcomed her good spirit, hard work, and dedication to the kids. Annie has become a role model, a good friend to the children in the program, and has become more immersed in the community. Marty's health is fragile but no large declines have occurred over these last few months. Her spirits remain high and Marty, too, has benefited from Annie's change in life. Sharing even more with each other, the two spend quiet days in the garden and rousing nights around the game boards. Annie has felt it a blessing to be home at this time.

Alex has faced the biggest change. One day in the early part of the summer, Laura had come home to announce that she was leaving. With regrets for the breakup of the family, Laura had said that she no longer can carry on the charade of the happy marriage, that she can no longer share her life with someone she doesn't really love. It had been difficult, involving and explaining the situation to the children. Tears had flowed and regrets were expressed but no blame was placed by husband or wife on each other. None of that shouting had taken place. The two of them had faced the situation with mature attitudes and had made responsible decisions. They had shared a large part of their adult lives together but now must find their own way, their own path, as they now seek different directions to their lives.

Laura has moved to a city in a nearby state to live with her unmarried sister. She had explained that a position was waiting for her and that within the year, she would have her own place and at that point, the children would begin their holiday and summer visits. For now, she remains in constant contact with her two children and has planned one trip before school starts to take them on a short vacation. Laura has remained a good mother but with the differences between her and Alex, she can no longer play the good wife.

Alex had been devastated in the beginning. Although being a realist about the sad situation of their marriage, the importance and stability of having two care providers in the household had overshadowed and walled off his personal feelings on the matter. The decision had been made for the children to remain with him, to remain in the same house, in the same school, near the same friends. Aaron will be entering his last year of high school and any other course of action concerning him didn't make sense. Katie is younger and could adapt but splitting apart siblings wasn't even considered. Although doing what was right for her, Laura continued to do what was right for the children.

Katie is the one to miss her mother the most with the tears and a slight sadness especially coming at bedtime. But Alex was always there to assure her that her mother loved her and that Laura would always be in the young child's life. Laura communicates with Katie often and is available for her anytime that her daughter might want or need her mother. Alex would strengthen the bonds with his children and his commitment to them while continuing to enjoy his most important job of being a father. For years, that had been enough to sustain him and that satisfaction and purpose continue to drive him on.

Luckily, a sweet older woman, one of their neighbors whom the kids have known for years, has started helping with the household duties. Erica, who is a widow, enjoys the time spent with Alex's children. The extra money from some cleaning and grocery shopping duties is simply icing to her. She comes over at seven in the morning, prepares the lunches, and stays with the children until they leave for school. And often, she will stay with Katie some afternoons with Alex working late or running errands and a few evenings when Alex attends a meeting or an event. At almost eighteen now and a good kid, Aaron needs little supervision and has immersed himself even more into his music. The teenager enjoys it greatly but Alex wonders if it is not also for diversion from their broken home, from that 'failed family.' But he is at the age where talking about one's feelings, especially to a parent, is usually not an area that they enter easily. Alex has respected his privacy and his personal feelings but has let Aaron know that he is there if he ever needs him.

Jeremy's situation remains the same. Nothing has changed at work. It is still uninspiring employment and Paul continues his taunting of him. But, the summer breezes and the longer days have taken him outside in the evening to his side yard. He has several targets arranged there to practice his casting skills. Jeremy can spend hours at this and some nights only the absence of light in the evening sky chases him inside.

And with neighbors out for evening walks, Jeremy has even gotten to the point of waving to one or two familiar faces as they move past. Appreciating one particularly kind face on that of an older man, Jeremy tells himself that some night he will walk to the edge of the fence and be close enough to introduce himself. He knows the gentleman's last name is Weston from the mailbox with his apartment number on it. But he doesn't know his first name. Someday he is going to find out, someday he will make his move, someday Jeremy will ask him.

*　　　*　　　*

"Daddy," Katie says to her father as he stands at the sink rinsing dishes and cleaning up from dinner.

"What, honey?" answers Alex.

"Emily and Tara are both going to be gone next week. What am I going to do all day if they won't be here?" she asks with true concern about how to lead a life without her friends in it.

"Erica will be here," says Alex of the full-time summer help from his kind neighbor now that the children are out of school. "Maybe you girls could figure out some extra things to do. She could take you to the pool during the day and also maybe go to the park. She draws with you, too, doesn't she? I'm sure you'll be able to find something to do. Are their families going to be gone on vacation next week or what?"

"No, it's a summer camp. Emily called it the History Tour and said that Tara is going, too. Why do they get to go and I don't?" And a slight pout sits on the little girl's face.

"I don't know why. There's probably not any reason that you couldn't go, too. I can call Mrs. Martin tonight and ask her about it, if you want me to."

"Oh, would you?" says Katie. "Emily keeps saying how much fun she and Tara are going to have next week. I don't want them having fun if I don't get to."

"Well," Alex chuckles to himself at the comment. "It's okay for them to have fun but maybe you can, too."

Katie then comes over to where Alex is standing and hugs him tightly around the waist. "I love you," says the sweet little thing to her father before scampering off to her room, happy and satisfied for now with the situation.

Having straightened the kitchen, Alex moves to the living room to sit down while calling Emily's mother. "Oh hi, Lisa, this is Alex," starts the conversation between the two neighbors and two parents. "I hope I'm not interrupting anything." Assurances come back that dinner is also over for their family. "Katie was telling me about Emily attending a summer camp or something next week." And Mrs. Martin fills in Alex on the new summer programs offered by the Parks Department this year that involve nature study, crafts, and field trips to local points of interest. One such program is centered on historical sites in the area, the History Tour. "So, Katie really wants to go. She doesn't want to miss out on any of the action, you know," says Alex with a laugh. "Do you think spaces are still open?

"I think so, Alex. Tara's mother just told me about it two days ago and they didn't say anything about filling up when we went in yesterday. I would just call the Parks Department tomorrow. It would be great to have Katie go with them. It's from nine in the morning until four and they're supposed to pack a lunch," says Lisa, providing more information on the camp. Alex thanks her and hangs up, and adds one more thing to his list of parenting duties for tomorrow.

\*　　\*　　\*

The day is quickly proving to be exceptionally busy. Besides two meetings in the morning with planners from the Core's main office, the appearance of ground water in one of the trenches has occupied most of the afternoon with finding a temporary solution to allow work to continue. Alex just now returns to the office to call and sign up Katie for the camp next week. He sits at his desk after finishing the call for a moment with a look of fatigue and disarray on his face. Scott has been in the office working on reports for most of the afternoon and now looks across the room at his tired friend. "Are you hanging in there, dad?" comes the kind-hearted query.

Alex pauses and then looks in Scott's direction. "Oh, yeah, everything's fine. I just don't think that I should have sat down, though," explains Alex about his difficulty to get going again.

"I really don't know how you do it. Working all day and then making the meals and all the shopping for the household. And Jennifer and I think we're busy."

"Oh, it's not so bad. Erica does a lot of the work around the house. She usually gets a meal started, too. I just have to finish it when getting home and then clean up. I sure don't know what I'd do without her, though."

"Did things get figured out at Seventh Street?" asks Scott about the day's main problem.

"Yeah, we were able to dig out a holding reservoir to move the water away. They're bringing in a load of gravel now and are going to start the drain system in that area right away. I don't think it'll hold us back for tomorrow. Mike said that he and two of his guys would stay late to wrap it up if needed."

"So, what's Katie up to next week? It sounded like you got her into a class or something," asks Scott about the overheard conversation on the phone.

"It's a new program at the Parks Department. They're going to spend the week going around the area touring all the historical sites. Her two good friends are going so she wanted to be able to go, too. I was lucky, they still had openings. She'll go during the day all of next week."

"That must be the fun part of parenting. Kids are great, aren't they?" says the younger friend.

"It's all worth it," agrees the man who truly relishes his role as a father. "When are you guys making the move? I don't want you to miss out on changing diapers and getting no sleep."

"In about two years. Jennifer's going to continue working for at least that long before she would feel right about taking any time off," says Scott.

"Would you have a second?"

"Sure, we'd go for two. Maybe get lucky and get one of each, like you. Hey, why don't you just take off? There's not much left to do and I can close up the yard and the trailer," he says to his obviously tired boss.

Not having thought about leaving early, the diligent manager wavers and then begins to acquiesce to the offer. "Well, maybe, are you sure?" Alex asks again.

"Get out of here!" says Scott.

*  *  *

After throwing his pack into the back seat of the peetee, Alex makes his way down the hill and onto the commuter cruiseway. With Erica waiting for Katie's arrival after school, he actually has an hour or two before needing to be home. Taking advantage of the opportunity, Alex decides to stop by the business district.

In Travers, as in many towns and cities across the country, smaller and locally owned businesses are now the standard. Gone are the days of big box stores offering only little containers of service. The race to the bottom had finally pulled us all under. The low low prices had simply come with too high a cost. Having taken its toll on the environment with questionable sourcing and having destroyed local commerce with unfair business practices, big business had finally been recognized as being bad business. Benefiting executives, corporations, and stockholders in distant locations is not something that everyday citizens want done with their hard-earned dollars. Those advantages need to stay closer to home, in their and their neighbors' own pockets.

Once again, cities and towns and neighborhoods have their own hardware stores and clothing stores and office supply stores. No longer do we need to get into a vehicle and drive to an expanse of parking lots and large buildings that are miles from one's home just to shop. No longer are we paving over the countryside to destroy town centers. And no longer do we drain the life and economic vitality from our local communities.

Alex is somewhat of a tool junkie. Having been in the trades most of his life, he knows the old adage 'the right tool for the right job' is not an empty statement. And knowing that Thompson's Hardware has one of the best power tool sections in the area, he heads there now. And if he is lucky, Alex might run into Nate Thompson, the owner and a long time friend.

Entering the store, he first scans the aisles for any sign of him before heading to the tool section. First looking at the sanders, Alex next moves on to one particular router that offers a new base and guide design that he has never seen before. Picking it up, he hears someone speaking from behind him.

"You've never seen a router before or what?" says Nate who had just spotted Alex from across the room after coming out of the back of the store.

Alex recognizes the voice and turning around, he extends a welcome handshake to his old friend. "I thought you must be somewhere nearby. I've never really known you not to be taking care of the store or your customers," says Alex about the hard working small business owner.

"Oh, I take Sundays off, mostly because my wife makes me," he explains about the long hours required when running one's own business. But Nate, like many other new entrepreneurs in this new world of business, wouldn't have it any other way.

"The store looks great, business must be good. I think I see a new face or two from the last time I was in."

"Yeah, we've expanded into a couple of areas that nobody else was really doing in town, like camping. And with the increased business, I've brought on two more people in the last year. We're up to five full time and three part-timers now. You'd think that I'd have less to do, not more, huh?"

"I think you'd even be busy on a desert island by yourself," says Alex jokingly.

"A desert island, huh? I might just like to try that sometime," says Nate. "And how are the kids, are they doing good?" And Alex spends a minute telling him about Aaron and Katie. Inquiring about his own family, Alex then listens as Nate runs down a short synopsis on everyone's activities.

"How's Laura? She used to drop in occasionally to pick up a few things but I don't think I've seen her for quite a while now. She must be one of those busy moms."

"We're not together anymore. Laura has moved out of town," answers Alex in a matter of fact manner. "It's been a couple of months now since she's left."

"Oh...oh, I'm sorry," says Nate, reacting as though he has just put his foot in his mouth.

Being very familiar now with this typical reaction from others when told of the separation and impending divorce, Alex gives his standard response. "Don't be, everything's fine. It's probably better this way," he then says, informing his friend while still trying to convince himself. After exchanging more conversation, they wish each other well and Alex leaves the store.

After checking the time, he figures that he has at least another forty five minutes to kill and begins walking the streets, looking in the windows. Passing the local coffee house and bakery, he is tempted to partake but decides that he doesn't really want anything right now. Crossing the street, Alex strolls the sidewalk and observes the people passing. It feels good to have some time without chores or responsibilities but something is missing, something is taking the joy from the moment. And Alex returns to his peetee that is parked nearby.

Sitting behind the wheel, he pauses before engaging the gear. Growing up with two other siblings and a host of nearby cousins, Alex always knew the Galway household as a busy place. Alex simply hasn't had any training in being alone and now, as he sits in his vehicle, he realizes that he is not really very good at it. So with a sigh, he backs out of the parking place and heads home.

\*     \*     \*


Now coming into their kitchen where Erica and Katie are busy making cookies, Alex is greeted by his young daughter running to him and hugging his waist. "Hi, sweetie, how's my best girl?" he says affectionately in a true statement of how he feels about his daughter. Katie is the rock in his life now, along with Aaron who has remained a warm and considerate son. Children, the pure unaffected essence of humankind, still provide the basis around which families thrive, in which love is given a platform. And with their futures once again bright and secure, the younger generations have built on the solid changes made in the years that had followed after the Great Mistake.

No longer do our children need to worry about going off to war or about slipping backwards while having to climb artificial ladders of success. With education and equitable economies at the forefront of public policy and with a new social conscience flowering in the decades following the debacle, we have created new generations that are leading us down unbelievable paths of potential and of achievement. No longer does there exist only a few winners with those many losers. And finally, finally, it has come down to how the game is played.

"Erica's making oatmeal cookies for us. I bet she makes the best cookies in the world," says the young girl. Erica laughs at the comment as she exchanges a big smile with Alex.

"I think you're probably right," he says. "And what are you working on?" Alex asks Katie who is standing on a stepstool near the sink washing something for dinner.

As the father moves closer to her to take a look, Katie says, "I'm washing the apricots. First you wash them real good, then you put them on the paper towel to dry, and then Erica is going to cut them into pieces to put in the cookies," explains the assistant cook. "And this half of the cookies," she goes on, directing Alex's attention to the dough already placed on the cookie sheet, "are going to get one chocolate chip, right on top. Erica said I could have one of those after dinner if it's okay with you. Is it Daddy, is it okay with you?" pleads Katie.

"I think we could probably work that out," he says.

Erica then quickly gives instructions to Alex on the status of their evening meal, passes on a few more pieces of needed information, and takes her leave to return to her own home. Katie and Alex remain in the kitchen preparing the rest of the dinner and then work together on setting the table as they wait for Aaron to arrive home.

\*     \*     \*

"Are you taking off?" asks Nick as Aaron opens his guitar case to put the instrument away.

"Yeah, I told my Dad that I'd be home by six tonight. I better get going," says Aaron as the band finishes their practice session in Nick's garage. "You know, the family that eats dinner together, stays together."

"Does he push you on that stuff?" says Nick, knowing of the recent series of events and of his mother's leaving.

"No, not really. I was just kidding but it's been a while since we've had a chance for all three of us to eat at the same time. I'm actually kind of looking forward to it. My dad's got this lady that helps out around the house and she's been doing a lot of the cooking for us. We're probably eating better than when my mom was there." Picking up the case and scanning the room for anything else of his, Aaron takes his leave of Nick and Jason who are the other two guitarists in the group.

"See you tomorrow then, about the same time?" calls out Nick as he reaches the door.

"Yeah, I'll be here. And when is the whole group practicing again?" asks Aaron.

"Saturday morning at Sam's. His parents are leaving Friday night on a trip so they said it was cool to use their place. We'll be way out in the country so bring your amp. We can make as much noise as we want," says Jason.

Aaron straps the guitar into the back of his peetee and drives away from Nick's house. Moving through the neighborhoods, he waves to a couple acquaintances as he passes. Soon, he is on one of the cruiseways heading home as the day begins to turn into early evening. Aaron relaxes into the natural beauty of the many green trees that now parallel most routes in the city. They act as a buffer, a balancer, that cleans the air and clears the mind. Aaron is in a very good mood when he arrives home.

Alex is sitting in the living room, watching video, when he sees Aaron's peetee pass the window. He shouts to Katie in the other room, "Hey, Aaron's home." The little sister jumps up and runs to meet her brother at the garage door.

"Hey, kiddo," says Aaron when seeing Katie there to meet him. "What's up?"

"Erica and I made cookies today and you've just got to see them. They all came out perrrrr...fect!" she exclaims excitedly. "Come on, they're in the kitchen," and the young girl grabs her brother's hand to lead him there. Aaron hurries to find a place to set down his guitar case.

"Hi, Dad," is the son's friendly greeting to Alex as he passes the living room. Katie then dutifully shows Aaron the cookies, explains the process of making them, and for the finale, displays the ones with a chocolate drop on top. She finishes by saying that both of them can have one after dinner. Alex then joins them in the kitchen.

"What's for dinner? I'm starved," asks the teenage boy with one of those hollow legs.

"Don't worry, there's plenty of food. Erica makes sure that we don't go hungry, eh?" says Alex as he begins to fill the plates. "Go wash your hands and dinner will be on the table when you get back." Katie helps her father serve the food and fills the glasses with something to drink.

The three of them have managed to continue a family lifestyle even with the absence of their mother. In the first few weeks after Laura left home, Katie had struggled with the loss and it had greatly concerned Alex. Laura would contact Katie almost every day at the beginning but now has been reduced to twice a week as the small girl has readjusted to their new situation. Her young age is a benefit in this area but also a detriment as she still requires that nurturing and connection to a motherly influence.

Erica has helped in this area and Alex feels extremely lucky to have found such a pleasant woman to have in their home.

Aaron has rolled with the punches quite well and has handled the situation without complaint or victimization. He is older but the young man is also a very even, thinking individual. Aaron is reaching the age where life begins to throw things at us, to see what we are made of, and he has passed all the tests with his continued quiet resolve and positive manner. But that quietness, that lack of complaint, somewhat bothers Alex. He just hopes that his son is doing as well on the inside as he appears to be doing on the outside.

"Did you have practice today?" Alex asks Aaron as they sit at the dining room table

"Yeah, over at Nick's house. Just the guitarists, though. This weekend we're all getting together," he says.

"How's it going? Are you guys still working on some of your own stuff?"

"About half of the songs we play are covers but the other half are all our own. Actually, Sam just wrote one of his first songs and it's better than the stuff Nick and I have been doing. I didn't think the drummer would come up with the best song. We're trying to work it out now."

"I want to play an instrument," says Katie as she joins in the dinner conversation. "Daddy, would you buy me something to make music with?"

"It's not that easy, you have to practice a lot, and it usually takes a really long time to get good at it," is the older brother's honest assessment of the challenge of learning to play a musical instrument. Katie's face then turns into a pout and she is upset at this response. Aaron picks up on it. "The best place to start is probably with a piano, don't you think, Dad?" he quickly adds. Alex lends his agreement.

"But we don't have a piano," says Katie.

"Yes, we do. I have the keyboard in my room, that's just like a piano," says Aaron. Katie's eyes light up at the comment. "I could give you your first lesson after dinner if you want."

Alex smiles at his son, expressing his appreciation for the offer of his time to his younger sibling. At the end of the meal, he volunteers to do the clean up by himself and the two scurry off to Aaron's room. "What about the cookies, don't you want them?" Alex yells down the hall after them.

"After my music lesson," shouts back Katie who now has other priorities on her mind.

Alex stays in the kitchen, putting things away and cleaning dishes. He then retires to the living room to do some reading and relaxing as he listens to the music lesson being given by Aaron. He smiles at the sounds and the laughter coming from the room. As long as things are all right with his children, everything is all right with Alex.

\*　　\*　　\*

Annie comes through the door with groceries in hand. Marty had spotted her arrival and now, standing in the front room, offers to take one of the bags from her.

"No, no, I've got it," says Annie as she struggles some with the heavy bags.

"Nonsense," says Marty. "Let me carry one of those for you. I'm just old, not helpless."

"But you shouldn't be lifting things," Annie protests.

"Give me that bag," and Marty takes it from Annie's arms. The two of them make their way into the kitchen.

"Oh, Marty, I wish you wouldn't do that. You're just going to make things worse," says Annie as they place the groceries on the countertop. Recently, the swelling of Marty's abdominal area has increased and although not complaining, Annie knows that it bothers her. She is very concerned about her grandmother's health and now greets her each morning to help with dressing. And each evening, Annie prepares dinner while Marty rests in the other room.

Marty has started regular biweekly appointments with the doctor, every other Wednesday. Dr. Granger has counseled with Annie on two separate occasions about what to expect in the coming months. Marty's health is not good and the doctor has leveled with her. He has said that possibly only six months may remain before her body will simply give out.

"And how did your day go, dear?" asks Marty as they begin putting the groceries away.

"Fine, just fine. The kids are so great, with all that energy and enthusiasm, and I have a really good group this week. They are so curious and are always asking questions. As soon as one craft is finished, they go around the room looking at each other's creations and then start lining up to begin the next one. I'm kind of glad when lunchtime and exercise break comes to try and clean up the room some," says Annie. "I'm also looking forward to next week. It's Lynn's turn at the crafts table and I'll get to do something outside with them."

"So, the instructors trade off, that's nice."

"Yes, it really is. Colin gave us free reign to organize anyway we wanted and we all just decided to rotate each week. It should help keep us fresh and won't stick anybody with being inside all the time, like with the crafts."

"What will you be doing next week, Annie?"

"Oh, something we call the History Tour. It's going around the area looking at and talking about historical places. It will be my first time, should be a lot of fun for me, too," Annie ends as the two of them slowly slip into their evening.

*       *       *

Jeremy is in the side yard practicing his casting. He has been working on a new fly design and wants to check the action one more time before the light leaves the evening sky. If it needs a little adjustment, he wants to be able to work on it yet tonight. The weekend is nearing and he is planning a two day trip to one of his favorite spots in the mountains which is about two hundred miles to the northeast of Travers.

There is a pleasant lake that attracts many anglers to this location but Jeremy's sights are set on the beaver ponds that lie above, at the higher sources of the stream that feeds it. He has fished them before but without much luck. Jeremy just needs to come up with the right fly for the job and he thinks he knows what will work this time. 'I think this is it,' he thinks to himself as he whips the fly back and forth in the air. Jeremy likes the action that he is getting from his new design.

Jeremy is engrossed in his work and is slightly startled as a voice calls out from behind him. "So, are they biting tonight?" Turning around, Jeremy sees one of his neighbors standing near the fence to his yard.

"Well, would you believe me if I said that a big one just got away?" he answers.

"Of course I would, you're a fisherman, right?" the neighbor replies and then both men break into laughter at the comment. Putting down his rod, Jeremy moves closer to the gentleman standing there and recognizes Mr. Weston as the person doing the talking.

"Do you fish?" asks Jeremy.

"Used to, probably been years now since I've done it, though. They didn't have much to fear from me, usually just did it so I could get outdoors. I always liked lakes and rivers when I was growing up, Minnesota, you know."

"Oh, Minnesota, I've been planning a summer trip there for years. I don't ever seem to get any closer to doing it, though," says Jeremy about his lack of confidence in exposing himself to anything new or unfamiliar.

"You should, you'd like it."

"Yes, I am sure that I would. You know, I've never met you officially. My name is Jeremy Lucas," offers the normally shy man as he extends his hand for shaking.

"Nice to meet you, Jeremy. My name is Robert Weston," says the kindly older gentleman.

"Nice to meet you, too. So, is it Bob or Robert that you prefer to be called?"

"It's Wes, from Weston. I was a Bobby growing up which I didn't like as I got older and Robert always seemed too formal. Friends started calling me Wes when I was in middle school and it just seemed to stick."

"Alright, Wes," says Jeremy as they end the handshake.

"Well, I better be moving along. I usually take a walk just before dark, it kind of helps me sleep. Looks like it's going to be a beautiful night," he comments while looking up at the first few stars of the evening coming out.

"Yes, it does," agrees Jeremy, also looking at the sky.

"It was nice meeting you Jeremy. I'll probably see you again around the neighborhood."

"I'm sure that you will. It was nice meeting you. Take care and have a good night," says Jeremy.

"You, too," ends Wes as the two take leave of each other.

Jeremy now hurries to put his equipment away and get back into the house to begin making his dinner. It is past eight thirty and he usually has the dishes done by now. The casting and conversation has upset his normal routine and now jeopardizes the nine thirty bedtime. It has upset his routine but for some reason, it has not in the least upset Jeremy. For some reason, tonight, Jeremy doesn't even care.

*　　*　　*

Alex sees Katie getting out of Lisa's car in the front of their house. He rises to meet her at the door. "Hey, cutie, how was the History Tour today? Did you have fun?" he asks her with a true interest in his daughter's daily activities.

"Hi, Daddy, yes I did. We saw an old log cabin that somebody lived in over two hundred years ago. They didn't have lights or bathrooms or even any video shows. I don't think that I would have liked living back then."

"No, it's definitely easier now."

"Tomorrow is the last day and all of us are going to put on a play. My teacher told us that our parents can come if they want. We're going to practice in the morning and then the play is at two in the afternoon. Can you come, Daddy, will you come?" Katie lightly pleads, looking up at her father.

"Uh, I don't know," Alex begins, not having been given much notice to be absent from his job. "Maybe I can, if I can get away from work," he answers.

Katie smiles back at him. "Okay," she says. "Just try, Daddy, just try." And she skips away to place some things in her room before going next door to Emily's house.

Alex returns to the living room and his mind quickly scans tomorrow's work requirements at the site. He is trying to figure a way for him to leave work early. It would be difficult as Friday can be a push sometimes to wrap up the bigger projects before the weekend. It would be difficult but Alex has already made the decision that it was going to happen.

\*     \*     \*

Lunchtime has arrived and the workers are gathered in the yard taking their well-deserved break. Alex sits in the trailer with Scott working on some end of the week reports. Glancing at the clock, Scott asks, "I was going to run down the hill to Savano's and grab a sandwich. Do you want to come along?"

Alex looks up from his desk. "No, I think I'll just stay here and try to get these reports done."

"What's the hurry? You have to eat."

"Oh, Katie's got a play that she is doing at the summer camp this afternoon and I was going to try and make it. I don't know if I can pull it off, though," says the father whose is slightly torn between his commitments.

"What do you have left?" asks the good friend and also the assistant manager of the project.

"I'm finished with authorizing the time sheets and I'm almost done with all the progress reports. I'll only have the materials usage for the last few days to do and then next week's requisitions to put into the order system."

"I can do those for you. Williams is running the digging crew and Dave says everything is going great with the repaving. He already said that he wouldn't need me this afternoon."

"Yeah, you could?" says Alex, contemplating the possibility. 'That sure would be great,' he thinks to himself. "You know, I might take you up on that. I don't think I can finish in time and still make it to Katie's play."

"Not a problem," says Scott. "A dad's gotta do what a dad's gotta do," he says, truly respecting his friend for his unselfish devotion to both of his children. "Oh, and by the way, what kind of sandwich do you want?"

\*     \*     \*

One thirty soon arrives and Alex hurries from the trailer to his waiting peetee. The camp is located on the edge of town and about twenty minutes from the job site. He knows that he will be cutting it close. Entering the cruiseway, Alex sets the course on his onboard computer and sits back to enjoy the ride.

The cruiseways form the basis of the new transportation system, especially within the many larger metropolitan areas. Blanketing the landscape with concrete and asphalt and an ever increasing complexity of roadways had not been the answer. The main facilitator for making cities livable again had been a reduction of traffic. And with commerce now based on a more local level, people live closer to their employment. Frustrating and wasteful commutes became a thing of the past.

With the development of smaller short distance vehicles for these local trips, there had actually been a reduction in the number of roadways. Because the peetees were much more compact, four and six lane freeways were easily converted into roadways half the width on routes solely for the use of personal transports. This allowed for the removal of thousands of miles of concrete highways that have been ground up, recycled, and reused elsewhere. And it has provided much needed drainage opportunities for the previously over-paved urban areas.

The cruiseways are electronically controlled as to the speed and the location of each personal transport. Once entering the thoroughfares, a person inputs his destination and is assigned an exit number. Then moving to the outermost lane, a peetee engages the tracking device and is placed a safe distance between the others also traveling this route. When nearing one's exit, the system moves the individual peetee back into the entry and exit lane until disengaging from the system when ushered onto their exit. The operator then takes back control of the vehicle.

The system creates a constantly flowing situation by which gridlock, stop-and-go traffic, and accidents are a thing of the past. By limiting these roadways to only peetees and implanting the access device in only those size vehicles, commutes and trips around town are now a predictable, less time-consuming activity. With hands off operation and time for other activities while driving, it had simply become a cruise, the cruiseways.

Alex hears the beep-beep of the warning signal, indicating that his exit is approaching. He is familiar with the location of Katie's summer camp as it has been used by the city for several special events over the years. One of its wealthier residents had deeded this large, rambling stone house to the city in the gift exchange program now available at municipal and federal levels. Located in a wooded setting, the property is a perfect spot for the hosting of the summer youth camps.

And in this new world with its new way of thinking, excess consumption is no longer socially acceptable. Simply because one could afford to use more energy or to use more resources doesn't give one the right to have a larger footprint upon the planet. And because of this acceptance, personal residences have been reduced in scale. If a large property or a building could be converted to a public or educational or greenspace use, the owner may receive vouchers that allow for the exchange of other smaller properties also in the program. With local economies reemerging as the main force in business, these individuals may turn a single large holding into several smaller opportunities in another part of the country or just down the street.

The world had always been a rich place and it had never been a problem of enough resources, it had always been a problem with the distribution of those resources. Because we previously failed to solve our social problems, individuals had felt the need to protect themselves and their families by amassing ever greater personal wealth, by building barriers and buffers around themselves. In a more equitable world with basic human needs now being met, the necessity to fight for and defend one's piece of the pie has disappeared. And the idea of personal wealth is slowly being replaced by the more real acknowledgment that it is a public wealth coming from a shared and bountiful earth.

Moving through the city streets, Alex checks the time, less than ten minutes before the program starts. Reaching the camp, he searches quickly for a parking spot and rushes inside to find signs that point him to the back of the house for the event. Emerging onto a patio, he sees the stage set with rows of chairs in the foreground that are filled with parents and friends of the children. Alex quietly takes a seat at the back as he sees the kids in costumes walking about behind the stage.

The program begins and all are then treated to an interesting presentation of what the children had learned during the week. Several adults would comment later that they had also learned several new things about their area's history. Luckily, Katie had spotted Alex sitting in the audience early in the program and a big smile with a sneaky wave had greeted him. An equally secretive greeting had been returned by the father.

At the conclusion of the program, Colin Everett, one of the directors of the summer programs, comes onto the stage to thank the children for their performance and to introduce the docents, teachers, and aides who have contributed. One of the teachers looks familiar to Alex but he can't remember how or why he might know her. Saying that a reception area with snacks and drinks is set up inside the house, Mr. Everett invites all to partake before leaving. Katie quickly rushes out to meet Alex when he finishes speaking.

"Hi there, sweetie. I thought you were really good," the father says about her role in the play.

"Oh, thank you, Daddy, come on," Katie then says hurriedly. "There's a table inside with a whole bunch of different types of cookies on it. And I want you to meet my teacher, she's the best. Her name is Ms. Sullivan but everyone calls her Annie. She said it was okay for us to call her Annie," she adds with an explanation for the familiarity with her teacher.

'Annie,' thinks Alex to himself. 'That's it, that's her name.' Thinking back to a few months ago at the Dance with Scott and

Jennifer, he remembers the limeade episode. Katie leads her father by the hand into the reception area. Spotting Annie at the other side of the room, Katie continues pulling on Alex until they are standing in front of her.

"Hi, Katie," is the nice greeting to the child from Annie when seeing her there. "You did great, you didn't have one mistake in your whole speech. I guess you must be an old pro at this acting thing, huh?" she teases.

"No, I'm not. It was only my first time doing it," says Katie. "Miss Sullivan, this is my Dad," and Annie's gaze focuses on Alex for the first time. She is taken aback for a minute as she attempts to put a place with a face that she, too, recognizes. The remembrance doesn't come as easily for her so Annie shakes it off and simply greets him. Katie then quickly excuses herself to join Emily who is already enjoying the cookie table.

"Annie, isn't it?" says Alex.

"Yes, yes that's right. And it seems like I've met you before from somewhere else but I'm sorry, I don't remember the name," answers Annie.

"It's Alex and I didn't expect you to remember. We only met once before and I kind of had a cheat sheet. Katie just told me your first name again."

"Where was it?" asks the attractive woman.

"Does limeade strike any bells?"

"Oh, it was that night at the Dance when I was with my friend, Julia," as things now come into full focus for Annie. "You were that nice guy who let us have the limeade."

"Yeah, and then you told me about your grandmother liking tangerines so much," offers Alex with more information about that first meeting.

"Well, I must say, you have an equally nice daughter. Katie is just a sweetheart, one of my favorites. She and her friend Emily kind of ran the show this week. They were great energy to have around, you should be proud."

"I'm a lucky dad, that's for sure. Thanks for saying such nice things about her," says Alex.

The conversation lapses for a moment as the two struggle slightly with the strong and mutual physical attraction to one another. When seeing her face again, Alex had remembered that bright smile and honest countenance and it attracted him, made him feel as though Annie would be a nice person to know. And for Annie's part, she now thinks back on Julia's teasing after their first meeting. This man is thoughtful and caring and yes, she admits to herself now, good looking. Alex does truly seem to be one of those nice guys.

"Have you been doing this for a long time, teaching and working with the children?" asks Alex.

"No, only just this summer. I had been a tour guide for almost twenty years. I only recently took a leave of absence to stay with my grandmother," says Annie.

"That's nice of you. Does she live with you?"

"Yes, but her health is failing now and I didn't want to be away from home so much." Other children now come running up to Annie and also want her to meet their parents. Accommodating them, she looks over her shoulder at Alex and gives a wave as the kids pull her away. He blurts out a quick 'Nice to see you again' and then Annie blends back into the crowd.

Alex looks around and sees Katie, Emily, and Lisa sitting on chairs near the refreshment area, munching on their cookies. He joins them and soon they are ready to leave. "Can Emily ride home with us?" asks the young girl who is usually ushered around by other mothers. The father answers in the positive and Emily's mother gives her approval. The two young girls pick up their mementos from the week and then race each other to Alex's peetee for the ride home.

Saying good-bye to Lisa, Alex hesitates and glances around the patio. His eyes scan and search the sea of people, seeking one particular face. But Annie is not to be seen, she is in one of the rooms organizing and passing out the children's creations. Knowing that the girls are waiting, Alex quickly goes through the house on his way to the front door. Peeking into one or two rooms, he hesitates when reaching the front entrance and then turns around one more time, just in case.

Annie is very happy with all the smiling faces coming at the conclusion of the week and at the end of her first History Tour. She notices that Katie and Emily have already picked up their items. Asking another teacher to take over for a minute, Annie explains she has something that she needs to do. Leaving the room, she makes her way back to the patio where the crowd is thinning as parents and students begin to head home. Not seeing Katie or Alex there, Annie goes into the house and also looks into the rooms on her way to the front door. Walking into the sunlight, she glances at the remaining vehicles in the parking lot. 'Well, I guess they left already,' Annie thinks to herself. With a few new thoughts excitedly bouncing around inside her head, Annie returns to the classroom and to her regular life.

\*　　\*　　\*

Several weeks have passed and the end of summer is quickly approaching. The Parks Programs are almost over with regular school soon beginning again. Annie and Marty sit at the kitchen table on a Saturday morning drinking tea. The conversation is minimal and Annie is less animated, less high energy than usual, and the keen grandmother picks up on it.

"So, there's just one more week of summer camp left," says Marty. "What will you being doing next week, dear?"

"Oh, it's going to be an open week. Those who sign up can choose from any of the activities we did this summer except the History Tour. All of us will be helping out at the Stone House. Friday will be a half day and then we will work the afternoon putting things back into storage. I guess it was pretty successful. They're talking about funding it again next year."

"Well, I think it's just great that they provide activities for the kids in the summer. They need something to keep them busy and keep learning," says Marty. Annie doesn't acknowledge the statement, her expression is somewhat vacant and concerned. The grandmother allows a few more minutes to pass and then says, "Everything okay, Annie?"

Annie stops the thinking process for a moment and turns toward Marty. "I'm sorry, what did you say?"

Marty gives a slight laugh and a half smile appears on her face as she accepts Annie's absentmindedness. "What were you thinking, dear?" she then asks.

Coming back into the moment, Annie answers, "Nothing." Having always been a positive and directed person, this feeling of uncertainty is new to her. Annie doesn't quite recognize it, definitely doesn't understand it, but she now knows something about it. And she is beginning not to like it.

With her job coming to an end soon, Annie has mulled over different options for the last few weeks. Her steady employment with the tour company for those many years has allowed her to have reserves that don't require her to immediately find other employment. But as she nears the age of forty, direction and purpose don't seem to come as easily as she remembers when younger. Annie hasn't really lacked in life, no large holes have appeared, but the absence of a close personal relationship with a mate or a life partner is disappointing to her.

Marty has always worried that Annie's putting her life on hold to take care of her grandmother's needs could wind up having some other consequences. She is beginning to see the signs of just such an occurrence and besides feeling guilty, Marty wants more for her granddaughter. She wants more gifts for one who has given so much to others.

"Are you concerned about not having a job when the summer camps are over?" is the straightforward question now asked of Annie by her grandmother.

"Not about a job, I know we'll be okay financially. I just, oh, I don't know, nothing. I wasn't really thinking about anything," Annie ends as she stands to clear the dishes from the table. Marty's eyes follow her to the sink. Sensing that she needs to interact and spend more time with others, the wise grandmother makes a suggestion.

"Have you talked to Julia lately? I haven't seen her for a long time," says Marty.

"No, it's been a while for me, too."

"Why don't you call her up and see what she is doing today? It's a Saturday, maybe you girls could get together. You know, do something or just spend some time together."

"I don't know if I should. She and Mark are probably already doing something. I don't want to bother her," sums up Annie as a good enough reason not to make the effort.

"Oh, I don't think you'd be bothering her. Julia used to tell me all the time how she missed not having you here in Travers. You've been friends for a long time, friends rarely bother each other," is the logic used to get Annie to act.

"She said that she missed having me around?" asks Annie, somewhat incredulous that others could possibly miss her.

"Yes, all the time," answers Marty.

"Well, maybe," and Annie gets busy with the dishes.

\*　　\*　　\*

The morning moves along quickly and Annie has spent most of the day so far doing housework. Having a job during the week has meant most of the cleaning tasks are relegated to the weekend. But the small four room house doesn't require much time and when finished, Annie enters the kitchen to get a glass of water. Looking down, she sees the phone on the counter.

'Marty's right,' Annie thinks to herself. 'I do need to make a bigger effort to reconnect with friends.' To bring about the change that she wishes in her life, she realizes more action is needed. Annie reaches for the phone to take that step now.

After a few rings, Julia picks up on the other end. "Julia, it's Annie." And the two friends spend the next twenty minutes in conversation, talking about many different things. Asking her friend if she is busy today, Annie is told that Mark is out for the afternoon and that she has no plans. Deciding to get together for a late lunch, they pick a time and a place and soon meet.

\*　　\*　　\*

"I want to hear more about the summer camps. Mark said that everyone at the Parks Department was just thrilled with the turnout and response. I heard several times about this 'new girl' in town who was doing such a wonderful job," says Julia when they meet at the restaurant.

"New girl, huh?" says Annie. "I have lived here for years and I'm known as the new girl."

"Well, now you really live here. And I'm so glad you do," adds Julia, reaching over to lightly touch her good friend's hand.

The two will enjoy a pleasant lunch at a comfortable smaller restaurant in the downtown district. And with a bright blue day upon them, they decide to take the River Walk after finishing eating. Of course, the conversation will continue as two good friends, and as two women, can so easily do. Eventually, Annie asks what Julia's husband, Mark, is doing for the day.

"Oh, he has two good friends who are kayakers and that is something he's always wanted to try. Mark is going along with them today and he was like a kid last night, got all excited. I think he was awake past midnight researching and reading all he could about the sport."

"He's such a great guy, everyone at the Parks Department only had good things to say about him. How long have you been married now? It's over ten years, isn't it?"

"Thirteen, and we were together four years before that. It seems like he's always been there. I can't really remember when he wasn't," says Julia.

Annie stares down into the water as they pause near a large rock in the river. She is quiet and a few minutes pass as the two women enjoy the warmth of the sun streaming down on the spot where they stand. Annie slowly lifts her head and turns toward her close friend. "You're lucky, you know, very lucky," she says about the quality relationship with her husband. And then she smiles broadly in Julia's direction.

Nodding her head while still just gazing straight in front of her, Julia answers, "I know I am."

They soon return to Annie's vehicle. The afternoon has been a pleasant respite for the both of them but especially for Annie. She needed to get outside of herself for a while, has needed a diversion and an activity to quiet that recently very noisy mind.

When reaching Julia's house, Annie is refreshed and recharged and says, "We have to do this again soon, real soon."

Julia thanks her for the ride and then she agrees with the proposition. "Yeah, we will, for sure. I had been wanting to get together with you for the last week or two. But, you know, I didn't want to bother you."

Annie immediately breaks into a loud laugh that surprises Julia and she just laughs back with a slightly puzzled look on her face. "What?" she finally asks.

Annie continues her laughter while just saying, "I'll tell you next time, next time. I love you."

"Love you, too," says Julia.

Driving away, Annie thinks to herself, 'She didn't want to bother me,' and bursts into laughter again.

\*     \*     \*

With one more holiday remaining before the end of summer, many people are preparing for that special weekend and Jeremy is no exception. Not having to work on Monday, he plans on staying overnight on Sunday to get in two days of fishing this time. But his new flies aren't ready yet, so he will use Saturday to finish the task and to do the packing.

Saturday comes early for Jeremy and he finds himself in his fly tying studio before even getting dressed or having breakfast. He allows his routine to vary because he has become very engrossed in his new design, a good one for the beaver ponds he thinks. Jeremy wants to finish this morning so that he can use his side yard for a test run, in case adjustments need to be made. By eleven that morning, he is outside practicing his casts and pulling his fly through a large tub of water. Jeremy is pleased because the action is perfect.

"So, it looks like you might make your own flies?" comes the friendly comment from his neighbor, Wes, as he turns the key in his mailbox that sits near Jeremy's fenced yard.

"Oh, hey there, Wes," answers the rather animated Jeremy. "Yeah, I do. I have been working on this one for over a week now. I always liked the looks of it but only just this morning made the adjustments to get the right action."

"Those fish don't stand a chance," says Wes.

"You know what, I think you're probably right about that," and both men release a short laugh.

The older gentleman moves nearer to the fenced yard and Jeremy puts down his rod to go and visit with him. Some polite conversation ensues and then Wes asks him where he is headed. He has lived next door long enough to know that his neighbor is usually gone on the weekends.

"It's an area in the Pitkin Hills. Lake Channing is the main lake but I plan to fish the beaver ponds that are above it. I went there a year or two ago and have always wanted to go back, going to spend two days this time. If they see me coming the first day, I'll circle back and sneak up on them the next," says Jeremy, providing lots of information to Wes and being much more talkative than is normal for him.

"That sure sounds good to me. I don't think that I have been out of town for over a year."

"What do you have going for the weekend, anything special?" Jeremy asks of Wes' plans.

"No, I just heard there might be some fireworks down by the River Walk on Saturday night. I'll probably take that in. I'm not going to be doing much else, though," says his neighbor. "Well, enjoy your trip and let me know how you did when you get back." And Wes turns to go back to his apartment.

Jeremy thanks him and then remains standing by the fence. He is thinking of something, something that is out of character for him but something that has presented itself to him at this moment and without taking any more time to deliberate his decision, he quickly says, "Hey, Wes, wait a minute. I want to talk to you about something."

Stopping in his tracks, Wes turns around and heads back to the fence where Jeremy is standing. "Yeah, Jeremy, what is it?" he asks in a friendly manner.

"Well, I don't know if you would be interested or not, but I have plenty of room in my car for another passenger if you would like to come along. I mean, you're welcome to do what you want, but I wouldn't mind having the company on the drive. And it would be a chance for you to get out of town, like you said," comes the surprising offer from such a private man.

"Really, you would want an old guy like me tagging along? Wouldn't it mess up your fishing?"

"No, it wouldn't at all, not at all. The cabins at the lake have great porches for just sitting and relaxing. There are a few short nature trails nearby, too. It's really a beautiful setting but not that many people know about it. I called earlier in the week to make a reservation and they said I didn't need to, only half were booked. I think you'd like the place," says Jeremy. "I'm sure you could find some things to do during the first part of the day. I usually knock off by two in the afternoon anyway. I might just fish the lake a little in the evening."

"Oh, I don't have any trouble passing the time. I've had lots of practice these last few years, you know. I'm about half way through a book, might be able to polish it off over the weekend. You know, I'd like that, if you have room, if it's no trouble," says Wes, allowing Jeremy a last out if needed.

"It's done," Jeremy shoots back. "You're coming and we leave tomorrow morning at five sharp, sound okay?"

"Sounds great. But you have to let me share in the expenses, let me pay for half the room if you're going to do all this for me," Wes volunteers.

"With you paying for half the room, I think things are already working out in my favor," returns Jeremy. And then the two men talk a bit more about their plans. Wes' mood is elevated, the change of scenery that the trip promises will get him out of his tiny one bedroom apartment and back into the bigger world. Jeremy is excited, having someone to go with for the first time on one of his fishing sorties. And Jeremy feels good about himself for asking Wes and for taking that first big step.

\*　　\*　　\*

It is four forty five and Jeremy is not sure if Wes has gotten up yet. When a light shines from the kitchen window when looking next door, he reasons that his friend must already be awake. He goes over and knocks quietly on his neighbor's door. The door opens quickly and Jeremy is welcomed into the room.

"So, you look like you're ready to go. You must have some of those fishing genes in you to get up so early," says Jeremy.

"Mostly old man genes, comes with the territory, you know. And I don't think I know any man my age that can sleep past six anyway, unless they're a drunk," says Wes.

Jeremy laughs at the comment. "Well, I'll run back to my place and finish loading the car. So, just come over whenever you're ready."

"Be there in five. I made us some sandwiches, so I just need to clean up the kitchen and I'll be right over," ends the kindly older gentleman.

\* \* \*

Jeremy and Wes have now been driving for almost two hours. Following the Central Valley route, they have headed north and are beginning to gain elevation as the road turns east, moving into the foothills. The day is clear but some clouds are gathering and the discussion turns to the possibility of rain.

"Those look like they have a little moisture in them," says Wes as they change direction and the clouds come into view directly in front of them.

"I think you're right. Usually, it's later in the afternoon when it starts, though," says Jeremy.

"Does it affect your fishing?"

"Actually, a light rain can help sometimes. It kind of makes the surface of the water opaque for the fish below and the low light causes them to start feeding. A hard rain isn't any good, though," states Jeremy with his considerable fishing knowledge. "A few sprinkles on those beaver ponds might be a good idea, maybe keep those fish from seeing me coming."

Another hour passes before the two new friends turn into the parking area for the Channing Lodge. It is a picturesque wooden structure, modest in size, with about ten cabins encircling it. The cabins serve as the sleeping quarters with meals and social activities taking place at the lodge. The two men approach the office as Jeremy stares out wistfully at the lake.

"I tell you what," jumps in Wes. "Let me check us in. I can do the unpacking, too. Why don't you just go get your fishing gear and get started?"

Jeremy looks over at Wes. "Really, are you sure?"

"Yeah, I'm sure. Is there anything special that I need to know about the rooms?"

"No, the cabins are pretty much the same as I remember. They all have two beds in them, I think."

"Well, get going and see what you can come up with then. But I don't want to just hear stories at the end of the day. Maybe you can bring us back a couple if you get lucky."

"Great idea, they'll cook them for us at the lodge," and Jeremy returns to the vehicle to get his gear.

Soon, Wes returns from the office and Jeremy passes off the keys to the car. Wes digs into his pack and pulls out a sandwich to hand over to Jeremy. "Here, take this with you. I don't expect this to be our dinner, too, though."

"It won't be. One fish dinner coming up," and with a few more words about timing and plans for the rest of the day, the two take leave of each other. With Jeremy almost running to the trail head that will take him to the ponds, Wes is glad that he offered to set up camp for the both of them.

*　　*　　*

Early afternoon arrives and only a few sprinkles have come from the darkened skies but the deep rumbling in the distance portends more on the way. Wes glances down at his watch, it is approaching two in the afternoon. Sitting on the front porch of their little cabin with book in hand, he hopes that his friend makes it before the main rains begin. Shortly, Jeremy is spotted coming across the broad meadow that is near the lake.

Putting down his book, Wes rises to meet him halfway. "So, how'd it go?" he asks when reaching him.

Without saying anything, Jeremy lifts the lid of his creel to reveal the marbled colors of two quite nice looking brookies. "Dinner, anyone?" he says.

"Alright, those are beautiful!" gasps Wes and gives his new buddy a high five. They soon make their way back to the cabin with Jeremy then running the fish over to the cook at the lodge. Coming back, Jeremy washes up quickly and joins Wes sitting comfortably on the front porch.

"So, how's it's been going? Have you been finding things to do?" asks the returned fisherman.

"Oh, yeah, it's been very nice. I've knocked fifty pages off my book and have been conversing with one of the jays that keeps coming around. He wants me to feed him, I think," says Wes. "Don't quite have a view like this out my front door, you know," spreading out his hand at the beauty and peacefulness of the quiet lake scene in front of them.

"It's really pretty, isn't it? I've been trying to get back up here for two years now, glad that I finally did it."

"Glad that you brought me, I appreciate it."

Jeremy had been right with his assumption that Wes seems a nice person and was someone worth knowing and he answers honestly by saying, "I'm glad that you could come."

The two men exchange warm smiles.

\*   \*   \*

"Are you ready?" asks Jeremy.

"Let me just change my shirt," answers Wes and then they make their way to the lodge for dinner. There are four or five tables of other diners as they enter the restaurant. When they sit down, the cook spots them and comes over to their table.

"Well, hello, Mister Lucas," he says to Jeremy. "I have your fish cleaned and everything is ready to go. Is there any certain way you would like it prepared tonight?"

"No, the chef special will be just fine." And the three of them exchange a laugh.

"And it will be, special. I don't see many brookies like this coming out of here much. What part of the lake did they come from?" asks the cook.

Jeremy smiles broadly and stays silent.

"Oh, I get it," and the likeable chef returns to his kitchen.

"Weren't telling, huh?" chuckles Wes.

"For me to know and for everyone else to find out," answers Jeremy. And they settle into a wonderful meal with courteous and attentive service in this warm, comfortable setting. Things are working out and both men appreciate the change of scenery and the respite that the trip is providing. With dinner complete, the two men retire to the sitting area of the lodge where card tables and reading material are provided. A few other diners are also relaxing there.

Wes strikes up a conversation with one of the gentlemen as Jeremy looks over the reading selections. In the next moment, Wes can be heard saying, "I don't know, I'll ask him." And then calling out to Jeremy, he says, "You don't happen to be a bridge player, are you?"

Turning around and surveying the scene, Jeremy answers, "Yes, I am. Why?" Wes says that the gentleman and his wife have been asking everyone and when finding out that Wes plays, only needed that most important fourth. "It's been a while but I could be easily talked into it."

Smiles come back from both Wes and the gentleman as he then runs back to the room to get his wife.

"So, you're willing to take them on?" asks Wes when the other man is gone.

"Yeah, and we're going to beat them, too," as Jeremy throws in a uncharacteristically strong statement for him.

"You're that type of player, huh?" says Wes while laughing. "I'm sure glad that you're going to be on my side."

Soon, the man returns and the four of them will play three rubbers. And, yes, the team of Weston and Lucas will win two of them, but all done gracefully with friendly competition and lots of laughter. The man's wife has Minnesota roots and she and Wes reminisce in-between bids. All in all, a pleasant, enjoyable, and late evening for the two new friends. Making their way back to the cabin, they sit for a moment on the front porch before retiring for the night.

"Where did you learn to play bridge? You must have spent some time doing it, we cleaned up," Wes asks Jeremy.

"In college. A few of us probably used up two full semesters on it. It was kind of like having a second major."

"And what was the first?"

"Accounting, business, not very exciting stuff," answers the mostly shy and reserved man. "And how about you, where did you learn to play?"

"From my wife. She loved playing, you know, the social side of it. Our house became the main venue for the local bridge club. It was either learn or hide in the basement," answers the easy going and amiable older man.

"You were married?"

"Oh, yes, for thirty seven years. Madeline was her name, I called her Maddy. She was a great gal and a good friend."

Jeremy is quiet, reluctant to ask the next question but in a few moments says, "And she's no longer with you?" The younger man looks over at Wes, waiting for his response.

"She passed four years ago. Some health problems put her in the hospital and then she contracted pneumonia. It took her a week later, just like that she was gone," Wes ends sadly but not with unpleasantness at the thought. He only concentrates on the good times when returning to memory lane these days.

"I'm sorry to hear that," says an empathetic Jeremy.

"Thank you, Jeremy. But what about you, I don't even know what kind of job you do," asks Wes.

"I work for an insurance company. I've been doing the same job ever since college. Like I said, not very exciting stuff," adds a less than confident Jeremy.

"Well, people need those products. You're probably helping them out, you should feel good about that," offers Wes as a validation for his employment.

Jeremy is just sitting quietly, without responding to Wes' last remark. He is concentrating deeply and Wes feels now is not the time to interrupt with more idle talk. Wes moves to get up from his chair and starts to say that it's probably time to turn in when Jeremy starts speaking again while just staring directly ahead into the darkness of the evening.

"So, did you ever feel disappointed with things, Wes, you know, like disappointed with your life when you were younger?" asks Jeremy, but still not looking in his direction.

Wes then sits back down and pauses, giving his answer some thought before continuing. He senses Jeremy's doubt and self-questioning. He is familiar with it and knows the longing and uneasiness that such a thought can perpetuate on one's self. Wes knows the damage that such thinking can do, so he begins slowly. "We all can get disappointed, Jeremy. It's not always our fault, circumstances can have a lot to do with it."

"But what happens when you get older and as your life path stretches in front of you, it seems like a path with no alternate routes, that you are stuck with no chance to change direction. Do you just give up and accept it, learn to live with it, learn to live with less?" The introspective, now more serious companion then looks over toward Wes, seeking the experience and wisdom of the older man.

"Making a living and making a life are two different things," says Wes. "When young, we all dream of doing great things, of accomplishing all our goals. But most of us don't become the scientist that cures cancer or the leader of a nation or the writer that writes the bestseller. It's okay to want those things, it's just tough reaching them. When we don't, we can be disappointed or we can make another life.

"Believe it or not, forty years ago I was headed to the Major Leagues in baseball. I'd worked my way up through the Minors, traveling from city to city, not earning much money but thinking that I was getting closer to getting my chance. I had given up college for baseball, left my friends and hometown for baseball, and had lived a solitary life without a lot of personal connections for baseball.  At twenty two, I was called into the farm club's office one day, fully expecting to be the next second baseman for the main club when I was told that my services were no longer needed and I was let go.

"Without an advanced education or any job training, I didn't know what to do.  But I entered an apprentice program in the trades, became a tile and stone mason, and spent the next thirty years as a skilled laborer.  It wasn't what I would have chosen maybe, but I earned a decent living.  And while in the program, I became good friends with one of the guys also going through it, and he had this sister.  Well, you can guess the rest.

"Now, life dealt me a blow, at least to my aspirations and my dreams.  But it handed me another gift at the same time, my dear dear Maddy.  And I know that if someone had asked me to make a choice between having been a Major League second baseman or a husband to her at anytime in the last forty years, well, you know, it wouldn't have even been close.

"We can push, we work hard, we dream, and yes, sometimes we can be disappointed.  But at my ripe old age, Jeremy, I think that if someone is just a good person and treats others fairly and honestly that they are a success, that they have made a contribution.  It's not what we do, it's who we are.  And in that department, I'd say you've pretty much reached the top, you truly seem to me to be one of those good people."

Jeremy glances over at Wes and smiles.  He's been needing to say what he did for years but no one had ever been there to hear it.  Just getting it out has been cathartic, listening to Wes' story has been enlightening.  And Jeremy is glad that he brought it up. Jeremy is glad that he has finally made a friend.

\*     \*     \*

It is now October and the crispness of the autumn air and the clarity of the seasonal sky fall on the countryside as Annie makes her way toward Donovan's orchard.  The past six weeks have passed quietly and quickly. With the end of the summer programs, Annie has simply stayed at home with Marty, doing some gardening, pruning their fruit trees, and sharing laughter around the game boards. She and Julia see each other often now and exchange phone calls almost daily.

Just recently, Annie has begun searching the job market as she knows the time is approaching for employment again, to obtain that income to balance the 'outgo' but also to put some direction and goals back into her life. Except for that letdown after her summer job ended, Annie's spirits have remained high and she looks forward to creating a new life in her hometown. Julia has been an immense help in this area with her support and friendship as the new girl is rapidly becoming a strong thread in that community fabric, fitting in and feeling comfortable.

The orchard is located a short distance from town on rolling hills and is comprised of about eighteen acres. The Donovans have owned them for over thirty years, having previously been in Marianne's family. Mr. Donovan had worked as an engineer with the city before retiring two years ago. While employed, he would still work in the orchard on the weekends, driving the tractor or helping with the pruning, and now devotes full time to the enterprise. Before Harry's retirement, Marianne had both helped in the cultivation and in running the retail outlet on the property but now basically just does the selling. But the hours are still long, early on the land in the morning and working the stand late into the afternoon.

Annie parks her peetee and reaches in the back for a shopping bag. Hers is the only vehicle in the lot and as she approaches the stand, she doesn't see Marianne or anyone manning the tables. Annie begins looking over the bins of just picked apples, pears, and other fruits. Soon, Marianne reemerges from the equipment shed and gives her a greeting.

"Oh, hi, Annie" she says. "So what do you think? We're going to try the self-service method. It's where you make your selection and then just pay whatever amount you think is reasonable and leave it on the table. Do you think it'll work?"

"I don't know, maybe," says Annie with a laugh.

"Well, I'm about ready to try it. Harry is always kidding me. He says that if I'm going to chain myself to these tables, I ought to get a longer chain," jokes the older and hard working woman. "It's great to see you, Annie," she then says.

"And it's great to see you, too, Marianne. Are these that new variety of pear already? And I didn't know you were doing nuts, these pecans look delicious."

"We're now trading product with a grower down south on a regular basis," explains Marianne. "We just started selling his pears recently and are now stocking his nuts, too. We send him our extra apples and other fruits. It allows both of us to move the produce when it's the freshest and keeps the spoilage to a minimum. Another grower has already approached us about doing the same thing. It's probably what we should be doing. And it has freed us up to just grow and not have to worry so much about the sales part of it."

"Sounds like a good idea," agrees Annie.

"Yes, it probably is," answers Marianne. "We're just not sure how far we want to take it. Harry's always complaining that he didn't retire so that he could just work harder. And I understand, we let one of the tractor operators go when he quit working for the city. He used to like driving the tractor back then but now it's just become something that has to get done. We're talking about hiring a new operator but aren't sure about taking on the extra overhead. And I'm not getting any younger. We've actually talked about selling once or twice but it's kind of hard to let go of the land, you know?

"But that's enough about us, how are you doing? I was talking to one of my customers a while back and your name came up as a teacher or counselor or something?" questions the affable orchard owner. And Annie will spend a minute informing Mrs. Donovan about the summer job that she had held.

Purchases are made and after more conversation between the women, Annie picks up her bags bulging with fruit. Marianne walks her to the car and with a kiss on the cheek from each, Annie prepares to leave. Pausing for a moment with the door open and thinking deeply on something, she then says, "You know, if you and Harry ever do want to sell or just need some help around here, would you let me know?"

With a surprised look on her face for a moment because of the unexpected comment, Marianne then replies, "Well, sure, dear, we would. We would definitely think of you."

"Thanks," says Annie.

\*　　\*　　\*

Both of Alex's children are back in school. It is Aaron's senior year and his enthusiasm is contagious. There is something about that final year of high school that is stimulating and exciting with all those possibilities and opportunities on a closer horizon. It is a time to give flight to your dreams and to reach for your aspirations. It can be that one time in life that is completely open and where the next step can have a profound effect on the rest of your journey. The world is wide and welcoming to its new stewards and the choices are many for these new citizens.

Innovative programs have been implemented over the past three decades that have led to better trained, better qualified, and better prepared individuals to go out into the world. Besides traditional college and university training, the trades have taken their rightful place in the hierarchy of education. For too many years, those with money had run and ruined the world in the name of progress and of growth and had felt entitled to self-enrichment at the expense of others. But now, those with the skills who actually did the building and created that wealth are on an equal footing with their capital counterparts.

Consequently, Aaron has several options available to him. With the government's successful two year service guarantee toward funding for higher education in place for many years now, a high school graduate can take two years to work on community outreach or international work service and then later pursue his or her education at a trade school or in a college setting. Conversely, you can attend school and receive financial aid, and then use those skills working in selected areas or locations throughout the world that need attention and pay back that aid. It is not so much an idea that allows young people to afford higher education, those costs have come down substantially over the years, it has become a way to involve them in the planning and direction of our new world. A world in which giving back is equal to receiving, a world in which your personal value is measured by your contribution to the social value.

Aaron is unsure at this stage of his plans after high school. Because music is an important and a growing part of his life, his first wish is to continue in that direction. And with public arts programs throughout the schools and communities, the ability to work in the field while studying or performing is a real possibility. But architecture is also another interest for him, having taken and enjoyed drafting classes while in high school. Aaron is unsure for now but who isn't at eighteen.

Katie is in the fourth grade. An energetic and bright student, she tackles all tasks and all responsibilities with full vigor. Katie is one of those doers and usually doesn't stop until everything is finished and in its right place. Young girls still remain quite different from young boys in this category. Requirements aren't chores to them, they are things to be accomplished and are things to be completed. And Alex feels fortunate that Katie's homework doesn't become his problem at the end of the work day.

Another new activity for the young girl has been participation in the after school soccer program. With Emily deciding to sign up, it was always, of course, a foregone conclusion that Katie would also join. Both of them are immensely enjoying the sport and the accompanying great exercise. A new soccer ball has been purchased for practice whenever a brother or a tired father can be talked into joining her in the back yard.

And Alex's life has settled into a comfortable and workable arrangement. With Erica almost becoming part of the family, things are mostly routine for the four of them. Both children greatly like this older woman who has come into their lives. Katie always has someone to go to for conversation or companionship and Aaron feels comfortable asking Erica to mend a shirt or make a dish for a club potluck. The household runs smoothly, efficiently, and Alex is greatly appreciative of the situation.

With six months having passed since Laura's leaving, Alex has been able to see things more clearly and to better understand them. His marriage had never developed into that partnership, had never contained that sharing or giving of one another that can lift people above their short term problems. With very little communication over the last several years between husband and wife, they had just continued to 'go on' as Laura had said on a few occasions. They had never really gotten to know one another as odd as that sounds after living together for so many years. When Laura had faced the problem and made her decision, it had forced Alex to make his, or at least, accept hers. Without a strong foundation to the marriage, the walls were always going to collapse. It had never been a question of if, it had always been that disheartening question of when.

For Alex, the idea of living outside the home of his children was the worst possible consequence of a divorce. Not being there to share in their lives as they were growing up was unacceptable to him. And it had kept him in the marriage, although being a disappointment to him as it was to his wife. But with the passing of time, Alex has finally begun to look forward to that next stage of his life, to the new possibilities that may lie ahead for him. The divorce settlement is only days away from being final but it won't be a celebration, it will just be a release.

\*　　\*　　\*

Annie and Marty are busy at the sink, washing some of the fruit from their backyard that had been picked earlier in the morning. Soon, the phone is heard ringing and the grandmother hurries to pick up the receiver. "Oh, hi, I'm doing just fine. And you?" Marty asks of the person who had called. "No, it's not a problem at all. Let me get her for you." Annie gives her grandmother an inquisitive look. "It's Marianne Donovan," she whispers, passing the phone over to her.

"Hi, Marianne," says Annie and then remains silent for a few minutes as she listens to the conversation from the other end.

"Tomorrow would be fine, what time?" she asks. "I'll be there, thanks for the call."

Putting the receiver down, she turns toward Marty who asks, "What did she want, dear? Did you leave something at their place the other day?"

Somewhat incredulous about what she has just heard, Annie just shakes her head. "No, it's not anything like that. Marianne and Harry want me to come work for them and then they want me to take over the orchard and to buy the business from them. She said they've been talking about it nonstop for the last two days and have come up with a plan that they want to discuss. They asked me to stop by tomorrow morning at ten," she ends with a fistful of information for her grandmother.

"They want you to work at the orchard?" asks Marty. "How did they decide to call you about it?" And Annie takes a minute to tell Marty about her discussion with Mrs. Donovan from the other day. Adjourning to the patio, the two women take their tea outside and continue the conversation.

"I don't know," Annie answers when asked by Marty about where she got the idea of buying the orchard. "When Marianne mentioned that they might sell it the other day, the idea just popped into my head. I haven't really thought about it since. I guess I'll just go out tomorrow morning and see what they say," she says.

"Is that something you would want to do, what about your guide job?" asks Marty.

"I don't think that I want to go back to that," states Annie with certainty. "I'm just now kind of settling in, you know, with friends and everything. I don't really want to tear out the roots again next year if I were to go back. I think I'm done with that nomad part of my life. It was fun, I enjoyed it, but I don't really need it anymore. Waking up in the same bed, in the same town, with the same people in my life kind of seems more important to me now," she says.

Marty sits quietly and thoughtfully while looking over at her granddaughter. Annie is a strong woman, a resourceful woman, and Marty knows that she wouldn't do anything that was flippant or capricious. A weight lifts from Marty after all these years as she realizes the next decisions that Annie makes will also take her own life into account, not just her grandmother's. Speaking in a soft voice, Marty then says, "You know what, that orchard might just be a good thing."

Annie takes a few slow sips of tea. "You think so, huh?" she says and then adds, "Me too, Marty, me too."

\*    \*    \*

It is the next morning. Drying her hands, Annie then places the dish towel back in its place. Breakfast is over, the kitchen is cleaned, and she hurries outside to check on Marty.

"You doing okay, need anything before I leave?" she asks. Assurances come back that everything is fine. "Well, I guess I'll take off then," Annie says somewhat hesitantly, with that 'I don't know what to expect next' look on her face.

"I can't wait until you get back and fill me in," shoots back Marty with positive energy and expectations.

"Well, here goes," and Annie gives her grandmother that light peck on the cheek before going out the door.

\*    \*    \*

On the way to the appointment, more serious thoughts and some doubts creep into her thinking. Annie wonders if she truly would be able to afford such a business. She hadn't really given any thought to the financial aspects of such a venture. 'Who am I kidding?' she starts to think. 'I can't afford to buy eighteen acres of land and a business.' Annie has considerable savings from participating in the Eighteen Percent Tax Rate Savings Program and could tap the Entrepreneurial Fund that the government offers but wonders if even that would be enough. Giving up on these thoughts for the moment, she simply decides to wait until talking with the Donovans before stressing about the situation.

The Entrepreneurial Fund is connected to the Public Savings System where a pool of money is made available to citizens for small business development. With the new emphasis on local commerce, a need had arisen for start up funding for all types of businesses and services. And it had been decided that the wealth of the nation should support and promote the wealth of the individual. For those who complete a business plan and make the case for the need of a certain service or product or company, low cost loans are made available from public money. A citizen has access to this fund three times over the period of their life with increasing amounts available at the completion of timely and full repayment of any previous loan.

Pulling into the parking area, Annie is quickly spotted by a smiling Mr. Donovan. "Hi Annie, welcome," comes the friendly greeting from Harry who had never been around at the time of her previous visits. "It's really good to see you. It's been a long time." Annie is everyone's favorite, as the true goodness of an individual is now treated as your most important attribute. Giving of yourself and contributing is recognized and valued these days, more than status, more than the things that you own or the power that you may possess.

Harry hurries off to find Ben, who helps out part time with the tractor and pruning work. He has been called in today so that the three of them are undisturbed while discussing the matter. When they return, they move into the small structure nearby that serves as an office, bathroom, and break room for the orchard. It also gives Marianne a place to escape for that quick lunch or to make a cup of tea to get through the long afternoon.

Offering Annie a place to sit first, the older couple pull up two more chairs to join her. "Well, Marianne tells me that you plan to stay around Travers, that you aren't doing the tour guide job anymore," starts Harry. "And that you might be looking for something else to do."

"Yes," says Annie. "I need to be here for Marty, you know, but I'm also looking for a change, a new challenge maybe."

Mr. Donovan gets to the point and explains the plan that they have come up with, the gestation of the ideas that the couple had been bouncing around for the past few days. The basic premise is this: they want Annie to come in and relieve Marianne from having to work the selling bins and tables. Annie would also be trained on the tractor operation, the soil monitoring, and the pruning work. Harry would stay on two days a week for now and Ben would move to full time. She would be able to draw a base salary each month and participate in the profits. Within one year, they would execute a buy agreement in which Annie becomes the sole owner of the business at an agreed upon price while the Donovans would retain ownership of the land and lease it back to Annie. This way they don't need to sell or lose the land, can earn income later from the leasing, and can move comfortably into their well-earned retirement years. Basically, it appears to be a win-win situation for everyone.

Annie is surprised by the generosity of their offer and almost immediately accepts. "I don't know how to thank you. It sounds great, just great!" she says excitedly.

"Well, you'll be helping us out of what was starting to be a problem. We're getting tired of all the work and quite honestly, the fun has gone out of it. We've already felt better over the last few days just thinking that we might have an escape plan. Haven't we, Marianne?" says Mr. Donovan.

"And we couldn't think of a better qualified person to do it. Harry and I have always worried that you and Marty might just buy that land out back and start your own orchard. Just trying to buy out the competition ahead of time," jokes Marianne. "No, all kidding aside. Both of you already know a lot about the trees and about caring for them. And you have the passion, you have the passion. That's what it takes sometimes to tend the land," she adds as further proof they have picked the right person.

On the drive home, Annie's spirits and energy are soaring. She would have to discuss the financial aspects with one of her father's friends who is familiar with business matters but the price quoted had sounded reasonable enough. Not having to buy the land has made that easier and if everything went right, she could be the owner of Easthills Orchard in a year. 'Imagine that,' she thinks to herself. 'Annie Sullivan, a business owner.' Annie decides that has a nice sound to it as she arrives home.

"I'm back," she shouts out when coming in the front door. "Where are you, Marty, where are you?" Annie continues with unbridled enthusiasm and rushes into her room before receiving an answer. "Oh, there you are. You won't believe it, you just won't believe it!" she begins and then relays the whole story of her meeting with the Donovans to her grandmother. Annie's excitement is contagious and both begin to brainstorm on the possibilities and opportunities that it may present.

"And I could help in the mornings. I could work the tables while you get some training on the equipment. It's about time that I made myself useful around here," says Marty.

Annie agrees that could work out and the women exchange animated conversation throughout the rest of the morning, coming up with idea after idea on marketing and promotion. They dream of days to come and of dreams that may come true. Purpose and direction are necessary in all lives and these two women are now starting down a new path, together.

*　　*　　*

A few weeks have passed and Annie is immersed in her work. Wanting to learn as much as she can, she has taken every chance to question Ben and Harry about each facet of the job. Annie's upbeat, positive attitude and energy have spilled over to the others. Mr. Donovan has even thrown in an extra day or two on occasion. Marianne stops by often and brings some baked item for all the workers to enjoy during their morning break.

Marty comes to the job each day with her. After setup, Annie will disappear into the orchard as the grandmother takes over the tables. With a simple cashbox, the task is easy with most customers bagging and weighing their own items. Marty only has to be the personable salesperson that she is, with a pleasant greeting to all that arrive. The crafty grandmother has come up with the idea of offering samples for soon to spoil items. It has worked well with Marty regularly pushing product out the door faster than anyone.

Before lunch, Annie takes over and Marty can retire to her comfortable chair nearby in a favorite spot under the fruit trees. From there, she has the wide green vista to gaze upon and her thoughts can drift lazily and easily into the afternoon. By two or three, though, Annie has one of the men watch the stand so that she can take Marty home to rest. Things are running smoothly, the system is working.

\*     \*     \*

"So, kiddo, how was school today?" asks Alex as Katie returns from next door after playing with her best friend.

"Hi Daddy, good, really good. I like my teacher a lot this year and I really like my Three Step teacher even more. Today was our first day for that class. It's really cool, all of the fourth grade classes meet in the assembly room and after Mr. Kenyon talked to us, we watched a movie, and then we got to pick from three different activities. Emily and I picked the sack race. They said every other Friday afternoon from now on, we get to do that. It's way more fun than school," gushes the young girl.

The Three Step Program has been in the school systems for years. With the mission of creating healthier, better informed individuals who can then avoid the many pitfalls of maturation, programs within the local educational system on nutrition and exercise, sexual education and hygiene, and personal finance and entrepreneurship have grown exponentially after hugely successful initial courses had appeared almost thirty years earlier. As a result, out of shape and overweight and low energy students are now a thing of the past. And no longer are children raising children as families and love and life are now planned and consequently welcomed. And no longer did we allow others to rob our young adults of their financial security later in life by enticing them and cheating them and enslaving them in the previously institutionalized schemes of debt entrapment. And we had finally been able to turn down the volume on the ad machine, to eliminate the confusing of wants with needs, and had provided other avenues of fulfillment for the satisfaction and enjoyment of our young people.

Therefore, nutrition with an emphasis on exercise is being taught to children while in elementary school, early in life so those better decisions can provide a lifetime of health benefits. Explanations on the physiology of the human body, sexual reproduction and health, and personal hygiene are taught at the middle school level. And each student graduating from high school must have taken a personal finance and business basics course with an emphasis on entrepreneurship. The 'three steps' that will start our young people down their long journey of life now promises a better beginning.

"The film talked about proteins, fats, and car...car," Katie continues. The word carbohydrates is supplied by Alex. "I didn't know food had all that stuff in it."

Alex laughs to himself. "Yes, all that's in food. You're going to learn a lot," he says smiling and gives his daughter a hug. "And it sounds like you're going to have fun doing it."

"Oh, yes," the little girl answers quickly. "And the next time, Emily and I are going to do the obstacle course. Daddy," Katie then says, "Erica said if I wanted to do some baking with her on Sunday, at her house, that I could help her. She makes such good pies and I really like doing it."

"Well, sure, honey, you could do that with her. What do we need to get for it?" asks Alex.

"She said to just bring the fruit. I want to get apples, apple pie is the best there is," says Katie.

"I'll pick up some tomorrow." And the deal is struck between father and daughter.

\*     \*     \*

Alex has been working in the yard all day. Certain annuals have run their course and now need to be pulled out. Raking the debris into a pile, he then retrieves the yard waste container from beside the garage. Checking the time, he realizes that the afternoon is slipping away. He quickly cleans the area and puts back the tools. Hurrying inside, Alex heads to the shower.

Getting Katie's apples are next on the list of the day's chores. Remembering that the Donovans seem to consistently have the best in the area, he now drives to their Easthills Orchard on this beautifully bright blue afternoon. A parking lot full of vehicles greets him as he arrives. Many are gathered around the tables, squeezing and smelling the fruit offered for sale. Alex joins the shoppers. As he stares down at the bins holding the different varieties of red and green apples, the father realizes that he has no idea what kind of apple makes a good pie. After standing idly for a few minutes, Alex then asks the woman standing next to him about her recommendations.

"You know, I'm not sure either. I never was much of a baker. You can ask the lady that works here, though. I think that's her over there," says the woman, pointing in Annie's direction.

It is a Saturday and the stand is busy as usual but even more so today. The wonderful fall weather probably has something to do with it as people enjoy driving out into the country on such a day. Alex notices that Annie is very busy ringing up sales and waits until a break occurs to approach her.

Annie's head is lowered as she quickly organizes and sorts an overflowing cashbox. She doesn't notice Alex approaching and he now stands in front of her. "Looks to me like business is pretty good," he says.

Annie looks up and easily recognizes the face this time and answers pleasantly, "Oh, hi," and then gives a slight laugh. "Yes, we're really busy. How have you been, how's Katie?"

"She's doing really good and everything's been going just fine with her. But how about you, how are you doing? This looks like something new, isn't it?"

"Only been doing it a couple of months now."

"So, you work for the Donovans?" asks Alex who also knows the long time, well-known local residents.

"Well, yes, kind of. I'm going to be buying the business from them over the next year."

"Ah, that's great, congratulations," comes the sincere, warm response from Alex. He then explains his reason for coming, the apples needed for Katie's pie. Annie will make her suggestion of the Jonathans or the Winesaps, with a stronger recommendation for the firmer Jonathan before being pulled away to attend to another customer. Alex makes his way back to the tables and bags a few pounds of the smaller red variety. He waits until Annie is free to take them to the register for payment.

Having to hurry as the parking lot empties only to fill up again quickly, Annie apologizes to him for not having more time for conversation. She then asks Alex for the time with almost three being his answer. With a concerned look, Annie quickly glances toward the orchard and then back to the crowd of waiting customers in front of her.

"Something wrong?" asks Alex.

"Oh, my grandmother is here. This is usually the time I take her home." During the week, one of the men will watch the tables so that Annie can take Marty back to the house. She begins to tire at this time of day and even though it's only a short distance, Annie is not quite sure how she is going to pull it off today. The stand is busier than usual and the customers just keep coming.

"I can take her home," offers Alex.

Annie stops in her tracks, surprised for a moment at this easy solution to her problem. "Well, I think that it would probably be fine with her. But are you sure that it's not inconvenient for you?" she asks. His kind face and pleasant smile assure her that it isn't. "Well, let me go see what she wants to do," and Annie looks down at the cashbox sitting on the table.

"I'll watch it." And Alex steps behind to fill in.

Marty is sitting in her special chair and in her special place in the orchard. Annie reaches where she rests and discusses the situation with her. She is happy to accept the offer as Marty is, indeed, starting to tire. After introductions, Alex and Marty then prepare to leave. Annie walks them to the car and repeatedly thanks Alex for his kind gesture. With a wave, they are off down the hill and back into town.

When Annie returns home that evening, Marty will relate the delightful conversation that she shared with Alex on the ride home. She will talk about how nice a man that he seems to be, how thoughtful and caring, and how good-looking he is. Annie will just brush the last comment off with a rather noncommittal, "Oh, you think so?" But she is very appreciative of the kindness shown and reminds herself to call Alex to thank him. Annie thinks that she probably has Katie's phone number somewhere on one of those rosters from summer camp.

*   *   *

Tuesday of the next week arrives and Annie is sitting at home after work, going through some bills and correspondence on her desk. Uncovering a pile of papers, she sees the phone numbers of the summer students sitting there. Looking down the list, Annie finds Katie's name and then checks the parent's contact number. 'Alex Galway,' she thinks to herself. 'Where else have I heard that name Galway?' Straining mentally for a moment, she soon gives up trying to remember.

It has been a few days since Alex took Marty home and she feels guilty for not having called yet to thank him for it. But she is hesitant to do so and has been putting it off intentionally. It shouldn't be a big deal, to just call someone and thank them, but with Alex there is something else in play. A feeling that has been absent in her life for many years has now surfaced again with his appearance. That possibility for connection, for sharing, and yes, maybe even spiritual and physical love with another has been placed right in front of her. And for the first time in a long time, she doesn't want to turn away from it or to push it into the background. And upon seeing Alex again the other day, she is somewhat giddy and excited, like a school girl, about something new coming into her life.

So, Annie is apprehensive, a little nervous about calling him. 'I'll just call him, thank him, and that will be the end of it,' she decides. 'It's no big deal,' Annie tries to tell herself again while dialing the number. But the nervousness rises again as the phone rings once, twice, and then three times before a voice answers, "Hello, this is Alex."

"Alex, this is Annie Sullivan."

"Oh, hi, Annie. How is that grandmother of yours doing?" he says to her.

"She's fine, that's what I'm calling about. I want to thank you again for what you did the other day. I never expected we'd be so busy. If you hadn't come along, I don't know what I would have done." Alex says that it was a treat for him talking with Marty and that it hadn't been any problem at all.

"Well, that's nice of you to say but counting the limeade that you gave me at a Friday Dance, that's two favors I owe you now. You're going to have to let me do something for you sometime if you're going to do all this for me."

"I'd probably be able to come up with something," he answers her with a laugh.

The conversation continues for a few minutes more about Katie's activities and the orchard duties and the weather before the discussion wanes. Beginning to feel a little awkward, Annie prepares to end the conversation by, once again, thanking him. But suddenly, coming from who knows where, she quickly blurts out, "You know, there's a little seafood restaurant nearby that Julia and I like a lot. It's really good and I haven't been there for a long time. Do you like fish?" An enthusiastic, positive response is returned by Alex. "Could I treat you to dinner sometime then? I really would like to make it up to you."

"Sure, that sounds great," says Alex.

"Are you busy at all this Friday night? I mean, we don't have to do it this Friday night, we can do it anytime," and Annie begins stumbling over her words.

Smiling inwardly, Alex then quickly eases over the situation. "This Friday or next Friday or any Friday is fine with me. This old single dad really doesn't have too busy of a social schedule, if you know what I mean," he says.

Annie appreciates the lightheartedness of the comment and says, "Well, let's do it this Friday then."

And dinner plans are made. Placing down the receiver, Annie pauses, wondering what's she done and where that came from, and then excitedly walks to the backyard to tell Marty.

\*     \*     \*

Alex has made arrangements with Erica to stay later on Friday until he returns from dinner. Katie has been allowed to ask a friend to stay over and has picked her new 'best friend' from the soccer team. Excited and having planned the night all week, Katie now helps her father get ready. "The blue one, definitely the blue one," she answers when asked to pick from one of two shirts. "And your hair's all messed in back, I'll fix it for you," she says and runs off to find a brush.

When telling his family this week about meeting Annie for dinner tonight, Alex has presented it as a 'thank you' from her for helping out with Marty. Alex has overly stressed this when discussing it with either the children or Erica. And, of course, the kids don't care anyway. Aaron is out with his friends for the weekend night and Katie had simply said, "Oh, she's so nice, you're really going to like her."

And Erica, for her part, is glad that he is finally getting out and doing some things for himself. All she had added one time was a, "Katie says that she's very pretty," and then had flashed a big smile back in Alex's direction.

It had been returned with a, "Yes, I guess she is."

Katie comes running back into the room. "Okay, sit down on the bed," she instructs and then proceeds to smooth out the rough spot on Alex's head. "Alright, that's it. You look great now, Dad! So, you're ready to go," and she grabs her father's hand to begin leading him down the stairs.

"Whoa, let me just get one thing," and Alex quickly returns to the bedroom.

"Come on, Daddy, you have to hurry," says Katie. "Kirsten's going to be here really soon."

Now, he understands the urgency. It is women's night at the house. With Erica supervising and probably joining in, Katie is looking forward to a night with just the girls, boys aren't allowed. Checking the time, he realizes that he's not supposed to meet Annie for another forty five minutes. But the father takes his clue, is glad that Katie is excited about the evening, and decides to drive over early to wait at the restaurant.

It's a new feeling for Alex, to be out for the night, especially with a woman. He basically hasn't thought on those things, love and relationship, ever since Laura left. And even while married, they had been absent from his life and he had simply learned to live without them. Intellectually, you may know that such action is not healthy, may not be honest, but the requirements of daily living had overshadowed his ability to work on change.

After Laura's leaving, Alex felt that those things would come back into his life again, later, maybe when the kids were grown and gone. He wasn't in any hurry and didn't really need it as the love from his children offered great sustenance and great purpose. But Alex is not one of those people who does well on his own, who can go to a movie or go to a restaurant by himself. So, having simply passed on these activities for the past six months, he welcomes the chance for conversation and connection with another. And he now sees that connection entering the parking lot as he waits on the bench in front of the restaurant.

"Hi," Alex calls out as Annie approaches.

"Have you been waiting long? I'm not late, am I?" she asks, noticing the comfortable repose shown by him on the bench.

"No, you're not at all, I think you're five minutes early," he says, checking his watch. "Katie kicked me out of the house so I just came over early and waited for you," and then he explains about her friend spending the night at their house.

"So, she didn't want her dad hanging around anymore, huh? She's so sweet, she's so cute," says Annie.

They make their way into The Salmon and sit at a small table near the window. The early evening is settling in and the porch lights come on out front. With only a few other diners at the moment, the setting is quiet and relaxing. Annie and Alex will order, exchange conversation about her past job, and discuss his current employment. They will ask each other about their family history. They will find out more about each other's lives.

Eventually the conversation turns to Marty. "I really enjoyed talking with your grandmother the other day. She is really a sweet person and doesn't seem to have a bad bone in her body. What an amazing woman," says Alex.

"Yes, she really is," agrees Annie. "And after all she's been through. If I ever start to complain about something or feel sorry for myself, I just need to remember my grandmother. In an instant, my problems seem small and temporary. It's been kind of a good measuring stick for me over the years."

"I hope you don't mind my asking but what happened to her face and hand? Is that from the fire, too?"

"No, Marty wasn't in the fire with my parents," says Annie. "Remember, about forty years ago, the Great Mistake?"

"Who doesn't?" is Alex's reply.

"Well, she was in that and suffered thermal burns over most of that side of her body. Her health had basically been okay when she was younger, but as she got older she began having more problems." And Annie tells Alex about Marty's advancing leukemia and on the doctor's dire prognosis of only the short time left for her grandmother to live.

"Oh, that's just awful," says a disheartened Alex with true concern for the woman that he has just met. "Oh, that's terrible, I feel so sorry for her. Is she in pain, does it bother her much?" he then asks.

"Some days it does, mainly the discomfort from the swelling and the joint pain. Of course, Marty won't let on if it does. She tires easily now, though, and I can see it in her eyes when it gets worse. The poor thing..." and then Annie pauses.

"Isn't there something they could do for her, something to treat the cancer?" asks Alex.

"No, not much. She could go through some treatments but it wouldn't really cure anything, probably only just prolong things. And Marty doesn't want any part of that. She says when it's her time to go, it's her time to go. She knows what the doctor has said about it," ends Annie.

With a somberness settling over the table, they move on to other topics. The conversation between them is easy, spirited, and natural. The spell of sadness is soon dispersed and the two will enjoy laughter and companionship for the rest of the dinner. Sharing a piece of berry cobbler for dessert with a pot of rich black tea, the two soon fight over the bill, with Annie winning as the sole purpose of the 'date' was to repay Alex's kindness from the other day. Soon, the couple find themselves on the front porch, thanking each other and preparing to take leave from one another for the evening .

"Thanks, Annie. I knew about this place but had never tried it before, it's great," says Alex.

"Yes, it's always been one of my favorite places. They are only open Wednesday through Saturday but it's worth coming when they are. Julia and I used to come here as often as we could when I wasn't traveling," says Annie. They then make their way toward the parking lot with Alex walking Annie to her car.

They both stand awkwardly for a moment, seemingly putting off the parting. But then Alex says, "Well, good night, Annie. I really enjoyed it," and opens the door for her to get in. Lowering the window, she thanks him once again for his help in taking Marty home the other day. As Annie begins backing out of the parking place, Alex waves good-bye and then suddenly stops her and runs over to the car.

"Hey, I was thinking, there is this Thai place over near where I live and the food is really, really good. And they always have lots of seafood on the menu. I think you'd like it, want to try it with me sometime?" offers this warm and gracious man.

"Sure, I love Thai food," says Annie.

"Good!" answers Alex quickly. "It'll give me a chance to pay you back," he then adds.

"But we are even. I thought I was paying you back with this dinner," observes Annie wryly.

"Oh, yeah, that's right. Well, maybe if I take you to dinner, you'd feel kind of guilty and have to pay me back by taking me out to dinner again."

"I probably would," says Annie as she sweetly smiles back at him before leaving the parking lot. Alex will watch her tail lights disappear into the night. Alex will watch for a long time before walking back to his peetee and returning home.

\*      \*      \*

Several months have now passed and Annie and Alex have continued to see each other. He will stop by the orchard on his way home to visit with her and on Saturdays to buy fruit which is never in short supply at the Galway household these days. Alex has kept Erica and Katie very busy making pies and crisps to use up all that fruit. And he will take time to visit with Marty, dragging another chair to her special spot to join her and while away a Saturday afternoon in conversation before giving her that ride home again.

Annie has stayed busy with the orchard. She is learning all areas of the business from the Donovans, has a great relationship with her farm hand, Ben, and wakes up every morning with energy and excitement for each coming day. Marty has slowed down considerably and now only works the stand for about two hours in the mornings before retiring to her chair. But those two hours allow Annie to take care of a few things before having to take over the selling tables so Marty continues to come to work with her. Annie will worry some that she should be at home resting more. She will check on her regularly during the day and ask if anything is needed but is always just greeted by that slight sweet smile that says, 'No, everything is fine, just fine.'

Annie and Alex have continued their respective life paths, in their unique direction, but with a side trip on occasion that has been welcomed and needed by both. Each has contributed to the other and has provided counsel and caring whenever needed. They have strengthened one another's lives while expanding and strengthening their own. They have come into each other's life with a purpose and for a reason. Annie and Alex have been given a gift and each feels the responsibility to return the favor.

\*     \*     \*

Even in mild climates, the seasons have their subtle changes. And in the spring, the lengthening of the days foretells of the change and the growth to come, the summer surge. The blooms are burgeoning on the fruit trees as Marty sits beneath them in her chair. A beautifully bright day with wisps of clouds floating through the sky create patterns with which the imagination can take flight. The dreams of the day, or of the past, come easily and Marty, in her frailty and small stature, feels as though she is big enough to fill that sky today. The presence of a man, a friend, in her darling Annie's life has been a blessing to her. Having always wanted more for her granddaughter, the grandmother feels as though that prayer, that concern, has been answered. Nothing may be sure or forever, Marty knows that, but for now it is a comfort and a release from that long felt remorse at having been a reason for the narrowness in Annie's life.

She is deep in thought, in reflection, when Alex's interruption with his soft question asks, "Got room for another daydreamer on this train?" Marty assures him that she does and he pulls up another chair to join her, on her good side.

"I don't know where it's headed or how far I'm going on it but you're welcome to ride along," quips the grandmother as she joins in the metaphor.

"How are you, Marty?" Alex then asks her with more than one meaning to his question.

"You know what, my boy, I feel good today, really good. It's probably the best that I have felt in weeks, I don't know why. Maybe it has something to do with the weather or the summer coming on or," and Marty pauses for a moment, "maybe because I was going to have a friend visit me today."

"Well, it's an honor to be called a friend of yours. I enjoy the time we spend together, it kind of gives me something to do with the day. My kids always seem to have something going on, you know, busy with their friends and things. But old farts like me, well, we kind of twiddle our thumbs sometimes."

"You're not old, I know what old is. And farts are just part of life, you know, and an important part at that, plus they're funny as hell," says the down to earth grandmother.

Alex laughs heartily at the joke and then makes the comment, "You're one of a kind, Marty, one of a kind."

Marty sits quietly, pensively, staring out to the far horizon before continuing. "Well, I'm one of a few. There are some of us left, but not many, not many," she ends oddly. Alex can only think that she is referring to her deformity, her survival from the nuclear explosions. Marty has never mentioned this, in all their hours of conversation in those chairs over the past few months, she has never even hinted at any sorrow or pity felt. That is one of the things that endears her so with others. Marty never complains about the hand that life had dealt her. Others have commented often they are not so sure that they would have had the same attitude if it had happened to them.

The subject is quickly changed by Marty as she inquires about Alex's work week and the children's activities and anything new since they had last spoken. A cool, light breeze then rustles the leaves above them. The 'kaw kaw' of the crows can be heard in the distance. Butterflies and moths flit in and out of the tall grasses surrounding their chairs. A serenity envelopes the orchard and the two friends sitting side by side float into its peacefulness. Even without conversation, these two souls easily intermingle in thoughts and value the presence of one another in their lives. Words are not needed, the feelings are clear.

"Alex," Marty says after a few minutes pass. "We've talked on many things over the past months and I have really enjoyed the conversations and you sharing time with me."

"It's been my pleasure. I have enjoyed talking with you, too," he replies to her kind comment.

"So, you wouldn't mind my asking you a personal question, would you?" she asks a little hesitantly.

"No, not at all," he says. "Go right ahead."

"You talk about your job, you talk about your children, a lot," begins Marty and Alex chuckles at the comment. "You even talk about Annie but you've never mentioned your wife, not once in all this time. Why is that?"

Alex is taken aback somewhat by the question. With the day going so well and so beautifully, the thought of bringing in clouds to cover that brightness is unappealing. But he has been asked a direct question and it will deserve a direct answer. Slowly and deliberately, he starts. "Well, there isn't much to say, not a lot of good came out of it, except for the children, of course. I couldn't make her happy and in retrospect, I guess that I wasn't happy. She finally had enough and made the change. It was her decision to move out, to move on to a different life. There was no reason to fight it, she was right, whatever had been there had been dead for years. There was no bringing it back to life," he ends plaintively, with obvious regret at the failed marriage.

"What brought you together, why did you get married in the first place then?" Marty gently presses.

"We liked spending time together and had both been single for quite a while. We seemed to share the same values and had the same view of the world. And in the beginning, I thought we wanted the same things out of life. We both wanted a family, you know, children. It just seemed like she was the 'right' one, that it was time to get married and move on to the next phase of my life. I was the type of guy who liked having others around. I don't do well by myself, you know," says Alex with his self-assessment about facing the world alone and without a partner.

"And how is it now, with your wife, I mean?"

"Oh, it's fine. She communicates with the kids often and stays in their lives. We don't have much to say to each other, but I'm starting to feel better about it."

"Well, I think you're a great guy. And I know that Annie does, too. I want to thank you for all you've done for us. It gives me a lot of comfort knowing that you two have become friends. She needs other people in her life. For way too long, she's only had me and that job. She has Julia and you and this orchard now, my prayers have been answered," says the devoted grandmother with a certainty to her words.

The breezes pick up again and climb the hillside as the sun warms the land. Annie soon joins them, bringing drinks and, of course, fresh fruit on a plate for a light snack. "What are you guys talking about?" she asks, noticing the earnest expression sitting on each of their faces.

Breaking the spell, both just laugh with Marty answering, "The weather, just the weather, what else do people talk about?" And she gives a wink in Alex's direction.

Annie notices and then under her breath says, "You two, you two," as she hurries back to the waiting customers.

"I shouldn't be keeping you. You ought to go see Annie," says Marty when she is gone.

"I will, in a minute," answers Alex. "This feels awfully good, just sitting down after the work week." And both are quiet again for a moment as they gaze out peacefully at the verdant hillsides. The grandmother is the next one to speak.

"Alex, is there anything that you want to ask me?" Marty then asks somewhat curiously.

"Ask you?" he says with a slightly perplexed look on his face. "No, not really. Why?"

"I mean, I asked you a personal question. Is there anything that you want to ask me?" queries the grandmother again. Alex just shakes his head side to side, hunches his shoulders, and says no, that he doesn't think so.

"Could I get something off my chest then, can I lean on you some? You know, I just kind of feel that I want to say it before it's too late," comes the seemingly serious request from this sweet and gracious older woman.

"Marty, you can tell me anything, anytime," and Alex moves to angle his chair closer to hers, for full attention, to be able to look more deeply into her eyes.

"Has Annie ever spoken to you about her parents, about my daughter?" He says that she had related the fire story to him one time, but that was about it. "Well, I didn't raise my daughter, Annie's mother. My husband did, on his own.

"I was married to John when I was only twenty two. He was two years older and had attended the same high school, grew up in the same town as I did. We had always been sweethearts, even when apart. John had gone to trade school and had been working for a few years already when I graduated from college. Against everyone's advice to wait a few years, we got married. We wanted to start our life together. We felt that we had already waited, while he started a career and I finished school.

"And Annie's mother was born after two years of marriage. We were happy, excited to have our first child, and thought that nothing could ever change that. We were committed to each other, needed each other, and loved each other. Everything was perfect," and Marty takes a deep sigh before continuing.

"When Annie's mother was only eight months old, John took her on a short trip to visit his parents. I stayed at home as I had just started working part-time for a tree nursery and taking time off right away wasn't a good idea. Well, that is when the Great Mistake happened, while they were gone. And thank goodness, if they had been there, they might have suffered the same fate, or worse. I'm glad that they weren't there," a sincere Marty then adds with emphasis and certainty.

Alex shifts in his seat, sensing the seriousness and the need of this 'confession.' Marty continues speaking, continues the story. "They were unable to return for days, for weeks, as all hell had broken loose. After finding me, I was transported to a nearby hospital and then to another, where John and Leslie were finally able to visit me. I was horribly burned and bruised and a terrible thing to look at. Leslie would just cry and turn her head to hold on even tighter to her daddy whenever John would try to let me hold her or be near her. It tore him apart, he felt so badly about it. But it wasn't his fault. I looked like a monster to such a young child, to such a baby." Tears well in the poor woman's eyes and she chokes some on the next words. "And I sure wasn't the pretty young thing that my husband had married.

"Well, long story short, I slipped into deep deep depression that lasted for years. I just couldn't imagine how my handsome young John could ever love or make love to me again. I didn't want my child to be scared or embarrassed by her ugly mother for the rest of her life. I hated everything, hated everyone, hated what had happened to me, and I became a completely different person. And I made it extremely difficult for John to carry on any kind of normalcy for Leslie.

"He tried, oh, how he tried, but in the end, he had no choice. I chased him away and with him, my child, Annie's mother. John had said that he didn't care what I looked like, that I was still the same person he had always so dearly loved. But I didn't believe him, didn't want to believe him. I simply wallowed in that old self-pity. And I was, pitiful." Marty pauses for a moment. "So, I'm not that really great person everybody always talks about. 'Poor Marty,' everyone says. Well, poor Marty did it to herself. I didn't lose my looks, I lost my life."

Alex is stunned, silenced by what he has just been told. And the pain and regrets that are coming from the woman are also painful for him and he moves to comfort her. "Oh, Marty, that must have been really hard, I'm so sorry. But Annie said that her mother and father had wanted you to come live near them. You must have reconciled with your daughter about it."

"Oh, yes, Leslie is just like Annie, she's always looking for the good in people. She forgave me, told me over and over how she understood what I did. But I couldn't bring back those years for her, those years of not having a mother around."

"And what about your husband, did the two of you ever work it out?" asks Alex.

"For many years, I refused to see him and just left unopened all the correspondence that he sent me. I just couldn't face him, if you get my meaning." Alex bites his lip and half smiles in Marty's direction to indicate that he understands the double entendre. "John never remarried, he still lives alone back East. He said..." and then Marty begins choking up again, "that there had only been one person in life for him and that had been me. And when that woman had disappeared, had gone away from him, he had no interest in searching for another. He said that another would just be a stand in, a replacement, for what we had shared, not the real thing. In the end, John had needed me as much as I had needed him. But I couldn't see that, not at my young age. So, I lost out on that great gift of sharing and coming together that occurs between two individuals who love and value one another and decide to spend their lives together," and then the soft, sweet voice of the saddened woman simply stops speaking.

Alex sits quietly beside her while still offering solace just with his presence. The chirping of the birds then comes back into the foreground. The wind stirs and rustles the leaves above them. The two companions stare at the clouds slipping through the sky. Silence seems the best avenue for the moment as each digests the exchange. Marty shifts in her chair, trying to reach a comfortable position. "Can I get you anything?" asks Alex.

"No, thank you," and then Marty continues. "You're probably wondering why I am telling you all this. It's not for pity's sake, god knows I've had enough of that in my life."

"But what you went through was horrible, disgusting. I can't believe that people used to drop bombs on each other, that they were capable of unleashing such devastation and horror upon others. And just because they didn't happen to agree with you or had different ideas from you. It was crazy, just crazy," says Alex of the previous use of war to resolve conflicts.

"Yes, it was. But what I want to say is that when two people finally find each other that they shouldn't let go, shouldn't give up when things get rough because things will get rough at times. Life still throws us those curves, but if we just hang in there and face what's coming our way, we'll be fine, we'll make it," observes the wise and worldly woman.

"So, you believe in that soul mate then, that one person to love and share your life with?" asks Alex.

"Oh, there's probably more than just one out there. It's a big world so we're not going to have the time or the chance to search all of it. But, we only need to find that one true and loving and sharing connection with another human being that nourishes us. And what I'm saying is when you find it, cherish it and value it and don't let go of it. For heaven's sake, Alex, don't let go of it, don't ever let go," and the conversation comes to an end.

\*　　\*　　\*

It is later that evening and Alex is in Katie's room reading with her. They had finished dinner earlier and are now about ready for bed. Aaron is gone for the night because his band is, once again, practicing. A peaceful and quiet evening settles on the Galway household as Katie's bedtime nears. "Okay, let's read a few more pages and then you'd better get to sleep."

"Alright, Daddy," says the little girl sweetly.

Alex cherishes that word 'Daddy.' There's nothing quite like hearing those words dad or daddy or his favorite, papa, from either one of his children. It serves as that daily reminder of his responsibility and of a main purposes in his life, to nurture their lives and the world around them so that the promise of a better life will not be an empty one.

The book is soon closed and Katie then scurries off to the bathroom to brush her teeth. Alex straightens the room and pulls down the covers on the bed. He will sit beside her, talking softly and giggling with her, as they rerun the events of the day and the plans for tomorrow.

The light goes out and Alex makes his way downstairs to the living room. Sitting down, he watches television for a short time. Then looking at the clock, he decides that the best course of action is to also retire for the evening. Aaron will be home late and has his own key. And he has his own good sense, so Alex can fall to sleep comfortably and without worry.

Feeling tired now and in the bathroom when the phone rings, he is startled back into the present and hurries to answer before it wakes Katie. Reaching the receiver, a small amount of worry about Aaron creeps into his thinking. If someone is calling this late, it usually doesn't forebode of anything good. "Hello, this is Alex," he answers quickly.

"Alex, oh no, Alex, it's Marty, poor Marty," comes Annie's distressed voice over the phone. Alex can tell that she has been crying, that she is very upset.

"What, Annie, what's wrong!"

"It's Marty, she...she," and the next words, the next reality is hard for her to admit, "she died." And Annie chokes on the emotion and breaks down over the telephone.

"Where are you?" asks Alex.

"I'm at the hospital. Marty was having trouble breathing so I called emergency and they brought her here. But she died on the way, they said she just gave out. There wasn't anything they could do," answers a slightly more composed Annie.

"I'll be right there," he says. "I'll be right there, Annie."

He hurriedly dials another number as he peels his pajamas and dresses again. The voice comes on the other line. "Erica, this is Alex. I need you to watch Katie. Can you come right over?" Sensing the urgency, she answers that she will.

Alex waits in the kitchen for his neighbor to arrive. All sorts of thoughts bounce around in his head, about Annie being upset and her loss, about the time spent and his friendship with the grandmother, and about that unusual conversation that he had with Marty just today. And one comment keeps coming to the foreground of his thinking. "Before it's too late," she had said, "before it's too late."

Erica arrives at the side door. "Thanks, thanks so much for coming," says Alex and then tells her of the situation. "I don't know when I might get back. Is it okay if I just call you later?" asks a rushed Alex, anxious to get to the hospital.

"I brought a few things, I plan on staying the night. Just do what you have to do and we can talk about it in the morning," offers the considerate woman.

Relieved and out the door, Alex drives quickly to the hospital. Giving them Marty's name at the desk, he is directed to a waiting room where he finds Annie. She stands to meet him and the two embrace before sitting down again. "I'm sorry, Annie, so sorry. Marty was wonderful, we're all going to miss her."

"Thanks," says Annie. "And thanks for coming by, it means a lot to me." Alex simply nods back at her without comment. "They said just wait here and someone would come talk to me in a while. I don't know what to do, just wait, I guess."

"Yes, let's just wait," and Alex reaches over to lightly touch her on the arm. Annie tear stricken eyes look up at him and she just gives a slight smile in his direction.

Soon, the doctor and a staff person come to talk with them. They explain what will be done with the body and that they should just go home now, that there is nothing further they can do. Thanking them, they leave the hospital and are now on the front steps. Annie begins to thank Alex for coming and to say good night. "Let's leave your car here, I'll take you home," he interrupts. "We can just come get it tomorrow." Glad not having to drive or navigate her way home, Annie agrees. And they make the slow and sorrowful journey back to her house.

\*　　\*　　\*

Entering into the quiet home, Annie passes Marty's room and pauses for a moment at her doorway before continuing into the kitchen. "Can I get you something to drink? I'm going to put on some water for lemongrass tea if you would like a cup of that?" asks Annie.

"I'd take some tea, thanks," answers Alex.

She returns to the living room and places the tea and two cups on the table by the couch. Sitting quietly, Annie peers into the pot to see how the brewing is progressing. She straightens some magazines in front of her and looks about the room, releasing a long sigh. "Well, it's sure going to be different around here now without Marty in it."

"I know you two were very fond of each other. I'm sure it's going to be a little tough on you for a while."

"Yes, but I guess things will work out. We just have to move on, right?" says Annie with a tinge of hope in her voice.

"That's what we do," agrees Alex. "You still have your friends and that orchard probably isn't going to let you slack off much. Being busy at times like this isn't a bad thing, though."

"No, you are right about that." Then pensive for a moment, Annie continues. "I always knew that it was coming, Alex. And I even knew that it could be at any moment but when it happens, well, it doesn't seem quite real."

"Nor should it, not yet," says Alex.

Annie slowly pours the tea into the two cups. She and Alex sit together and talk softly into the night. Annie will break down occasionally and need to be comforted. Soon, the hour is late, very late, and Annie says that she ought to let him go home and get back to his family. Telling her of Erica's being with Katie, Alex replies that there is no hurry, that he could stay on the couch for the night if she wants, if she would like to have someone there with her. Saying that he has already helped, Annie assures him that she will be fine. Alex stands to leave and Annie also rises to walk him to the door.

"Get some sleep and I'll stop by tomorrow. Is around noon okay?" asks Alex. Annie says that noon would be fine but, that he doesn't need to, doesn't have to come by. "I'll see you at noon," he says again.

"That would be nice," she says.

\*     \*     \*

"So, is everything okay with you, sweetie?" says Alex to his young daughter the next morning as he walks into the kitchen after coming downstairs later than the others. Erica and Katie are busy at the stove carefully monitoring the pancakes for that just right time to flip them.

"Oh hi, Daddy. Yes, everything's fine," answers Katie. "Erica came in this morning and said that you had to go somewhere last night. She said that we could make whatever I wanted for breakfast so I asked for pancakes."

Alex goes over to Erica to thank her for staying the previous evening. He stresses again and again how appreciative he is that she was able to come over. "Oh, hush," she finally says to him. "You know that I think of these kids as my own now. You don't have to thank me for helping take care of them."

"I don't know what I would do without you," says Alex and he gives the older woman a kiss on the forehead. Erica blushes and smiles backs at him. "Do you know what time Aaron got home last night, did you hear him?"

"Not very late, I think it was only a little after midnight. I was still up watching some television and told him the situation. We both went to bed after that, I slept on the couch. I told him we would wake him for breakfast. Do you want to go see if he wants some of these pancakes?"

Alex heads upstairs to retrieve his son. Knocking lightly on the door, he calls out, "Aaron, are you awake?"

"Yeah, come on in, Dad," he answers.

"Hi, Erica said that you might be interested in breakfast. She and Katie are making pancakes and they're almost ready. Do you want to come down and have some?

"Sure, that sounds good, I'm starved," he says and then asks, "Was there was a problem last night? Erica said something bad had happened to one of your friends."

Alex will then spend a few minutes telling Aaron about the circumstances from the previous evening. He will mention the death of his friend's grandmother and talk about how he had met the two women at the orchard last fall. Alex tells of his fondness for Marty and explains about her being a survivor of the Mistake. He doesn't say much about Annie on purpose, not knowing what his son might think about a woman other than his mother being in his life. For now, Alex skirts the issue.

"You're kidding me, she survived the nuclear explosions! I knew about the Great Mistake but I didn't know anyone was still alive from that time," says Aaron. Alex adds that there are only a few survivors left, that Marty was one of the last. "That's too bad she died. I'm sorry, Dad. Is your friend doing okay?"

"Yes, she's sad but she knew that her grandmother didn't have long to live. That's something I wanted to talk to you about. I want to go over and check on her today but I need someone to stay with Katie. I don't really want to ask Erica again after her spending last night here. Could you be around for a couple of hours at noon to watch her?"

"Sure, that's not a problem. I'm just going to hang at home today anyway. I'm kind of tired from last night."

"Oh, that's right. How did it go, was it fun?" asks Alex about his son's and the band's first performance.

"It was great, just great! We were all really nervous at first so we started with some simple stuff, you know, popular songs that we knew the kids would like. But then Nick told the crowd that we were going to do one of Sam's songs and when we finished it, everybody stood up and clapped really loud for us. We couldn't believe it. After that, we mainly stayed with our own stuff and I guess everybody liked it."

"Aaron, I think that's wonderful, really wonderful. Are you guys going to do it again sometime?"

"Yeah, we had a guy come up to us after we had finished and say that he had an event soon that he wanted us to play for. It just blew us away. I don't know why we put off performing for so long. It's really fun!" says his talented son.

"Well, I'll head down and tell them you're coming," says Alex about the impending breakfast.

"Thanks, I'll just get dressed real quick and be right there. What's her name?" he then asks his father as Alex enters the hallway to return downstairs.

He stops and turns toward Aaron with a questioning look on his face. "Whose name?"

"Your friend whose grandmother died."

"Oh," Alex feigns interest, "it's uh, it's Annie."

\*     \*     \*

It is about five minutes before twelve when Alex pulls into Annie's driveway. Exiting the vehicle, he makes his way to the front porch and gives a light knock on the door. Through the glass, he sees Annie coming from the kitchen and takes a step back to wait for her. "Hi," is the pleasant greeting from this lovely woman. "Thanks for coming by, you're right on time. Are you always so punctual?" she teases.

"I think I am, kind of pathetic, huh?" says Alex.

"No, not at all. I think it's a good attribute," she says as they walk to the patio in the back. "Let's sit out here, it's so nice today. I made some fresh lemonade, would you like some?"

"Sure, that sounds good. Can I help you with anything?" he asks as Annie heads back to the kitchen to get the drinks.

"That's okay, I'll be right back," she says. And Annie quickly returns with a pitcher and two very tall glasses. Placing them on a small side table, she joins Alex who is already sitting in one of the chairs. The soft, warm breezes swirl around the patio. It is a pleasant setting, a peaceful moment, except for the dark cloud of last evening that still hangs in the air.

Slowly sipping his lemonade, Alex is the first to speak. In an earnest, caring voice he says, "Did you get some sleep last night, Annie?" And then he looks in her direction with sincere sad eyes for his loss, too. Alex had grown fond, very fond, of Marty over the last few months. He had felt comfortable in her presence, had appreciated her insights and the conversations, and had been welcomed by her into the family.

"Well, I wandered the house for a while and at one point, I just sat in Marty's room and kind of stared at her things. But then I got pretty tired and went to bed. I tried to quit thinking about things. It worked, I fell asleep."

"That's good, I'm glad you were able to get some sleep. Now, if there's something that you need help with in the next few days, you'll let me know, won't you?"

With a wide smile on her face, Annie looks over at him. "Yes, I will," she answers. "Julia is coming by tomorrow afternoon and she's going to help me plan the service. I think I just want to have a small ceremony at the orchard."

"Oh, that sounds nice. I think Marty would have liked that," says Alex. "But I mean it, if you need to do something or to go somewhere, please let me go with you. I can easily get away from work on short notice and I don't want you having to do all those things by yourself."

Annie just nods her head and remains pensive for a moment before saying, "Well, there is one thing that you can help me with. I don't think that I can face talking to the funeral home people by myself. It just seems so morbid, having to deal with someone's body after their spirit has left it. I still need to set that up. I was thinking about doing it on Tuesday."

"Done," answers Alex right away. "Do you want to do it in the morning or in the afternoon?"

"I was thinking about the morning," says Annie.

They will make plans on the time and location to meet and will continue sitting on the back patio in conversation for the next two hours until the time for Alex to return home draws near. Before leaving, he makes her promise to call him if she needs something, if she needs anything, he says again.

Walking Alex to the door, Annie repeatedly thanks him for visiting and for coming to the hospital last night. Alex, for his part, keeps saying that he was glad that he was able to help out. "She became a good friend of mine, too, you know."

Pausing on the front porch, the two companions run out of words and simply look at one another for a moment. Tears well in Annie's eyes as she thinks about the loss of her beloved grandmother and she is unable to hold back her emotions any longer and breaks down. Alex moves to comfort her and Annie then collapses into his arms. They hold on to each other tightly. They hold on to each other so as not to seem so alone.

\*　　\*　　\*

Monday arrives and Alex is back at work. Sitting in the office with Scott, he is checking the work requirements for the coming week. "It seems like things are in good shape. All the requisitions have come in and the extra equipment that we need was ordered. Do you see anything that's missing?" asks Alex.

"No, I don't. I ran over the staffing situations with Emery this morning. Two backhoe operators from the Fleming project came in early this morning and we can use them through Wednesday according to district headquarters. I think we can complete the southwest section by the end of the week."

"So, if I leave you to run things a couple of times this week, do you think that would be okay?"

"Sure, I can run the show," he says.

"Thanks, Scott. I have something that I need to do tomorrow morning for a couple of hours. But I should be back after lunch." Alex then says, "Do you remember that woman I told you about who had been in the Great Mistake?" Scott answers that he does. "Well, she passed away on Saturday and I'm going to go with her granddaughter to arrange the cremation."

"Oh, Alex, I'm sorry to hear that. They're the people you were telling me about who are going to buy the Donovan's orchard, aren't they?" he asks.

"Yes, that's right. Well, I kind of became good friends with the grandmother and Annie, that's the granddaughter's name. She and I have spent some time together, so I want to kind of help her out on this."

"I didn't know you were dating anybody. I never heard you say anything about that."

"Well, we're not really dating. I stop by the orchard to visit sometimes and, I guess, we've gone out to dinner a few times," says a not-so-honest Alex.

"So, it's just a platonic thing, huh?" slyly asks his co-worker. "Is she pretty?"

Alex looks across at his good friend, at a person who knows him well and just laughs. "She's beautiful, Scott, just beautiful. But you know, that's not what attracted me to her. From the very beginning, which was that night last summer when you made me go to the Friday Dances with you and Jennifer by the way, there's something in her eyes and something about her smile that is just appealing and approachable."

"Really, you met her that night!" says Scott.

"Yeah, and then when Katie took the summer camp class. She was Katie's teacher that week. And then again at the orchard a few months later. I gave her grandmother a ride home one time and after that, we became friends."

"So, she's single? Has she ever been married?"

Alex answers no and then fills in Scott on Annie's history as a tour guide, about her caring for her grandmother all these years, and about her buying the orchard and deciding to set down roots. He speaks glowingly and with admiration for the woman. He speaks fondly and warmly of her attributes, many that he felt he sought but never found in Laura.

"Is it serious, between the two of you?" asks Scott.

"I'm not sure. I don't know how she feels about it and I don't know how I feel about it. I like being with her and think about her often. But, you know, I'm a father first. I probably shouldn't complicate things with romance. And besides, she just needs a friend now. I don't want to make things harder for her."

"Do you know how she feels about you?" questions the friend who has harbored worries about this man always putting himself last on the list.

"No, not really. Her grandmother just used to say that Annie thought I was a nice guy. That's about it, I guess," Alex answers with a shrug of the shoulders.

"Well, there's one thing I've learned about relationships over the years. I think that it's probably one of the reasons Jennifer and I do so well together. We talk, often and about everything, especially things that are important to each of us as an individual. You know, no matter how well you know someone, you can't read their mind. If you think you can, you're probably wrong anyway. If a relationship is important to you, then it's important enough to talk about. Maybe try it sometime, you might be surprised at the answers you get back."

Alex fidgets at his desk, scribbling with a pen on a piece of paper, kind of like a schoolboy struggling with the thought of asking the pretty girl next to him in math class to go to the prom. He wants to do it but, what if she says no? Alex looks across the room at his friend. "Just ask her, huh?"

"Just ask her," says Scott.

*　　*　　*

Annie rises very early that morning. She has kept herself busy for the past twenty four hours, avoiding that down time for reflection when sorrow may want to creep back into her thinking. She had called Julia yesterday but there were several others to contact about Marty's death. Each call has been difficult and has brought emotions to the surface that she is trying to hold down and keep in check. On more than one occasion, Annie has weakened and simply broken down.

The house is quieter and seemingly larger now that Marty is gone. Annie knows how much she enjoyed coming home to her grandmother at the day's end for the companionship and the sharing. She worries about the emptiness that might greet her on the return home each day. We all need family, for connection and support, for love given and love received. We all need someone in our life who cares for us and for whom we can give care. With her parents gone and no family of her own, Marty had provided that link. It wasn't much of a family, Annie knew that, but at least, she had Marty, until now.

She has gone into her grandmother's room often to straighten things, to put away some of her clothing, to sit by her bed and quietly speak to her. Annie will say how she is going to miss her, how sorry she is for the pain and trials that Marty had faced in life, and for her best wishes now that she can rest. Annie will place fresh flowers and a bowl of fruit on Marty's side table to brighten the room and to let her know that she is thinking of her. And the strong, resilient woman will allow herself to grieve and be sorrowful at times, granting herself the right to mourn.

Annie is in the kitchen washing dishes when she hears the knock on the front door. Drying her hands on a towel, she turns and sees Julia standing there, waving. Annie waves back and hurries to open the door to let in her friend. "Hi, Julia, come in. Thanks for coming by."

"Oh, honey, I'm so so sorry about Marty," says Julia as she embraces her friend. "I know how you must miss her already. Are you doing okay?"

"Yes, mostly I guess. But, I must admit I've had my moments, too," answers the granddaughter.

The two women stand in the living room. Annie asks if she can get her something to drink. A glass of water is requested and Julia follows her host into the kitchen to get it. Julia glances into Marty's room as she passes and sees the vase of flowers near her bed. She asks, "Did someone bring flowers by?"

"No," Annie says. "I put those there. I just thought that they would brighten the room some, make it more cheerful. Marty always liked daffodils. She used to say it was like having sunshine even if the day was gray and dreary. Marty had all sort of sayings, they keep coming to me over the last couple of days. I can still see her smile, that mischievous look in her eye," and Annie pauses some before continuing. "I think I'll miss her optimism the most, though, that ability to always stay happy and to always be hopeful. If I have any part of her in me, I hope it's that part," and the sad woman ends her thoughts.

Julia then moves closer to her friend and is able to reach her hand. Holding it now, she strokes it softly and with tenderness. Looking into Annie's eyes, she sees the sadness and sense of loss that her friend is feeling. "I know how much she meant to you," says Julia. "We're all going to miss Marty," and she falls silent, just looking in Annie's direction.

"Julia, you were so nice to her, she liked you so much. And I don't think I can ever repay you for all you did for us over the years. Every time Marty needed you or I would ask for a favor, you always helped out. I really, really appreciate it," says Annie. "I hope I can help you as much sometime."

"Don't be silly, Annie. Our friendship is as important to me as it is to you. Even though we didn't get to spend a lot of time together, I always knew you were there and could count on you for anything. And now, with you living here for the last year, it's been wonderful. You know that," says Julia. And the two women exchange soft smiles with one another.

"So, you're probably going to need some help with things," says Julia, getting down to business right away. "I already told Mark not to count on me for much this week, so whatever you need, just let me know."

"Thanks, I do need some help in figuring out the memorial service. I thought about having it at the orchard and maybe plant a tree or something near the place where Marty would always sit. I think she would like that."

"And what about the orchard? I have to work tomorrow and Wednesday at the optometrist but I'm free after that. Do you need help at the selling tables or anything?"

"I've closed the orchard until Saturday. Ben is going to put out a sign this morning saying that we would be selling again on the weekend. I'm going to the funeral home tomorrow and I would like to have the service on Thursday or Friday."

"If I didn't have to work, I could go with you. I don't want you having to do all that on your own. Oh, darn it, maybe I should call Dr. Abrams and try to get it off," proposes a disappointed Julia at not being available to help.

"No, I'll be fine. Alex is going with me," says Annie.

"Oh, good for him. And did you say he came to the hospital the other night and drove you home?"

"Yes, and he came by yesterday."

"That's so considerate of him. I only met him that one time at the Dance but he sure seemed nice. Have you two been seeing each other some then?" asks Julia.

"Well, we're not really dating if that's what you mean. Alex sometimes drops by the orchard on his way home from work. And usually on Saturdays, he comes out to buy fruit and then will stay to talk with Marty. He got into the habit of taking her back to the house for me so I wouldn't have to leave the tables. We've gone out to dinner a few times."

"And...?" Julia questions with a tilt of her head.

"And what?" returns Annie.

"And would you like to be seeing him? I mean, do you want to spend more time with him?"

"Yeah, I think so. I like him and Marty was always pushing me to go out with him. She kept telling me that she thought the world of him. She was always saying that they don't come much better than Alex."

"So, why didn't you?" asks Julia.

"Well, you know, Marty was so sick. I shouldn't be thinking about myself at a time like that and I didn't want to complicate things by getting involved with someone. I needed to be home with her, and, he never asked me out anyway."

"What do you mean, he never asked you out?"

"Except for going out to dinner those few times, no, not really. But he has a family, Julia, and Alex takes being a father very seriously. I just don't think he probably has the time or room for a girlfriend or anything like that at this point in his life. It's fine. Alex has become a good friend and I should just be happy with that," says Annie.

"Dear, dear Annie," Julia begins, "when are you going to learn that you deserve good things in life, too? I'll have to agree with Marty on this one. She would always talk about how she wanted so much more for you, that you were always doing things for her and others but not for yourself. You've put yourself second in line for as long as I've known you and now it's time for you to move to the head of that line, Annie. Marty would want that for you," says Julia. "And how do you know that Alex doesn't want to spend more time with you?"

"I don't know if he wants to. But if he did, wouldn't he ask me out more often or at least talk about it?" wonders the long lonely woman who now acutely senses those potential pangs of loneliness may soon be arriving again as the love and care for another is no longer required of her.

"Maybe he's afraid."

"Of what?" asks Annie.

"Of the same thing you are," says Julia.

\*       \*       \*

Thursday is the day that is decided for Marty's service. A dozen of her closest friends will be attending a simple service at the orchard. It is scheduled for two in the afternoon, about the time of day that Marty would usually return home to rest. Annie knows that her grandmother loved sitting in that comfy chair, staring out at green hillsides, watching the clouds move past, and seeing the scurrying of life around her as the birds and the squirrels and the bugs went about their daily routines. Marty had felt a part of things in this setting, a part of the ongoing process of life. And Annie wants her remains to rest here forever.

Several people have arrived and the service is short, sweet, and filled with some tears. A tree is planted near Marty's spot with her ashes as a foundation for the new growth. A light meal and refreshments are served on the selling tables as friends of the well-liked grandmother mingle and exchange reminisces of her life. Soon, the guests begin to peel away and only Annie and Alex are left to clean and put things away. A look of sadness has stayed on Annie's face most of the day. More than once, Alex has asked if she is doing okay. The response has always been just a quiet nod of the head while fighting back the emotion.

"Let me finish," says Alex as the chores are mostly completed. "I'm just going to load a few things in the car and put the tables back in the shed. Why don't you sit down for a while?"

Annie looks in his direction and acquiesces wearily as she is tired and worn out from the emotional drain of her loss. She has wondered privately to herself all week about what next may lie ahead for her. A big phase of Annie's life is over, the caring and providing for her grandmother. And, of course, it is not a sense of relief or release but a feeling of doubt and of momentary lack of direction in her life. Annie has the orchard and those responsibilities will keep her busy. But, she won't have anyone to come home to, anyone with whom to share her experiences of the day. She won't have anyone who needs her now. Annie will have to redefine her life, without Marty in it.

Alex returns from the parking lot and his eyes search for Annie. He spots her on the hill, sitting in Marty's chair. As he had done so many times before, the good friend to both women pulls up a second chair. Quietly and without comment, Alex sits down beside her. Conversation is absent as each sit with their own thoughts of the day and with their own thoughts of Marty. A few minutes pass as the wind rustles the leaves overhead and the lazy afternoon breezes brush past them.

Annie is the first to speak. "Alex, do you ever think about the choices that you have made in life and wonder why it was that you did what you did?"

"Yes, I guess there's been one or two."

"What were they?" she asks.

"Oh, the biggest one is probably why Laura and I even got married in the first place because the relationship never really went anywhere. We never offered much to each other and except for the children, it was kind of a waste," says Alex half-heartedly at the memory.

"Why did you do it then?"

"In retrospect, I think I wanted to get married at that point in my life, you know, wanted to have a family. I was ready for a change from the single life. I was fairly old when I got married," explains Alex.

"Is there anything else, anything else that you might question now?" she presses a bit further.

Alex smiles, lets out a small laugh, and looks over at Annie. "So, what's this all about?"

"I was just wondering if there's anything else in life that you regret, if there's anything else that you would do differently if you were given a second chance?"

Alex is quiet for a moment and takes his time in answering. "Maybe just one other thing, Annie. But it's kind of silly, kind of stupid. It's not really worth mentioning."

"I want to know. If it's something that was important to you, I want to know," the sincere woman asks of her companion.

"Ah, it's just kind of a stupid thing and I don't think it makes any difference now," and Alex stops talking, turning in Annie's direction. Her gaze at him is persistent so he continues. "I never finished my book," he says.

"You were writing a book, when?"

"Before the marriage and family came along."

"Did you want to become a writer?" she asks.

"Well, I didn't grow up wanting to be an underground utilities manager if you know what I mean," he answers with a laugh. "I feel that our creative side can be just as productive and can contribute to society just as much as our nuts and bolts jobs. I think that's why I'm so excited about Aaron's music, maybe he will be able to make a living at it someday."

Both of them are again quiet for a moment. Afternoon at the orchard is a peaceful time, a tranquil time, when the busyness of the day begins to wind down to the relaxing promise of early evening. Often it has been a time when Annie reflects on the day's work, her luck at being able to buy the orchard, and on Marty who waits for her return. But not today, not from now on, as there is no reason to hurry home anymore.

"What about you, Annie?" asks Alex. "Is there anything that you might have done differently?"

The pensive woman sitting beside him takes a deep breath before she begins speaking again. "I always thought that I had it made, Alex. You know, with traveling all over the world and having all these great adventures. Everybody was always telling me how lucky I was, how they wish they could be doing what I was doing. And I did feel lucky, I felt fortunate. But sometimes, I would look at others with a family or with friends and wish that I could have that, too. Not when I was younger maybe, but later on, in the last few years especially. And now I'm older and don't know if those things will ever happen for me."

"Is that something you want, a family?"

"Of course, most of us want that in our lives, don't you think?" says Annie, looking over in his direction.

"Yes, I do," says Alex.

"And I had a family, you know with Marty, but not anymore. Oh, I know it will pass but I feel kind of lost now. I probably just need to get back to work. I'm afraid taking the week off has given me too much time to think."

"Well, we all need that connection to others. I was talking to Marty about the same thing recently. She told me how she found out that her husband had needed her as much as she needed him. Sounded like she had some regrets about it."

"Marty told you about John!" comes the astonished response from Annie.

"Yes, just last week."

"Unbelievable," she says. "Marty never told anyone about her marriage or about the separation. She had kept it inside all those years and then she told you," reflects Annie. "Marty must have thought the world of you to share that," she says and then asks. "Did you say last week?"

Alex is reserved, hesitant to compromise Marty's trust even though she is gone. But he is talking to her granddaughter, to Annie, and he feels as though there is nothing that he wouldn't share with her. Sadly Alex answers, "Last Saturday, Annie, it was last Saturday."

And immediately Annie makes the connection to the night that Marty died. Lingering in the thought for a moment, Annie then asks, "What did she tell you, Alex, what did she say?"

"She told me about being in the hospital and feeling sorry for herself. She told me about her depression and her refusal to see her husband and her daughter. Marty had asked me a few questions and then said that she wanted to tell me something, to get it off her chest. And then she told me the story of your mom growing up without a mother."

"Marty must have really liked you. She never confided that to anybody over all those years."

"Well, I liked her," says Alex. He pauses and looks over in her direction. Alex is reflective and quiet for a minute before adding, "And I like you, Annie."

Annie is taken aback for a moment by this personal comment. It is the first time that she has heard such words coming from Alex. She glances in his direction with a quixotic expression and a half smile on her face as if not quite believing what she has just heard. "You do?" she says.

"I do," Alex answers directly and assuredly. "You're the best thing to come into my life for a long time, Annie, and I want you to know that." Sitting close to each other, Alex reaches for her hand and Annie extends it to him. He grasps it gently, lightly, but with firm commitment and Annie feels the energy and the connection between the two of them. It is their first real touch and it is comforting and soothing to both.

"And there is something else that Marty said to me," Alex continues as they sit side by side. "She said that when two people find each other, that they shouldn't let go," he says, squeezing Annie's hand a little tighter while still staring straight ahead. "She said, 'Whatever you do, don't ever let go.'"

The late afternoon sun lowers in the sky. The wind rises and stirs the grasses on the hillside where they sit. The peacefulness and serenity are welcome relief from a hectic week. Annie and Alex sit in the chairs in the orchard as the early evening settles around them, holding hands and holding onto each other.

\*     \*     \*

The next morning finds Alex back at work. He had taken a day off for the funeral and is now in the office catching up on some reports. Noon arrives and Alex is surprised at how quickly the morning has moved past. Scott enters the trailer from the yard and says that he is heading to get sandwiches, a usual Friday event for the two of them, and what would he like. "Just whatever you get," says Alex and he goes back to his work.

"Okay, be back soon," says Scott and he exits the trailer.

Alex watches him as he walks across the parking lot and then continues staring out the window, absentmindedly. His mind drifts to thoughts of Annie, which has been a frequent occurrence for him over the last twenty four hours.

\*     \*     \*

Annie has spent most of her morning straightening the small house. She has washed and remade Marty's bed, has put the grandmother's clothing into drawers and closets, and has placed some of her private possessions into a box tucked underneath the bed. Annie knows that a time will come to give away the clothing and other items but for now, she just cleans and tidies Marty's room. Tomorrow she will go back to work at the orchard. Today is a reorganization day, a day to restart her life.

Melancholy can set in from time to time and Annie responds by busying herself and by reminding herself that Marty is free of her pain now, by thinking only good thoughts about her beloved grandmother. The worry of impending uncertainty will creep in every so often but Annie relies on her strength of resolve to assure herself that she will get through it. But at times, the empty house reminds her how alone she really is now and how different things will be moving forward.

Because it isn't a change that one can look forward to, with anticipation or any eagerness. It is one of those changes in which the outcome is unknown, in which tomorrow may be better, or worse. Annie is sinking into one of those down moments when the ringing of the phone startles her back into the present. Rushing to the kitchen, she picks it up.

"Annie, it's Alex," says the voice at the other end.

A broad smile crosses Annie's face as the previous negative thoughts immediately evaporate. "Hi, Alex. Are you at work?" she asks, wondering the purpose of a call from him in the middle of the day.

"Yes, I'm just at the end of a lunch break. Hey, uh, I wanted to know if you'd like to go to Katie's soccer game with me tonight? It's at five and then maybe we could get something to eat after that," offers Alex as a proposal. "I mean, if you're busy or have things to do, I understand. I just thought you might like to see her play."

"That sounds like a lot of fun, I'd like that," answers Annie, eager to have something to do with her evening. "But do you think it would be okay with Katie if I came along?" she then adds as a second thought.

"Sure, she thinks you're great," says Alex. And with the plans made between the two, the conversation is ended.

*　　*　　*

Alex and Annie make their way from the parking lot to the soccer fields. Katie had received an earlier ride from a friend's mother as they were required to be to the field by four for warm-ups and stretching. They take seats near the edge of the field where they join the other families and friends. Alex scouts the field for Katie. Seeing her, he waves and receives a cheerful wave back. He eagerly points out Emily to Annie, whom she already knows, and two other good friends of Katie's whom she met by playing on the team. The energy is high, the weather is perfect, and the game is exciting to watch.

"How long have these kids been playing?" asks Annie. "A lot of them seem to be really good players."

"A few of them for a couple of years now but Emily and Katie have been playing only since last summer. She really likes it and her coach tells me she has turned into one of the better players, that she takes it seriously and is a good learner," brags the papa and always proud parent.

Soon, the game is over and as the others and the players mix on the field, Katie then comes running over to where her father is standing with Annie. Rushing up to him, she says, "Did you see my pass, Daddy? I was the one that passed it to Sarah when she got the goal. Did you see it, did you see it!"

"Yes, honey, I did, that was a great pass. I thought you played a really good game," and he gives his daughter a quick hug. Alex then turns toward Annie and says, "You remember Ms. Sullivan, don't you, your teacher from last summer?"

"Oh, yes, I do," says Katie. "Did you watch the game, did you see me play?" she asks Annie.

"Yes, I did, Katie. I thought that you played really well." And the little girl beams back brightly at her.

"Did you bring my stuff, Dad,?" asks the young girl about her overnight bag. Katie is going to be spending the night at one of her girlfriend's house. And that is why Alex is free to go to dinner with Annie tonight.

"I'll go get it. Do you mind waiting while I go back to the car?" Alex asks Annie.

"Not at all," is the response from this woman who is greatly enjoying the activity and energy of the young children around her. Katie then asks Annie to wait just where she is standing with a 'promise' not to move. Katie makes a quick exit but explains that she will be right back.

Annie soon spies Katie and two friends coming across the field to the spot where she waits. Running up to her and a little out of breath, Katie proudly announces to her friends, "This is Annie, my Daddy's friend. She's nice and a really good teacher. Annie, this is Jessica and Taylor." Both young girls blush and giggle a little and then offer their hands for shaking. Grasping each, Annie shakes them and says that it is very nice to meet them. All three girls soon turn and begin to run back toward the other players with Katie's words being overheard by Annie, "See, I told you she's really pretty."

Alex comes back from the car and asks Annie for directions to find Katie. He crosses the field and passes her bag to Jessica's mother. Returning, he says that they are free to go and asks if Annie is hungry yet. She replies that she is and they walk back to the parking lot and then drive toward the restaurant. They share a relaxing and enjoyable meal and the evening is welcomed greatly by both as a diversion to an otherwise unpleasant week. The reality of Marty's passing is slowly being replaced by the necessity of moving on, of moving past the sorrow and the pain and into the realm of only fond memories.

Arriving at Annie's house, the couple sit in the car for quite a while just quietly talking with each other. After twenty minutes, Annie says that she should be going in, tomorrow is a work day. Alex offers his help if she could use it and the kind offer from him is readily accepted by her. "So, about the same time as usual?" Annie asks of his regular Saturday visit to the orchard.

"Yes, about the same time," says Alex.

As she reaches for the handle, Annie prepares to get out of the peetee. Alex, always the gentleman, begins to open his door to go around when Annie's hand comes over and touches his arm. "I can do it," she says.

"Alright," he answers.

Annie then leans over and kisses him softly on the cheek. "Thank you, Alex, thank you for everything." He is mesmerized, surprised by this show of affection, and just sits quietly, not knowing how to respond but enjoying it immensely.

Annie exits the vehicle and with a wave walks up her front steps and into the house. Turning on the lights, she looks around her house of these many years and feels the warmth and welcome that it exudes. It is here that Annie and Marty had shared their lives and the positive energy of all those years is instilled in its walls. So, tonight, she doesn't feel lonely. Tonight, she doesn't worry about tomorrow. Tonight, everything is 'just fine.'

\*     \*     \*

Jeremy Lucas now excitably looks forward to the coming of each and every day. Having become friends with Wes has been an immense boost to his self-esteem and to his outlook on life. The two have continued spending time together during the week for that occasional dinner out and Wes joins Jeremy about once a month on one of his fishing trips. But the biggest attraction for the both of them has been the twice monthly bridge club that they have joined. Jeremy's talent and competitive drive have made them something of a cause célèbre in the community. Wes is a strong reliable player and with Jeremy's risk taking ability, they are seldom beaten in local club tournaments.

Work is still mundane and unchallenging for Jeremy but he has stood his ground with Paul and has actually converted a few of his fellow workers to his side. So, Paul can no longer muster support for his taunts and more than once, Jeremy has made him look foolish. It has made the task of going to the office each day easier for him and has lightened that old load of self-doubts. It is just a job, he continually tells himself, and with the fishing and with Wes as a new friend and the bridge club, he has other things in his life to look forward to now.

Jeremy is slowly becoming a new man. The shell that had closed around him for so many years has broken apart in recent months and has released a different person into the world, one who now chooses to lead a life without self-imposed limitations and without reduced expectations. And this honest, quiet man is determinedly proceeding in that new direction.

*    *    *

Annie has been back at the orchard for a few weeks now. There is much to do with the weeding, the watering, and the soil monitoring. With Ben working on a better water delivery system to the trees, it has left most of the tilling and testing to Annie. Having reduced the selling hours to the afternoon has freed her to drive the tractor in the morning. Mr. Donovan has not worked since last spring and with only the two of them, there is always much to do and the days are long.

Often Annie won't get home until after six in the evening, having started at seven thirty that morning. And with the main selling day still being Saturday, six days a week are required to get the job done. But Sunday remains a day off and she looks forward to it this week with excitement and a little apprehension. This Sunday, Alex has invited her to a midday dinner at his house with his family.

Annie knows Katie, has met Erica, but Aaron has never been at home the few times that she and Alex have stopped by the house. The Sunday dinner is, more or less, an introduction to the family and Annie is slightly nervous. She has always worried what the children might think of her coming into Alex's life. Annie gets along fine with Katie, of course, but meeting Aaron is a different matter. He is older, more adult, and may have stronger feelings about the situation. 'Or not,' Annie thinks to herself. But she is not sure and Annie struggles to keep the expectations within reason. Looking at the clock, she realizes that it is time to be in the shower and stops her chores.

*　　*　　*

Driving down the hillside and toward the cruiseway, Annie is buoyed by the wonderful early fall weather. Her house is tucked tightly into the hillside on the south side of town while Alex's house is in the eastern section of town with older homes and large yards. She has always felt comfortable in that neighborhood, having known a few friends over the years who have lived there. Annie makes her way across town and soon parks in front of the Galway house. She takes a deep breath, exits her peetee, and walks to the front door. Alex had spotted her and opens it before a knock is required.

"Hi," comes the soft greeting from him.

"Hi," answers Annie with a warm smile.

And they make their way toward the kitchen where Erica and Katie are busy preparing the dinner. In the hallway, Annie teases him a bit, "So, what part of the meal did you make?"

"I made the trips to the grocery store, lots of them," says Alex. "I volunteered to help but the girls of the house didn't want me messing it up, I guess."

Katie soon spies Annie and jumps down from the stool to go greet her. Grabbing one of her hands, Katie quickly ushers her into the kitchen where she tells Erica that, "This is Annie, she was my teacher at camp last summer."

"I know that," answers Erica with a laugh. "I have met Annie before and it's so nice to see her again," she says, addressing their dinner guest.

"Come on," says Katie, taking over again. "Let me show you what we're having. I helped wash the vegetables, Dad and I set the table, and Erica let me put the pie crust in the dish. You have to spread it out with your fingers and make it even all around," she explains for Annie's benefit.

Alex then excuses himself from the kitchen and goes upstairs to see how Aaron is coming along. Knocking on his son's door, he explains that Annie has arrived and that Aaron should come down when he is ready.

"Thanks, Dad. I'm just finishing up a chat with Sam. I'll be right down," answers Aaron.

The father returns to the kitchen to find Erica by herself. "Where did everybody go?" asks Alex.

"They're out back. Katie wanted to kick the soccer ball with Annie. And then she said something about showing her room to her. Katie sure seems excited to have Annie here, doesn't she?" observes the older woman.

"Yeah, this morning she asked me twice what time Annie was going to be coming over today," says Alex.

"Well, she's very nice. I don't blame her."

"Thanks, Erica," he says but then adds, "Do you think it could have anything to do with Laura not being at home anymore?" Alex has tried his best to be both parents to each of his children but knows that he can't really fill the shoes of that mother. It saddens him sometimes to think that his little girl is growing up without that influence in her life. Laura's leaving left a hole in his life that has slowly been filling, but worries that it may be one that is only getting deeper for his daughter.

"Oh, I don't know, maybe it could be. It's normal, though, for little girls to be excited about guests and company and special events. That stuff is really important to them, that's probably most of it," says Erica.

Aaron has made his way downstairs and enters the kitchen. "Hi, what are we having?" is his first question. Erica fills him in quickly and then tells both to get out of her way and let her finish. Laughing, they beat a hasty retreat to the backyard. There they find Katie and Annie giggling as the little girl is trying to show her how to use your head to pass the ball. Soon, they notice the two men standing there.

"Annie, this is Aaron," says Alex, proud of the son who is now turning into a young man.

Annie walks over to greet him and extends her hand. "I've heard so much about you. I'm glad that we finally get to meet."

Still a little shy of older women, or more correctly, women in general, he smiles back and says "Nice to meet you, too."

Annie knits her brow and takes a very long look at Aaron. "I've seen you before, you look very familiar to me. Your dad says that you are a musician, is that right?" Aaron nods his head. "What instrument do you play?"

"Guitar and keyboards, but guitar mostly."

"That's it!" exclaims Annie "You were playing last year for the Art Show at the high school. My grandmother and I came to it and you were playing the guitar."

"Yeah, yeah I was," says Aaron as a wide smile begins to grow on his face.

The day goes splendidly. Erica stays for dinner and with the five of them around the table, the house is alive with laughter and conversation. The afternoon moves along quickly and soon Annie realizes that she should probably be going home, having a few things yet to do before the work week starts again. Alex, Aaron, and Katie walk her to the door to say good-bye. Waving to all, Annie drives away on her way home.

Katie then immediately runs over to Emily's house to file her report of the day's activities with her friend as Alex and Aaron retire to the living room. "So, you met Annie before?" asks Alex, surprised at the coincidence. "Do you remember it?"

"Sure, this lady came up to me as she was leaving and thanked me for playing. She asked about the music and I told her that the students had composed it. She said something about really liking it and asked me my name," says Aaron about the recollection. "I like her, Dad, she's nice."

"Thanks, Aaron. I wasn't sure about inviting her over, but I wanted you to meet her," says Alex.

"Why not?"

"Why not what?"

"Why weren't you sure about inviting her over?"

"Oh, uh, I don't know. I guess just because of your mother," answers Alex.

"But you and Mom have been divorced for quite a while now," says Aaron.

"I know but all those years it was Mom and me and now…" and then Alex's voice trails off. He's not sure where he's headed with this and just stops talking.

"Things can change, Dad. I don't expect you not to see any women ever again just because you and Mom were married," says the rapidly maturing older teenager.

"So, it doesn't bother you if I spend time with Annie then?" Alex asks of his son.

"Not at all, it's probably a lot better than spending all that time by yourself," says Aaron.

"But what about Katie? I know how much she missed Mom at the beginning. Do you think she'd be comfortable with it?" asks the parent turned child for the moment.

"Are you kidding me? All Katie's been talking about for the last two days is that Annie is coming over to dinner on Sunday. I think she likes her a lot."

"You really think it wouldn't be a problem then?" is the final question from the father.

"I don't," answers Aaron.

Alex smiles, pats his son on the shoulders, and relaxes his own as a huge weight has just been lifted from them.

\*     \*     \*

Annie has been busy at the orchard. Some of the trees have quit producing for the year. She and Ben have used every spare moment to try and get ahead on the pruning. During the winter months, there is quite a lot of work with this task and any trees that they can get done now only helps later. But on the days that they do prune, both must start work an hour earlier and it has made for a long week.

It is now Thursday night and Annie and Alex have exchanged phone calls a couple of times since last Sunday's dinner but have been unable to see each other. On the drive home, Annie tells herself to give him a call tonight. She wants to have Alex over for dinner tomorrow night if he is free. Annie worries that she may have waited too long to ask.

Stopping at the market on the way home, she goes ahead and buys two beautiful pieces of ono and several fresh vegetables. If Alex can't make it, she can always freeze one fillet. But if she doesn't get groceries now, there's no way that tomorrow she will have time to do that and cook dinner after work. Annie moves ahead with her plans and hopes for the best.

Upon entering the house, she quickly puts the groceries away and picks up the phone to call Alex. After three rings, he answers on the other end. "Hi, this is Annie. I hope I'm not interrupting dinner or anything," she starts. After assurances that she isn't, Annie continues. "I've been meaning to call you since yesterday, but didn't want to bother you at work and I'm just getting home from the orchard. I know it's kind of late to ask you but I thought if you weren't doing anything tomorrow night, you might like to come over for dinner? I probably should have given you more notice about it, I didn't know if Erica was going to be at the house then or not," says Annie.

"Well, she's here now, let me ask her. I'll be right back." And Alex turns away to ask the kindly woman with Annie listening in the background. "Erica, it's Annie. She's invited me over to dinner tomorrow night. Do you have anything going on, could you maybe watch Katie for me?" There is a pause. "No, it's not a problem at all, it was just kind of a last minute thing anyway." And Alex returns to the conversation with Annie.

"I'm sorry, I guess we'll have to do it some other time. Erica's busy tomorrow night," he says. But before Annie has a chance to say anything Alex then interrupts her. "Excuse me, Annie, just a minute." And she listens to the conversation from the other end again. "What? What's that, Aaron? Really, you don't have anything planned, are you sure that would be okay with you? Well, thanks, thanks a lot."

"Aaron says he'll stay with Katie, so I guess it's a date. I mean, dinner sounds great," says the father, somewhat stumbling over his words. "What time should I be there?" Annie tells him seven o'clock and the conversation ends.

Annie quickly puts down the phone and dances a little jig. Her spirits immediately soar and the fatigue from the work day is wiped away in a single moment as off to the kitchen she dashes to retrieve her recipe book. There is a ginger and mango glaze that would be perfect on the ono. She just has to find it.

Annie is up late that night. She cleans and tidies the house, takes time to arrange and set the table, and goes through her closet to seek out what she might wear for the occasion. If she is able to get some tasks done tonight, it wouldn't be such a mad dash after work tomorrow. And Annie plans on enjoying the evening, the entertaining, and the sharing of time with someone who now means very much to her.

*   *   *

"Knock, knock," Alex shouts out through the screen door and then he sees Annie running in from the back patio.

"Oh, hi, come on in," she answers sweetly and greets him with a hug. The two make their way into the kitchen where the dinner preparations are under way. Annie opens the oven to check the contents before joining Alex, sitting at the table. "So, I'm glad it worked out," she says. "I should have given you more notice but Wednesday was way busy at the orchard and when I got home, I thought it was probably too late to call."

"That's fine. I can't believe that Aaron offered to watch Katie, wonders never cease, I guess," says Alex with a chuckle.

"He's a great guy. I really enjoyed talking to him last week," says Annie about last Sunday's dinner.

"Yeah, he's a good kid, I'm pretty lucky. Aaron's taking Katie to dinner and then they're going to a movie and he is letting her pick both of them. Katie's really excited about it."

Annie stands to begin making the salad as the conversation continues. It is a pleasant setting, in the kitchen. Annie's house backs to the hillside and her yard is overflowing with plants and flowers. She has always enjoyed gardening but it was Marty who was the driving force behind all the plantings, especially of the five mature fruit trees. Annie tends to them as a tribute to her grandmother. She feels as though it will always provide that connection to her beloved Marty.

And, at times, Annie marvels at the connection to her new employment that it had provided. Without Marty's great love of tangerines and her energy to create their backyard orchard, she wonders if things would have turned out like they did. Annie wonders at times about fate and destiny and the serendipity of life when events like this occur. She doesn't know how but Annie knows that Marty had something to do with her buying the orchard before it was her grandmother's time to go.

"Everything's almost ready. Let me just finish one thing and then we can move to the living room. Is it okay if we eat in about a half hour?" asks Annie.

"Sure, I'm in no hurry. Can I help?" says Alex.

"Well, I have a bottle of wine, white, in the refrigerator and if that sounds good, you could open that," says Annie, looking in his direction. "The opener is in the top drawer to the right of the sink and the glasses are in that cabinet," she says, pointing with knife in hand.

Alex carefully pours into the two glasses and carries one to Annie who is standing at the counter. "I'm done, let me just wash my hands." Picking up her glass, she raises it toward Alex and offers a toast, "To Fridays." Slowly sipping the crisp and clean Sauvignon, the couple exchange glances and a broad smile crosses Alex's face. "What?" asks Annie.

"Oh, nothing," says Alex. "Just looking at you."

"Yeah, why's that, do I have some food stuck on my face?" wisecracks the hostess for the evening.

"Because I like to," is his simple reply. "And because I can't believe how lucky I am to know you," is the sincere compliment from this very appreciative man of the turn that his life has taken. After years of shallowness with Laura, Annie's unselfish nature and her true concern for others is refreshing and empowering to him. And her attention to him has been a sorely needed tonic for this very thirsty soul.

"You're awfully sweet to say that, Alex," Annie says to him. "Come on, let's go sit down in the living room. I'll start the fish in a little while."

The conversation is easy, natural, and laughter arises often between the two of them. This is one of the first times that they have been able to truly relax and simply enjoy one another's company. Previous 'dates' usually involved others or took place within certain time frames and didn't allow for any relief from the responsibilities or duties of their regular lives. But things are different now and both of them feel this and understand this. And it has provided a freedom to their relationship that hadn't existed previously for them.

The dinner is excellent and compliments continually come from Alex. In the low light of candles and with the soft sounds of music, they will sit at the table for almost an hour after dinner and just talk before getting up to share the task of cleaning away the dishes. After the kitchen is straightened and any leftovers placed in the refrigerator, Annie and Alex and the last third of the wine bottle make their way back to the living room. Alex begins to sit in his same chair when Annie speaks up. "No, over here," she says, patting the cushion on the sofa beside her.

"Don't mind if I do," says Alex.

The energy and excitement that can flow between two people who feel strongly and who feel love toward one another can be overpowering in the moment. Thought and intellect and control give way to feeling and emotion and abandonment. Annie and Alex sip their wine in quiet reflection as the conversation lapses. Then both begin speaking at once and laughter follows.

"You go ahead," says Annie, while still laughing. "What was it that you were going to say?"

Alex looks over at her and their eyes meet. Without further words, he just continues staring at Annie and she back at him. Wide smiles then grow on each face as they begin to move closer together. As their heads tilt to the side and Annie's eyes slowly close, their lips meet and their arms comfortably wrap around one another. The warmth of their embrace fills the room and removes time from the evening. These two souls have waited months for just such a moment and the release that it offers is real and reciprocal as they slip into their night.

*　　*　　*

Two months have passed and the couple have integrated each other into their lives. Alex contributes Saturdays to helping at the orchard while Sundays are reserved for being at home with the children but that day is also now shared with Annie. Both of the children have warmed to her easy graciousness and helpful manner. She has been welcomed into her new 'family' and any worries that she may have held about intruding or taking away Alex from his responsibilities have been removed. And for Alex's part, with the sad passing of Marty, he doesn't fear that he may complicate Annie's life at a time when she may not have needed distractions. Both had respected each other's position and the wait has been both beneficial and worthwhile.

Annie's presence in the household has been especially good for Katie. The young girl has, indeed, missed her mother and has reached out to Annie for that female connection and that motherly nurturing. Annie has taken Katie to get her hair cut, has run with her to the grocery store for that one needed item for the night's dinner, and has been a regular attendee at all her soccer games. Annie even picks up Katie and her friends after practice some nights. The young girl had confided in the older woman one night at bedtime that everyone else always has a mother to provide rides but that she never does. After hearing that, Annie is sure never to miss her turn.

In speaking with Aaron, Annie has found out that the young man is floundering some after graduation from high school. He is battling within himself about whether to continue with his education now or to work on his music to see where that might lead. With the sometimes difficulty of a father offering advice to a son, Annie has substituted as a good listener and confidante whenever approached. While Aaron has continued his practicing and playing with the band, he has expressed some guilt at not yet finding a job and earning his own way. With pruning season upon them and only two people working the orchard, Annie had offered Aaron a job after discussing it with Alex. He now drives the tractor, works the selling tables on occasion to free Annie for other tasks, and loves working outdoors at the orchard. Last week, they even converted one of the outbuildings on the property into a practice studio for Aaron and his band. This new arrangement has, indeed, been a very good fit for all.

With the harvest season coming to an end for a few months and the work at the orchard on track, Annie and the others plan on taking a deserved weekend and traveling north to Whiskey River. Aaron will be unable to come because his band plays regularly now and this weekend, they have gigs on both Friday and Saturday nights. But Katie is excitably looking forward to it, along with both adults. They will drive up early on Saturday and stay the night, returning on Sunday afternoon.

*     *     *

Jeremy now heads over to Wes' apartment to pass off his key. Whenever he is to be out of town, Jeremy makes sure that his neighbor has access to his place. There is no reason for this. He has no plants or pets and a package delivery on Saturday is unlikely but Jeremy feels that if something ever came up, at least Wes could get in. And deep down inside, it gives him solace to know that there is someone that he can count on. He knocks on that person's front door now.

Wes opens it and welcomes Jeremy inside. "So packing up, huh? And you're coming back tomorrow night?"

"Yeah, it's about three hours away, so I won't be back until late. I'll come by to see you on Sunday to get the key back," says Jeremy. "I'm heading over to the market now to get a few things, can I pick you up anything?"

"No, I'm pretty well set. I appreciate the offer though, thanks. Where are you heading to this time?" questions the neighbor and now good friend.

"Whiskey River, it's up north."

"I know that place. It's a big river, isn't it?"

"Yes, big and fast, but there are lots of quiet pools along the edges. I've pulled quite a few large black bass out of there over the years. I was thinking about keeping a few this time. If I get lucky, do you want to come over for a fish dinner on Sunday?" comes the offer from Jeremy.

"Sure, count me in," says Wes.

"Good, I guess I better come through then."

"Somehow, I don't think that's going to be a problem. I know I'd never bet against your chances of finding fish or at winning a bridge game. That's for sure."

"Well, thanks for watching the place, Wes, and I'll see you on Sunday." And Jeremy returns to his apartment to finish packing the gear and the food for tomorrow's trip. The morning will come early and bedtime is only two hours away.

*     *     *

Alex, Annie, and Katie have spent the morning driving north on the inland route. They are heading to McAfee's River Resort. Scott and Jennifer, Alex's friends, come here at least once a year. It is located in the beautifully wooded hills only a short distance from the ocean. With the prevalence of fog at the coast, it is the best of both worlds, guaranteed sunshine with beach activities only a short drive away. Alex has also been told that it is child-friendly, with outdoor ping pong and shuffleboard, and boasts one of the best restaurants in the area. Camping is provided but the real draw for most guests are the graciously restored rustic wooden cabins with porches that provide an excellent view of the trees and of the river.

Arriving now, they check in at the lodge and then Katie runs ahead with the key to their cabin. Annie follows her as Alex begins unpacking the suitcases from the car. The trail winds up the hillside and Katie excitedly looks for Cabin Eight. "Here it is,

Annie," she calls out when finding it. And Annie arrives in time to help the small girl with the lock.

"Look, look," Katie says once inside. "It has a little kitchen, I've never seen such a little kitchen. Isn't it cute, Annie?" Annie quickly agrees with her assessment. "And look, this bed is just perfect for me," she goes on, lying down on the single bed. "You and Daddy can have the big bed. I want this one." Running out to the porch, Katie shouts to her father walking up the path with the luggage. "You can see the river from here. It's all bright and shiny," she says of the sun reflecting off the water.

Alex soon arrives and joins in the inspection of the cabin and its surroundings. "This really is pretty, Alex. That was a good tip from Scott," says Annie. Alex is happy that the cabin is clean, comfortable, and offers such a lovely setting in the trees. He is glad that they have taken the time to get out of town and have some down time. And he is glad that Annie could join Katie and him as it will truly be more fun with her along, for both himself and for his daughter.

They will unpack, go back to the main lodge, and get involved in a fun game of shuffleboard. Having a wonderful lunch will confirm Scott's recommendation of the local restaurant. By late afternoon, the three of them walk down to the river and sit on its banks, watching it flow past and listening to its soothing gurgling. Alex is soon standing, educating his young daughter on the art of skipping rocks across the water's surface. The center of the river runs deep and fast, but large rocks and fallen trees line its banks and provide quiet pools of water that are good for skipping. Katie has taken on the task of finding just the right flat rocks that make the best skippers and she runs up and down the river's edge in search of them. Coming back to the spot where Annie and Alex sit, she eagerly shows them her finds.

The sun beats down on them as the afternoon wears on. Alex says that he is thirsty and wonders if either of the girls might like a drink. Katie asks for an orange juice if they have it. Annie says that she needs to use the bathroom. The lodge and small store are just above them, very near. Katie is engrossed in tossing her pile of rocks into the water and asks to stay while they go. Both adults look at one another and decide that it should be okay, they will be gone only a few minutes. With warnings to stay back from the water and with promises of a quick return, Annie and Alex scramble up the bank and make the short walk to the lodge. Annie excuses herself at the bathroom as Alex enters the store to buy the drinks.

\* \* \*

Jeremy has been fishing all day. He has caught several small fish that have been released and a large one that now resides in his creel. With the late afternoon sun lowering in the west, he knows that feeding time is coming and, with a little luck, that second dinner should be netted before too long. He works the still pools by the banks with an occasional cast into the main current just below some large rocks. Jeremy deftly and expertly works the line as he continues his fishing.

\* \* \*

Alex waits near the bathrooms for Annie with drinks in hand. Down below, Katie has become engrossed in perfecting her new found skill at skipping rocks. Counting aloud each time, she has reached four and strives to attain her goal of five. Throwing into the main current has presented its problems, though, as the rock is grabbed and pulled down quickly. Having been educated on the need for smooth calm water, Katie climbs onto the trunk of a large fallen tree projecting into the river. From this angle, she can throw parallel to the shore and can use the whole of the quiet pool that the three of them have been enjoying.

With a fistful of stones, she begins letting them fly. But from the increased height of the log, it is proving a difficult task. Katie saw her father crouching low when he did his tosses and has picked up on the technique. The young girl now emulates him and moves to lower herself when she steps on a mossy patch on the fallen tree. Katie's feet go out from under her and she lands hard on her bottom before falling into the water. The girl is stunned for a moment as the current then begins moving her downstream. She tries to swim back to shore but panics and calls out loudly, "Daddy, Daddy! Help, help...help!"

Alex hears the cries and the drinks are thrown to the ground as he begins running back to the spot where they left Katie. Annie emerges from the bathroom in time to see him racing down the bank toward the river. She immediately runs after him yelling, "Alex, what's wrong? What's wrong!"

Cresting the bank, Annie sees Alex at the water's edge but no Katie and immediate concern overwhelms her. The father is scanning the river and now sees the young girl caught in its main current. "Katie!" he yells. "Oh, my god, Katie!"

Alex begins running down the road that parallels the river as fast as he can. Annie follows quickly behind. The young girl is scared, very scared, but she is moving her arms and trying to stay on top of the water. After a few hundred yards, Alex stops as the river bends to the left and leaves the roadway. The banks are steep and Alex scrambles down one of them. He is about to jump in the water when Annie reaches the spot above him.

"No, Alex!" she screams at him. "You won't be able to catch up to her. We have to get ahead of her, we have to get ahead!" Looking down the riverbed, Annie sees the river curving back to, once again, follow the road. She takes off running.

Alex climbs back up the bank to follow her, shouting at the top of his lungs, "We're coming, Katie, we're coming!"

Jeremy glints into the late afternoon sun as he prepares to try a few more casts before calling it a day when he hears the loud voices and shouting coming from the road. Turning, he sees Annie and Alex in a panic running toward him. Immediately he knows there is a problem and searches his surroundings to find the peril. Looking up river, he soon spots Katie moving in the water just above the large rocks that he had fished earlier in the day. She is no longer swimming or moving her arms. The young girl is tiring and heading directly for a falls in the river that rushes between the rocks. Jeremy sees Katie enter the falls and then she disappears underneath the water.

Throwing his rod to the ground, he rapidly peals his waders and shoes while watching for her to resurface. Coming back up, the girl now floats listlessly face down in the water. Not wasting a second, Jeremy dives in and quickly begins swimming toward Katie. The current is strong, very strong, and he fights it as he tries to keep his head above the water and tries to maintain eye contact with the small child.

Alex and Annie have now reached the broad bend in the river. They race down the bank and begin running across the gravelly shore toward the water. Jeremy reaches Katie and pulls her head above water. Both are rapidly moving downstream in the central current of the river with Jeremy holding on tightly to the child. His attempts at swimming back to shore are proving difficult. Struggling in the water, he sees two people running along the now flatter, wider river bed and chasing after them.

Looking downstream, he sees that the river narrows and runs through another series of rocks. Jeremy knows that he needs to get the small girl to shore now. He will never be able to hold on to Katie going through the rapids that are approaching. With one arm around the child's waist, Jeremy uses the other and with his feet kicks wildly, determinedly, toward the river's edge. Spotting a sandbar just above the falls, he sets that as his goal.

Jeremy is getting a little closer but the water remains deep and cold and fast. He continues kicking furiously and summons his last bit of strength to literally throw Katie onto the edge of the sandbar before the current pulls him back into the river. Annie and Alex are sprinting full speed toward the spot where Katie now lies, lifeless and without movement. Reaching the young girl, they pull her farther onto the land. Not breathing, Annie immediately begins an attempt to resuscitate her. Alex is a mess and can only say, "Oh, Katie. Oh, poor, poor Katie."

Annie stops for a second to address him. "Help him, Alex," she says with a quick toss of her head, meaning Jeremy who now finds himself in trouble after all his exertion. Alex is frozen, not wanting to leave Katie's side. Annie then states firmly and loudly, "Go help the man, Alex! I know what I'm doing." And she immediately goes back to working on the young girl.

Alex stands and with one last look at his child, his precious Katie, takes off again running down the bank. With another bend in the river coming, he races along the edge trying to get ahead of Jeremy. Soon reaching a broad sandbar, he looks up river to see Jeremy moving toward him, out of fight and tiring. Looking around, Alex then spots a broken limb lying near him. It is about ten to twelve feet long with several branches coming out of it. Quickly breaking them, he leaves a few that will give him handholds. His plan is to use this to help pull Jeremy from the rushing water.

Standing on the shore, Alex prepares himself for the rescue effort. Besides timing the toss into the water correctly, he knows that he will have to brace himself to hold on against the strong current and the weight of the man. Practicing, he places one hand on the end of a broken branch and realizes that another branch can wrap around behind his back. Alex shouts out and begins gesturing to Jeremy of his plan with the man weakly nodding back that he understands.

The time has come and Alex moves to the water's edge. As Jeremy nears, he lets go with the branch that does, indeed, land near him. The exhausted man grabs onto the piece of wood. The current and the considerable weight of his body are great and almost rip the branch out of Alex's hands. His feet dig in as the broken ends of the branches gash into the hands and back of him. He falls to the ground and is pulled along but he holds on, holds on. And the worn out and tired body of Jeremy is pulled to shore as Alex rushes to his side.

"I'm okay," Jeremy says quickly. "You go back, you go back," he says about the spot where Katie lies.

Alex hesitates for a minute and then rapidly begins running for his life, for the life of his daughter whose precarious situation now comes back into its horrible reality for him. Alex is scared, scared to death. With all the exertion and fear, his heart is about to explode out of his chest as he races back to her.

Annie continues working on Katie when she suddenly starts to cough up the swallowed water. Katie begins to come back into consciousness and when the realization of what has just happened comes to her, a look of terror crosses her face and she reaches out for Annie. The two hug each other and hold on as the tears pour out of the little girl. "Oh, Annie," she cries out.

"It's all right, Katie, it's all right now," the older woman says soothingly. Annie then has Katie lie back down on her side. She is lying still, resting, with Annie holding her hand when Alex reaches them. Annie looks up at his worried expression and says, "She's okay, Alex. She's going to be fine."

The relief is total and complete with his worst nightmare not having come to pass. Alex then drops weakly to the ground beside them and begins stroking Katie's hair with tears welling in his eyes. "Oh, honey, oh, sweet sweet Katie," are the only words that he is capable of speaking. He turns in Annie's direction and says, "Thank you, thank you."

"Alex, where is the man that rescued Katie from the water? What happened to him!" asks a worried Annie. Alex relates the story of pulling Jeremy out of the river before returning to help him make his way back to the lodge. Others had witnessed the event and the sound of the ambulance can now be heard in the distance as it approaches. Katie and Jeremy are then both placed inside and transported to the hospital for care and observation. Alex has sustained deep gashes on one hand and on his back where the branch had dug into him. He will also be treated and bandaged while at the hospital.

After a few hours, all are then released and after exchanging names and addresses, Jeremy and the Galway group both head back home. Having found that they are from the same city, they make plans to have Jeremy out to the orchard next weekend to properly thank him. He had risked his life to save Katie's life, something that Alex feels he will always owe to this stranger who had come into their lives at the right time and who had definitely been in the right place.

*　　*　　*

It is late and the house is dark. Alex parks in the driveway and then hurries to open the front door. Katie and Annie follow behind on the sidewalk. With Annie sitting beside her in the back seat, the young girl has slept most of the way home. Entering the house, they all now climb the stairs to her bedroom. Alex turns down the bed while Annie undresses Katie and helps put on her pajamas. The young girl is exhausted but she has made it through an incredible ordeal, something that she will always remember and that may even shape the rest of her life.

Katie asks Annie to stay in the room with her and the strong and comforting woman pulls up a chair to sit down beside the bed and hold onto one of Katie's hands.

"You won't leave me until I fall asleep, will you?" says the little girl in her small, soft voice.

"No, I won't leave you."

"Good," says Katie. "Annie, will you make pancakes with me in the morning?"

"Yes, honey, I'll make pancakes with you."

"Good," she repeats and that is last word from Katie's mouth as she then easily drifts off to sleep.

\*　　\*　　\*

Alex is downstairs in the kitchen, gulping down a glass of water. He is tired, shaken, and somewhat in a state of disbelief about what has happened to them on this day. A simple trip to the country had turned into a fight for survival. Alex is so grateful, so relieved that everything had been fine in the end. He can't even contemplate the situation if things had turned out differently. And what would he have done if Annie hadn't been there? Alex then notices Aaron's peetee parking out front.

Seeing lights on in the house, the teenager is surprised that his family is back so soon. 'I thought they were supposed to stay overnight,' he thinks to himself as he enters the front door and is immediately greeted by his father.

"Dad, what are you guys doing home? Weren't you going to spend the night?" says Aaron. And then looking down, he sees his father's bandaged hand. "Dad, what happened to your hand! Did you get hurt, are you okay?"

"Yes, yes, I'm fine, Aaron," Alex answers quickly. "We had a problem, we had an accident, so we came home right away." And then the story of Katie's falling into the water and of her subsequent rescue is briefly explained.

"Oh, no, that's awful. Katie almost drowned?" says Aaron. "Where is she?" he wants to know. In her bedroom he is told, and the brother starts to run up the stairs to see her when he is stopped by his father.

"No, wait a minute, Aaron. She's already in bed now, Annie is staying upstairs with her. Katie's okay, your sister's okay," says Alex, trying to reassure him.

Soon, Annie joins them in the kitchen. She informs them that Katie has fallen asleep and is resting fine. The three will sit at the table discussing the day's events for the next half hour. With things calming down, Alex inquires about Aaron's evening and about his band's first live performance.

Remarking that things had gone very well, Aaron says that they were all going to meet at Sam's for pizza and to celebrate. But, Aaron is not so sure that he should go with all that has just happened to his family.

"You go ahead, everything's fine now," says Alex.

"Are you sure? I came home to grab a few things and then I was going to spend the night over there. I didn't think anyone would be home." Assurances again come back from his father. "Alright, then," says Aaron and he goes up the stairs to his room. And he will peek at Katie and just watch her for a few minutes. He will watch her to make sure that she is truly okay.

Aaron returns to the kitchen and says he will be home early in the morning. Taking his leave, he is nearly out the front door when his father calls to him. Stopping and turning around, he waits for Alex to reach him.

"So, you be careful driving over to the Sam's. It's late...so be careful, will you? Make sure that you pay attention to the road," says Alex a little haltingly, a little awkwardly.

"Yeah, yeah, I will," Aaron answers back. 'Just like I always do,' he thinks to himself. "Is everything okay, Dad?" he says next, picking up on something.

"Sure, I just want you to be careful, promise?" says Alex and with an uncharacteristic gesture between the man and his older son, he hugs Aaron tightly for a few moments.

"I promise," says Aaron. "And I'll make sure I'm back early in the morning," he says, still looking at his father somewhat peculiarly as he leaves the house.

Alex returns to the kitchen where Annie sits. He is visibly shaken, with a tired and weary expression on his face. "Are you okay, Alex?" she asks, concerned about his appearance. The worn out man drops his head and his shoulders begin moving up and down in great sobs. The tears and worry from the day pour out of him. Annie rises quickly to hold him and ushers Alex to a chair to sit down. His tear streaked face looks up at her.

"Oh Annie, I was so scared today, so scared," the poor man pleads. "If something bad had happened to Katie, I don't know what I would have done," says Alex as he struggles to hold back the emotion and the crying.

"I know," she says. "It scared all of us. But she's okay, Alex, she's okay now."

"But, if I ever lost Katie or Aaron, it would be so hard to go on living. If anything ever happened to one of my kids, well, that's just got to be the worst thing that could ever happen to a parent. I love them so much, so much," Alex says and then the weakened man starts to cry again.

Annie holds him closer and tighter and Alex releases into her arms and her embrace. A few minutes pass before he can regain his composure. "I'm sorry, Annie," he says, feeling a bit better. "I should try to be stronger but I guess it just all came back on me now that it's over."

"I know how much you love your children, Alex, I do. I think it's great, there's nothing to be embarrassed about," says Annie. They continue talking at the kitchen table while holding on to one another's hand.

"When you love someone, you take it for granted that they will always be there. When the threat of that loss comes in front of you, it can be frightening," says Alex and then pauses for a minute. Looking deeply into Annie's eyes, he continues, "It's the way I feel about you now, Annie. I'm in love with you," he says sincerely and with conviction. A broad smile comes over Annie's face as she sits beside him. "And I'm afraid that I might lose you. I just never want you to go away."

Annie then reaches for Alex's face and caresses it with both of her hands. "Oh, Alex," she says in a softer voice. "I love you. You're not going to lose me. I'm not going away." And the two of them exchange a long heartfelt kiss in the bright glare of the kitchen light. They will sit for several minutes longer as calm and comfort now come over the both of them.

Glancing at the clock, Alex sees that it is late, very very late. "I better let you get home. Do you mind just taking my car and I'll get it in the morning? I shouldn't leave Katie here by herself," he says to Annie.

"No, I don't think I want to take your car home," says Annie. Alex then looks her way with a perplexed expression on his face. "I'm going to stay here tonight."

"Really, staying here? No, I'm okay now, you can go home," Alex says to her.

"Ah, it's not because of you, although that's pretty appealing. It's the pancakes," says Annie. The puzzled look comes back to Alex's face. She lets out a small laugh.

They will slowly climb the stairs to the bedroom with arms draped around each other as the end to the day finally folds around them. Annie and Alex will then settle down for a well-deserved rest but not before making love to each other for the first time. And it will now definitely not be their last.

\*       \*       \*

Sunday has arrived and the party for Jeremy has been in the planning stages all week. On Monday, Alex had invited him to the orchard for an afternoon meal and as a way to thank him for his unselfish and courageous act. Alex was sure to mention that Jeremy was free to ask any friends that he would like to come with him. Wes had been approached later in the week and had readily accepted. He was already very proud of his friend because of an article appearing in the local newspaper about the 'Rescue on Whiskey River.'

Several people have been invited to join in the celebration and honoring of this man. When informed of the party, Katie had immediately rushed next door to tell and invite her best friend Emily. And, of course, the young girl has related the story of her rescue over and over again to the many who were eager to listen. And Katie always ends with, "He is really strong and he didn't even think about himself. Jeremy's my good friend."

Scott and Jennifer are coming, Julia and Mark are invited, Erica is coming, and a few other close friends who had expressed an interest in meeting Jeremy. And Aaron plans on inviting Sam as a companion for the teenage boy.

Alex, Katie, and Emily arrive two hours before the party is to begin to help Annie set up. The girls carry pies that they and Erica had baked the day before and Alex carries a cooler packed with drinks. Setting them down, the young girls scamper away into the orchard to play. Alex then goes to help Annie spread the tablecloths over the two selling tables that will serve the banquet. "Hi," he says to her when they finish and he then gives her a light kiss on the lips.

"Well, hi there," returns Annie and then asks, "Alex, can you help me get a few more things out of the car?" And they retrieve more goodies from her trunk that had been lovingly and expertly prepared by Annie the previous evening.

"This stuff looks great. I hope it wasn't too much trouble. You must have stayed up late doing it," says Alex.

"Oh, don't worry, it really wasn't any trouble at all. It feels kind of good to have someone to cook for and to have nice people to share it with. I don't think I'd want it any other way," she says with a wink in his direction.

Then with no one else around them, Alex reaches for Annie and holds her close to him. "I don't think I'd want it any other way, either," he says and the two exchange a long and passionate kiss. Pulling back, the two people look at each other as broad and genuine smiles grow on each of their faces.

"Maybe we can come back to that later today," Annie muses as they let go and continue the work of setting up.

"I'll be sure to nearby," says Alex. The two of them are a good match, a strong union. And each is mature enough to know that what one contributes to a relationship is as important as what one gains from a relationship.

Guests arrive and the party begins. Jeremy and Wes come a little later than the others and when showing up are greeted by applause and cheers as they cross the parking lot. Wes even stops in his tracks to join in the clapping and slaps his good friend on the back. Jeremy smiles and just gives a little wave. Katie then rushes up to him and reaches for his hand to lead him back to a spot at the table next to her and Emily. Introductions are made and everyone takes their turn approaching the man to commend him and thank him for his bravery.

The day is perfect, a clear bright sky and a fresh slight breeze. The setting is idyllic with the fruit trees and the green hillsides with the tall grasses. Early winter rains have nourished the land and all of nature's glory is, once again, alive and well after the dry summer. Laughter and conversation continually arise from those sitting around the tables and then drift away toward the late afternoon sun. Aaron has brought his guitar and with Sam by his side drumming a water bucket, all enjoy the music. Mark and Jeremy talk and when Mark learns of his fishing abilities, a plan is hatched for next year's summer camps in which Jeremy will teach the children about fishing on Saturdays, a special weekend class. Jeremy readily accepts and jumps at the chance to instruct others on his hobby and on his passion.

With things now winding down, some begin taking their leave and start back home. Soon, it is only Annie and Alex and the girls left with Jeremy and Wes as they sit at a table engaged in quiet conversation. A short time later, the two men stand to excuse themselves and begin thanking the hosts for such a special day. Alex and Annie then walk them to their vehicle. Alex shakes hands warmly and sincerely with Jeremy and says,

"I don't know how I can ever really thank you. I will always owe my child's life to you. Thank you, thank you."

Jeremy simply smiles back at the father.

Annie also thanks the guest of honor. Annie especially liked meeting Jeremy's friend and now addresses Wes directly. "And I'm so glad that you were able to come today, too. I hope we can all get together again sometime."

"It was nice meeting you and your family, ma'am," says the kindly, older gentleman.

"Oh, they're not my family," says Annie just to set the record straight. "Not yet, that is," she says, placing her arm around Alex who is standing next to her. Alex then reciprocates with his hand going around Annie's waist. They continue holding on to each other and wave as Jeremy and Wes drive away.

"That was fun," Annie says, turning to Alex when their guests are gone and disappearing down the road.

"That was fun," he agrees.

*   *   *

Several months have passed and these lives that have come together continue sharing time in friendship. Of course, Annie and Alex's relationship has grown stronger and they are now able to spend more private time together, at the urging and with the encouragement of all around them. Katie and Aaron are extremely fond of this new woman in their father's life. The love and respect that Annie offers them is immensely valuable and appreciated by both of the children. This has especially been heartwarming to Alex who had worried what bringing Annie into his life might mean for the family.

Jeremy has stayed connected. He and Wes are the occasional dinner guests at the Galway house and every few weeks all meet at a nearby restaurant. With summer approaching, Jeremy has finalized the fishing classes with Mark that will start soon. Katie has already enlisted Emily to be in the first group that will spend Saturdays for a month at nearby lakes and rivers before taking a final overnight to a more distant fishing location. For three months over the summer in three different sessions, Jeremy will give up his Saturdays to share with others and to share with the children. The first session is already filled with the second filling fast. And with his reputation as a local hero, many of the young people want a chance to meet the man.

Aaron has blossomed at the orchard along with the trees. Taking his responsibilities seriously, Aaron has proven to be a dedicated hard worker who contributes greatly to the operation of the business. It was exactly what he and Annie had needed. Along with Ben, the three of them are operating an efficient and profitable business. It has freed Annie to reduce her hours, and her worry, and to more enjoy the job. And Aaron can still continue practicing and composing his music.

Katie has benefited greatly from, once again, having a mother figure in her life. The bond with Annie from the accident has grown their relationship and has provided a closer connection between the two that otherwise might have taken longer to develop. The trust that the young girl has in the older woman is complete and unwavering. And a family has been put back together with all of their members now having their needs met and their contributions appreciated by one another.

Alex is a good man with a good heart who had deserved more and now reaps the benefits of a true, sharing, loving relationship with a life partner. The old worries about the problems for the children from a broken home have now lessened greatly. And to have another to love and receive love from has completed the man who never knew the hole in his heart was so large.

And then there is Annie, sweet, sweet, dear Annie Sullivan. With distance coming from Marty's passing, she can now devote more time and pay more attention to her needs and to her wishes. And what she had wanted more than anything has come to pass, a true family in her life. It didn't matter that the children weren't hers, biologically, because in the realm of life and love they had become hers, truly hers, to love and respect and nurture. And Annie has found that they need her, too.

\*　　\*　　\*

It is now the first Friday night of the summer after the end of the school year. Annie hurries to fold the selling tables and to put the produce back in the shed. It is late afternoon as she and Ben prepare to leave for the night. Having closed the stands a half hour early, they are making good progress.

"Thanks," Annie says to her worker when the shed door is closed and locked. "I really appreciate you staying late to help." Usually Ben is gone by this time of the day. He arrives early and will usually end his shift by the middle of the afternoon. But, Aaron is the one who has left early today.

"So, Aaron is playing music tonight, is that right?" asks Ben as they both cross the parking lot toward their peetees.

"It's the first time that his band is performing for one of the Friday Dances. He's pretty excited about it."

"Good for him, that is exciting. I'm glad the boys get to do it. I think music is important for our children's education."

"So do I," says Annie as she quickly agrees with him. "Music is and art is and writing is and dance is, too."

"Oh, dance is always great fun and exercise. My wife makes me go to the ballroom dances with her almost every Sunday. She loves it and it makes her happy, which you know, makes me happy," says the hard working man and husband.

Annie thanks him again and says, "See you Monday."

"On Monday," is Ben's warm response.

\*　　\*　　\*

Annie looks at the time as she drives toward Alex's house. Having brought a change of clothes with her, she plans on getting ready there. Already splitting her time between the residences, the ratio now weighs heavily in favor of the Galway household. And there has been talk recently of her selling the house and making the transition official. Both Annie and Alex have agreed on the start of the next school year as a final move in date. But for now, the system works well with the two of them sneaking away to Annie's house on some special evenings that allows time just for themselves.

"Hello, hello," Annie calls out as she comes through the front door after arriving at Alex's.

"I'm upstairs, Annie, come on up," he answers.

"Where's Katie?" she asks when entering the bedroom.

"She's been ready for an hour and is over at Emily's helping her. She told me I have to wear this," he says, holding up a freshly ironed blue shirt. "Katie had Erica iron it while I was at work. What do you think?"

"Just like a woman, she has good taste. I'd go with it," says Annie and then plants a kiss on Alex's cheek.

"Yeah, I thought it was a pretty good choice, too," he says and then smiles back at her. "Katie said that we absolutely have to be there by six o'clock. Does that give you enough time to get ready for the dance?"

"Sure, done with the bathroom?" asks Annie. Alex answers that he is and the conversation will continue as Annie changes clothes and gets ready. "Did you talk with Aaron?"

"At about three o'clock when he was leaving the orchard. He seemed a little apprehensive about performing tonight. Aaron kept saying that he hoped they sounded good enough. I know a lot of his friends are going to be there."

"I think he's probably a little nervous about the whole thing." Then emerging from the bathroom, Annie pronounces that she is finally presentable for the evening.

Alex lends his agreement and adds, "I guess I'm going to have to stand in line tonight to get a dance with you. You are beautiful, Annie, truly beautiful," as he expresses his opinion of her good looks and, more meaningfully, of her good nature.

"Thank you, honey. You're sweet," says Annie. "I'll move you to the head of the line anytime."

\* \* \*

Soon, the four of them are heading to The Dance. Katie and Emily giggle in the back seat as they make their way past the green and clean neighborhoods that surround this thriving city. A new social responsibility has arisen in society where private desires no longer take precedence over communal needs. The wealth of the world was never meant to be parceled out and owned, it was meant to be shared. The bounty that has always been in the world now touches every person's life.

We had almost reached the breaking point, the point of no return, but when facing a severe threat, humankind had risen to its potential for goodness and reason. With the world coming together and with the fear of our differences disappearing, the possibilities are now endless. And with the blessings of health, safety, and a more fair distribution of resources, we have finally achieved the 'heaven on earth' that had always been within our reach. Alex and Annie now drive toward the horizon of that new reality, strong and confident in the knowledge that the life ahead for them and all others will, indeed, be a good one.

Arriving at the Harvest Hall, they quickly find a parking spot and then join the crowd moving toward the front doors as the good wishes from one to another flow from friend to friend, from neighbor to neighbor, and from citizen to citizen. All are in good spirits and all now have fewer worries and far fewer concerns as they are truly the recipients of this better world.

Approaching the front door, Alex then lets Katie and Emily run ahead and say hello to Aaron before the music starts. He and Annie stop to make their contribution at the door. Seeing other friends on the way in, they slowly wind their way through the crowd toward the bandstand. When glancing up from arranging the equipment, Aaron sees the two of them and with a nod of the head, smiles back in their direction. Alex acknowledges the sign and Annie gives him a little wave.

"He looks like he's doing fine now," she says.

"Yeah, I think he is," says Alex. "You know, I've never heard the whole band together. I'm kind of excited about it. I didn't get past the recorder in fourth grade, can't carry a tune in a bucket. I don't know where he gets it."

"From inside," says Annie.

Looking over at his mate, Alex just smiles and nods his head in agreement. He then asks, "I'm kind of thirsty, want something to drink before the dance starts?" Annie answers that she would. "You can stay here, I'll be right back. What do you want?"

A broad smile comes over Annie's face as she moves closer to Alex and grabbing his arm with both of her hands, gives it a squeeze. Standing close and looking long into his eyes, she says, "Oh, maybe a limeade."

When immediately picking up on that remembrance of their first meeting, he says with a laugh, "Are you sure you want that? You don't know what that might lead to."

"It's okay. I'm willing to take the chance."

*　　*　　*

The music energizes and activates the crowd. Aaron's group has gotten good, really good, and most of the music they now perform is their own. All present are having a great time. Katie and Emily have danced almost every dance, with Katie telling all, "That's my brother's band." And it has made for a very special night for the young girl.

With good vibes and good energy abounding, Annie dances with the girls and with her Alex, several times. Annie will enjoy herself immensely tonight as she dances into the evening and into the warmth and comfort of friends and now family, as she dances into her new life.

Dedicated to Hillary and Morgan

My children

May we leave you that better world

CPSIA information can be obtained
at www.ICGtesting.com
Printed in the USA
BSHW021410170520
0264FS